BLACK OXEN

broadview editions
series editor: L.W. Conolly

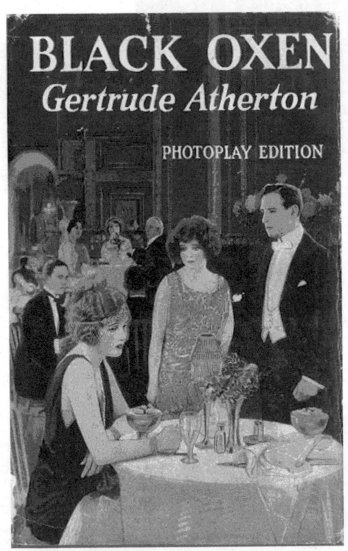

Dust jacket of the 1924 *Photoplay* edition of *Black Oxen*.

BLACK OXEN

Gertrude Atherton

edited by Melanie V. Dawson

broadview editions

Library and Archives Canada Cataloguing in Publication

Atherton, Gertrude, 1857-1948
      Black oxen / Gertrude Atherton ; edited by Melanie V. Dawson.

(Broadview editions)
Originally publ.: New York : Boni and Liveright, 1923.
Includes bibliographical references.
ISBN 978-1-55481-025-3

      I. Dawson, Melanie, 1967- II. Title.
III. Series: Broadview editions

PS1042.B5 2012   813'.4   C2012-900308-5

Broadview Editions

The Broadview Editions series represents the ever-changing canon of literature in English by bringing together texts long regarded as classics with valuable lesser-known works.

Advisory editor for this volume: Michel Pharand

Broadview Press is an independent, international publishing house, incorporated in 1985.

We welcome comments and suggestions regarding any aspect of our publications—please feel free to contact us at the addresses below or at broadview@broadviewpress.com.

North America
PO Box 1243, Peterborough, Ontario, Canada K9J 7H5
2215 Kenmore Ave., Buffalo, New York, USA 14207
Tel: (705) 743-8990; Fax: (705) 743-8353
email: customerservice@broadviewpress.com

UK, Europe, Central Asia, Middle East, Africa, India, and Southeast Asia
Eurospan Group, 3 Henrietta St., London WC2E 8LU, United Kingdom
Tel: 44 (0) 1767 604972; Fax: 44 (0) 1767 601640
email: eurospan@turpin-distribution.com

Australia and New Zealand
NewSouth Books
c/o TL Distribution, 15-23 Helles Ave., Moorebank, NSW, Australia 2170
Tel: (02) 8778 9999; Fax: (02) 8778 9944
email: orders@tldistribution.com.au

www.broadviewpress.com

This book is printed on paper containing 100% postconsumer fibre.

Typesetting and assembly: Eileen Eckert, Calgary, Canada.

PRINTED IN CANADA

MIX
Paper from
responsible sources
FSC
www.fsc.org   FSC® C004071

ANCIENT FOREST ™
FRIENDLY

Contents

Acknowledgements

I am grateful to the Department of English at The College of William and Mary for its support of this project, and to chairs Susan Donaldson and Liz Barnes for allowing me to work with student researchers (Paolo Jasa, Ben Christian, Chris Tracy, and Will Carmines) on this project. Thanks also go to Christy Burns, Director of Women's Studies at the college, for research funds. I also thank Dean Teresa Longo, Dean of Educational Policy, Arts and Sciences at The College of William and Mary, for her generous contribution to the edition's permission costs.

I owe intellectual debts to members of my writing group at William and Mary, Liz Barnes and Jenny Putzi; their enthusiasm and sound advice have been unwavering across the years it took to bring this project to fruition. Work throughout the project was also sped along by Marjorie Mather of Broadview Press. I have benefitted enormously from the intellectual generosity of Dale Bauer, Stephanie Foote, Erin Gentry Lamb, and Karsten Piep as well as insights offered by the press's anonymous reviewers. Elizabeth Morrow Clark, Eastern European historian at West Texas A & M University, provided valuable insights far outside the realms of my expertise. In addition, Judy Robinson provided expert help at the Bancroft Library, University of California, Berkeley. Thanks go as well to Susan Snyder at Bancroft Library in regard to the Gertrude Franklin Horn Atherton collection, the Bancroft having graciously allowed the reprinting of various materials cited in the introduction and appendixes. I am also grateful to the staff at the Library of Congress, both in the General Reading Room, and in the Motion Picture Reading Room, where many of the materials pertaining to the *Black Oxen* film are located. Thanks also to the New York Public Library, Manhattan branch, for making one of the only extant copies of the film available for viewing. More immediate help throughout the project came from Swem Library's intrepid Interlibrary Loan department, where staff were able to procure many necessary and hard-to-find materials for me. And last, but certainly not least, are many thanks to John Nichols for expert technical support, equally significant psychological support, and illuminating conversation about this project, in all its phases.

Thanks for permission to reprint materials in the appendices of this edition are due to Kathleen Dell, of the Floyd Dell Estate, and to Bruce Kellner and the Carl Van Vechten Trust, for permission to reprint Van Vechten's review of *Black Oxen* (Appendix D1). Thanks go as well to The New York Times/PARS International for permission to quote a 1923 review in the introduction, Penguin/Viking for permission to reprint the Eugen Steinach excerpt (Appendix A2), and Harper Collins Publishers for permission to reprint an excerpt of Frederick Lewis Allen's work (Appendix B2).

Introduction

When *Black Oxen*'s central character, Mary Zattiany, claims, "I do not merely *look* young again, I *am* young. I am not the years I have passed in this world, I am the age of the rejuvenated glands of my body" (p. 188), she offers readers a fantasy of controlling one's experience of age, if only readers would embrace the opportunities afforded them by modern science. As a medical rejuvenation drama that sheds light on women's confrontation with age and its varied effects, *Black Oxen* speaks to the issues facing mature women in the 1920s, issues that have not waned in contemporary society. Experience, physical beauty, and romantic love (particularly across generational lines) continue to emerge in current conversations about age and its value. As a best-selling 1923 novel and the inspiration for a popular film of 1924, *Black Oxen* in many ways launched a set of questions about generational positions and how to value them relative to one another. The novel queries not only what it means to be and to remain young (a question that may have been unthinkable just a generation earlier), but also how youth and age may be hybridized in modern life. In a society that appeared to worship youth unambiguously, Atherton's novel appropriated for its heroine the physical features commonly associated with youth, while also insisting that creative thought, integrity, and subtlety could be acquired only over long and, at times, difficult years of life.

Atherton's Mary Zattiany enters the plot of *Black Oxen* as a vibrantly lovely woman who refuses to treat the concept of physical age as anything other than voluntary and controllable. Although the character was once unrecognizable because of age, and worn because of her volunteer work during the war years, she has experienced a "rejuvenation" treatment at the age of 58, a procedure that leaves her looking as if she were in her late 20s. While this treatment sounds far-fetched, rejuvenation therapies were distinctive products of 1920s culture. Atherton herself participated in the procedure in 1922, at the age of 64, and was so pleased with the results that she made medical rejuvenation a significant part of the novel's plot, calling attention to the treatment's possibilities and, along the way, dissecting the age-specific dimensions of American culture during the 1920s. The procedure involved a series of X-ray treatments directed at the ovaries, a therapy that was later modified to involve the concentration of light rays.[1] The process, known as the "Steinach treatment," was intended to stimulate the sex organs and to bring about a more youthful appearance, along with greater energy and mental acuity.[2] (See also Appendix A.)

Black Oxen opens just as youth was becoming a dominant force in American culture generally and particularly in the US's premiere intellectual city, New York, the novel's setting. With its placement of Mary Zattiany in this context, the novel raises the question of what an energetic and experienced woman could accomplish in the world, once she possessed all the energy and personal appeal of youth and once she saw herself as unencumbered by expectations of family life (for the treatment destroyed the generative capacity of the sex organs). With her sophisticated understanding of politics, an interest in international relations, and an investment in humanitarian projects in the post-war era (which

---

1 As early as 1923, a year after Atherton's X-ray procedure, the treatment was modified to include heat rays and to minimize the X-ray's use; just after the turn of the century, there was proof that X-rays were dangerous. Early deaths (and amputations) such as those of Thomas Edison's assistant, Clarence Dally, however, did not stop X-ray based experiments, particularly ones connected with rejuvenation. As Atherton's doctor wrote to her in 1923, in regard to a new round of therapy,

> The treatment that professor Steinach wanted me to give you is an electrical one consisting of penetrating heat rays. It is given about every other day. The patient just feels a certain amount of pleasant heat over the regions of the ovaries, which organs are likewise heated and therefore better nourished by blood circulation, thus giving out more hormones into the blood stream. In many cases Steinach replaces the X-Ray by this treatment, but only, in these cases, where he can assume that still many well-functioning ovary cells are present. I am using a combined treatment; stimulating by the X-Ray and increasing this effect by the heat rays. (Letter, Dr. Harry Benjamin, 25 September 1923, quoted with the permission of Bancroft Library, University of California, Berkeley.)

2 Eugen Steinach (1861-1944) was an Austrian physician and medical researcher who pioneered endocrine therapies. In the 1910s his work was primarily focused on male sexuality in relation to testosterone. He advocated vasoligation to improve men's sexual potency; the parallel operation (developed years later), for which he was best known, involved the irradiation of the ovaries so as to improve women's vitality and rejuvenate their appearance.

See Julie Prebel, "Engineering Womanhood," *American Literature* 76.2 (2004). Prebel notes that Atherton's treatment "consisted of eight sessions of X-rays directed at the ovaries" (307).

become important in the novel's final chapters), Mary Zattiany exhibits her independence from American culture and its preoccupations. She owes allegiance to no man, no one country, and no narrow social milieu, particularly one obsessed with personal pleasures. Her versatility is in part indicated by the various names by which she is known; at times she is referred to as Mary Ogden (her maiden name), the Countess Zattiany (from her Hungarian marriage), and also Marie (the European version of her name, used by a former lover). In the novel's early chapters, the Americans she meets do not know how to refer to her, a sign of her ambiguity as well as her determination to live her life on her own terms, aloof from others' judgments.

This aloofness aids Atherton's 58-year-old character as she descends into youth-worshipping New York. This was, after all, the era of the young generation's rise, as exemplified by the flapper. Mindful of the world outside of romantic interests, Mary Zattiany, who is by nature serious and ambitious, is poised to explore what a woman can accomplish if free from all conventional expectations, particularly those of her immediate milieu. The novel thus sheds light on what it meant to live during "the age of Youth,"[1] as is it somewhat mockingly termed in *Black Oxen*'s chapter 25, but to live in this era as a older woman. As another middle-aged figure in 20s fiction describes it, the era during which "youth so indisputedly ruled," left an older generation struggling to find its place.[2]

Because the novel suggests that rejuvenation practices could lengthen a lifespan and exponentially multiply an individual's productive years, it treats experience as an overlooked commodity that far exceeds the value of youthful energy alone. However, while youth appears synonymous with adolescent narcissism, rejuvenation, as Atherton depicts it, had the potential to introduce into society a heightened sense of social responsibility, now combined with recovered energy. Mary Zattiany makes such assertions soon after she reveals the story of her rejuvenation, asserting her belief in exploiting the "best period of usefulness, and philosophical as well as active enjoyment of life" (p. 187):

> Certainly, man's span is too brief now ... He withers and dies at an age when, if he has lived sanely ... he is beginning to see life as a whole, with that detachment that comes when his personal hold on life and affairs is relaxing, when he has realized

---

1 *Black Oxen*, 148. All subsequent citations appear parenthetically in the text and refer to this Broadview edition.

2 Edith Wharton, *The Mother's Recompense* (1925), 71.

his mistakes, and has attained a mental and moral orientation which could be of inestimable service to his fellow men, and to civilization in general. (p. 187)

Such passages create an argument for the value of experience (which is the one aspect of age that Atherton will treat positively), particularly in the suggestion that mature "detachment" serves the interests of many. The passage also associates a "philosophical" attitude with service to humanity. In the post-World War I context, Mary Zattiany's strong sense of social responsibility contrasts with the antics of the flapper generation, with its vapid youth and vigorous pursuit of personal pleasures.

Despite the novel's critique of pleasure-obsessed New York, it nonetheless begins with the somewhat paradoxical assertion that youthful beauty and audacity are unassailable values, when paired with a mature mind. Detailing Mary Zattiany's sensational appearance in New York at the theater, where she first exhibits her young form and self-assurance, the novel records much speculation about her identity. She resembles a young New Yorker known years ago as Mary Odgen, who would now be in her late 50s. Yet the disinterested stranger refuses to answer questions about her identity. Despite the machinations of a jealous flapper, she becomes involved with playwright Lee Clavering, who is in his mid-30s. Mary Zattiany eventually tells Clavering her story, revealing that she is not Mary Ogden's illegitimate child or niece (as some believe), but that she is the same woman, now possessed of a romantic and political past. She unapologetically reveals that she has relieved the boredom of a loveless marriage by engaging in romantic affairs and in Hungarian political intrigue. Her history also involves an account of her medical rejuvenation, which followed her work as a nurse in World War I. Finding herself spectacularly changed after the treatment, she has returned to New York on business. The responses of Clavering and her childhood friends follow.

Emerging near the middle of Atherton's career, *Black Oxen* effectively positioned Atherton as one of the most widely discussed American novelists of the 20s, alongside Sinclair Lewis and Edith Wharton.[1] Not only was the rejuvenation story widely discussed,

---

1 Frank Luther Mott, *Golden Multitudes* (1947), 253. Also see Emily Wortis Leider, *California's Daughter* (1991). By the 1920s, contends Leider, "Atherton's books ... were the most popular of all American novels" in Europe, "far outdistancing titles by Sinclair Lewis or Edith Wharton" (4).

but the character of Mary Zattiany was heralded by reviewers as stunningly new. Commonly portrayed figures such as the staid and backgrounded middle-aged woman (satirized by authors such as Lewis) and the vapid flapper—visible in novels such as *Flaming Youth* (1923), *The Great Gatsby* (1925), and *Gentlemen Prefer Blonds* (1925)—have little in common with Mary Zattiany, who appears as a woman free from all familial, financial, reproductive, sexual, and social limitations. In every way, Madame Zattiany counters the 20s ideal of the youthful girl-woman who embodied "not merely youth, but unripened youth," the type of figures who became "men's casual and light-hearted companions," in the words of 1920s social commentator Frederick Lewis Allen.[1] The flapper, as Atherton envisioned her, was a creature apart from the subtle, sophisticated rejuvenate. Somewhat like literary characters such as Wharton's Ellen Olenska in *The Age of Innocence* (1920) and Fitzgerald's Benjamin Button in "The Curious Case of Benjamin Button" (1922), Mary Zattiany exhibits a youthful form, while embodying the complexity that so many of the era's actual youth were perceived as lacking. In her case, experience in conversational, political, sartorial, and intellectual arts suggests Atherton's investment in highlighting the fact that sophistication can be gained only across time and through a daring life. Real, guileless youth, in other words, appears less compelling.

Mary Zattiany's multidimensionality, along with her analytical mind, worldly experience, and independence meant that she, as one reviewer asserted, "is an arresting figure, splendid as a diamond—and with more than a little of a diamond's hard and shallow quality. Rich, young, beautiful, of course, fascinating, with ... a power of magnetism no man can resist ... she was in every sense a woman with a past. For this past she has no shame and no regrets."[2] Such comments address Mary Zattiany's fascinating modernity, which is in part defined by her resistance to easy categorization. Childless in her youth and rendered sterile after her rejuvenation treatment, she has engaged in a unique type of reproduction—reproducing herself—and in her own image. Recreating the image of her youth while investigating her unique place in the world as a rejuvenated woman, Mary Zattiany is at once unpredictable and formidable. Experienced yet apparently youthful, aged yet apparently ageless, she is neither young nor old, but

---

1 Frederick Lewis Allen, *Only Yesterday: An Informal History of the Nineteen-Twenties* (1931), 108-09. See Appendix B2.
2 "Latest Works of Fiction," *New York Times*, 21 January 1923, BR 14, 3.

essentially both and, as a consequence, possessed of the qualities of two generations. Rather than feeling a double constraint, however, she remains profoundly independent.

Gertrude Atherton's Life and Career

As a professional who led a long, unusual, and peripatetic life, Gertrude Atherton was as restless as she was ambitious. Though her early career was characterized by lackluster and, at times, sharply critical reviews, Atherton achieved widespread fame over the course of a 60-odd-year career and authored more than 50 books. While *Black Oxen* was the author's most famous novel, Atherton was also known for her California-based fiction; she was also recognized, and at times soundly critiqued, for her depictions of strong, independent, and sexualized women. As biographer Charlotte McClure contends, Atherton envisioned herself as a "correct historian" of her times and upheld the value of "a novelist's instinct, unmolded by literary traditions, to imagine unusual circumstances that would develop the latent potentialities of selected types of characters."[1] Favoring unusual settings, uniquely motivated figures, and occasionally outrageous action, Atherton privileged densely populated social worlds, whether elite Manhattan, the Federal-era US, old California, or ancient Athens; in these worlds, the women of her fiction shine in relief to ordinary customs and social inhibitions.

In her autobiography, Atherton recounts how the perceived problem of her originality affected her early career. "The word original was a red rag to the American publisher," she contends, depicting the publishing community as blindly bound to tradition; one of Atherton's early novels, *Hermia Suydam* (about an "ugly woman" who "made herself over into a beauty" and who took a lover while rejecting the institution of marriage), produced a storm of criticism that was "venomous, vituperative, and personal," as Atherton viewed it.[2] One reviewer described the novel as "an aggressive story of that ugly kind which necessarily follows when romance has for its leaven human coarseness," a novel "not fitted to be brought into the family."[3] Taking pride in her work's deviation from the expected, Atherton seemed to measure herself by her willingness to chart a combative personal course. "There is

---

1 Charlotte McClure, *Gertrude Atherton* (1979), 38.
2 Gertrude Atherton, *Adventures of a Novelist* (1932), 138, 146, 148.
3 Leider, 82.

only one way in which man or woman can develop real strength," she would write, "and that is to fight unceasingly and to stand absolutely alone."[1]

Perhaps as a consequence of her belief in individualism, many contradictions characterize Atherton's life. She was said to possess much charm, but developed few lasting and warm relationships. She eloped suddenly at the age of 18, but later shunned marriage after the death of her husband, arguing, "no writer with a real gift and with a real ambition has any business with a home, children, the unintermittent comforts of life which stultify and stifle. If a man has the gift to write, to create,—the greatest of all gifts—what more does he want?"[2] As Atherton made her way alone, she owed allegiance to no family and no coterie of authors.[3] Perhaps most unconventionally, in her mid-to-late twenties, she became interested in reincarnation, feeling a particular affinity for the ancient Athenian, Aspasia, and wrote a fictional account of Aspasia's marriage to Pericles (based on Atherton's interpretation of the relationship), even as she simultaneously insisted on the uniqueness of any personality, particularly her own.

Born Gertrude Franklin Horn in October 1857 in San Francisco, Atherton was raised by her mother and, during various periods of financial and social difficulty, with the assistance of her maternal grandfather, Stephen Franklin. After Atherton's mother's divorce from Thomas Horn (an alcoholic), the family moved to the Franklin ranch near San Jose. In 1864, they returned to San Francisco; in 1865 Mrs. Horn married a man by the name of John F. Uhlhorn, who would desert the family in 1870, after losing his business, gambling, and committing forgery. While young Gertrude's formal education included her attendance at several girls' schools in San Francisco, biographers note that the child's most significant educational experiences occurred when her grandfather Franklin took charge of her literary education. When he moved in with his daughter's family, he requested that 14-year-old Gertrude read aloud to him two hours each evening, and he held

---

1 Gertrude Atherton, "Why is American Literature Bourgeois?" *North American Review* 178 (1904): 781.

2 Atherton, "Why?" 780.

3 Even California drew Atherton's ire, for in frustration, she once termed it "The Black Hole of Calcutta"—as stifling as a nearly airless dungeon in India where British soldiers of the East India Company, who had been taken prisoner, were said to have died from extremely cramped conditions in 1756. See Jennifer Bradley, "Woman at the Golden Gate: The Last Works of Gertrude Atherton," *Women's Studies* 12.1 (1986): 18.

her to exacting standards.[1] In 1874, Gertrude was sent to a great aunt in Lexington, Kentucky, for a year, where she attended the Sayre Institute; her formal schooling would end with her return to California a year later. Some accounts of her departure from Kentucky stress the failure of the Bank of California, in which the Franklins were invested, as precipitating her return; other renditions of this event, Atherton's among them, suggest that a year of high-spirited behavior prompted her relatives to send their young charge home. As Atherton records the moment in her autobiography, *Adventures of a Novelist* (1932), her Kentuckian Aunt Mary remarked at their parting: "You have your points, Gertrude, and I can't help liking you, but I am free to say that I was never so glad to see the last of any one in my life. I think you are headed straight for the devil, and I shall pray for you."[2]

Atherton married within six months of her return to California; her hasty union to George Atherton, then 24, was unexpected, not only because of the bride's youth, the couple's brief acquaintance, and their secretive elopement, but primarily because Atherton had been courting Gertrude Horn's mother, Gertrude Uhlhorn, who was 14 years his senior. In this strange scenario of generational crossing, mirror first names and similar surnames, and overlapping attractions, some of the themes that would appear in *Black Oxen* are visible. Reportedly greeted by her mother with the query, "'Do I look any older?'" upon her return from Kentucky, Atherton essentially aged Mrs. Uhlhorn by marrying her beau and then by bearing two children in quick succession, thereby transforming Gertrude Uhlhorn into a grandmother and not the young lover she had seemed, so recently, to be.[3] The Atherton marriage took place in 1876. Later that year, a son, George Goñi Atherton (Georgie) was born, followed by a daughter, Muriel, in 1878.

Atherton found family life confining, in part because her wealthy in-laws participated in a social sphere that conscripted women's social interactions and because of her limited time for pursuing anything other than domestic and social interests. In addition, the Athertons' distrust of women authors hampered Atherton's literary pursuits. According to Atherton, her husband's family disapproved of her reading and actively attempted to hamper it. When she received her first paycheck for a serial novel, she indulged in a book-buying spree, and did not, as her husband had hoped, offer

---

1 Leider, 32.
2 Atherton, *Adventures*, 43.
3 Atherton, *Adventures*, 45.

to pay his debts.[1] That fiction, *The Randolphs of Redwoods* (1883), published in *The Argonaut*, a San Francisco weekly, appeared under a pseudonym, but the eventual revelation of the novel's authorship brought about Atherton's ostracism in both Menlo Park, where the Athertons summered, and in San Francisco, where the family wintered, especially because the novel's events were seen as mirroring a local high society scandal of female alcoholism.[2] Yet Atherton continued to write, publishing short fiction in various San Francisco magazines and composing a second novel, *What Dreams May Come*, which was published in 1888.

By 1887, Atherton's life had changed dramatically, for both her husband and older child, Georgie, were dead (one of complications related to a kidney stone and the other, at age six, of diphtheria). As a widow of 30, Atherton characteristically decided to live on her own terms, illustrating a scenario that would become significant across her work—that of a woman who exercises the strength and assertiveness necessary to change her life. Her daughter, Muriel, was sent to live with her paternal grandmother, while Atherton devoted herself to her profession in New York. This relocation reflected her sense that both the West coast and a married state made for a difficult entrée into the realm of American letters.[3] Yet despite her hopes, Atherton found the New York literati cold and the reviewers unappreciative of her work. She departed for Paris after the publication of her third novel, *Hermia Suydam* (1889), which dealt with sexual relationships outside of marriage and which was condemned for its frankness. From 1889-99, Atherton was particularly peripatetic, moving from the US to London and then to Paris, returning to California, then moving back to England, and eventually making her home in Washington, DC. It would be decades before she would settle into any home.

When Atherton returned to California in 1890, she assessed the literary potential of her native state as never before, gaining a new perspective after her European travels. As a result, regional subjects formed the basis of *Los Cerritos* (1890) as well as two collections of stories featuring California, *Before the Gringo Came* (1894) and *The Splendid Idle Forties* (1902). Along with Atherton's embrace of California's land and history came unprecedented critical praise, which suggests that Atherton's expansionist work with gender was most comprehensible when wedded to the

1 Leider, 59.
2 Leider, 57-58.
3 Bradley, 18.

regionalist subject of early, unpredictable life in California. As early as 1891, Atherton was being asked by magazines such as *Cosmopolitan* to compose essays about the literary representation of California. Articulating her awareness of her California-based fiction's value, Atherton claimed, "If I ever get any literary reputation, it will be over these stories, and I should like everything else I have ever done forgotten."[1] Atherton's regionalist writing was especially appreciated in England, where she was viewed as representative of the US and of the unique culture of the American West. With the appearance of *The Californians* (1898), she was considered, according to a British review, "one of the most vivid and entertaining interpreters of the complex characteristics of American womanhood."[2] Another reviewer (also British) claimed "in point of sheer power there is not a living woman novelist who comes near her."[3] This period of her career "made" her as a writer, Atherton would later claim.[4]

When Atherton later wrote of her efforts to achieve success in the literary world, she frequently compared herself to other strong, professional women, whom she viewed as kindred spirits, particularly when they, like her, challenged their professional establishments. In an account of opera singer Sybil Sanderson, whom Atherton met in San Francisco in the mid-1880s, Atherton's sympathetic approach to career struggles can be observed, particularly in her telling of Sanderson's 1889 debut at the Opéra Comique. Possessed of a three-octave range and an unusually clear voice, Sanderson was an outsider to the musical world of Paris.[5] Stressing both Sanderson's work ethic as well as her disregard of the critical establishment, Atherton describes what Sybil faced in the "sharp cynical faces" of the critics, as well as the "Sneers. Ridicule. Pens tipped with venom ... offering Sybil up on a platter, disemboweled and dismembered."[6] Braving the negative reviews and pursuing her work, even when success seemed unlikely, Sanderson triumphed. Atherton concludes Sanderson's

---

1 Quoted in Leider, 112.
2 *The Spectator: A Weekly Review of Politics, Literature, Theology and Art*, 1 October 1898, p. 445. Atherton quotes this review in her autobiography, 292.
3 From the British newspaper *The Sketch*, quoted in advertisement, *The Pall Mall Gazette*, 25 November 1898, p. 191. Atherton also quotes from this review in *Adventures*, 292.
4 Atherton, *Adventures*, 292.
5 Atherton, *Adventures*, 153-54.
6 Atherton, *Adventures*, 155, 156, 157, 158.

story, noting, "The French themselves quickly forgot the adverse criticism and pronounced her a great artist. As time went on she became the idol of Paris, and one of the most brilliant figures in Europe," thereby authoring the kind of story Atherton liked best: that of the upstart woman achieving greatness on her own terms.[1] It was, significantly, the story she authored in regard to her own career as well.

Favorable reviews of Atherton's work by English reviewers made her pointedly critical of what she saw as the imaginative deficits of American literature, which she attributed to the nation's insular attitude and conservative literary culture. Casting American writers as a flock of "literary sheep" who are "almost invariably without style, distinction," Atherton viewed successful authors as devoted to "the little and the obvious."[2] The US, thus, was characterized by a "distinctly middle-class" attitude, in that it is "afraid of doing the wrong thing" in every respect. "It is as correct as Sunday clothes and as innocuous as sterilized milk," Atherton argued.[3] By contrast, Atherton cast herself as striving to adopt the role of an artist whose imagination, not her publishing community, determines her inventive work. Not surprisingly, Atherton's attitudes took the form of a rebellion against the dominant trends in late nineteenth-century publishing, particularly realism. Atherton claimed to loathe William Dean Howells and his realist principles, decrying realism's "fatal influence," along with "the excruciating boredom of [Howells's] novels." When these comments were circulated with unexpected publicity, Atherton responded, "Well, I am glad of it. I only wish I had been old enough and bold enough to extinguish him before he got in his deadly work. He was a curse."[4] "Howells's star," she wrote elsewhere,

> was also in the ascendant, but he made all life seem commonplace and I detested him. I think it a pity he ever lived, for he was a blight on American letters. He founded the school of the commonplace, and to any young writer who hated the commonplace as I did, the Howells tradition was an almost insurmountable obstacle on his upward path. Those who followed in his footsteps were reasonably sure of success, not only because

1 Atherton, *Adventures*, 159.
2 Atherton, "Why?" 776, 775.
3 Atherton, "Why?" 778.
4 Gertrude Atherton, "Wanted: Imagination." *What is a Book? Thoughts about Writing* (1935), 56.

the critics, largely of his own ilk, decreed that realism (littleism would have been a better word) was the fashion, but because the majority of fiction readers were necessarily commonplace and enjoyed reading about their own kind.[1]

Not only does realism represent the banal, in Atherton's view, but it in turn *reproduces* the commonplace. Working outside the confines of realism, for Atherton, meant imagining a new breed of characters altogether.[2] Atherton would later claim, "What I am looking for is more superwomen in history."[3]

Novels such as *Hermia Suydam* (1889), *The Doomswoman* (1892), *Patience Sparhawk* (1894), *American Wives and English Husbands* (1898), and *Black Oxen* (1923) attempted to represent "superwomen," as they stressed the challenges experienced by unusual women, but also highlighted women's eventual successes. In part, Atherton's objections to realism appear rooted in her commitment to creating fictional women who are socially progressive as well as non-conformist; these creations closely resemble the projection of self in which Atherton was most invested—that of a controversial beauty, quick of wit, by turns feminine and coldly intellectual, and rich in sexual or "animal" magnetism.[4] Both Atherton's regional writings and her audacious women characters continued to define her career. *Black Oxen*, her most popular novel, revitalized her career, and its topics reappeared in *The Crystal Cup* (1925), which like *Black Oxen* was made into a film by the First National Film Company. Novels about the ancient world followed, including *The Immortal Marriage* (1927), which featured Pericles and Aspasia, *The Jealous Gods* (1928), and *Dido, Queen of Hearts* (1929). In 1940, Atherton was named first among California's Most Distinguished Women, and in 1942, she was described in the *San Francisco Chronicle* as uniquely able to "grasp of the new thing ... what people had just begun to think about."[5] As reviewers came to understand Atherton's career, she was depicted as a woman of her time, firmly and unapologetically engaged in its debates and controversies.

---

1 Atherton, *Adventures*, 101-02.
2 See McClure, 39. Atherton's style, according to McClure, was "a judicious blend of the Romantic and the Realistic" and "had become for her the only type of novel that was 'true to life.'"
3 McClure, 52.
4 See McClure on Atherton's friendships, 23-24.
5 Joseph Henry Jackson, "Watch the Parade: Write It All Down," *San Francisco Chronicle*, 1 November 1942, 11.

Age in the Flapper Era

In querying the conditions that enabled women to achieve individuality in the early twentieth century, Atherton emphasized
such qualities as maturity and intelligence. The 1920s, as Atherton presents them, enabled women to define their position in
the world, especially if they were as strong and non-conformist
as Mary Zattiany, who begins, notably, by redefining her relation
to age. By championing her character's experience, sophistication, and investment in political power, Atherton issued a direct
challenge to the primacy of youth's appeal, just as she challenged
masculinity's claim to elder statesman-like qualities, for Mary
Zattiany is both youthful in appearance and a formidable political negotiator (if not in the present, then in her European past).
If, as the novel's title (borrowed from Yeats) suggests, "The years
like great black oxen tread the world, And God, the herdsman
goads them on behind," then Zattiany avoids this pummeling, and
in spectacular fashion. Atherton makes this point in the novel's
epigraph by cutting the quotation before Yeats's next line, which
reads "And I am broken by their passing feet."[1] The medical procedures at the center of the novel challenge not only age's ability
to break an individual, but also God and the mechanisms of age
He controls. Instead, Atherton allows Mary Zattiany to control
her age with her espousing of modern medicine.

While the medical dimensions of this novel's history constitute the book's most frequently discussed aspects, they are fas-
cinatingly multi-dimensional. Atherton claimed that her decision
to partake in rejuvenation therapy (also known as "reactivation"
therapy or "being Steinached") stemmed from the fear that her
"mind had really gone sterile," or more specifically, that despite
a life of regular literary productivity, she had reached a moment
when she could not create.[2] Admitting that "I had been satisfied
with nothing I had written since *The Perch of the Devil*" (1914) and
that "my mental dynamo refused to tune up,"[3] she pursued the
treatment after reading about a prominent physician who was able
to recapture "all the energy and endurance" of a much younger man after the treatment.[4] After the operation, the physician,

---

1   These are the penultimate lines from Yeats's play *The Countess Cathleen*.
    The Countess Cathleen (1999), 738-39.
2   Atherton, *Adventures*, 554.
3   Atherton, *Adventures*, 554.
4   Atherton, *Adventures*, 555, 556.

Atherton notes, would work "fourteen hours a day, and hardly knew what it was to feel fatigue."[1] In the narrative of her experience with the procedure, Atherton focuses primarily on its merits for working professionals. Mary Zattiany, too, describes her decision to undergo the Steinach procedure as based on a "growing mental lassitude, a constant sense of effort in talking everlastingly on subjects that called for constant alertness and often reorientation" (186). As a result, Zattiany claims, "I was really aghast and began to look toward the future not only with a sense of helplessness but of intolerable weariness," engaging in a holistic argument for rejuvenation. The novel thus echoes physicians' claims that a number of complaints could be traced to endocrine deficiencies, including arteriosclerosis, premature senescence, and "diabetes, gout, cancer, metabolistic disturbances of every description, impotence and nervous diseases" as well as insanity.[2] Like Steinach, Charles Evans Morris, whose *Modern Rejuvenation Methods* was published in 1926, believed that rejuvenation techniques could affect the entire body. In particular, he explained that the technique's method of "attacking ... sluggish cells" meant infusing the body with energy.[3]

After her medical examination by Dr. Harry Benjamin, who would remain a life-long correspondent, Atherton was told that her "pituitary and thyroid glands were likely depleted and that there should be a fresh release of hormones into the blood stream."[4] As a consequence, in 1922, at the age of 64, Atherton decided to partake in "X-Ray stimulation in a laboratory," which was a "painless and rather boring process."[5] What followed, according to Atherton's description, was a period of lethargy, and then, as she recounts it, a marked change occurred:

And then, one day—it was about a week after the finish of the treatments—I had the abrupt sensation of a black cloud lifting

---

1 Atherton, *Adventures*, 556.
2 George F. Corners, *Rejuvenation: How Steinach Makes People Young* (1923), 54. (See Appendix A1.)
3 Charles Evans Morris, *Modern Rejuvenation Methods* (1926), 123.
4 Atherton, *Adventures*, 558. See Dr. Harry Benjamin, "Steinach-Therapy against Old Age (A Review of Ten Years' Experience)," 11. Manuscript, Bancroft Library, University of California, Berkeley. Dr. Harry Benjamin, Atherton's physician, saw his practice increase dramatically after the publication of *Black Oxen* and would later reference Atherton as one of his great successes.
5 Atherton, *Adventures*, 558.

from my brain, hovering for a moment, rolling away. Torpor vanished. My brain seemed sparkling with light. I was standing in the middle of the room when this miracle happened and I almost flung myself at my desk. I wrote steadily for four hours; marched [Countess Zattiany] triumphantly out of the theatre, with a complete knowledge of who she was, what had happened to her, what was going to happen to her and the hero came to life in the first paragraph.... It all gushed out like a geyser that had been "capped" down in the cellars of my mind, battling for release.[1]

As Atherton mentions her character, Mary Zattiany, she refers to the fact that she had previously envisioned this character in a theater setting, though she had been unable to create the full plot. In many ways, Atherton linked the vitality of her character to the mental flexibility she attributed to her own regenerated state. In her account, Madame Zattiany becomes an emblem of restored creativity.

During the years just before and following the publication of *Black Oxen*, "glandular science" was the frequent subject of newspaper articles and medical studies. As may be imagined, not all of this conversation was sympathetic to the goals of those seeking rejuvenation. Atherton would address the procedure's skeptics with typical ardor, identifying them as Americans of the "narrow-minded, ignorant, moronic, bigoted, cowardly, self-righteous, anemic, pig-headed, stupid, puritanical, hypocritical, prejudiced, fanatical" type, or "cocoa-blooded atavists, who soothe their inferiority complex by barking their hatred of anything new. The very word Science is abhorrent to them, and, if they ruled the world, progress would cease."[2] Atherton concludes by raining vituperation upon doubters, noting, "We live in an age of scientific marvels, and those who do not take advantage of them are fools and deserve the worst that malignant Nature can inflict upon them."[3]

According to Julie Prebel, the moderns' desire to "change undesirable social behavior" through medicine emerged in relation to eugenic interests, immigration debates, sexology (or the study of sexual difference), and age therapies.[4] In *Sex and Life: Forty Years of Biological and Medical Experiments*, Dr. Eugen Steinach,

---

1 Atherton, *Adventures*, 558-59.
2 Atherton, *Adventures*, 561.
3 Atherton, *Adventures*, 562.
4 Prebel, 308.

rejuvenation's pioneer, lists the principal problems he viewed as related to hormonal deficiencies, or what he referenced as "endocrine depletions," including painful menstruation, headaches, knee and joint pain, skin disorders, brittleness of the finger nails, hair loss, vascular spasms, migraines, nervous over-excitability, vomiting, visual derangements, and sexual frigidity.[1] According to its proponents, the Steinach operation was less extreme than invasive gland grafting (which involved organs from other species), for it meant that "the functions of the patient's own glands are stimulated and re-energized into a more youthful activity."[2] Discussions of the new, age-related therapies had become deeply enmeshed in the popular culture of the modern era. At this juncture, experimental procedures included injections of the "extract of canine testicles," vasoligature, work with "prepared fetal sheep cells," electrical currents, and the "gland grafting" experiments of Dr. Serge Voronoff, which served as radical interventions into hormonal and reproductive therapies.[3] Yet by focusing on a politically motivated woman's rejuvenation, Atherton drew attention to the possibilities of women's social (and not biologically reproductive) productivity.[4]

---

1 Eugen Steinach, *Sex and Life: Forty Years of Biological and Medical Experiments* (1940), 200-01. (See Appendix A2.)

2 Harry Benjamin, "'The New Fountain of Youth': How the Famous Steinach Operation Checks the Progress of Old Age—A Record of Its Success to Date," *McClure's Magazine* (1924): 106.

3 See Susan Squier, "Incubabies and Rejuvenates: The Traffic between Technologies of Reproduction and Age-Extension," *Figuring Age: Women, Bodies, Generations* (1999), 89. Throughout the 1920s, as Susan Squier reports, *The New York Times* and *Time* magazine frequently covered innovations in glandular science. Also see Laura Davidow Hirshbein, "The Glandular Solution: Sex, Masculinity, and Aging in the 1920s," *Journal of the History of Sexuality* 9.3 (2000). In part, glandular science became popular because of an interest in prolonging "masculine power indefinitely through renewal of their sex glands" (280).

4 Squier, 88-98. Atherton, who was not opposed to invasive therapies, would later participate in the "surgical implantation of ovarian tissue from sheep—an adaptation of the notorious 'monkey gland' experiments of Dr. Serge Voronoff." When the treatment yielded no spectacular results, Atherton was reportedly disappointed (Leider, 305-06). Atherton's definition of rejuvenation's goal was particularly significant in the context of ongoing experiments that took an interest in women's fertility, as in the implantation of chimpanzee ovaries into women and one case of the "grafting" of human reproductive organs into a female chimpanzee, which was impregnated with a human fetus (which did not live) in 1926.

Throughout the 1920s, Atherton was an ardent champion of the modernity she equated with increased possibilities for self-definition. Physical beauty, elasticity, and "fresh" faces were of great importance to her, as much as she was invested in medicine's effect upon mental vitality. Atherton was frequently described by friends and associates as a physically conscious individual, even a vain one (much to the amusement of reporters who interviewed her in her advanced years). In *Black Oxen*, too, physical beauty is an intrinsic part of the narrative. While Mary Zattiany triumphs over an ageist society, it is also notable that Atherton insists that her protagonist is a beauty, not *because* of her age, but *in spite* of it, thereby upholding a traditional fascination with youthful forms, which she combines with an experienced psyche in Mary Zattiany. Notable hostility toward advanced age is evident in the novel's representation of Mary Zattiany in her pre-activation state.[1] Even before he knows her secret, Lee Clavering contends (in reference to the New York stage), "we are too young a country to tolerate middle-age heroines" (p. 76). When he discovers that his lover is in fact *past* middle age, the revelation conjures for him the vision of a skeletal and withered hag, and he wonders, "Should he not always see the old face under the new mask, as the X-rays revealed man's hideous interior under its merciful covering of flesh?" (p. 191). At such moments, the novel maintains the larger culture's obsession with youthful forms, just as it upholds such qualities as beauty, slimness, and patrician coolness, often without complication.

When Zattiany reveals her identity-based secret to the now-aged contemporaries from her youth (in the novel's dramatic chapter 26), they react with conservative horror, voicing moral outrage at her escape from age's outward signs and, notably, articulating a sense of horror directed at the aging process itself. They display a "chill of terror, in some cases revulsion" as Mary Zattiany describes the procedure that has prevented her from "growing old with themselves; as any natural Christian woman would" (p. 157). The assembled women understand any deviation from the norm, even a welcome deviation, as "not only mysterious and terrifying but subtly indecent" (p. 157), but they also express horror at their own aging forms. "Time," according to the grand dame,

---

1 As Julie Prebel notes, she appears as an aging "grotesque," seen by observers as "an older woman ... 'faded! ... withered, changed, skinny where she had been slim, her throat concealed by a dog collar a yard long—her expression sad and apathetic—the dethroned idol of men'" (323).

Jane Oglethorpe, "is a brute to all women" (p. 201). By the time she was 50 and a widow, she claims, "my complexion was gone, my stomach high, and I had the face of an old war horse. But—and here is the damned trick that nature plays on us—I hoped—hoped—I dreamed—and as ardently as I ever had dreamed in my youth ... that these clever intelligent men would look through the old husk and see only the young heart and the wise brain—I knew that I could give them more than many a younger woman" (p. 204). Such confessions not only define the signs of age as a product of conventional thinking, but they also cement Atherton's representation of the US's cultural fearfulness, as she depicts the nation as immured in cultural norms, not because their manifestations are pleasing, but because everyone submits to them, however destructive.

In Mary Zattiany, however, the novel presents an endless circuit of youth and age as interwoven. At her first appearance, the stranger's face belies her body's apparent youth, and what emerges is a narrative of her idealized hybridity. Lee Clavering's first view of Mary Zattiany is full of suggestions of the ironic distance and self-possession that became attributable to age, once her history is known. Rather than serving as the object of an appropriating gaze, Mary Zattiany wields a gaze of her own, coolly objectifying Clavering, who notes that these eyes appear "inconceivably wise, cold, disillusioned. She did not look a day over twenty-eight. There were no marks of dissipation on her face. But for its cold regularity it would have looked younger—with her eyes closed. The eyes seemed to gaze down out of an infinitely remote past" (p. 45). Mary Zattiany's power, then, emerges in her unique combination of independence (born of experience) and her attractiveness. Impervious to the will of men because of her mind, which protects the youthful body from the overt sexual interests that make the flapper generation ridiculous, Mary Zattiany is both lovely and skeptical, youthful in appeal and experienced in worldly realms.

Atherton's depiction of a 58-year-old heroine, sexualized and lovely, challenged the mainstream American culture's obsession with raw youth, just as it complicated the comfortable reliability of an older generation. The jazz age in which the characters operate appears as a deeply hypocritical era, in Atherton's portrayal, for while youth are sentimentalized, they are also deeply distrusted. For Atherton, flapper youth are bereft of conversational abilities and subtlety alike. Critiquing the dangerous velocity of the "too pampered American girl," for whom "youth ... promised to be briefer than ever!" figures such as Clavering are clearly invested in youth's outward signs, but not the ideas or lifestyles associated with the younger generation (p. 129). The problem, then, is not youth so much as a culture that idealizes the crudely young and does nothing to socialize them. Fitzgerald's worldly, vain youth exemplify this pattern, as do the vapid young women of Anita Loos's works and the unbound women of *Flaming Youth*, a popular novel (and subsequent film) from the early twenties. With her indiscretions and adolescent narcissism, Janet Oglethorpe, the novel's flapper figure, stands as a reminder that those who are possessed of physical youth are often devoid of the ability to spend this resource wisely. When Janet appears with "big black eyes ... sparkling wickedly, her vivid little mouth [in] a twist that can only be described as a grin" (p. 129) or as a sneering grinning, boozing, ill-mannered, cigarette-smoking being with the "dark naughty little face" (p. 120) of a "glorified gutter-snipe" (p. 125), she is contrasted with Zattiany's brilliantly substantive conversation. It would be ironic that the actress playing Janet Oglethorpe, Clara Bow, would launch her career based on the perceived charm that her character embodied, in the eyes of the film's reviewers. (See Appendices D3 and D4.)

In the popular press, writers typically noted that the consequences of flapperdom would be dire, imagining a growing "looseness" in manners, minimal clothing, the liberal use of cosmetics, and fears of sexual promiscuity. With her irresponsible and short youth, the flapper must have seemed a prime candidate for future rejuvenation, particularly in light of fears that the flapper would squander her youth. Critics frequently predicted that flappers would never settle into mature society or become social leaders, mothers, or role models. More immediate concerns encircled reports of dancing, drinking, and other exhibitionistic behaviors. Specifically, flappers of the prohibition era were reportedly "getting stewed to the gills" while "shooting craps and playing bridge and poker for high stakes while under the influence of drink."[1] The flapper's sexual experimentation, or her permissiveness regarding "petting," along with "snugglepupping" (both of which allowed bodily, though clothed, contact), were frequently raised as concerns as the flapper craze spread.[2]

---

1 "Councilman Quinn and the Female Flapper," *Washington Post*, 22 January 1922, 65.

2 "Blame Girls for 'Snugglepupping' and 'Petting Parties' in Chicago," *Washington Post*, 12 March 1922, 21.

For critics of the flapper generation, maturity could not come into vogue too quickly. As early as the summer of 1922, a range of articles predicting the end of flapperism appeared. "The Younger Generation is going out of style more rapidly than short skirts," crowed one writer.[1] A number of stylists embraced the mature woman of thirty as an antidote to the flapper, an ideal that intersected with the heroine that Atherton would create. As a woman who appears to be in her late 20s, Mary Zattiany would have embodied a stark contrast to the flapper, for she was an embodiment of the "new," mature figure so enthusiastically embraced by the fashion reporters, a "woman whose soul has developed, whose mind has grown, whose heart has expanded—the full-bloom rose of 30."[2] "It is undoubtedly true," wrote one author in *The New York Times*, "that women are 'more beautiful, intelligent, poised and attractive' at twenty-eight than at the 'sweet sixteen' of Victorian romance."[3] Despite the fact that "the stores bought the longer skirts and tried to sell them," the more subdued, "mature" styles failed to inspire consumers. Nonetheless, the press's willingness to oppose the 30-year-old to the teen-aged flapper suggests a significant move in its recognition that multiple generations of American women could be held up as ideal, albeit in regard to different understandings of beauty and in light of gradations of age suggested by the term "youth." (See also Appendix C.)

National and International Contexts

As it attends to varied alignments among its characters, *Black Oxen* raises a set of questions not only about personal maturity, but also about the nature of a mature, modern nation, treating an American obsession with youth as an index to a set of broader cultural limitations. In the view of Atherton's heroine, American culture appears immature, divisive, and unwelcoming to a true sophisticate, in part because society is divided into distinct subcultures. These divisions sever not only youth from the more mature, but the intelligentsia from the free thinkers, the teetotalers from the boozers, and the New Yorkers from the rest of the world. In many ways, the novel's social divisions appear as artificial as they are distinct, enforcing separations that contribute to the larger society's inability to reconcile its internal oppositions. As Frederick Lewis

---

1   "The Passing of Youth," *New York Times*, 11 June 1922, 38.
2   Helen Rowland, "Exit the Flapper," *Washington Post*, 5 August 1922, 9.
3   "Sweet and Twenty-Eight," *New York Times*, 14 June 1922, 15.

Allen wrote in 1931 of the nation's intellectual life, "the intellectuals of the country ... differed vehemently among themselves."[1] For such groups, "New York was their chief rallying-point," where they abutted various other subcultures.[2] Clavering, for example, is part of a social group that functions as a symbol of American intellectual urbanity. As a playwright and a "Sophisticate," he is part of the New York intelligentsia, the supposed best of the young, educated urban professionals, or a rarified and insular group.

The Sophisticates group, which also includes Clavering's author friend, Gora Dwight, is composed of socially affiliated writers and publishers. Reviews of *Black Oxen* attest to the fact that this depiction was understood as referencing the figures of the "Algonquin Round Table," who gathered daily at the Algonquin Hotel in Midtown Manhattan. As a review from *Time* noted, *Black Oxen* "deal[s] with literary New York of today" and represents "the famous 'round table' at which sit the supposedly elect."[3] Composed of dramatists, writers, magazines editors, press agents, and reviewers connected to publications such as *The New Yorker*, the *Saturday Tribune*, and *Life*, the group included such figures as Heywood Broun, Ruth Hale, George Kaufman, Carl Van Vechten, Dorothy Parker, Edna Ferber, Harpo Marx, Robert Sherwood, Robert Benchley, Harold Ross, and Donald Odgen Stuart, to name but a few affiliates, a group that acquired an air of insularity and elitism, despite the socialism (and feminism) of its various members. Although their individual careers varied, the group was recognizable and, for the matter of a decade or so, home to witty repartee and discussion of current events.

Aspects of this subculture may be understood as an engaging what Ann Douglas has termed the modern tendency to produce "terrible honesty," or direct confrontations with contentious issues.[4] Yet *Black Oxen* paints the group as purely superficial, suggesting that despite their reputation, the Sophisticates are not truly advanced, their endless repartee constituting an enclosed circuit of conversation. Readers acquainted with Freud (as many might have been by 1923), would have been prepared to interpret the group's endless attention to wit as evidence of "pleasure in

---

1 Allen, 228.

2 Allen, 228.

3 "Books: Sophisticates," *Time*, 3 March 1923, 12. The review depicts Van Vechten vividly, with "imposing ... white hair and youthful face, bitter, with his tongue, clever with the somewhat too facile pen."

4 See Ann Douglas, *Terrible Honesty: Mongrel Manhattan in the 1920s* (1996), chapter one.

nonsense," or a limited developmental phase akin to the "child [who] learns to control the vocabulary of its mother tongue" and as it "apparently takes great pleasure in 'experimenting playfully," with that material.[1] Isolated within a verbally oriented, aggrandized social circle possessed of a particularly located urban sensibility, the Sophisticates appear as limited as the Algonquin Round Table's members, who were readily satirized, as in Lorelei Lee's comment from *Gentleman Prefer Blonds* (1925) that "it is wonderful to have so many internal resources that you never have to bother to go outside of yourself to see anything."[2] The Sophisticates reappear in a later Atherton novel, and the main character adopts a similarly critical stance toward the group, noting that "it was pleasant to bask in the atmosphere of people so thoroughly pleased with themselves."[3] Eventually, this character comes to believe that these "clever people could be ... monotonous in time."[4] Late in *Black Oxen*, Mary Zattiany recognizes that her interest in the group is born merely of Clavering's prominence, and she recognizes that the group members "were not for her. Their conversations, interests, shallow mental attitude to life, bored her" (p. 245). As a Sophisticate, Clavering is poised to enter a relationship with Mary Zattiany that will either challenge his strong affiliations with the group or force Mary to conform.

If the Sophisticates stood for an "aristocracy of intellect," then this new "aristocracy" promised to replace the real gentry Zattiany left in Europe.[5] Such a comparison reveals hints of trouble as Zattiany attempts to accommodate herself to her lover's milieu. The most damning portrait of the Sophisticates appears when she and Clavering journey to a mountain retreat near the novel's end. Hoping for a much-needed rest and time alone with Clavering, Zattiany is immersed into a group holiday. Ironically, what she discovers is proof of the Sophisticates' indebtedness to cultural primitivism. Upon examining the Native American décor of their camp, they burst into "war whoops" (p. 245) and appear "no less primitive in soul than woodsmen who had never seen a city," whooping and dancing until Mary believes that "They were no longer doing a stunt, they were atavistic" (p. 275). Such

---

1 Sigmund Freud, *The Basic Writings of Sigmund Freud* (1938), 717.
2 Anita Loos, *Gentlemen Prefer Blondes and But Gentlemen Marry Brunettes* (1998), 142.
3 Atherton, *Crystal Cup*, 135.
4 Atherton, *Crystal Cup*, 244, 221.
5 Nina Miller, *Making Love Modern: The Intimate Public Worlds of New York's Literary Women* (1999), 93.

behaviors are not restorative, however, despite the era's belief in the regenerative powers of the primitive. For these New Yorkers, primitive investments in romance, physicality, and escapism reign, despite their claims to cultural evolution. On a national level, too, the novel hints, backwardness reigns in American culture.

The novel maintains a critical stance toward an intellectual culture that excludes more than it includes, that exists on the trading of witticisms and insular jokes, and that has no interest in international affairs in the post-World War I decade. In this milieu, Mary Zattiany's early allusions to her war-relief work fall on indifferent ears, as do her interests in the plight of European orphans, especially those in Hungary and Austria, for whom she wants to establish a "relief committee" so as alleviate their sufferings (p. 153). In New York, the talk remains of New York, and so Mary Zattiany's sense of responsibility as a Countess exists at the periphery of the text from its earliest pages. As she notes, "I am told that Americans avoid serious topics in Society. I, alas, have become very serious," or "very serious" in a context that is not (p. 70). If American "sophistication," as Atherton suggests, was but a synonym for slick and stylized insularity, then it would necessarily appear limited to the experienced eyes of a true cosmopolitan, for whom elitism is balanced out by a sense of social responsibility. A lovely, youthful-looking woman with a mature sense of civic engagement would need to look beyond the US for her ideal environment.

Mary Zattiany's aloofness from American attitudes draws attention to the fact that during the post-war years, Americans turned inward, both socially and politically. In the wake of World War I, immigration law, for example, was altered so to exclude peoples considered culturally and ethnically undesirable; in addition, the economic depression in 1920 overlapped with a new wave of immigration, resulting in a "new nationalism demanding a greater homogeneity than seemed to be emerging from the melting pot" as "ethnic homogeneity" grew in popularity.[1] Moreover, "a highly developed ... wariness of the dangers of too-close communion with trans-Atlantic developments—a wariness at times bordering on childishness" became visible in American foreign policy.[2] Mary Zattiany, however, stands for an international awareness that challenges the dominant social trends. By creating a transnational dimension to Zattiany's experience, Atherton implicitly critiques

---

1   L. Ethan Ellis, *Republican Foreign Policy, 1921-1933* (1968), 15.
2   Ellis, 78.

the childish nature of US isolationism, treating it as an analogue to the youthful Americans' focus on selfhood. By contrast, Mary Zattiany is a singular figure and true cosmopolitan; she is a citizen of the world. She stands aligned with beauty and intellect (even the beauty *of* intellect), the audacity of logic that supersedes personal interests, and the recognition that diplomacy in the wake of an international war is a necessary and worthy enterprise. By the novel's end, in foregoing a romantic liaison within the US in order to organize relief work in Europe, Mary Zattiany is willing to sublimate sexual desire to social productivity; her children will be Europe's orphans, her adoption of the many superseding interests that are merely personal.

Willing to enact her sense of social responsibility, her sense of her "old mind in the young brain," (p. 301) and not, like the flapper, to elude it under the guise of charming irresponsibility, Mary Zattiany is a figure possessed of what Tyrus Miller terms a "reserved and diplomatic face," in contrast to the "fractious" early modernist figure imbued with optimism and energy.[1] Youthfully energized, experienced, and aloof from the US, she exists in a position that allows her an enormous ability to stand aloof from the world she views, a world which admires her, however cautiously.

---

1 Tyrus Miller, *Late Modernism: Politics, Fiction, and the Arts between the World Wars* (1999), 11.

Gertrude Atherton: A Brief Chronology

1857   Gertrude Horn born, 30 October in San Francisco, California.

1860   Gertrude Horn's parents (Gertrude Franklin Horn and Thomas L. Horn) divorce on the grounds of Horn's intemperance; family moves to Franklin ranch near San Jose.

1864   Horn family returns to San Francisco when Gertrude Franklin Horn marries John F. Uhlhorn.

1870   Gertrude Horn attends Clark Institute; Uhlorn deserts the family.

1873   Gertrude Horn attends school at St. Mary's Hall.

1874   Gertrude Horn is sent to live with relatives in Kentucky and to the Sayre Institute in Lexington, Kentucky.

1875   Gertrude Horn returns to San Francisco and attracts the attention of George Atherton, who had been courting her mother, Gertrude Horn Uhlhorn. Atherton later describes her future husband's interest in her as "The old story of youth calling to youth against the declining charms of middle-age" in her autobiography, *Adventures of a Novelist* (p. 50).

1876   Eighteen-year-old Gertrude Horn elopes with George Atherton in February; the couple live in Valparaiso Park with the well-to-do Atherton family, who attempt to teach domestic duties to Gertrude and to limit her literary interests; in November, George Goñi Atherton (Georgie) born.

1878   The George Athertons move to a rancho in Jolon, Monterey County, which George manages for his family.

1878   The Athertons return to Valparaiso Park; Muriel Atherton born.

1882   The Athertons move outside of San Francisco to a grape farm in Oroville; death of George Goñi, who is in San Francisco with his paternal grandmother, Dominga Atherton.

1883   Atherton's first novel, *The Randolphs of Redwoods*, published serially in *The Argonaut*, a San Francisco paper; the Atherton family reacts negatively.

1885   The Athertons move to San Francisco at Gertrude's insistence, amid protests from George.

1887	George Atherton dies while at sea on a merchant ship; Gertrude takes Muriel to Dominga Atherton and moves to New York, supporting herself in part by writing for *The Argonaut*.
1888	*What Dreams May Come*, a story of reincarnation, published.
1889	Atherton travels to Paris; *Hermia Suydam* published and critiqued as immoral; journeys to London.
1890	Grandfather Stephen Franklin dies; Atherton returns to San Francisco; Dominga Atherton, Gertrude's mother-in-law, dies; *Los Cerritos* published.
1891	Atherton becomes interested in writing about California; "The Literary Development of California" appears in *Cosmopolitan*; *A Question of Time* published.
1892	Leaves California for the East; *The Doomswoman* published as serial; *A Christmas Witch* published in *Godey's*; moves to New York City.
1893	Trip to the Chicago World's Fair and Columbian Exposition; *The Doomswoman* published in book form.
1894	Moves from New York to England; *Before the Gringo Came* published.
1895	Travels in England; *A Whirl Asunder* published.
1896	Travels in Brittany.
1897	Travels in Normandy; *Patience Sparhawk and Her Times* and *His Fortunate Grace* published.
1898	*The Californians, American Wives and English Husbands*, and *The Valiant Runaways* published; Gertrude Franklin Horn Uhlhorn dies.
1899	Daughter Muriel marries; Atherton settles in Washington, DC; travels to Belgium and London; *A Daughter of the Vine* published.
1900	Visits Cuba; summers in the Adirondacks; *Senator North* published.
1901	Visits both New York and West Indies; *The Aristocrats* published.
1902	Visits Denmark; returns to San Francisco; *The Splendid Idle Forties* and *The Conqueror: Being the True and Romantic Story of Alexander Hamilton* published; meets James D. Phelan, who will go on to serve as US senator from California and remain a close friend.
1903	Visits Hungary; settles in Munich; *A Few of Hamilton's Letters, Heart of Hyacinth* and *Mrs. Pendleton's Four-in-hand* published.

1904	Travels to England; "Why Is American Literature Bourgeois?" appears in *North American Review*; *Rulers of Kings* published.
1905	Returns briefly to San Francisco; travels to Petaluma; *The Bell in the Fog and Other Stories* and *The Traveling Thirds* published.
1906	*Rezánov* published; San Francisco earthquake and fire, which destroy many of Atherton's papers.
1907	Divides time among Munich, San Francisco, and London; *Ancestors* published.
1908	*The Gorgeous Isle* published.
1909	Lives in Munich, travels to Chicago and California; "The Present Unrest among Women," an essay on women's suffrage, published.
1910	Leaves Munich for England, returns to San Francisco; *Tower of Ivory* in print.
1911	Tours US by train; travels to London; supports suffrage in California.
1912	Returns to California and campaigns for Woodrow Wilson; *Julia France and Her Times* published.
1913	Travels to Italy, then to Montana; *Perch of the Devil* and *California: an Intimate History* published.
1915	Sees pro-suffrage work published in *New York Times*.
1916	Writes from France for the *Delineator* and *The New York Times*.
1917	Resides in New York City; *The Living Present* published.
1918	*The White Morning: A Novel of the Power of the German Women in Wartime* published.
1919	Reports from Paris for *New York Times*; returns to California; publishes *The Avalanche*, writes *Don't Neglect Your Wife*, a filmscript; *The Avalanche* (film) released.
1921	*Sisters-in-Law* published.
1922	Receives Steinach rejuvenation treatment from Dr. Harry Benjamin in New York; *Sleeping Fires* published.
1923	Takes apartment in San Francisco; *Black Oxen* published; Boni and Liveright contracts for reprint of *Black Oxen* by publisher A.L. Burt.
1924	First National Pictures releases *Black Oxen* film in January; the ending has been altered so as to leave Clavering in the company of Janet Oglethorpe, who appropriates Clavering after Madame Zattiany leaves the country. Reviewers admire the film's faithfulness to the novel, Corinne Griffith's portrayal of an elegant Mary Zattiany, and the novelty of the rejuvenation topic.

1925   Travels to Paris and meets Gertrude Stein; travels to Switzerland, then Athens to research novel about Pericles and Aspasia; *The Crystal Cup* published.

1926   *Vein of Gold* (film version of *Perch of the Devil*) released.

1927   First National releases film of *The Crystal Cup*; *The Immortal Marriage* published.

1928   *The Jealous Gods: A Processional Novel of the Fifth Century B.C.* published.

1929   Travels to Boston, then to Rome on family trip; *Dido, Queen of Hearts* published; "Gertrude Atherton Day" celebrated at the Golden Gate International Exposition.

1930   Visits Egypt; settles in New York City.

1931   *The Sophisticates* published.

1932   Autobiography, *Adventures of a Novelist*, published.

1933-42 Moves between New York and San Francisco; *The Foghorn, Golden Peacock, Can Women Be Gentlemen?* and *The House of Lee, The Horn of Life* published.

1935   Hosts Gertrude Stein on her San Francisco visit.

1940   At the Golden Gate International Exposition, Atherton is named California's Most Distinguished Woman on Women's Day.

1941   Settles into daughter Muriel's house in San Francisco.

1945   *Golden Gate Country* published.

1946   *My San Francisco, A Wayward Biography* published.

1947   City of San Francisco presents Atherton with Gold Medal.

1948   Death of Gertrude Atherton, 14 June.

1966   At a court hearing, where she seeks to divorce her much younger husband, Corinne Griffith, star of *Black Oxen* film, declares that the original Griffith is dead and that she is Griffith's sister, who is 25 years younger, and that she took her sister's place years earlier.

A Note on the Text

This Broadview edition of *Black Oxen* is based on the 1923 first edition, published in New York by Boni and Liveright. This edition maintains the characteristic flavor of the original text. Only when words have been dropped have insertions been made; they appear in brackets. On the rare occasion when a typographical error appears in the original, a footnote is provided and indicates a likely intent. There are a number of 1920s colloquialisms, characteristic phrases (or slang), and casual contractions, which are considered nonstandard today, that are left unamended in the text. In the case when typographical features such as accents are commonly used today, the text has been left in the original format.

Original copies of the novel sold for two dollars. Across 1923, Horace Liveright and Atherton maintained a lively interest in the book's sales, speculating on when they would top a hundred thousand copies (the definition of a modern best seller).[1] Liveright praised the novel's early title, *Her Infinite Variety,* which he pronounced "highly provocative and not one bit conventional," and which he considered an improvement on Atherton's earlier working title, *Tides of Time.*[2]

In the fall of 1923, Liveright sent Atherton a telegram announcing a contract for the novel's second run with reprint publisher, A.L. Burt. It read, "HAPPY TO REPORT HAVE SOLD TO AL BURT REPRINT RIGHTS BLACK OXEN TEN CENTS A COPY THEN GUARANTEEING ONE HUNDRED THOUSAND COPIES MINIMUM AND EXPECT TO SEE SEVERAL TIMES THIS AMOUNT."[3] This edition would sell for 75 cents a copy and was produced in tandem with the January 1924 film, *Black Oxen,* released by First National

---

1 See Letter, Horace Liveright, 18 October 1923, for his first announcement that sales had topped 100,000. In the same letter, he predicts an eventual sale of 300,000 copies and notes that both he and Atherton will earn 5 cents a copy on the reprint. Quoted by permission of the Bancroft Library, University of California, Berkeley, as are all of Liveright's subsequent letters and telegrams cited here.

2 Letter, Horace Liveright, 15 August 1922.

3 Telegram, Horace Liveright, 22 September 1923. The "ten cents" cited by Liveright refers not to the sale price of the edition, but the amount of royalty earned by the Liveright firm.

Film Company.[1] Also timed in relation to the film's release was the novel's serialization in newspapers across the country (over 200 of them, according to advertisements placed in film journals in early 1924). Some of these included *The Buffalo Evening Times, The Times Union* (Toronto), *The Pittsburgh Press, The Chicago Herald and Examiner, The Courier Journal* (Louisville), and *The North American* (Philadelphia).

---

1 Telegram, Horace Liveright, undated (likely fall 1923, item number 112).
   Also see Letter, Harry Burt, A.L. Burt Company, 22 December 1923,
   which assures Atherton of the company's "pleasure at the appearance of
   our new photoplay edition of BLACK OXEN," along with news that the
   copy was being sent to Atherton. It continues "We feel there is not the
   slightest question but what we can make BLACK OXEN the biggest-
   selling title in all the popular copyright class for the year 1924." In all,
   the publication of *Black Oxen* made a considerable amount for Atherton,
   based on the 15 per cent per copy royalty she received. Atherton was paid
   $31,383.40 in October 1923; later in the year, she received an additional
   $10,913.25 (Royalty statement, Boni & Liveright, period ending 31
   October 1923, quoted with permission of the Bancroft Library). In contemporary dollars, this would be a little more than half a million dollars.
   The only extant complete copies of the film are at the New York Public
   Library and at George Eastman House, Rochester, New York.

BLACK OXEN

by

GERTRUDE ATHERTON

Author of "Sisters-in-Law"

The years like Great Black Oxen tread the world
And God the herdsman goads them on behind.
—W.B. Yeats.[1]

---

1   W.B. Yeats, *The Countess Cathleen*. Ed. Michael J. Sidnell and Wayne
    K. Chapman. Ithaca, NY: Cornell UP, 1999. 738-39. These are the
    penultimate lines from Yeats's play *The Countess Cathleen*, which was first
    published in 1892 and printed in its final form in 1912.

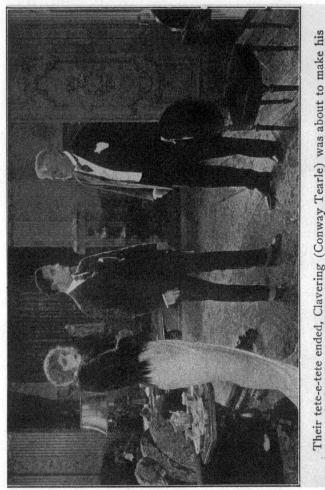

Their tete-e-tete ended, Clavering (Conway Tearle) was about to make his departure when Judge Trent (Tom Guise), who held buried in his mind the secret of the charming Madame Zattiany's (Corinne Griffith), entered.

(Screen version of "The Black Oxen.")

I

"Talk. Talk. Talk.... Good lines and no action ... said all ... not even promising first act ... eighth failure and season more than half over ... rather be a playwright and fail than a critic compelled to listen to has-beens and would-bes trying to put over bad plays.... Oh, for just one more great first-night ... if there's a spirit world why don't the ghosts of dead artists get together and inhibit bad playwrights from tormenting first-nighters? ... Astral board of Immortals sitting in Unconscious tweaking strings until gobbets[1] and sclerotics[2] become gibbering idiots every time they put pen to paper? ... Fewer first-nights but more joy ... also joy of sending producers back to cigar stands.... Thank God, no longer a critic ... don't need to come to first-nights unless I want ... can't keep away ... habit too strong ... poor devil of a colyumist must forage ... why did I become a columnist? More money. Money! And I once a rubescent[3] socialist ... best parlor type ... Lord! I wish some one would die and leave me a million!"

Clavering opened his weary eyes and glanced over the darkened auditorium, visualizing a mass of bored resentful disks: a few hopeful, perhaps, the greater number too educated in the theatre not to have recognized the heavy note of incompetence that had boomed like a muffled fog-horn since the rise of the curtain.

It was a typical first-night audience, assembled to welcome a favorite actress in a new play. All the Sophisticates[4] (as Clavering had named them, abandoning "Intellectuals" and "Intelligentsia" to the Parlor Socialists) were present: authors, playwrights, editors and young editors, columnists, dramatic critics, young publishers, the fashionable illustrators and cartoonists, a few actors, artists, sculptors, hostesses of the eminent, and a sprinkling of Greenwich Village[5] to give a touch of old Bohemia to what was otherwise almost as brilliant and standardized as a Monday night at the opera. Twelve years ago, Clavering, impelled irresistibly from a dilapidated colonial mansion in Louisiana to the cerebrum of the Western World, had arrived in New York; and run the usual gamut

---

1 An unappealing lump of something, such as raw meat.
2 A patient with the hardening of bodily tissues, as in multiple sclerosis.
3 Blushing.
4 The "Sophisticates," a fictitious social group, modeled after the Algonquin Round Table members, who luncheoned daily at the Algonquin Hotel in Manhattan.
5 Home to a concentrated Bohemian subculture of New York in the 1910s, which ceded prominence to the Manhattan subcultures in the 1920s.

of the high-powered man from reporter to special writer, although youth rose to eminence less rapidly then than now. Dramatic critic of his newspaper for three years (two years at the war), an envied, quoted and omniscient columnist since his return from France. Journalistically he could rise no higher, and none of the frequent distinguished parties given by the Sophisticates was complete without the long lounging body and saturnine[1] countenance of Mr. Lee Clavering. As soon as he had set foot upon the ladder of prominence Mr. Clavering had realized the value of dramatizing himself, and although he was as active of body as of mind and of an amiable and genial disposition, as his friends sometimes angrily protested, his world, that world of increasing importance in New York, knew him as a cynical, morose, mysterious creature, who, at a party, transferred himself from one woman's side to another's by sheer effort of will spurred by boredom. The unmarried women had given him up as a confirmed bachelor, but a few still followed his dark face with longing eyes. (He sometimes wondered what rôle he would have adopted if he had been a blond.) As a matter of fact, he was intensely romantic, even after ten years of newspaper work in New York and two of war; and when his steel-blue half-closed eyes roved over a gathering at the moment of entrance it was with the evergreen hope of discovering the consummate woman.

There was no affectation in his idealistic fastidiousness. Nor, of late, in his general boredom. Not that he did not still like his work, or possibly pontificating every morning over his famous name to an admiring public, but he was tired of "the crowd," the same old faces, tired of the steady grind, of bad plays—he, who had such a passionate love of the drama—somewhat tired of himself. He would have liked to tramp the world for a year. But although he had money enough saved he dared not drop out of New York. One was forgotten overnight, and fashions, especially since the war, changed so quickly and yet so subtly that he might be another year readjusting himself on his return. Or find himself supplanted by some man younger than himself whose cursed audacity and dramatized youthfulness would have accustomed the facile public to some new brand of pap flavored with red pepper. The world was marching to the tune of youth, damn it (Mr. Clavering was beginning to feel elderly at thirty-four), but it was hard to shake out the entrenched. He had his public hypnotized. He could sell ten copies of a book where a reviewer could sell one. His word

---

1 Gloomy, dark, and mysterious, as in an individual's temperament.

on a play was final—or almost. Personal mention of any of the Sophisticates added a cubit to reputation. Three mentions made them household words. Neglect caused agonies and visions of extinction. Disparagement was preferable. By publicity shall ye know them. Even public men with rhinocerene hides had been seen to shiver. Cause women courted him. Prize fighters on the dour morn after a triumphant night had howled between fury and tears as Mr. Lee Clavering (once crack reporter of the gentle art) wrote sadly of greater warriors. Lenin had mentioned him as an enemy of the new religion, who dealt not with the truth. Until he grew dull—no grinning skeleton as yet—his public, after hasty or solemn digestion of the news, would turn over to his column with a sigh of relief. But he must hang on, no doubt of that. Fatal to give the public even a hint that it might learn to do without him.

He sighed and closed his eyes again. It was not unpleasant to feel himself a slave, a slave who had forged his own gilded chains. But he sighed again for his lost simplicities, for his day-dreams under the magnolias when he had believed that if women of his class were not obliged to do their own housework they would all be young and beautiful and talk only of romance; when he had thought upon the intellectual woman and the woman who "did things" as an anomaly and a horror. Well, the reality was more companionable, he would say that for them.... Then he grinned as he recalled the days of his passionate socialism, when he had taken pains, like every socialist he had ever met, to let it be understood that he had been born in the best society. Well, so he had, and he was glad of it, even if the best society of his small southern town had little to live on but its vanished past. He never alluded to his distinguished ancestry now that he was eminent and comfortable, and he looked back with uneasy scorn upon his former breaches of taste, but he never quite forgot it. No Southerner ever does.

The play droned on to the end of the interminable first act. Talk. Talk. Talk. He'd go to sleep, but would be sure to get a crick in his neck. Then he remembered a woman who had come down the aisle just as the lights were lowering and passed his seat. He had not seen her face, but her graceful figure had attracted his attention, and the peculiar shade of her hair: the color of warm ashes. There was no woman of his acquaintance with that rare shade of blonde hair.

He opened his eyes. She was sitting two seats ahead of him and the lights of the stage gave a faint halo to a small well-shaped head defined by the low coil of hair. She had a long throat apparently, but although she had dropped her wrap over the back of the seat he had no more than a glimpse of a white neck and a suggestion of sloping shoulders. Rather rare those, nowadays. They reminded him, together with the haughty poise of the head, of the family portraits in the old gallery at home. Being dark himself, he admired fair women, although since they had taken to bobbing their hair they looked as much alike as magazine covers. This woman wore her hair in no particular fashion. It was soft and abundant, brushed back from her face, and drawn merely over the tips of the ears. At least so he inferred. He had not seen even her profile as she passed. Profiles were out of date, but in an old-fashioned corner of his soul he admired them, and he was idly convinced that a woman with so perfectly shaped a head, long and narrow, but not too narrow, must have a profile. Probably her full face would not be so attractive. Women with cendré hair[1] generally had light brows and lashes, and her eyes might be a washed-out blue. Or prominent. Or her mouth too small. He would bet on the profile, however, and instead of rushing out when that blessed curtain went down he would wait and look for it.

Then he closed his eyes again and forgot her until he was roused by the clapping of many hands. First-nighters always applaud, no matter how perfunctorily. Noblesse oblige.[2] But the difference between the applause of the bored but loyal and that of the enchanted and quickened is as the difference between a rising breeze and a hurricane.

The actors bowed en masse, in threes, in twos, singly. The curtain descended, the lights rose, the audience heaved. Men hurried up the aisle and climbed over patient women. People began to visit. And then the woman two seats ahead of Clavering did a singular thing.

She rose slowly to her feet, turned her back to the stage, raised her opera glasses and leisurely surveyed the audience.

"I knew it!" Clavering's tongue clicked. "European. No American woman ever did that—unless, to be sure, she has lived too long abroad to remember our customs."

He gazed at her eagerly, and felt a slight sensation of annoyance that the entire house was following his example. The opera glasses concealed her eyes, but they rested upon the bridge of an indubitably straight nose. Her forehead was perhaps too high, but it was full, and the thick hair was brushed back from a sharp point. Her eyebrows, thank Heaven, were many shades darker than her

---

1 Ashen colored.

2 Obligation to be generous by those who are well-to-do.

hair. They were also narrow and glossy. Decidedly they received attention. Possibly they were plucked and darkened—life had made him skeptical of "points." However, Clavering was no lover of unamended nature, holding nature, except in rare moments of inspiration, a bungler of the first water.

In spite of its smooth white skin and rounded contours above an undamaged throat, it was, subtly, not a young face. The mouth, rather large, although fresh and red (possibly they had lip sticks in Europe that approximated nature) had none of the girl's soft flexibility. It was full in the center and the red of the underlip was more than a visible line, but it was straight at the corners, ending in an almost abrupt sternness. Once she smiled, but it was little more than an amused flicker; the mouth did not relax. The shape of the face bore out the promise of the head, but deflected from its oval at the chin, which was almost square, and indented. The figure was very slight, but as subtly mature as the face, possibly because she held it uncompromisingly erect; apparently she had made no concession to the democratic absence of "carriage," the indifferent almost apologetic mien that had succeeded the limp curves of a few years ago.

She wore a dress of white jet made with the long lines of the present fashion—in dress she was evidently a stickler. The neck was cut in a low square, showing the rise of the bust. Her own lines were long, the arms and hands very slender in the long white gloves. Probably she was the only woman in the house who wore gloves. Life was freer since the war. She wore a triple string of pearls.

He waited eagerly until she should drop her glasses.... He heard two girls gasping and muttering behind him.... There was a titter across the house.

She lowered the opera glasses and glanced over the rows of upturned faces immediately before her, scrutinizing them casually, as if they were fish in an aquarium. She had dropped her lids slightly before her eyes came to rest on Clavering. He was leaning forward, his eyes hard and focal, doing his best to compel her notice. Her glance did linger on his for a moment before it moved on indifferently, but in that brief interval he experienced a curious ripple along his nerves ... almost a note of warning.... They were very dark gray eyes, Greek in the curve of the lid, and inconceivably wise, cold, disillusioned. She did not look a day over twenty-eight. There were no marks of dissipation on her face. But for its cold regularity she would have looked younger—with her eyes closed. The eyes seemed to gaze down out of an infinitely remote past.

Suddenly she seemed to sense the concentrated attention of the audience. She swept it with a hasty glance, evidently appreciated the fact that she alone was standing and facing it, colored slightly and sat down. But her repose was absolute. She made no little embarrassed gestures as another woman would have done. She did not even affect to read her program.

II

Clavering left his chair and wandered up the aisle. He felt none of his usual impatience for the beneficent cigarette. Was he hit? Hardly. Inquisitive, certainly. But he had seen so many provocative shells. Vile trick of nature, that—poverty-stricken unoriginal creature that she was.

He glanced over the rows of people as he passed. It was not the play that was animating them. The woman was a godsend.

His gaze paused abruptly on the face of Mr. Charles Dinwiddie. Clavering's grand-aunt had married Mr. Dinwiddie's father and the two men, so far apart in years, were more or less intimate; the older man's inexhaustible gossip of New York Society amused Clavering, who in turn had initiated Mr. Dinwiddie into new and strange pleasures, including literary parties and first nights—ignored by the world of fashion.

All New York men of the old régime, no matter what their individuality may have been twenty years earlier, look so much alike as they approach sixty, and more particularly after they have passed it, that they might be brothers in blood as in caste. Their moustaches and what little hair they have left turns the same shade of well-bred white. Their fine old Nordic faces are generally lean and flat of cheek, their expression calm, assured, not always smug. They are impeccably groomed and erect. Stout they may be, but seldom fat, and if not always handsome, they are polished, distinguished, aloof. They no longer wear side-whiskers and look younger than their fathers did at the same age.

Mr. Dinwiddie's countenance as a rule was as formal and politely expressionless as became his dignified status, but tonight it was not. It was pallid. The rather prominent eyes were staring, the mouth was relaxed. He was seated next the aisle and Clavering hastened toward him in alarm.

"Ill, old chap?" he asked. "Better come out."

Mr. Dinwiddie focussed his eyes, then stumbled to his feet and caught Clavering by the arm. "Yes," he muttered. "Get me out of this and take me where I can get a drink. Seen a ghost."

Clavering guided him up the aisle, then out of a side exit into an alley and produced a flask from his hip-pocket. Mr. Dinwiddie without ceremony raised it to his lips and swallowed twice, gasping a little. He had reached the age of the mild whiskey and soda. Then he stood erect and passed his hand over the shining curve of his head.

"Ever seen a ghost, Lee?" he asked. "That woman was there, wasn't she?"

"She was there, all right." Clavering's face was no longer cynical and mysterious; it was alive with curiosity. "D'you know who she is?"

"Thirty-odd years ago any one of us old chaps would have told you she was Mary Ogden, and like as not raised his hat. She was the beauty and the belle of her day. But she married a Hungarian diplomat, Count Zattiany, when she was twenty-four, and deserted us. Never been in the country since. I never wanted to see her again. Too hard hit. But I caught a glimpse of her at the opera in Paris about ten years ago—faded! Always striking of course with that style, but withered, changed, skinny where she had been slim, her throat concealed by a dog collar a yard long—her expression sad and apathetic—the dethroned idol of men. God! Mary Ogden! I left the house."

"It is her daughter, of course——"

"Never had a child—positive of it. Zattiany title went to a nephew who was killed in the war.... No ... it must be ... must be ..." His eyes began to glitter. Clavering knew the symptom. His relative was about to impart interesting gossip.

"Well?" he asked impatiently.

"There were many stories about Mary Ogden—Mary Zattiany—always a notable figure in the capitals of Europe. Her husband was in the diplomatic service until he died—some years before I saw her in Paris. She was far too clever—damnably clever, Mary Ogden, and had a reputation for it in European Society as well as for beauty—to get herself compromised. But there were stories—that must be it! She had a daughter and stowed her away somewhere. No two women could be as alike as that except mother and daughter—don't see it too often at that. Why, the very way she carries her head—her *style* ... wonder where she kept her? That girl has been educated and has all the air of the best society. Must have got friends to adopt her. Gad! What a secret chapter. But why on earth does she let the girl run round loose?"

"I shouldn't say she was a day under twenty-eight. No doubt she looked younger from where you were sitting."

"Twenty-eight! Mary must have begun sooner than we heard. But—well, we never felt that we knew Mary—that was one of her charms. She kept us guessing, as you young fellows say, and she had the devil's own light in her eyes sometimes." His own orb lit up again. "Wonder if Mary is here? No doubt she's come over to get her property back—she never transferred her investments and of course it was alienated during the war. But not a soul has heard from her. I am sure of that. We were discussing her the other night at dinner and wondering if her fortune had been turned over. It was at Jane Oglethorpe's. Jane and a good many of the other women have seen her from time to time abroad—stayed at her castle in Hungary during the first years of her marriage; but they drifted apart as friends do.... She must be a wreck, poor thing. She ran a hospital during the war and was in Buda Pesth for some time after the revolution broke out.[1] I hope she had the girl well hidden away."

"Perhaps she sent the girl over to look after her affairs."

"That's it. Beyond a doubt. And I'll find out. Trent is Mary's attorney and trustee. I'll make him open up."

"And you'll call on her?"

"Won't I? That is, I'll make Trent take me. I never want to look at poor Mary again, but I'd feel young——Hello! I believe you're hit!" Mr. Dinwiddie, having solved his problems, was quite himself again and alert for one of the little dramas that savored his rather tasteless days. "I'd like that. I'll introduce you and give you my blessing. Wrong side of the blanket,[2] though."

"Don't care a hang."

"That's right. Who cares about anything these days? And you can only be young once." He sighed. "And if she's like her mother—only halfway like her inside—she'll be worth it."

"Is that a promise?"

"We'll shake on it. I'll see Trent in the morning. Dine with me at the club at eight?"

"Rather!"

---

1 A reference to the 1918 "Aster revolution" in Hungary. A liberal democratic party overturned the government of King Charles IV and founded the Hungarian Democratic Republic. In March of 1919, this republic would be overturned by the Hungarian Soviet Republic, then by the Kingdom of Hungary. In 1920 the Treaty of Trianon redefined the borders of the Kingdom, amid much contestation, with Hungary losing more than seventy percent of its territory. A push to overturn this treaty and interact more forcibly with the rest of Europe dominated Hungarian politics during the rest of the 1920s.

2 "Wrong side of the blanket," an illegitimate child.

The critics left after the second act to damn the play at leisure. Clavering remained in his seat. Forty minutes later, while the performers were responding to faint calls and amiable friends were demanding the author of the doomed play, the lady of mystery (who, Clavering reflected cynically, was doubtless merely an unusual looking person with a commonplace history—most explanations after wild guesses were common-place) left her seat and passed up the aisle. Irresistibly, Clavering followed her. As she stood for a moment under the glare of the electric lights at the entrance he observed her critically. She survived the test. A small car drew up to the curb. She entered it, and he stood in the softly falling snow feeling somewhat of a fool. As he walked slowly to his rooms in Madison Square he came definitely to the conclusion that it was merely his old reporter's instinct that burned so fiercely, even when he had prodded Dinwiddie and shaken hands in a glow of anticipation. Certainly there was no fire in his blood. His imagination had not toyed for a moment with the hope that here at last ... He did not feel in the least romantic. But what man, especially after Dinwiddie's revelations, wouldn't feel a bit curious, a bit excited? Thank Heaven he was young enough for that. He must know who she was. Certainly, he would like to talk to her. She knew the world, no doubt of it—with those eyes! European women, given the opportunity, could cram more of life into ten years than an American woman into forty. She had had her experiences in spite of that madonna face; he'd bet on it. Well, he wasn't falling in love with a woman who had too heavily underscored in the book of life. But he enjoyed talking to European women of the world. New York had been overrun of late with Russian princesses and other ladies of title come over in the hope of milking the good old American cow, and when he could divert them from their grievances he found them clever, subtle and interesting. It was unlikely that this woman had a grievance of that sort or was looking for a chance to get at the generous but elusive udder. Her pearls might not be real, but her gown was superlatively expensive, her evening wrap of mauve velvet lined with ermine, and her little car perfectly turned out. He'd look like a fortune-hunter with his salary of fifteen thousand a year and a few thousands in bonds ... not if he knew it! But find out who she was, know her, talk to her, learn what he *felt* was an interesting history—quite another matter.

The next evening when he arrived at the club he found Mr. Din-widdie fuming.

"What do you think!" he exclaimed as he led his guest to his favorite table in the corner. "That old rascal bluffed me! Bluffed me. Said there was no relative of Countess Zattiany in the country that he knew of. Looked blank as a post when I told him of the extraordinary resemblance of that girl to Mary Ogden. Said he never heard of her. Laughed at the idea of a sub-rosa[1] daughter. Pretended to be angry at such an aspersion on Mary's fair fame—was in love with her himself like the rest of us. But he was lying and he knew that I knew he was lying. What'll you have?"

"Anything. Go ahead. I know by the glitter of your eye that you haven't finished."

"You're right, I haven't." He gave his order and leaned forward. "I've done a little prospecting on my own account. Mary inherited the old Ogden house over on Murray Hill. I happen to know that the lease ran out last year and that it hasn't been rented since. Well, I walked past there today, and some one is living in it. Boarding off. Windows open. Fresh curtains. A servant receiving a parcel at the area door. She's there, mark my words."

"Not a doubt of it. Why didn't you walk boldly up and send in your card?"

"Hadn't the courage. Besides, that girl never heard of me. I hadn't the ghost of an excuse."

"Why not put Mrs. Oglethorpe on the scent? She could call. Women are always fertile in excuses."

"I can't see what pretext she could trump up. She'd be keen enough, all right, but she hardly could tell this haughty creature with the unmistakable stamp of the great world on her that she knows she must be the left-handed daughter of Mary Ogden. Even Jane hasn't assurance enough for that."

"She might assume that this young woman is a member of the Countess Zattiany's family—daughter of a cousin or something—those extraordinary resemblances do recur in families.... That indeed may be the explanation."

"Not a bit of it. That girl is Mary's daughter."

"I'm inclined to agree with you. But it is understood that you can't hurl it at her. Mrs. Oglethorpe, however, could invent a pretty pretence—saw her at the theatre—struck by her likeness to her

---

1 Literally "under the rose," or secret; here, an illegitimate child.

old friend—discovered she was living in the family mansion—felt that she must seek her out——"

"Um. That's not quite the sort of thing the New York woman does, and you know it. True, the war has upset them as it has every one else. They are still restless. I have met two opera singers, two actresses, three of these juvenile editors and columnists at dinners and musical evenings during the last month alone. I believe they'd lionize Charley Chaplin if he'd let them, but I understand he's more exclusive than we are. God! What is New York Society coming to?"

"You like straying outside the sacred preserves yourself occasionally."

"I do. But I'm a man. We always did stray a bit. But when I think of the exclusiveness of only a few years ago! Why, New York Society was a Club. The most exclusive club in the world. London Society was Bohemia compared to it. It's the democratic flu, that's what! Aristocracy's done for."

"I'm not so sure. The reaction may be devastating. But it's a sign of grace that they've at last discovered sufficient intelligence to be bored with their somewhat monotonous selves. And Mrs. Oglethorpe always does exactly as she pleases. Better drop her a hint."

"Well, I'll try it. But while Jane may be high-handed, she has certain rigid ideas when it comes to Society and who shall enter its gates. So far she's made no concessions. She and a few others still keep a tight rein. Their daughters though! And granddaughters! Jane's girls are replicas of herself with every atom of her personality left out—but Jim's daughter, Janet, is her grandmother over again plus modern bad manners, bad habits, and a defiance of every known convention. Wretched little flapper. Gad! What are we coming to!"

"Never mind Janet——"

"Why don't you suggest it to Jane? She thinks more of you than of any one else. I doubt if you could ask her anything——"

"Not much. She'd twig at once. I've had several hints lately that she has her eye on somebody she wants me to marry. You must do it yourself—and you *must*!"

"Well! If she won't, Mrs. Jim might. The younger women would know this girl like a shot if they thought there was any fun in it—then drop her if she didn't measure up. I don't know that I care to place her in such a position."

"I've an idea the fair unknown can take care of herself. I don't see her picked up and dropped. Probably it would be the deuce and all to meet her. I think my plan is best. You can rouse any woman's curiosity, and no one has more than Mrs. Oglethorpe. That would be the wedge. You'd meet her and then you could give her a dinner and invite me."

"All right. I'll try it. Something must happen soon. My arteries won't stand the strain."

V

"Madam is not at home, ma'am."

"Is she not? Then I'll wait for her."

Mrs. Oglethorpe swept by the butler and he had the sensation of chaff scattering before a strong wind. In truth Mrs. Oglethorpe was an impressive figure and quite two inches taller than himself. He could only stare at her in helpless awe, the more so as he had recognized her at once. Leadership might be extinct, but Mrs. Oglethorpe was still a power in New York Society, with her terrible outspokenness, her uncompromising standards, her sardonic humor, her great wealth, and her eagle eye for subterfuge. How could a mere servant hope to oppose that formidable will when his betters trembled at her nod?

Mrs. Oglethorpe had made her usual careful toilet. Her full long dress of heavy-pile black velvet, almost covered with a sable cape, swept the floor; changing skirts meant nothing to her.[1] Like all women of the old régime in New York, she wore her hair dressed very high and it was surmounted by a small black hat covered with feathers, ruthlessly exposing her large square face with its small snapping black eyes and prominent nose. A high-boned collar of net supported what was left of her throat. She wore no jewels, as she clung to the rigorous law of her youth which had tabued[2] the vulgar display of anything but pearls in the daytime. As she was too old and yellow for pearls she compromised on jet earrings and necklace. She carried a cane.

Mr. Dinwiddie to his surprise had found no difficulty in persuading her to investigate the mysteries of the Ogden mansion, for she had leapt at once to the conclusion that the friend of her youth was in some way menaced by this presumptuous stranger of the fantastic resemblance. There had been a time when, while indignantly repudiating the stories so prevalent for many years

---

1 A reference to changes in skirt length, which could vary by the season.
2 An alternate spelling of "tabooed."

after Mary Ogden's marriage to Count Zattiany, she had secretly believed and condoned them; not only because she had loved her devotedly and known something of her heavy disillusionment, but because the wild secret life the exalted Countess Zattiany was believed to be leading fed her own suppressed longings for romance and adventure. With the passage of years, which had taken their toll of Mary's beauty and fascination, and brought complete disillusionment to herself, she had almost forgotten that old phase; moreover, it was many years since she had visited Europe and correspondence between the two friends, once so intimate, had almost ceased before the war. During that long interval she had heard nothing of her except that she was running a hospital in Buda Pesth, but shortly after the close of the war she had been distressed to learn from a member of one of the various commissions to Vienna that Countess Zattiany was ill in a sanitarium. She had written at once, but received no reply. Now she feared that some adventuress had taken advantage of a superficial resemblance—she dismissed Mr. Dinwiddie's protestations of the exactness of that resemblance as the maunderings of a weakened memory playing about among the ghosts of its youth—to scheme for the Ogden fortune. When told that Judge Trent was evidently shielding the woman her suspicions were redoubled. She had consistently hated Judge Trent for fifty years.

If, on the other hand, the creature were really Mary's daughter—and could prove it—well, she would make up her mind what course to take when she met her.

"I'll wait in the library," she announced, and moved majestically down the hall. Then at a sound she paused and glanced toward the stair which rose on the left, opposite the library. A woman was descending, a woman only an inch or two shorter than herself and no less stately, with ashen blonde hair coiled low on her graceful neck and wearing a loose gown of pale green crepe with a silver girdle.

"My God!" exclaimed Mrs. Oglethorpe in a loud imperious voice, as if commanding the Almighty to leap from his throne and fly to her assistance. Then she leaned heavily on her cane.

The lady came quickly down the stairs and made a peremptory signal to the butler. As he disappeared she walked forward more slowly and paused within a few feet of her agitated guest. Her eyebrows were slightly raised, her face impassive. Not even those sharp old eyes staring at her guessed that she had been completely taken by surprise and was inwardly quaking.

Mrs. Oglethorpe could not speak for a moment. The years had dropped from her. She was once more a young woman come to spend the day with her favorite friend ... or to attend a reception in the stately formal house on Murray Hill ... high rooms filled with women wearing tight basques, bustles, full sweeping skirts, small hats or bonnets perched on puffs and braids[1].... Mary, the most radiant and beautiful and enchanting girl in the world, coming forward with hands outstretched, while her more formal mother frowned a little at her enthusiasm ... or were they both risen to haunt the old house?

But confusion could reign for only a few seconds in Mrs. Oglethorpe's indomitable soul. She drew herself up to her imposing height, and her voice was harsher than usual as she addressed the vision that had confounded her.

"Pardon me. Your likeness to my old friend, Countess Zattiany, startled me. Who are you, may I ask?"

"Does it really matter?" And once more Mrs. Oglethorpe started, although the accent was foreign.

"Yes, it does matter," she said grimly. "That is what I have come to find out."

"Oh!" Again there was a slight lift of the eyebrows. "I had always heard that Americans were unconventional, but hardly that they carried their independence of the conventions so far as to invade the house of a stranger."

"I'll not be put off. Are you Mary Zattiany's daughter?"

For a second there was an expression of broad amusement on the beautiful cold face opposite, but it passed with a slight shrug of the shoulders. "No," she said evenly.

"Then who are you?"

"I do not choose to say—at present." Her tone was as arrogant as her interlocutor's and Mrs. Oglethorpe bristled.

"What does Trent mean by lying about your presence in this house?"

"Judge Trent respects my wishes."

"Your wishes! You've made a fool of him. But I am Countess Zattiany's oldest friend, and if she has been imposed upon, if she has come to any harm, if you are after her fortune by pretending on the strength of your singular likeness to be her heir, I shall know how to put a stop to it in spite of Judge Trent. I suppose you have never heard of me. My name is Oglethorpe."

---

1   Basque, a long, fitted Victorian-era jacket; bustle, a puffed and ornately draped back section of the skirt, both styles of the 1870s and 1880s, dating from the time when Jane Oglethorpe would have been a girl. The long skirts and hairstyles mentioned here also date from the late nineteenth century.

"I have heard of Mrs. Oglethorpe—from Countess Zattiany. But she failed to prepare me for your excessively bad manners."

"Manners be damned. I use what manners I choose and I've never done anything else. I repeat to you that Countess Zattiany was the most intimate friend of my youth and for many years after. If she has no one to protect her interests in this country, I shall protect them myself. Don't you suppose I am well aware that if you were in her confidence she would have sent you direct to me? It is the first thing she would have thought of. If you are not an impostor and an adventuress present your credentials and I will ask your pardon."

"Judge Trent has my credentials. Now, if you will excuse me——"

"I will not excuse you. I will get to the depth of all this mystery. I abominate mystery. It is vulgar and stupid. You will tell me who you are, or I will set the newspapers on your track. They'll soon ferret it out. I've only to say the word."

"Ah!" The lady seemed to falter for a moment. She looked speculatively at the indignant old face opposite, then made a vague little gesture toward her hair, and dropped her eyes. "No," she said softly. "Don't—please." She raised her eyes once more and looked straight into Mrs. Oglethorpe's. The two women stood staring at each other for several seconds. Mrs. Oglethorpe's eyes blinked, her jaw fell. Then she drew herself up in her most impressive manner.

"Good day," she said. "Your pardon for the intrusion," and although her voice had trembled, she swept majestically down the hall. The unwilling hostess touched a bell and a footman opened the door.

VI

Three weeks passed. There were almost twice as many first-nights. "Mary Ogden," as Clavering called her for want of the truth, was at each. She never rose in her seat again, and, indeed, seemed to seek inconspicuousness, but she was always in the second or third row of the orchestra, and she wore a different gown on each occasion. As she entered after the curtain rose and stole out before it went down for the last time, few but those in the adjacent seats and boxes were edified by any details of those charming creations, although it was noticeable that the visiting of both sexes was most active in her neighborhood.

For by this time she was "the talk of the town," or of that important and excessively active-minded section of Greater New York represented at first-nights. The columnists had commented on her. One had indited[1] ten lines of free verse in her honor, another had soared on the wings of seventeenth century English into a panegyric[2] on her beauty and her halo of mystery. A poet-editor-wit had cleped[3] her "The Silent Drama." Had it been wartime she would inevitably have been set down as a spy, and as it was there were dark inferences that she was a Bolshevik[4] agent who had smuggled vast sums of money into the country and passed it on to the Reds. There were those who opined she was some rich man's mistress, recently imported, snatched from some victim of revolution who could no longer afford her. Blonde madonnas were always under suspicion unless you knew all about them. Others, more practical, scoffed at these fancy theories and asserted roundly that she was either a Russian refugee who had sound American or English investments, or some American woman, educated abroad, who knew no one in New York and amused herself at the theatre. Indeed? Why then should an obviously wealthy young woman of as obviously good birth and breeding bring no letters?[5] Something crooked, not a doubt of it. A European girl or young widow of position would never come to America without a chaperon; nor an American brought up abroad. A woman with that "air" knows what's what. She's simply put herself beyond the pale and doesn't care. Some impoverished woman of the noblesse who has taken up with a rich man.

The men would have liked to put a detective on the track of every millionaire in town.

Clavering had confided in no one, and Mr. Dinwiddie, although he had attended a party given by one of the most hospitable of the Sophisticates where the unknown was discussed from cocktail to cocktail, and where, forgetting his arteries, he had befuddled himself at the generous fount,[6] had guarded his tongue. To Clavering he had been unable to extend either hope or information. Mrs. Oglethorpe had turned a bleak and rigid countenance upon the

---

1 Written.
2 A formal verse expressing high praise.
3 Archaic form of "called."
4 A revolutionary in 1917 Russia. The term was commonly used to refer to Communists, as was the somewhat derogatory term, "Reds."
5 Letters of introduction created avenues of social entrée for individuals (usually men) who travelled alone.
6 Became intoxicated.

friend of her youth when he had called with an eager ear, and forbidden him tartly ever to mention the subject to her again.

"Interview must have been devilish unpleasant to curdle poor old Jane like that," he had commented. "No doubt the girl showed her the door. Gad! Jane! But Mary's daughter could do it. None better."

Clavering was deeply disappointed. He turned a scowling back on the gossips rending The Topic to tatters. New York must have a new Topic every season. This girl had arrived in a season of dearth. And, unless she were discovered to be living in absolute flagrancy, they would throw down the carpet. Some went even further. After all, what about ...

But there seemed to be not the remotest prospect of meeting her, nor even of solving the mystery. She had been seen striding round the reservoir[1] in a short skirt and high laced boots of soft pale leather. One triumphant woman had stood next to her at a glove counter and overheard her observe to the clerk in a sweet and rather deep voice with an ineluctably refined—and *foreign*—accent that gloves were cheaper in New York than in Paris. She had been passed several times in her smart little car, and once she had been seen going into the Public Library. Evidently she was no hermit. Several of the Sophisticates had friends in Society and questioned them eagerly, but were rewarded only by questions as eager in return.

On the sixth of these first-nights, when the unknown slipped quietly from her seat at the end of the last act, she saw the aisle in front of her almost blocked. One after another the rows of seats were hurriedly deserted. Clavering, as usual, was directly behind her, but Mr. Dinwiddie, forced from his chair many aisles back, was swept out with the crowd.

When she reached the foyer she found herself surrounded by men and women whose frank interest was of the same well-bred but artless essence as that afforded a famous actress or prima donna exhibiting herself before the footlights. It was evident that she had a sense of humor, for as she made her way slowly toward the entrance a smile twitched her mouth more than once. Clavering thought that she was on the point of laughing outright. But he fumed. "Damn them! They'll scare her off. She'll never come again."

---

1   Probably a reference to the scenic Central Park Reservoir in Manhattan, built in late 1850s and early 1860s and known as the Jacqueline Kennedy Onassis Reservoir today.

One or two women had vowed they'd speak to her. After all a first-night was a club of sorts. But their courage failed them. The crowd made way for her and she crossed the pavement to wait for her car. Clavering, always hoping that some drunken brute would give him the opportunity to succor[1] her, followed and stood as close as he dared. Her car drove up and she entered. As it started she turned her head and looked straight at him. And then Clavering was sure that she laughed outright.

He started recklessly after the car, plunging between automobiles going in four different directions, and jumping on the running board of a taxi, told the man to drive like hell toward Park Avenue. There was amused recognition in that glance! She had, must have, noticed him before tonight!

And then he had his chance. To the brave belong the fair.[2]

VII

He dismissed the taxi at the corner of her street and walked rapidly toward the house. He had no definite object, but with the blood of romantic ancestors who had serenaded beneath magnolia trees pounding in his veins, he thought it likely he would take up his stand under the opposite lamp-post and remain there all night. The reportorial news-sense died painlessly.

Suddenly, to his amazement, he saw her run down the steps of her house and disappear into the area. She was once more at the gate when he hurried up to her.

"May I—am I——" he stammered. "Is anything the matter?"

For a moment she had shrunk back in alarm, but the narrow silent street between its ramparts of brown stone was bright with moonlight and she recognized him.

"Oh, it is you," she said with a faint smile. "I forgot my key and I cannot make any one hear the bell. The servants sleep on the top floor, and of course like logs. Yes, you can do something. Are you willing to break a window, crawl in, and find your way up to the front door?"

"Watch me!" Clavering forgot that he was saturnine and remote and turning thirty-four. He took the area steps at a bound. Iron

---

1 To provide with relief, shelter.
2 Title of a 1913 comedic film directed by Al Christie. Also a play on the Celtic phrase, "to the brave belong all things," which the Celts invoked when battling the Romans.

gates guarded the basement doors, but the old bars on the windows were easily wrenched out. He lifted his foot, kicked out a pane, found the catch, opened the window and ran up the narrow dark stairs. There was a light in the spacious hall and in another moment he had opened the door. He expected to be dismissed with a word of lofty thanks, but she said in a tone of casual hospitality:

"There are sandwiches in the library and I can give you a whiskey and soda."

She walked with a light swift step down the hall, the narrow tail of her black velvet gown wriggling after her. Clavering followed in a daze, but his trained eye took note of the fine old rugs and carved Italian furniture, two splendid tapestries, and great vases of flowers that filled the air with a drowsy perfume. He had heard of the Ogden house, built and furnished some fifty years ago. The couple that had leased it had been childless and it showed little wear. The stairs curving on the left had evidently been recarpeted, but in a very dull red that harmonized with the mellow tints of the old house.

She opened a door at the end of the hall on the right and he found himself in a large library whose walls were covered with books to the ceiling. Dinwiddie had told him that the Ogdens were bookish people and that "Mary's" grandfather had been an eminent jurist. The room was as dark in tone as the hall, but the worn chairs and sofas looked very comfortable. A log was burning on the hearth.

She took a key from a drawer and handed it to him.

"You will find whiskey and a syphon in that cabinet, Mr. Clavering. I keep them for Judge Trent."

"Mr. Cla——" He came out of his daze. "You know who I am then?"

"But certainly. I am not as reckless as all that."

Her accent was slight but indubious, yet impossible to place. It might be that of a European who spoke many languages, or of an American with a susceptible ear who had lived the greater part of her life abroad. "I was driving one day with Judge Trent and saw you walking with Mr. Dinwiddie."

"Trent—ah!"

He had his first full look into those wise unfathomable eyes. Standing close to her, she seemed somewhat older than he had guessed her to be, although her face was unlined. Probably it was her remarkable poise, her air of power and security—and those eyes! What had not they looked upon? She smiled and poured broth from a thermos bottle.

"You are forgetting your whiskey and soda," she reminded him.

He filled his glass, took a sandwich and sank into the depths of a leather chair. She had seated herself on an upright throne-like chair opposite. Her black velvet gown was like a vase supporting a subtly moulded flower of dazzling fairness. She wore the three rows of pearls that had excited almost as much speculation as her mysterious self. As she drank her mild beverage she looked at him over the brim of her cup and once more appeared to be on the verge of laughter.

"Will you tell me who you are?" asked Clavering bluntly. "This is hardly fair, you know."

"Mr. Dinwiddie really managed to coax nothing from Judge Trent? He called three times, I understand."

"Not a word."

"He had my orders," she said coolly. "I am obliged to pass some time in New York and I have my reasons for remaining obscure."

"Then you should have avoided first-nights."

"But I understood that Society did not attend first-nights. So Judge Trent informed me. I love the play. Judge Trent told me that first-nights were very amusing and that I would be sure to be seen by no one I had ever met in European Society."

"Probably not," he said drily and feeling decidedly nettled at her calm assumption that nothing but the society of fashion counted. "But the people who do attend them are a long sight more distinguished in the only way that counts these days, and the women are often as well dressed as any in the sacrosanct preserves."

"Oh, I noticed that," she said quickly. "Charming intelligent faces, a great variety of types, and many—but many—quite admirable gowns. But who are they, may I ask? I thought there was nothing between New York Society and the poor but—well, the bourgeoisie."

He informed her.

"Ah! You see—well, I always heard that your people of the artistic and intellectual class were rather eccentric—rather cultivated a pose."

"Once, maybe. They all make too much money these days. But there are freaks, if you care to look for them. Some of the suddenly prosperous authors and dramatists have rather dizzy-looking wives; and I suppose you saw those two girls from Greenwich Village that sat across the aisle from you tonight?"

She shuddered. "One merely looked like a Hottentot,[1] but the other!—with that thin upper layer of her short black hair dyed a greenish white, and her haggard degenerate *green* face. What do they do in Greenwich Village? Is it an isolation camp for defectives?"

"It was once a colony of real artists, but the big fish left and the minnows swim slimily about, giving off nothing but their own sickly phosphorescence."

"How interesting. A sort of Latin Quarter, although I never saw anything in Paris quite like those dreadful girls."

"Probably not. As a race we are prone to exaggerations. But are you not going to tell me your name?"

She had finished her supper and was leaning against the high back of her chair, her long slender but oddly powerful looking hands folded lightly on the black velvet of her lap. Once more he was struck by her absolute repose.

"But certainly. I am the Countess Zattiany."

"The Countess Zattiany!"

"The Countess Josef Zattiany, to be exact. I went to Europe when I was a child, and when I finished school visited my cousin, Mary Zattiany—I belong to the Virginian branch of her mother's family—at her palace in Vienna and married her cousin's nephew."

"Ah! That accounts for the resemblance!" exclaimed Clavering. And then, quite abruptly, he did not believe a word of it.

"Resemblance?"

"Yes, poor old Dinwiddie was completely bowled over when you stood up and surveyed the house that night. Thought he had seen the ghost of his old flame. I had to take him out in the alley and give him a drink."

She met his eyes calmly. "That was the cause of his interest? Cousin Mary always said that the likeness to herself as a young woman was rather remarkable, that we might be mother and daughter instead of only third cousins."

"Ah—yes—exactly. Is—is she with you?"

"No, alas! She is in a sanitarium in Vienna and likely to remain there for a long time. When Judge Trent wrote that it would be well for her interests if she came to New York she asked me to come instead and gave me her power of attorney. As my husband

---

1 Nineteenth-century European name for members of the Khoikhoi people in southwestern Africa. In 1810 a tribal woman, who went by the name Sarah "Saartjie" Baartman, was exhibited in London as the "Hottentot Venus."

was killed in the first year of the war and I had no other ties, I can assure you I was glad to come." She shivered slightly. "Oh, yes! Vienna! To see so much misery and to be able to give so little help! But now that Mary's and my own fortune are restored I can assure you it gives me the greatest satisfaction of my life to send a large share of our incomes to our agent in Vienna."

This time there was an unmistakable ring of truth in her deep tones. And she was human. Clavering had begun to doubt it, notwithstanding her powerful disturbing magnetism. But was he falling in love with her? He was attracted, dazzled, and he still felt romantic. But love! In spite of his suspicions she seemed to move on a plane infinitely remote.

"Shall you stay here?"

"Oh, for a time, yes. I cannot see Cousin Mary, and even Paris is spoiled. Besides, Judge Trent wishes me to learn something of business. He is growing old and says that women nowadays take an interest in their investments. I certainly find it highly diverting."

"No doubt. But surely you will not continue to shut yourself up? You could know any one you choose. Judge Trent has only to give you a dinner. Unfortunately most of his respectable friends are a great many years older than yourself——"

"I have no desire to know them. In Paris, off and on, I met many of those elderly New York ladies of position. They all have that built-up look, with hats too small and high for their bony old faces, which they do not even soften with powder or the charming accessories of the toilet known to every European woman of fashion. And feathers! Why are they so fond of feathers—not charming drooping feathers, but a sort of clipped hedge, all of a size, like a garden plot; sometimes oblong, sometimes round? And why do they never look *à la mode*, in spite of their expensive furs and materials?"

"That is the sign manual of their intense respectability. The old régime would not compromise with fashion in all its extravagant changes for the world. Moreover, it is their serene belief that they may dress exactly as they choose, and they choose to keep an old tradition alive. Are not English duchesses much the same?"

"So. Well, I do not bore myself."

"But the younger women. They are the smartest in the world. There is not the least necessity you should bore yourself with the elders. Surely you must long for the society of women of your age."

She moved restlessly for the first time. "They were always in Europe before the war. I met many of them. They did not interest me. I hardly knew what they were talking about."

"But men. Surely a woman as young—and beautiful——"

"Oh, men!" Clavering had never heard as profound disillusion in any woman's tones. And then a curious expression of fear flitted through her eyes and she seemed to draw herself together.

"What has some brute of a man done to her?" thought Clavering with furious indignation, and feeling more romantic than ever. Could it have been her husband? For a moment he regretted that Count Josef Zattiany had gone beyond human vengeance.

"You are too young to hate men," he stammered. And then he went on with complete banality, "You have never met the right man."

"I am older than you perhaps think," she said drily. "And I have known a great many men—and of a variety! But," she added graciously, "I shall be glad if you will come and see me sometimes. I enjoy your column, and I am sure we shall find a great deal to talk about."

Clavering glowed with a pride that almost convinced him he was not as blasé as he had hoped. He rose, however.

"I'll come as often as you will let me. Make no mistake about that. But I should not have stayed so long. It is very late, and you are—well, rather unprotected, you know. I think you should have a chaperon."

"I certainly shall not. And if I find you interesting enough to talk with until two in the morning, I shall do so. Dine with me tomorrow night if you have nothing better to do. And——" She hesitated a moment, then added with a curious smile, "Bring Mr. Dinwiddie. It is always charitable to lay a ghost. At half after eight?"

She walked with him to the front door, and when he held out his hand she lifted hers absently. He was a quick-witted young man and he understood. He raised it lightly to his lips, then let himself out. As he was walking rapidly toward Park Avenue, wondering if he should tramp for hours—he had never felt less like sleeping—he remembered the broken window. The "crime wave" was terrorizing New York. There was no policeman in sight. To leave her unprotected was unthinkable. He walked back slowly until he reached the lamp-post opposite her house; finally, grinning, he folded his arms and leaned against it. There he stood until a policeman came strolling along, some two hours later. He stated the case and told the officer that if anything happened to the house he would hold him responsible. The man was inclined to be intensely suspicious until Clavering mentioned his newspaper and followed the threat with a bill. Then he promised to watch the house like a hawk, and Clavering, tired, stiff, and very cold, went home to bed.

VIII

"Tommy rot. Don't believe a word of it. Mary's mother was one of the Thornhills. Don't believe there ever was a Virginia branch. But I'll soon find out. Also about this Josef Zattiany. That girl is Mary Ogden's daughter."

They were seated in a corner of Mr. Dinwiddie's favorite club, where they had met by appointment. Clavering shrugged his shoulders. He had no intention of communicating his own doubts.

"But you'll dine there tonight?"

"Won't I? And I'll keep my ears open."

Clavering privately thought that the Countess Josef Zattiany would be more than a match for him, but replied: "After all, what does it matter? She is a beautiful and charming woman and no doubt you'll have a very good dinner."

"That's all very well as far as it goes, but I've never been so interested in my life. Of course if she's Mary's daughter I'll do anything to befriend her—that is if she'll be honest enough to admit it. But I don't like all this lying and pretence——"

"I think your terms are too strong. There have been extraordinary resemblances before in the history of the world, 'doubles,' for instance, where there was no known relationship. Rather remarkable there are enough faces to go round. And she confesses to be of the same family. At all events you must admit that she has not made use of her alibi to force her way into society."

"Probably knows her alibi won't stand the strain. The women would soon ferret out the truth....What I'm afraid of is that she's got this power of attorney out of Mary when the poor girl was too weak to resist, and is over here to corral the entire fortune."

"But surely Judge Trent——"

"Oh, Trent! He's a fool where women are concerned. Always was, and now he's got to the stage where he can't sit beside a girl without pawing her. They won't have him in the house. Of course this lovely creature's got him under her thumb. (I'll see him today and give him a piece of my mind for the lies he's told me.) And if this girl has inherited her mother's brains, she's equal to anything."

"I thought that your Mary was composite perfection."

"Never said anything of the sort. Didn't I tell you she always kept us guessing? I sometimes used to think that if it hadn't been for her breeding and the standards that involves, and her wealth and position, she'd have made a first-class adventuress."

"Was she a good liar?"

"She was insolently truthful, but I'm certain she wouldn't have hesitated at a whopping lie if it would have served her purpose. She was certainly *rusée*."[1]

"Well, the dinner should be highly interesting with all these undercurrents. I'll call for you at a quarter past eight. I must run now and do my column."

Clavering, often satirical and ironic, was positively brutal that afternoon. The latest play, book, moving picture, the inefficiency of the New York police, his afflicting correspondents, were hacked to the bone. When he had finished, his jangling nerves were unaccountably soothed. Other nerves would shriek next morning. Let 'em. He'd been honest enough, and if he chose to use a battle-axe instead of Toledo steel[2] that was his privilege.

He called down for a messenger boy and strolled to the window to soothe his nerves still further. Dusk had fallen. Every window of the high stone buildings surrounding Madison Square was an oblong of light. It was a symphony of gray and gold, of which he never tired. It invested business with romance and beauty. The men behind those radiant panels, thinking of nothing less, made their brief contribution to the beauty of the world, transported the rapt spectator to a realm of pure loveliness.

A light fall of snow lay on the grass and benches, the statues and trees of the Square. Motors were flashing and honking below and over on Fifth Avenue. The roar of the great city came up to him like a flood over a broken dam. Black masses were pouring toward the subways. Life! New York was the epitome of life. He enjoyed forcing his way through those moving masses, but it interested him even more to feel above, aloof, as he did this evening. Those tides swept on as unconscious of the watchers so high above them as of the soaring beauty of the Metropolitan Tower. Ground hogs, most of them, but part of the ever changing, ever fascinating, metropolitan pageant.

The arcade of Madison Square Garden[3] was already packed with men and he knew that a triple line reached down Twenty-

---

1 Inclined to be crafty.

2 Toledo, Spain, was known for its steel and for its production of the finest European swords.

3 A multi-purpose arena in Manhattan, used to host sporting events, concerts, and conferences.

sixth Street to Fourth Avenue. There was to be a prize fight to-night and the men had stood there since noon, buying apples and peanuts from peddlers. This was Tuesday and there was no half-holiday. These men appeared to have unbounded leisure while the rest of the city toiled or demanded work. But they were always warmly dressed and indubitably well-fed. They belonged to what is vaguely known as the sporting fraternity, and were invariably in funds, although they must have existed with the minimum of work. The army of unemployed was hardly larger and certainly no bread line was ever half as long. Mounted police rode up and down to avert any anticipation of the night's battle. A loud barking murmur rose and mingled with the roar of the avenues.

The great clock of the Metropolitan Tower began to play those sad and sweetly ominous notes preliminary to booming out the hour. They always reminded him of the warning bell on a wild and rocky coast, with something of the Lorelei[1] in its cadences: like a heartless woman's subtle allure, poignantly difficult to resist.

There was a knock on the door. Clavering gave his daily stint to the messenger boy. He was hunting for change, when he recaptured his column, sat down at his desk, and, running it over hastily, inserted the word "authentic." New York must have its Word, even as its topic. "Authentic," loosed upon the world by Arnold Bennett,[2] was the rage at present. The little writers hardly dared use it. It was, as it were, the trademark of the Sophisticates.

The boy, superior, indifferent, and chewing gum, accepted his tip and departed. Clavering returned to the window. Gone was the symphony of gold and gray.[3] The buildings surrounding the Square were a dark and formless mass in the heavy dusk. Only the street lights below shone like globular phosphorescence on a dark and turbulent sea.

Two hours later he left his hotel and walked up Madison Avenue. Twenty-sixth Street was deserted and as littered with papers, peanut shells, and various other debris as a picnic train. The mounted police had disappeared. From the great building came the first roar of the thousands assembled, whether in approval or the reverse it would be difficult to determine. They roared upon the slightest pretext and they would roar steadily until half-past

---

1 A mermaid capable of luring men to their deaths with song.

2 Popular English novelist (1867-1931) who wrote a weekly column about literature for the *Evening Standard*.

3 American-born James McNeill Whistler (1834-1903) entitled many of his paintings "symphonies" in particular color combinations.

ten or eleven, when they would burst out of every exit, rending the night with their yells, while a congested mass of motors and taxicabs shrieked and honked and squealed and coughed; and then abruptly the silence of death would fall upon what is now a business quarter where only an occasional hotel or little old brownstone house—sole reminder of a vanished past when Madison Square was the centre of fashion—lingered between the towering masses of concrete and steel.

IX

When Clavering and Dinwiddie arrived at the Ogden house Judge Trent was already there and mixing cocktails in the library. He was a large man who must have had a superb figure before it grew heavy. He wore the moustache of his generation and in common with what was left of his hair it glistened like crystal. His black eyes were still very bright and his full loose mouth wore the slight smirk peculiar to old men whose sex vanity perishes only in the grave. Beside him stood a man some ten years younger who was in the graying period, which gave him a somewhat dried and dusty look; but whose figure was still slender and whose hard outlines of face were as yet unblurred by flesh. They were, of course, faultlessly groomed, but if met in the wilds of Africa, clad in rags and bearded like the jungle, to the initiate they still would have been New Yorkers.

"Come in! Come in!" cried the Judge heartily. "Madame Zattiany will be down in a minute—she prefers to be called Madame Zattiany, by the way. Thinks titles in America are absurd unless wearers were born to them—more particularly since continental titles today are worth about as much as rubles and marks[1].... Mr. Clavering, you know Mr. Osborne? Madame Zattiany kindly permitted me to bring him as she was having a little party. Families old friends."

Clavering placed two fingers in the limp hand extended and met the cold appraising eye calmly. The New York assumption that all other Americans are rank outsiders, that, in short, not to have been born in New York is a social and irremediable crime, had often annoyed him but never caused him to feel the slightest sense of inferiority. He had his own ancestors, as important in their day as

---

1 Rubles and marks, forms of Russian and German currency, were worthless by 1923.

any bewigged old Dutchmen[1]—all of whom, he reminded himself, had been but honest burghers[2] in Holland. But he admired their consistency. The rest of the country had been commenting bitterly on the New York attitude since the eighteenth century. And when you got under their protective armor they were an honorable and a loyal lot. Meanwhile it paid to be as rude as themselves.

"I am delighted that Madame Zattiany has decided to come out of her shell at last," said Judge Trent, shaking vigorously. "I've been urging it for some time. But she has had a long and harrowing experience, and seemed to want only to rest. I think the stir she made at your first-nights, Clavering, had something to do with it. There was a time, you know, when she never appeared without making a sensation—like poor Mary before her—but young as she is all that seems almost too remote to recall. Of course if she had been able to live in London or Paris after the war it would have been different, but she was stuck in Buda Pesth and Vienna—ah!"

Madame Zattiany had entered the room. She wore pale green chiffon with floating sleeves that left her arms bare. In the subdued light she looked like a girl playing at Undine.[3]

Clavering heard Dinwiddie give a sharp hiss. "Gad! More like Mary than ever. Nile-green was her favorite color."

She greeted the Judge and Clavering with her slight flickering smile and then turned to the other two men.

"This must be Mr. Osborne, as Judge Trent pointed out Mr. Dinwiddie to me one day on Fifth Avenue. It was kind of you both to come in this informal manner. I appreciate it very much."

Her manner was a little like that of a princess giving audience, Clavering reflected, a manner enhanced by her slight accent and profound repose, the negligent lifting of her hand to be kissed; and as she stood graciously accepting their expressions of unhoped for felicity she looked less American, more European, than ever. But Clavering wondered for the first time if that perfect repose were merely the expression of a profound indifference, almost apathy ... but no, she was too young for that, however the war may

---

1 Old New York was dominated by descendants of wealthy Dutch landowners.

2 Archaic term for members of a small-town middle class; predates term "bourgeoisie."

3 Heroine from an early German romance, extremely popular in the late nineteenth-century US, in which Undine, a mermaid, marries a human and assumes human form, except on Saturdays, when she returns to her mermaid form.

have seared her; and she was smiling spontaneously, there was a genuine note of pleasure in her voice as she turned to him.

"It was more than kind of you to watch my house until the policeman came," she said on a lower key. "I was really alarmed when I remembered that broken window and all those dreadful stories in the newspapers. But you kept watch beneath my windows like a *preux chevalier*[1] and I felt safe."

"I felt rather a fool if the truth be told." Her eyes had a curious exploring look and Clavering felt unaccountably irritated, in spite of all that her words implied. "I'd have done the same if you had been old and withered. Served me right. I should have thought before I left the house to telephone for a watchman."

"Ah! Quite so. American men are famous for their gallantry, are they not? Myself, I have always liked them." The smile rose to her wise penetrating eyes, and Clavering colored like a schoolboy. Then it faded and her face looked suddenly rigid. "I wonder," she muttered, then turned her back abruptly. "You must not forget your cocktail. And dinner has been announced."

Mr. Dinwiddie made a pretext of sipping his cocktail as the three raised their glasses simultaneously to their hostess. She had declined to join them, with a little grimace. "Perhaps in time I may become American enough to like your strange concoctions, but so far I think cocktails have a really horrid taste. Shall we go in?"

The Judge offered his arm with the formal gallant air he could assume at will and the other men followed at a discreet distance: her shimmering gown had a long tail. Mr. Dinwiddie's eyes seemed to bore into that graceful swaying back, but he was not the man to discuss his hostess until he had left her house, and Clavering could only wonder what conclusions were forming in that avid cynical old brain.

The dining-room, long and narrow, was at the back of the hall and extended along the entire width of the large house. Like the hall it was panelled and dark, an imposing room hung with family portraits. A small table at the end looked like a fairy oasis. It glittered and gleamed and the flowers were mauve, matching the tall wand-like candles.

"I do hope, Madame Zattiany," said Mr. Osborne, as he took a seat at her left, "that you won't succumb to the prevailing mania for white, and paint out this beautiful old walnut. Too many of our houses look entirely too sanitary. One feels as if he were about to be shown up to a ward, to be received by a hospital nurse with a

---

1 A gallant knight, or in modern times, a chivalrous man.

warning not to speak too loud." There was no chill formality in his mien as he bent over his young and beautiful hostess.

"Ah, you forget this is Countess Zattiany's house," she said, smiling. "But I will admit that if it were mine I should make few changes. White was quite *à la mode* in London long before the war, but, myself, I never liked it."

Judge Trent sat opposite his hostess at the round table. She had placed Mr. Dinwiddie and Mr. Osborne on either side of her, smiling at Clavering. "I am sorry I do not know any young ladies," she said graciously, although there was a twinkle in her eye. "You look rather lonesome."

"Why should he?" growled Dinwiddie. "He is young and you are young. The rest of us are the ones to feel out of it."

"Not a bit of it! Not a bit of it!" exclaimed Judge Trent. "You forget that Madame Zattiany has lived in Europe since infancy. She's talked to elderly statesmen all her life."

"Well, we're not statesmen, the lord knows." Dinwiddie could always be relied on to make the obvious retort, thought Clavering, although it must be admitted that he was seldom with none at all. "But you must have seen more young men than old during the war, Madame Zattiany. I understand that Mary turned her palace in Buda Pesth into a hospital and that you were her chief assistant."

"That is quite true, and I had by no means confined myself before that to elderly statesmen; but I had almost forgotten what a young man on his feet looked like before the war finished. Or Society, for that matter. My one temptation to enter Society here would be the hope of forming a relief organization—drive, do you call it?—for the starving children of Austria. Russian children are not the only pitiable objects in Europe, and after all, the children of civilized countries are of more value to the future of the world."

"Another drive!" Judge Trent groaned. "New York flees to cover at the word. Enter Society by all means, but to give your youth its rights. You have been deprived of them too long."

"I shall never feel as young as that again. Nor will any girl who was merely sixteen at the beginning of the war ever be the same as your care-free young ladies here. I sit in the restaurants and watch them with amazement—often with anger. What right have they ... however ... as for myself I shall not reenter the world for any but the object I have just mentioned. Luncheons! Dinners! Balls! I was surfeited before the war. And I have forgotten persiflage, small talk. I am told that Americans avoid serious topics in Society. I, alas, have become very serious."

She swept her favored guests with a disarming smile. They understood. There was no sting in her words for them.

Clavering spoke up eagerly. "Why should you bore yourself with social functions? If you want to raise money for the children I will not only start a drive in my column but take you to call on several powerful editors—or bring them here," he added hastily at the look of amazement in her eyes, "and they will be more than willing to help you. They have only to meet you——"

"That is all very well," interrupted Judge Trent, who, like the other elderly gentlemen, was glaring at the famous young columnist who daily laid down the law to his admiring readers. "But to raise money in large amounts you've got to have a committee, and no committee is of any use—for this sort of thing—without the names of fashionable women who are as well known to our democratic public, that daily devours the society columns, as the queens of the movies."

"Well—well—I do not know. I must think. It is not a step to take lightly."

Clavering intercepted a flash between her eyes and Judge Trent's and the old gentleman tightened his lips in a self-conscious smirk as he bent over his fish.

"Damn him!" thought Clavering. "He knows the whole truth and is laughing at us in his sleeve."

Madame Zattiany had turned the subject gracefully to European politics, and he watched her with a detached air. Trent's attitude toward her amused him. It was more deferential and admiring than infatuated.... Whatever her charm, she was no longer in her first youth, and only unripe fruit could sting that senescent palate. But the other two! Clavering smiled sardonically. Dinwiddie, hanging on her every word, was hardly eating. He was a very handsome man, in spite of his shining pate and heavy white moustache. His features were fine and regular, his eyes, if rather prominent, were clear and blue, his skin clean, and his figure but little amplified. He was only sixty-two.

Osborne, who looked barely fifty, was personable and clever enough to attract any woman. He, too, was astonishingly indifferent to the excellent dinner, and both these gentlemen had reached an age, where, if wary of excess for reasons of vanity and interior comfort, they derived their sincerest enjoyment at the table.

That she possessed sex magnetism in a superlative degree in spite of her deliberate aloofness, Clavering had, of course, been conscious from the first. Had not every male first-nighter been conscious of it? There was a surfeit of beauty in New York. A

stranger, even if invested with mystery, must possess the one irresistible magnet, combined with some unusual quality of looks,
to capture and hold the interest of weary New Yorkers as she had
done. Even the dramatic critics, who looked as if they hated everybody, had been seen to gaze upon her with rare approval.

But tonight Clavering had a glimpse of something more than
a magnetism for which she was not responsible and to which she
had seemed singularly indifferent. It was quite evident that he was
watching charm in action. She was sparkling and exerting herself,
talking brilliantly and illuminatingly upon the chaos still known
as Europe,[1] and it was patent that her knowledge was not derived
from newspapers or drawing-room gossip. Her personal acquaintance of public men had evidently been extensive before the war,
and she had as manifestly continued to see those in and out of
office in Vienna and Buda Pesth throughout all the later fluctua-
tions. Her detestation of the old German militaristic party was unmitigated and she spoke of the late ruler of the Dual Empire[2] and
of his yearning heir with no respect whatever. With other intelligent people she believed Bolshevism to be an inevitable phase in
a country as backward and ignorant as Russia, but, to his surprise,
she regarded the Republican ideal of government as the highest
that had yet been evolved from finite minds, still far from their last
and highest stages of development. She believed that the only hope
of the present civilization was to avert at any cost the successful
rise of the proletariat to power until the governing and employing
classes had learned sufficient wisdom to conciliate it and treat it
with the same impartial justice they now reserved for themselves.

---

1 In the wake of the Great War, Europe experienced economic, political,
   and social turmoil.
2 A reference to the Austro-Hungarian Monarchy, in place between 1867
   and 1918 and under which Hungary retained official power, which
   was largely a technicality, but important to those invested in defending
   Hungarian rights. As a Hungarian by marriage, Countess Zattiany is
   chafing under the Austrians' attempts to claim power over Hungary. The
   Empire's last ruler was Emperor Franz Joseph, who died of natural causes
   during World War I. Heir to the throne, Archduke Franz Ferdinand was
   assassinated in 1914, alongside his wife. His death led to the conflicts
   that initiated the Great War; next in line of succession was Charles I of
   Austria, who briefly ruled after Franz Joseph's death, but he renounced
   his right to the throne at the war's end. By 1918, the Austro-Hungarian
   Empire was dissolved, to the relief of Hungarian nationalists, although
   Charles would attempt to reclaim the Hungarian throne in 1921, before
   being exiled to Madeira.

("And to educate themselves along the lines laid down in 'The Mind in the Making,'"[1] interpolated Clavering.) Otherwise any victory the masses might achieve would be followed by the same hideous results as in Russia—in other words, the same results that had followed all servile uprisings since the dawn of history. When the underdog, who has never felt anything but an underdog, with all the misery and black injustice the word implies, finds himself on top he will inevitably torture and murder his former oppressors. He hasn't the intelligence to foresee the ultimate folly of his acts, or that the only hope of the world is equal justice for all classes; he merely gratifies his primitive instinct for vengeance—precisely the same today, as during the first servile uprising of Rome—he butchers and slaughters and wrecks, and then sinks with his own weight, while what brains are left reconstruct civilization out of the ruins. "The trouble is that the reconstructing brains are never quite good enough, and after a time it is all to do over again...."

This was by no means a monologue, but evoked in the give and take of argument with Mr. Osborne, who believed in never yielding an inch to the demands of labor, and with Mr. Dinwiddie, who, since his association with the Sophisticates, was looking forward vaguely toward some idealistic regeneration of the social order, although Socialism was rather out of date among them, and Bolshevism long since relegated to the attic.

But Clavering was not particularly interested in her political views, sound as they were. Foreign women of her class, if not as liberal, always talked intelligently of politics. What interested him keenly was her deliberate, her quite conscious attempt to enslave the two men beside her, and her complete success. Occasionally she threw him a word, and once he fancied she favored him with a glance of secret amused understanding, but he was thankful to be on the outer edge of that glamorous crescent. It was enough to watch at a comparatively safe distance. Would his turn come next, or was she merely bent on so befuddling these old chaps that there would be no place left in their enraptured minds for suspicion or criticism? No doubt he was too rank an outsider.... She shot him another glance.... Was his to be the rôle of the sympathetic friend?

Then she began to draw Dinwiddie and Osborne out, and it struck him that her attitude was not merely that of the accomplished hostess. They both talked well, they were intelligent and

---

1   *The Mind in the Making: The Relation of Intelligence to Social Reform* (1921) by James Harvey Robinson, explored the ways in which historical events inform social reform efforts in the present, invoking a type of history that encompassed social, economic, and intellectual dimensions.

well-informed, and he was himself interested in what they had to say on the subject of national politics. (The Judge, who had an unimpaired digestion, was attending strictly to his champagne and his dinner.) There was something of anxiety, almost of wistfulness, in her expression as she listened to one or the other doing his admirable best to entertain her. They had the charm of crisp well-modulated voices, these two men of her own class; she had met no better-bred men in Europe; and their air was as gallant as it had been in their youth. He had a fleeting vision of what gay dogs they must have been. Neither had married, but they had been ardent lovers once and aging women still spoke of them with tender amusement. And yet only the shell had changed. They had led decent enough lives and no doubt could fall honestly and romantically in love today. In fact, they appeared to be demonstrating the possibility, with the eternal ingenuousness of the male. And yet nature had played them this scurvy trick. The young heart in the old shell. Grown-up boys with a foot in the grave. Dependent upon mind and address alone to win a woman's regard, while the woman dreamed of the man with a thick thatch over his brains and the responsive magnetism of her own years. Poor old fighting-cocks! What a jade nature was ... or was it merely the tyranny of an Idea, carefully inculcated at the nativity of the social group, with other arbitrary laws, in behalf of the race? The fetish of the body. Stark materialism.... However, it was not as hard on them as on women outgrown their primary function. Theirs at least the privilege of approach; and their deathless masculine conceit—when all was said, Nature's supreme gift of compensation—never faltered.

It crossed Clavering's mind that she was experimenting on her own account, not merely bewildering and enthralling these estimable gentlemen of her mother's generation. But why? Joining casually in the conversation, or quite withdrawn, he watched her with increasing and now quite impersonal interest. He almost fancied she was making an effort to be something more than the polite and amiable hostess, that she was deliberately striving to see them as men who had a perfect right to fascinate a woman of her age and loveliness. Well, it had happened before. Elderly men of charm and character had won and kept women fully thirty years their junior. Possibly she belonged to that distinguished minority who refused to be enslaved by the Ancient Idea, that iron code devised by fore-thinking men when Earth was young and scantily peopled.... Still—why this curious eagerness, this—it was indecipherable ... no doubt his lively imagination was playing him tricks. Probably she was merely sympathetic.... And then, toward the end of the dinner, her manner changed, although too subtly for any but the detached observer to notice it. To Clavering she seemed to go dead under her still animated face. He saw her eyes wander from Dinwiddie's bald head to Osborne's flattened cheek ... her lip curled, a look of fierce contempt flashed in her eyes before she hastily lowered the lids.... He fancied she was glad to rise from the table.

X

"Well?" he asked, as he and Dinwiddie were walking away from the house; Osborne had driven off with Judge Trent. "Do you still think her a base impostor?"

"Don't know what I think and don't much care. She can pack me in her trunk, as we boys used to say. She's a great lady and a charming woman; as little doubt about the first as the last. She's like Mary Ogden and she isn't. I suppose she *might* be merely a member of the same family—with several thousand ancestors where types must have reappeared again and again. If she wants New York Society, especially if she wants money for those starving children, I'll go the limit. But I'm going to find out about her all the same. I'll hunt up Harry Thornhill tomorrow—he's a recluse but he'll see me—and I'll get on the track of some Hungarian refugee. She can't be the usual rank impostor, that's positive. She has the same blood as Mary in her veins, and if she's Mary's daughter and wishes to keep it dark, that's her business. I'll never give her away."

"Well, good luck. Glad it went off so well."

They parted at the door of Mr. Dinwiddie's rooms and Clavering walked slowly home in an extremely thoughtful mood. He felt an uneasy distrust of the Countess Josef Zattiany, and he was not even sure that he liked her.

On the following Monday night, however, he was by no means averse from making a notable personal score. As Abbott, a dramatic critic, who happened to sit next to Madame Zattiany, made his usual hurried exit at the falling of the first curtain Clavering slipped into the vacant chair. She smiled a welcome, but it was impossible to talk in the noise. This was a great first-night. One of the leading actresses of America had returned in an excellent play, and her admirers, who appeared to be a unit, were clapping and stamping and shouting: handkerchiefs fluttered all over the house. When the curtain descended after the fifteenth recall[1] and

---

1 Encore.

the lights went up and demonstration gave place to excited chatter, Madame Zattiany held out her hand toward Clavering.

"See! I have split my glove. I caught the enthusiasm. How generous your people are! I never heard such whole-souled, such—ah—unself-conscious response."

"Oh, we like to let go sometimes and the theatre is a safe place. One of the best things that can be said for New York, by the way, is its loyalty to two or three actresses no longer young. The whole country has gone crazy over youth. The most astonishingly bad books create a furore because from end to end they glorify postwar youth at its worst, and the stage is almost as bad. But New Yorkers are too old and wise in the theatre not to have a very deep appreciation of its art, and they will render tribute to old favorites as long as they produce good plays."

"But that is very fine.... I go to the matinee a good deal and I am often very bored. And I have been reading your current novels with the desire to learn as well as to be amused. I wish so much to understand the country in which I was born. I have received much illumination! It is quite remarkable how well most of your authors write—but merely well, that is. So few have individuality of style. And even in the best authors I find nearly all of the heroines too young. I had read many American novels before the war—they came to us in Tauchnitz[1]—and even then I found this quite remarkable preoccupation with youth."

"Well—youth is a beautiful thing—is it not?" He smiled into her own beautiful face. "But, if you will notice, many of our novelists, capable of real psychology, carry their heroines over into their second youth, and you can almost hear their sigh of relief when they get them there."

"Yes, but they are still behind the European novelists, who find women interesting at any age, and their intelligent readers agree with them. Young women have little psychology. They are too fluid."

"Quite right. But I am afraid we are too young a country to tolerate middle-aged heroines. We are steeped in conventionalism, for all our fads. We have certain cast-iron formulae for life, and associate love with youth alone. I think we have a vague idea that autumnal love[2] is rather indecent."

---

1   The Tauchnitz company published the Collection of British and American Authors in inexpensive reprints for European readers.

2   Love late in life; "Love Autumnal," a poem by Oliver Jenkins, appeared in the *Anthology of Massachusetts Poets* in 1922.

"And you—yourself?" She looked at him speculatively. "Are you too obsessed?"

"I? Good lord, no. I was in love with a woman of forty when I was seventeen."

His eyes were glowing into hers and she demanded abruptly: "Do you think I am forty?"

"Rather not!"

"Well, I am young," she said with a deep sigh of content. "But look! I see nothing, but I see everything."

Clavering glanced about him. Every neck in the boxes and neighboring seats was craned. It was evident that the people in front—and no doubt behind—were listening intently, although they could have caught no more than an occasional word of the murmured conversation. Eyes across the aisle, when not distended with surprise, glared at him. He laughed softly.

"I am the best hated man in New York tonight." Then he asked abruptly: "If you wish to avoid fashionable society why not see something of this? It would be quite a new experience and vary the monotony of books and plays."

"I may—some time, if you will kindly arrange it. But I am not a stranger to the cognoscenti.[1] In London, of course, they are received, sought after. In Paris not so much, but one still meets them.—the most distinguished. In Berlin the men might go to court but not the women. In Vienna—well, genius will not give quarterings. But alas! so many gifted people seem to come out of the bourgeoisie, or lower down still—whether they are received or not depends largely on their table manners."

"Oh, I assure you, our cognoscenti have very good table manners indeed!"

"I am sure of it," she said graciously. "I have an idea that American table manners are the best in the world. Is it true that one never sees toothpicks on the table here?"

"Good lord, yes!"

"Well, you see them on every aristocratic table in Europe, royalty not excepted."

"One more reason for revolution——Oh! Hang it!"

The lights had gone out. Clavering half rose, then settled himself back and folded his arms. A man stood over him. "Just take my seat, Billy, will you?" he asked casually of the eminent critic. "It's only two back.

The eminent critic gave him a look of hate, emitted a noise that resembled a hiss, hesitated long enough to suggest violence, then

---

1 Rarified group possessed of a particular type of information.

with the air of a bloodhound with his tail between his legs, slunk up the aisle.

"Will you tell me how you always manage to get one of these prize seats?" asked Clavering at the fall of the second curtain. "Nothing in New York is more difficult of attainment than a good seat—any seat—for a first-night. All these people, including myself, have a pull of some sort—know the author, star, manager. Many of us receive notifications long in advance."

"Judge Trent has a pull, as you call it."

"That explains it. There has been almost as much speculation on that point as about your own mysterious self. Well, this time I suppose I must. But I'm coming back."

He gave Mr. Dinwiddie his seat and went out for a cigarette. The foyer was full of people and he was surrounded at once. Who was she? Where had he met her? Dog that he was to keep her to himself! Traitor! He satisfied their curiosity briefly. He happened to know Judge Trent, who was her trustee. His acquaintance with the lady was only a week old. Well, he hadn't thought to mention it to such friends as he had happened to meet. Been too busy digging up matter for that infernal column. Yes, he thought he could manage to introduce them to her later. She had brought no letters and as she was a Virginian by birth and had gone abroad in her childhood and married a foreigner as soon as she grew up she knew practically no one in New York and didn't seem to wish to know any one. But he fancied she was getting rather bored. She had been here for a month—resting—before she even went to the theatre. Oh, yes, she could be quite animated. Was interested in everything one would expect of a woman of her intelligence. But the war had tired her out. She had seen no one but Judge Trent until the past week....

He kept one eye on the still resentful Abbott, who refused to enhance his triumph by joining his temporary court, and slipped away before the beginning of the last act. Dinwiddie resigned his seat with a sigh but looked flushed and happy.

"Poor old codger," thought Clavering as he received a welcoming smile, and then he told her of the excitement in the foyer.

"But that is amusing!" she said. "How naïve people are after all, even in a great city like New York."

"Oh, people as active mentally as this crowd never grow blasé, however they may affect it. But surely you had your triumphs in Europe."

"Oh, yes. Once an entire house—it was at the opera—rose as I entered my box at the end of the first act. But that was a thousand years ago—like everything else before the war."

"That must be an experience a woman never forgets."

"It is sometimes sad to remember it."

"Dinwiddie tells me that your cousin, who was Mary Ogden, once had a similar experience. It certainly must be a sad memory for her."

"Yes, Mary was one of the great beauties of Europe in her day—and of a fascination! Men went mad over her—but mad! She took growing old very hard. Her husband was handsome and attractive, but—well, fortunately he preferred other women, and was soon too indifferent to Mary to be jealous. He was the sort of man no woman could hold, but Mary soon cared as little about him. And she had her consolations! She could pick and choose. It was a sad day for Mary when men left her for younger women."

"But I thought that European men were not such blind worshippers of youth as we are?"

"Yes, within reason. Mary was too intellectual, too brilliant, too well-informed on every subject that is discussed in salons, not to attract men always. But with a difference! Quite elderly women in Europe have *liaisons*, but alas! they can no longer send men off their heads. It is technique meeting technique, intellectual companionship, blowing on old ashes—or creating passion with the imagination. Life is very sad for the women who have made a cult of men, and the cult of men is the European woman's supreme achievement."

The delayed curtain rose and the house was silent. First-nighters, unlike less distinguished audiences, never disgrace themselves by whispering and chattering while the actors are on the stage.

At the end of this, the last act, while the audience, now on their feet, were wildly applauding and fairly howling for the author of "the first authentic success of the season," Clavering and Madame Zattiany went swiftly up the aisle. A few others also hastened out, less interested in authors than in taxi-cabs.

He handed her into her car and she invited him to enter and return with her for a sandwich and a whiskey-and-soda. He hesitated a moment. "I'll go with pleasure," he said. "But I think I'll walk. It—it—would be better."

"Oh!" A curious expression that for the second it lasted seemed to banish both youth and loveliness spread even to her nostrils. Sardonic amusement hardly described it. Then it vanished and she said sweetly: "You are very considerate. I shall expect you."

He did not walk. He took a taxi.

XI

She opened the door as he ran up the steps. "I never ask my servants to sit up," she said. "Judge Trent warned me that the American servant is as difficult to keep as to get and must be humored. When I think of the wages I pay these pampered creatures and the amount of food they consume, and then of my half-starved friends in Austria, it makes me sick—sick!"

There being no reply to the axiomatic truth involved in these words, Clavering followed her silently into the library. The log fire was still burning and he hastily replenished it. They took their little supper standing and then seated themselves in easy chairs on either side of the hearth.

"Why don't you bring over your own servants?" he asked. "Time and democracy might ruin them, but meanwhile you would have comfort. Surely you brought your maid?"

"I've had no maid until now since the beginning of the war. I rarely left the hospital. Heaven knows where my other servants are. The young men were mobilized and those that returned alive were either killed in the revolution or turned revolutionists themselves. No doubt the new government would have turned Mary's palace in Buda Pesth into a tenement house if it had not still been a hospital. We left during the revolution and lived in Vienna. Servants with the virus of Bolshevism in their veins would be worse than these."

"Were you ever in danger?"

"Oh, many times," she said indifferently. "Who was not?"

"Was that what broke your cousin down?"

"That and the hard work in Vienna trying to relieve the distress—while half-starved herself. Of course we had almost no money until the United States Government restored our properties."

"Will she join you here when she is well?"

"No, Mary Zattiany will never be seen again."

"Ah? As bad as that? Her friends will be distressed. I understand they saw her abroad from time to time before the war—particularly Mrs. Oglethorpe. That old set is very loyal."

"Loyal! Oh, yes. They are loyal. Mrs. Oglethorpe was ready to give me over to the police. She seemed to think that I had murdered Mary—no doubt during the revolution, when it would have been quite easy. And she seemed to resent quite bitterly my resemblance to Mary in her youth—as if I had committed a theft."

"Probably it made her feel her age. I wonder you saw her."

"I was coming down the stairs as she crossed the hall. Be sure I would not have seen her if I could have avoided it."

"Why?" He left his seat restlessly and leaned against the mantelshelf. "That sounds impertinent. All my questions have been impertinent, I am afraid. But—I should warn you—I gather that both Mr. Dinwiddie and Mrs. Oglethorpe think there is something wrong—that is, unexplained."

"Really?" She looked intensely amused. "But that is interesting. Of course I knew of Mr. Dinwiddie's curiosity from Judge Trent—but I rather thought——"

"Oh, yes, you have floored him completely. But I fancy he's more curious than ever. I—I—wish you would confide in me. I might be better able to defend you if the necessity arose."

"Don't you believe I am what I represent myself to be?"

"It is a terrible thing to say to a woman like you, but——"

He expected her to rise in her majesty and order him to leave the house, but she merely smiled again and said:

"You forget Judge Trent. Do you think if I were an impostor he would vouch for me?"

"I believe you could make any man believe what you wished him to believe."

"Except yourself."

"Remember that a newspaper man——However, I'll speak only for myself." He thrust his hands into his pockets and tried to summon his saturnine expression, but he had an uncomfortable feeling that he looked merely wistful and boyish and that this highly accomplished woman of the world was laughing at him. "For my own sake I want to know," he blurted out. "I haven't an idea why I suspect you, and it is possible that you are what you say you are. Certainly you are far too clever not to have an alibi it would be difficult to puncture. But I *sensed* something that first night ... something beyond the fact that you were a European and did a curious thing—which, however, I understood immediately.... It was something more....: I don't think I can put it into words ... you were there, and yet you were not there ... somebody else seemed to be looking out of your eyes ... even when Dinwiddie thought he had explained the matter...."

"You mean when he assumed that I was the illegitimate daughter of Mary Zattiany. Poor Mary! She always wanted a daughter—that is, when her own youth was over. That is the reason she was so fond of me. Do you think I am Mary's bastard?"

"I did—I don't now.... I don't know what to think.... I have never lost that first impression—wholly."

She stirred slightly. Was it a movement of uneasiness? He was horribly embarrassed, but determined to hold his ground, and he kept his eyes on her face, which retained its expression of mocking amusement.

"But you think I am an adventuress of some sort."

"The word does not apply to you. There is no question that you are a great lady."

"Of course I might be an actress," she said coolly. "I may have been on the stage in Vienna when the war broke out, become accidentally associated with Countess Zattiany, won her confidence, owing to the extraordinary resemblance—our blood may have met and mingled in Cro-Magnon days—stolen her papers, led her to talk of her youth—of course every one knew Countess Zattiany's record in European Society—forged her power of attorney with the aid of an infatuated clerk, poisoned her—and here I am!"

He laughed. "Bully plot for the movies. That is a new angle, as they say. I hadn't thought of it. And a good actress can put over anything. I once heard a movie queen, who was the best young aristocrat, in looks and manner, I ever saw on the screen, say to her director—repeating a telephone conversation—'I says and he says and then I seen he hadn't heard me.'"

For the first time since he had known her she threw back her head and laughed heartily. Even her eyes looked young and her laugh was musical and thrilling.

Then she demanded: "And do you think I am an actress—who got an education somehow?"

"I think you are an actress, but not that sort. Your imaginative flight leaves me cold."

"Perhaps you think I had Mary's personality transferred and that it exists side by side with my own here in this accidental shell. There are great scientists in Vienna."

"Ah!" He looked at her sharply. "Button, button—I feel a sensation of warmth somewhere."[1]

She laughed again, but her eyes contracted and almost closed. "I fear you are a very romantic young man as well as a very curious one."

"I deserved that. Well, I am curious. But not so curious as—interested."

"I hope you are not falling in love with me." Her deep voice had risen to a higher register and was light and gay.

---

1   "Button, button, who's got the button?" is a children's guessing game, played in a circle and oriented to guessing who has been given a button while everyone in the circle attempts to disguise where the button actually is. The reference here deals with subterfuge.

"I am half in love with you. I don't know what is going to happen——"

"And you want to protect yourself by disenchantment?"

"Perhaps."

"And you think it is my duty ..."

"Possibly I'd fall in love with you anyway, but I'd like to know where I stand. I have a constitutional hatred of mystery outside of fiction and the drama."

"Ah." She gazed into the fire. "Mr. Dinwiddie, no doubt, is making investigations. If he verified my story, would you still disbelieve?"

"I should know there was something back of it all."

"You must have been a good reporter."

"One of the best."

"I suppose it is that."

"Partly. I don't think that if you were not just what you are I'd care a hang. Other people's affairs don't excite me. I've outgrown mere inquisitiveness."

"That is rather beside the point, isn't it? It all comes back to this—that you are afraid of falling in love with me."

"You don't look as if it would do me any good if I did."

"Why not let it go at that?"

"I think the best thing I can do is to get out altogether."

She rose swiftly and came close to him. "Oh, no! I am not going to let you go. You are the only person on this continent who interests me. I shall have your friendship. And you must admit that I have done nothing——"

"Oh, no, you have *done* nothing. You've only to *be*." He wondered that he felt no desire to touch her. She looked lovely and appealing and very young. But she radiated power, and that chin could not melt.

He asked abruptly: "How many men have you had in love with you?"

"Oh!" She spread out her hands vaguely. "How can one remember?" And that look he most disliked, that look of ancient wisdom, disillusioned and contemptuous, came into her eyes.

"You are too young to have had so very many. And the war took a good slice out of your life. I don't suppose you were infatuating smashed-up men or even doctors and surgeons."

"Certainly not. But, when one marries young—and one begins to live early in Europe."

"How often have you loved, yourself?"

"That question I could answer specifically, but I shall not."

He calculated rapidly. "Four years of war. Assuming that you are thirty-two, although sometimes you look older and sometimes younger, and that you married at seventeen, that would leave you—well, eleven years before the war began. I suppose you didn't fall in love once a year?"

"Oh, no, I am a faithful soul. Say three years and a third to each attack."

"You talk at times singularly like an American for one who left here at the age of two."

"Remember that my family went with me. Moreover, Mary and I always talked English together—American if you like. She was intensely proud of being an American. We read all the American novels, as I told you. They are an education in the idiom, permanent and passing. Moreover, I was always meeting Americans."

"Were you? Well, the greater number of them must be in New York at the present moment. No doubt they would be glad to relieve your loneliness."

"I am not in the least lonely and I have not the least desire to see any of them. Only one thing would induce me—if I thought it would be possible to raise a large amount of money for the women and children of Austria."

"Ah! You would take the risk, then?"

"Risk? They were the most casual acquaintances. They probably have forgotten me long since. I had not left Hungary for a year before the war, and one rarely meets an American in Pesth Society—two or three other American women had married Hungarians, but they preferred Vienna and I preferred Europeans. I knew them only slightly.... Moreover, there are many Zattianys. It is an immense connection."

"You mean you believe you would be safe," he caught her up.

"*Mon dieu!* You make me feel as if I were on the stand. But yes, quite safe."

"And you really believe that any one could ever forget you?"

"I am not as vain as you seem to think."

"You have every right to be. Suppose—suppose that something should occur to rouse the suspicions of the Countess Zattiany's old friends and they should start investigations in Vienna?"

"They would not see her—nor their emissaries. Dr. Steinach's sanitarium is inviolate."

"Steinach[1]—Steinach—where have I heard that name lately?"

---

1 Dr. Eugen Steinach (1861-1944), an Austrian physician and endocrinologist who pioneered the rejuvenation or "Steinach" operation. See Introduction, pp. 9-11 and Appendix A2.

Her eyes flew open, but she lowered the lids immediately. Her voice shook slightly as she replied: "He is a very great doctor. He will keep poor Mary's secret as long as she lives and nobody in Vienna would doubt his word. Investigations would be useless."

"She *is* there then? I suppose you mean that she is dying of an incurable disease or has lost her mind. But do not imagine that I care to pry further into that. I never had the least idea that you had——Oh, I don't know what to believe! ... Won't you ever tell me?"

"I wonder! No, I think not! No! No!"

"There *is* something then?"

"Do you know why you still harp on that absurd idea that I am what I am and still am not? Do you not know what it is—the simple explanation?"

"No, I do not."

"It is merely that European women, the women who have been raised in the intrigues of courts and the artificialities of what we call 'the World,' who learn the technique of gallantry as soon as they are *lancée*,[1] where men make a definite cult of women and women of men, where sincerity in such an atmosphere is more baffling than subtlety and guile—that is the reason your American girl is never understood by foreign men—where naturalness is despised as gauche[2] and art commands homage, where, in short, the game is everything—that most aristocratic and enthralling of all games—the game of chess, with men and women as kings, queens, pawns.... There you have the whole explanation of my apparent riddle. You have never met any one like me before."

"There are a good many women of your class here now."

"Yes, with avowed objects, is it not? And they do not happen to possess the combination of qualities that commands your interest."

"That is true enough. Perhaps your explanation is the real one. There is certainly something in it. Well, I'll go now. I have kept you up long enough."

He was about to raise her hand to his lips when she surprised him by shaking his warmly.

"I must get over that habit. It is rather absurd in this country where you have not the custom. But you will come again?"

"Oh, yes, I'll come again."

---

1 Launched into the world; literally, "thrown."
2 Crude, tactless.

XII

Madame Zattiany adjusted the chain on the front door and returned very slowly to the library. That broad placid brow, not the least of her physical charms, was drawn in a puzzled frown. Instead of turning out the lights she sat down and stared into the dying fire. Suddenly she began to laugh, a laugh of intense and ironic amusement; but it stopped in mid-course and her eyes expanded with an expression of consternation, almost of panic.

She was not alarmed for the peace of mind of the man who was more in love with her than he had so far admitted to himself. She had been loved by too many men and had regarded their heartaches and balked desires with too profound an indifference to worry over the possible harm she might be inflicting upon the brilliant and ambitious young man who had precipitated himself into her life. That might come later, but not at this moment when she was shaken and appalled.

She had dismissed from her mind long ago the hope or the desire that she could ever again feel anything but a keen mental response to the most provocative of men. No woman had ever lived who was more completely disillusioned, more satiated, more scornful of that age-old dream of human happiness, which, stripped to its bones, was merely the blind instinct of the race to survive. Civilization had heaped its fictions over the bare fact of nature's original purpose, imagination lashing generic sexual impulse to impossible demands for the consummate union of mind and soul and body. Mutuality! When man was essentially polygamous and woman essentially the vehicle of the race. When the individual soul had been decreed by the embittered gods eternally to dwell alone and never yet had been tricked beyond the moment of nervous exaltation into the belief that it had fused into its mate. Life itself was futile enough, but that dream of the perfect love between two beings immemorially paired was the most futile and ravaging of all the dreams civilization had imposed upon mankind. The curse of imagination. Only the savages and the ignorant masses understood "love" for the transitory functional thing it was and were undisturbed by spiritual unrest ... by dreams ... mad longings....

No one had ever surrendered to the illusion more completely than she. No one had ever hunted with a more passionate determination for that correlative soul that would submerge, exalt, and complete her own aspiring soul. And what had she found? Men. Merely men. Satiety or disaster. Weariness and disgust. She had not an illusion left. She had put all that behind her long since.

It seemed to her as she sat there staring into the last flickerings of the charred log that it had been countless years since any man had had the power to send a thrill along her nerves, to stir even the ghost of those old fierce desires. No woman had ever had more cause to feel immune. Too contemptuous of life and the spurious illusions man had created for himself, while destroying the even balance between matter and mind, even to be rebellious, she had felt a profound gratitude for her complete freedom from the thrall of sex when she had realized that with her gifts of mind and fortune she still had a work to do in the world that would resign her to the supreme boredom of living. During the war man had been but a broken thing to be mended or eased out of life; and she knew that there was no better nurse in Europe; it had always been her pride to do nothing by halves; and before that she had come to look upon men with a certain passive toleration when their minds were responsive to her own. Whatever sex charm they possessed might better have been wasted on the Venus in the Louvre.[1]

And tonight she had realized that this young man, so unlike any she had ever known in her European experience, had been more or less in her thoughts since the night he had followed her out of the theatre and stood covertly observing her as she waited for her car. She had been conscious during subsequent nights at the play of his powerful gaze as he sat watching for a turn of the head that would give him a glimpse of something more than the back of her neck; or as she had passed him on her way to her seat. She had been even more acutely conscious of him as he left his own seat while the lights were still down and followed her up the aisle. But she had felt merely amusement at the time, possibly a thrill of gratified vanity, accustomed as she was to admiration and homage.

But on the night when he had hastened up to her in the deserted street and offered his assistance, standing with his hat in his hand and looking at her with a boyish and diffident gallantry in amusing contrast with his stern and cynical countenance, and she had realized that he had impulsively followed her, something had stirred within her that she had attributed to a superficial recrudescence of her old love of adventure, of her keen desire for novelty at any cost. Amused at both herself and him, she had suddenly decided, while he was effecting an entrance to her house, to invite him into the library and take advantage of this break in the monotonous life she had decreed should be her portion while she remained in New York.

---

1 The Greek statue, Venus de Milo, displayed in the Louvre.

She had found him more personally attractive than she had expected. Judge Trent, whom she had deftly drawn out, had told her that he was a young man of whom, according to Dinwiddie, great things were expected in the literary world; his newspaper career, brilliant as it was, being regarded merely as a phase in his progress; he had not yet "found himself." After that she had read his column attentively.

But she had not been prepared for a powerful and sympathetic personality, that curious mixture of naïveté and hard sophistication, and she had ascribed her interest in him to curiosity in exploring what to her was a completely foreign type. In her own naïveté it had never occurred to her that men outside her class were gentlemen as she understood the term, and she still supposed Clavering to be exceptional owing to his birth and breeding. It had given her a distinct satisfaction, the night of the dinner, to observe that he lost nothing by contact with men who were indubitably of her own world. There was no snobbery in her attitude. She had always been too secure in her own exalted state for snobbery, too protected from climbers to conceive the "I will maintain" impulse, and she had escaped at birth that overpowering sense of superiority that carks the souls of high and low alike. But it was the first time she had ever had the opportunity to judge by any standards but those in which she had been born and passed her life. As for Clavering, he was a gentleman, and that was the end of that phase of the matter as far as she was concerned.

It was only tonight that she had been conscious of a certain youthful eagerness as she paced up and down the hall waiting to hear him run up the steps. She had paused once and laughed at herself as she realized that she was acting like a girl expecting her lover, when she was merely a coldly—no longer even bitterly—disillusioned woman, bored with this enforced inaction in New York, welcoming a little adventure to distract her mind from its brooding on the misery she had left behind her in Europe, and on the future to which she had committed herself. And a midnight adventure! She had shrugged her shoulders and laughed again as she had admitted him.

But she felt no disposition to laugh as she sat alone in the chilling room. She was both angry and appalled to remember that she had felt a quivering, almost a distension of her nerves as she had sat there with him in the silence and solitude of the night. That she had felt a warm pleasure in the interest that betrayed him into positive impertinence, and that a sick terror had shaken her when she saw that he was making up his mind not to see her again. She had not betrayed herself for a moment, she was too old a hand in the game of men and women for that, and she had let him go without a sign, secure in the confidence that he was at her beck; but she knew now, and her hands clenched and her face distorted as she admitted it, that if he had suddenly snatched her in his arms she would have flamed into passion and felt herself the incarnation of youth and love.

Incredible. Unthinkable. She!

What should she do? Flee? She had come to New York for one purpose only, to settle her financial affairs in the briefest possible time and return to the country where her work lay. But she had been detained beyond expectation, for the slow reorganization of one of the companies in which a large portion of her fortune was invested would not be complete without her final signature. There were other important transfers to be made, and moreover Judge Trent had insisted that she become thoroughly acquainted with her business affairs and able to maintain an intelligent correspondence with her trustees when he himself had retired. She had shown a remarkable aptitude for finance and he was merciless in his insistence, demanding an hour of her time every day.

Business. She hated the word. What did it matter——But she knew that it did matter, and supremely. She might have the beauty, the brains, and the sex domination to win men to her way of thinking when she launched herself into the maelstrom of politics, but she was well aware that her large fortune would be half the battle. It furnished the halo and the sinews, and it gave her the power to buy men who could not be persuaded. She had vowed that Austria should be saved at any cost.

No, she could not go now. She must remain for another month—two months, possibly. She was no longer in that undisciplined stage of youth when flight from danger seems the only solution. To wreck the lives of others in order to secure her own peace of mind would make her both ridiculous and contemptible in her own eyes, and she had yet to despise herself. She would "stick it out," "see it through," to quote the vernacular of these curious American novels she had been reading; trusting that she had merely been suffering from a flurry of the senses ... not so remarkable perhaps....

But her mind drifted back to the past month. Senses? And if it were not that alone, but merely the inevitable accompaniment of far stranger processes ... if it were what she had once so long sought and with such disastrous results ... She had believed for so many years that it existed somewhere, in some man ... that it was every woman's right ... even if it could not last for ever.... But while it lasted! After all, imagination had its uses. It helped to prolong as well as create.... She sank back and closed her eyes, succumbing to an ineffable languor.

It lasted but a moment. She started up with an exclamation of impatience and disgust; and she shivered from head to foot. The room was bitterly cold. There were only ashes on the hearth.

XIII

Clavering turned hot and cold several times during his walk home. He had been atrociously rude, impertinent. If she hadn't ordered him out of the house it must have been because she was a creature of moods, and he had merely amused her for the hour. No doubt she would wake up in a proper state of indignation and give her servants orders.... Or—was she sincere when she demanded his friendship, willing to put up with his abominable manners, trusting to her own wit to defeat him, lull his suspicions? Friendship! The best thing for him to do was to avoid her like the plague. He hated to admit it, but he was afraid of her, not so much of falling in love with her and going through tragedy, which was probably what it would come to, as of the terrible force so skillfully hidden in that white and delicate body, of a powerful personality fortified by an unimaginable past. She gave the impression of a woman who had been at grips with life and conquered it, from first to last. Formidable creature! An extraordinary achievement if true. But was it? Women, no matter how beautiful, wealthy, highly placed and powerfully organized, got the worst of it one way or another. When they fell in love they were apt to lose their heads, and with that the game. Technique crumbled. For a moment he imagined her in love, dissolved, helpless; then hastily changed the subject. He liked women to be strong—having long since abandoned his earlier ideal of the supine adorant—but not too strong. Certainly not stronger than himself. He had met a good many "strong" women in the last twelve years, swathed, more often than not, in disarming femininity. A man hadn't a chance with them, man's strength as a rule being all on the outside. Women grew up and men didn't. That was the infernal truth.

For the moment he hated all women and felt not only a cowardly but a decidedly boyish impulse to run away. He'd like to wander ... wander ... lie out in the woods and dream as he had done in his boyhood ... before he knew too much of life ... reading

Shelley and munching chestnuts.... Then he remembered that woods were full of snow in winter, and laughed. Well, he'd go and see Gora Dwight.[1] She was in Washington at the moment, but would be home on Friday. She was a tonic. Strong if you like, but making no bones about it. No soft feminine seductions there. She, too, had fought life and conquered, in a way, but she showed the scars. Must have had the devil of a time. At all events a man could spend hours in her stimulating company and know exactly where he stood. No damned sex nonsense about her at all. He knew barely another woman who didn't trail round to sex sooner or later. Psychoanalysis had relieved them of whatever decent inhibitions they might have had in the past. He hated the subject. Some day he'd let go in his column and tell women in general what he thought of them. Remind them that men were their superiors in this at least: they kept sex in its proper place and were capable always of more than one idea at a time. So was Gora Dwight. He believed he'd make a confidante of her—to a certain extent. At all events he'd refresh his soul at that tranquil font.

XIV

Gora Dwight, after the fashion of other successful authors, had recently bought a house. It was in East Thirty-fifth Street, not far from the one at present occupied by Madame Zattiany, but nearer Lexington Avenue. It was one of the old monotonous brownstone houses, but with a "southern exposure," and the former owner had removed the front steps and remodeled the lower floor.

The dining-room, on the left of the entrance, was a long admirably proportioned room, and the large room above, which embraced the entire floor, Miss Dwight had converted into a library both sumptuous and stately. She had bought her furniture at auction that it might not look too new, and on the longer walls were bookcases seven feet high. She had collected a small library before the war; and for the many other books, some of them rare and all highly valued by their present possessor, she had haunted second-hand bookshops.

The prevailing tone of the room was brown and gold, enlivened discreetly with red, and the chairs and lounges were deep and

---

1 Gora Dwight, one of the Sophisticates, had appeared in Atherton's novel *Sisters in Law* (1921). She is depicted as a successful author and a skeptic about romantic love.

comfortable. A large davenport stood before the fireplace, which had been rebuilt for logs. There was a victrola in one corner, for Miss Dwight was amenable if her guests were seized with the desire to jazz, and a grand piano stood near the lower windows. The only evidence of sheer femininity was a tea table furnished with old pieces of silver she had picked up in France. The dining-room below was a trifle gayer in effect; the walls and curtains were a deep yellow and there were always flowers on the table.

New York knew so much about this new literary planet that it took for granted there was nothing further to be discovered. There are always San Franciscans in the great city, and when she became famous they were obliging with their biographical data. Life had been hard on her at first, for although she came of old Revolutionary stock she grew up in poverty and obscurity. Her father had been a failure, and after the death of her parents she had kept a lodging house for business women, taking courses at the University of California meanwhile; later she had studied nursing and made her mark with physicians and surgeons. Her brother, a good-looking chap with fine manners, but a sort of super-moron, had unexpectedly married into the old aristocracy of San Francisco, and Gora, through her sister-in-law, the lovely Alexina Groome,[1] had seen something of the lighter side of life. During this period she had written a number of short stories that had been published in the best magazines, and one novel of distinction that had made a "howling success" in San Francisco, owing to the unprecedented efforts of the fashionable people led by young Mrs. Mortimer Dwight; but had fallen flat in the East in spite of the reviews. Then had come a long intermission when fictionists were of small account in a world of awful facts. She was quite forgotten, for she made not even a casual contribution to the magazines; shortly after the war broke out she offered her services to England and for long and weary years was one of the most valued nurses in the British armies. At the close of the war she had returned to California, intending to write her new novel at Lake Tahoe, but finding the season in full swing she had gone to some small interior town and written it there. When it was finished she had brought it on to New York and had remained here ever since.

So ended the brief biography, which was elaborated in many articles and interviews.

As for the novel, it won her instant fame and a small fortune. It was gloomy, pessimistic, excoriating, merciless, drab, sordid, and

---

1 See the author's "Sisters-in-Law." [Atherton's note]

hideously realistic. Its people hailed from that plebeian end of the vegetable garden devoted to turnips and cabbages. They possessed all the mean vices and weaknesses that detestable humanity has so far begotten. They were all failures and their pitiful aspirations were treated with biting irony. Futile, futile world!

The scene was laid in a small town in California, a microcosm of the stupidities of civilization and of the United States of America in particular. The celebrated "atmosphere" of the state was ignored. The town and the types were "American"; it would seem that merely some unadmitted tenuous sentiment had set the scene in the state of the author's birth, but there the concession ended. Even the climate was treated with the scorn that all old *clichés* deserved. (Her biographers might have contributed the information that the climate of a California interior town in summer is simply infernal.)

Naturally, the book created a furore. A few years before it would have expired at birth, even had a publisher been mad enough to offer it to a smug contented world. But the daily catalogue of the horrors and the obscenities of war, the violent dislocations that followed with their menaces of panic and revolution that affected the nerves and the pockets of the entire commonwealth, the irritable reaction against the war itself, knocked romance, optimism, aspiration, idealism, the sane and balanced judgment of life, to smithereens. More *clichés*. The world was rotten to the core and the human race so filthy the wonder was that any writer would handle it with tongs. But they plunged to their necks. The public, whose urges, inhibitions, complexes, were in a state of ferment, but inarticulate, found their release in these novels and stories and wallowed in them. The more insulting, the more ruthless, the more one-sided the disclosure of their irremediable faults and meannesses, the more voluptuous the pleasure. There had been reactions after the Civil War, but on a higher plane. The population had not been maculated[1] by inferior races.[2]

The young editors, critics, special writers were enchanted. This was Life! At last! Moreover, it was Democracy. These young and able men, having renounced their earlier socialism, their sense of humor recognizing its disharmony with high salaries and pleasant living, were hot for Democracy. Nothing paid like Democracy in this heaving world. The Democratic wave rose and roared. Symbolic was this violent eruption of small-town fiction, as realistic

---

1   Stained, defiled.
2   This stance is informed by both eugenics and nativism.

as the kitchen, as pessimistic as Wall Street. All virtue, all hope, all idealism, had gone out of the world. Romance, for that matter, never had existed and it was high time the stupid world was forcibly purged of its immemorial illusion. Life was and ever had been sordid, commonplace, ignoble, vulgar, immedicable; refinement was a cowardly veneer that was beneath any seeker after Truth, and Truth was all that mattered. Love was to laugh. Happiness was hysteria, and content the delusion of morons (a word now hotly racing "authentic"). As for those verbal criminals, "loyalty" and "patriotism"—*fecit vomitare*.[1]

Their success was colossal.

Gora Dwight caught the crest of the wave and sold three hundred thousand copies of "Fools." She immediately signed a contract with one of the "woman's magazines" for the serial rights of her next novel for thirty thousand dollars, and received a corresponding advance from her publisher. Her short stories sold for two thousand dollars apiece, and her first novel was exhumed and had a heavy sale.

It was difficult to be pessimistic with a hundred thousand dollars in bonds and mortgages and the deed of a house in her strong box, but Gora Dwight was an artist and could always fall back on technique. But although her book was the intellectual expression of wildly distorted complexes, owing to the disillusionments of war, the humiliation of her ego in woman's most disastrous adventure, and the consequent repression of all her dearest urges, she deserved her success far more than any of her adolescent rivals. She had formed her style in the days of complete normalcy, and not only was that style distinguished, vigorous, and individual, but she was able to convey her extremest realism so subtly and yet so unambiguously that she could afford to disdain the latrinities[2] of the "younger school." A marvellous feat. Most of them used the frank vocabulary of the humble home, as alone synonymous with Truth. Never before had such words invaded the sacrosanct pages of American letters. Little they recked,[3] as Mr. Lee Clavering, who took the entire school as an obscene joke, pointed out, that they were but taking the shortest cut—advantage of the post-war license affecting all classes—to save themselves the exhausting effort of acquiring a vocabulary and forming a style.

The spade as a symbol vanished from fiction.

---

1 Vomit-inducing.
2 Relating to a simple toilet; crassness.
3 Paying heed to something important.

Miss Dwight had her own ideals, little as she permitted her unfortunate characters to have any, and not only was she a consummate master of words and of the art of suggestion, but she had been brought up by finicky parents who held that certain words were not to be used in refined society. The impressions received in plastic years were not to be obliterated by any fad of the hour.

No one knew, not even her fellow Californians, that she had had a disastrous love affair which had culminated in an attempt to murder her beautiful sister-in-law. Her book had been a wild revulsion from every standard of her youth, and she loathed love and the bare idea of mutual happiness in fellow mortals as she recently had loathed blood and filth and war and Germans.

Success is a great healer. Moreover, she was a woman of strong and indomitable character, and very proud. She consigned the man, who, after all, was the author of her phenomenal success, to nethermost oblivion. You cannot sell three hundred thousand copies of a book, receive hundreds of letters from unknown admirers telling you that you are the greatest novelist living, see your name constantly in the "news," be besieged by editors and publishers, and become a popular favorite with Sophisticates, and carry around a lacerated heart. The past fades. The present reigns. The future is rosy as the dawn. Gora Dwight was far too arrogant at this period of her career to love any man even had there been anything left of her heart but a pump. Her life was full to the brim. She was quite aware that the present rage for stark and dour realism would pass—the indications were to be seen in the more moderate but pronounced success of several novels by authors impervious to crazes—but she was too fertile for apprehension on that score. She had many and quite different themes wandering like luminous ghosts about the corridors of a brain singularly free from labyrinths, ready to emerge, full-bodied, when the world was ready for them.

The last time Clavering had sat opposite a woman by a log fire both had enjoyed the deep luxury of easy chairs and his hostess had seemed to melt into the depths until they enfolded her. But Miss Dwight never lounged. Her backbone appeared to be made of cast-iron. She sat erect today on a hassock while he reclined in a chair that exactly fitted his spine and enjoyed contrasting her with the other woman. Gora Dwight had no beauty, but she never passed unnoticed in a crowd, even if unrecognized. Her oval eyes were a pale clear gray, cold, almost sinister, and she wore her mass of rich brown hair on top of her head and down to her heavy eyebrows. Her mouth was straight and sharply cut, but mobile and capable of relaxing into a charming smile, and she had beautiful teeth. The nose was short and emphatic, the jawbone salient. It was, altogether, a disharmonic type, for the head was long and the face short, broad across the high cheekbones; and her large light eyes set in her small dark face produced a disconcerting effect on sensitive people, but more often fascinated them. Clavering had been told that in her California days she had possessed a superb bust, but long years of unremitting work in France and England had taken toll of her flesh and it had never returned; she was very thin and the squareness of her frame was emphasized by the strong uncompromising bones. But her feet and her brown hands were long and narrow, and the straight lines of the present fashion were very becoming to her. She wore today a gown of dark red velvet trimmed with brown fur and a touch of gold in the region of the waist. It was known that she got her clothes at the "best houses."

She was a curious mixture, Clavering reflected, and not the least contradictory thing about her was the way in which her rather sullen face could light up: exactly as if some inner flame leapt suddenly behind those uncanny eyes and shed its light over the very muscles of her cheeks and under her skin. The oddest of her traits was her apparent pleasure in seeing a man comfortable while she looked like a ramrod herself; and she was the easiest of mortals to talk to when she was in the right mood. She was morose at times, but her favorites were seldom inflicted with her moods, and of all her favorites Clavering reigned supreme. This he knew and took advantage of after the fashion of his sex. He told her all his troubles, his ambitions, which he believed to be futile—he had written plays which his own criticism had damned and no eye but his own and Gora Dwight's had ever seen—and she refreshed and stimulated his mind when his daily column must be written and his brain was stagnant. She also knew of his secret quest of the one woman and had been the repository of several fleeting hopes. And never for a moment had she thought him saturnine or disillusioned. Not she! Gora Dwight had an extraordinary knowledge of men for a woman to whom men did not make love. But if she had neither beauty nor allure she had genius; and a father confessor hardly knows more about women than a nurse about men. Moreover, she had her arts, little as men suspected it. Long ago she had read an appraisement of Madame Récamier[1] by Sainte-Beuve:

---

1 Juliette or Madame Récamier (1777-1849), the beautiful and witty wife of a wealthy French banker whose home became a literary and political salon in Paris.

"She listens *avec séduction*."[1] Gora had no intention of practising seduction in any of its forms, but she listened and she never betrayed, and her reward was that men sound and whole, and full of man's inherent and technical peculiarities, had confided in her. Altogether she was well equipped for fiction.

XV

She was listening now as Clavering told her of his adventurous meeting with Madame Zattiany, of their subsequent conversations, and of his doubts.

"Are you sure she is not playing a part deliberately?" she asked. "Having her little fun after those horrible years? She looks quite equal to it, and a personal drama would have its attractions after an experience during which a nurse felt about as personal as an amputated limb. And while one is still young and beautiful—what a lark!"

"No. I don't believe anything of the sort. I fancy that if she didn't happen to be so fond of the theatre she'd have come and gone and none of us been the wiser. Her secret is *sui generis*,[2] whatever it is. I've racked my mind in vain. I don't believe she is the Countess Zattiany's daughter, nor a third cousin, nor the Countess Josef Zattiany. I've tried to recall every mystery story I ever read that would bear on the case, but I'm as much in the dark as ever."

"And you've thought of nothing else. Your column has fallen off."

"Do you think that?" He sat up. "I've not been too satisfied myself."

"You've been filling up with letters from your correspondents after the fashion of more jaded columnists. Even your comments on them have been flat. And as for your description of that prize fight last night, it was about as thrilling as an account of a flower show."

He laughed and dropped back. "You are as refreshing as a cold shower, Gora. But, after all, even a poor colyumist must be allowed to slump occasionally. However, I'll turn her off hereafter

---

1 "With seduction." From the essay "Madame Récamier" by Charles Augustin Sainte-Beuve (1809–69), the major French literary critic of his day, published in *Galerie de femmes célèbres tirée des causeries du lundi* (1859).

2 Latin for "of its own kind," unique.

when I sit down to my typewriter. Lord knows a typewriter is no Wagnerian orchestra and should be warranted to banish sentiment.... Sentiment is not the word, though. It is plain raging curiosity."

"Oh, no, it is not," said Miss Dwight coolly, lighting another cigarette, which she carefully fitted into a pair of small gold tongs: neither ink nor nicotine was ever seen on those long aristocratic fingers. "You are in love with her, my child."

"I am not!"

"Oh, yes, you are. I've never been misled for a moment by your other brief rhapsodies—the classic Anne—the demoniac Marian—but you're landed high and dry this time. The mystery may have something to do with it, but the woman has far more. She is the most beautiful creature I ever beheld and she looks intelligent and keen in spite of that monumental repose. And what a great lady!" Gora sighed. How she once had longed to be a great lady! She no longer cared a fig about it, and would not have changed her present state for that of a princess in a stable world. But old dreams die hard. There was no one of Madame Zattiany's abundant manifestations of high fortune that she admired more. "Go in and win, Clavey—and without too much loss of time. She'll be drawn into her own world here sooner or later. She confesses to being a widow, so you needn't get tangled up in an intrigue."

"You forget she is also a very rich woman. I'd look like a fortune hunter——"

"How old-fashioned of you! And you'd feel like nothing of the sort. The only thing that worries you at present is that you are trying to hide from yourself that you are in love with her."

"I wonder! I don't feel any raging desire for her—that I can swear."

"You simply haven't got that far. The mystery has possessed your mind and your doubts have acted as a censor. But once let yourself go ..."

"And suppose she turned me down—which, no doubt, she would do. I'm not hunting for tragedy."

"I've an idea she won't. While you've been talking I've written out the whole story in my mind. For that matter, I began it last Monday night when I saw you two whispering together. I was in the box just above—if you noticed! And I watched her face. It was something more than politely interested."

"Oh, she looked the same when she was talking to Din and Osborne that night at dinner. She is merely a woman of the world who has had scores of men in love with her and is young enough to be interested in any young man who doesn't bore her. To say nothing of keeping her hand in.... But there is something else." He moved restlessly. "She seems to me to be compounded of strength, force, power. She emanates, exudes it. I'm afraid of being afraid of her. I prefer to be stronger than my wife."

"Don't flatter yourself. Women are always stronger than their husbands, unless they are the complete idiot or man-crazy. Neither type would appeal to you. The average woman—all the millions of her—has a moral force and strength of character and certain shrewd mental qualities, however unintellectual, that dominate a man every time. This woman has all that and more—a thousand times more. A mighty good thing if she would take you in hand. She'd be the making of you, for you'd learn things about men and women and life—and yourself—that you've never so much as guessed. And then you'd write a play that would set the town on fire. That's all you need. Even if she treated you badly the result would be the same. Life has been much too kind to you, Clavey, and your little disappointments have been so purely romantic that only your facile emotions have played about like amiable puppies on the roof of your passions. It's time the lava began to boil and the lid blew off. Your creative tract would get a ploughing up and a fertilizing as a natural sequence. Your plays would no longer be mere models of architecture. I am not an amiable altruist. I don't long to see you happy. I'm rather inclined to hate this woman who will end by infatuating you, for of course that would be the last I'd ever see of you. But I'm an artist and I believe that art is really all that is worth living for. I want you to do great work, and I want you to be a really great figure in New York instead of a merely notable one."

"You've both taken the conceit out of me and bucked me up.... But I want you to meet her, and I don't know how to bring it about. I have an idea that your instinct would get somewhere near the truth."

"Suppose I give a party, and, a day or two before, you ask her casually if she would like to come—or put it to her in any way you think best. Nobody calls these days, but I have an idea she would. People of that type rarely renounce the formalities. Then, if I'm really clever, I'll make her think she'd like to see me again and she will be at home when I return her call. Do you think you could work it?"

"It's possible. I've roused her curiosity about our crowd and I'll plant a few more seeds. Yes, I think she'll come. When will you have it?"

"A week from Saturday."

"Good. You're a brick, Gora. And don't imagine you'll ever get rid of me. If she is unique, so are you. This fireside will always be a magnet."

Miss Dwight merely smiled.

XVI

Clavering walked rapidly toward Mr. Dinwiddie's club. He was in no haste to be alone with himself, although he should have been at his desk an hour ago. But it was time Dinwiddie had some news for him.

The club was deserted as far as he was concerned and he went on to Mr. Dinwiddie's rooms in Forty-eighth Street. There he found his friend in dressing-gown and slippers, one bandaged foot on a stool.

"Gout?"[1] he asked with the callousness of youth. "Wondered why I hadn't heard from you."

"I've tried to get you no less than four times on the telephone."

"When I'm at work I leave orders downstairs to let my telephone alone, and I've been walking a lot."

"Well, sit down and smoke. Standing round makes me nervous. You look nervous yourself. Been working too hard?"

"Yes. Think of taking a run down to Florida."

"Perhaps I'll go with you. But I've something to tell you. That's the reason I called you up——"

"Well?"

"Don't snap my head off. Got a touch of dyspepsia?"[2]

"No, I haven't. If you had to turn out a column a day you'd be nervous too."

"Well, take a vacation——"

"What have you found out?"

"It took me a week to get in touch with Harry Thornhill, but he finally consented to see me. He's lived buried among books for the last twenty years. His wife and two children were killed in a railway collision——"

---

1 Painful, hot, swelling condition of the joints, especially in the foot or big toe. The condition is caused by high levels of uric acid, which cause crystals to form at the joints. Gout was known as a wealthy person's disease based on the assumption that a rich diet contributed to the condition.

2 Indigestion.

"What the devil do I care about Harry Thornhill!"

"You're a selfish young beggar, but I would have cared as little at your age. Well—a cousin of his, Maynard Thornhill, did move to Virginia some thirty-five years ago, married, and had a family, then moved on to Paris and remained there until both he and his wife died. Beyond that he could tell me nothing. They weren't on particularly cordial terms and he never looked the family up when he went over. Has Madame Zattiany ever said anything about brothers and sisters?"

"Not a word."

"Probably married and settled in Europe somewhere, or wiped out. You might ask her."

"I'll ask her no more questions."

"Been snubbing you?"

"On the contrary, she's been uncommonly decent. I got rather strung up the last time I was there and asked her so many leading questions that she'd have been justified in showing me out of the house."

"You impertinent young scamp. But manners have changed since my day. What did she tell you?"

"Nothing. I'm as much in the dark as ever. What have you found out about Josef Zattiany?"

"Something, but not quite enough. I met an Austrian, Countess Loyos, at dinner the other night and asked her about the Zattianys. She said the family was a large one with many branches, but she had a vague idea that a Josef Zattiany was killed in the war. Whether he was married or not, she had no idea...."

Clavering stood up suddenly and looked down on Mr. Dinwiddie, who was smiling less triumphantly than ruefully. "Well?" he asked sharply. "Well?"

"I see you've caught it. It's rather odd, isn't it, that this Austrian lady, who has lived her life in Viennese Society, knows nothing apparently of any young and beautiful Countess Zattiany? I didn't give her a hint of the truth, for I certainly shall not be the one to loose the bloodhounds on this charming young woman, whoever she may be. Told her that I recalled having met a very young and handsome countess of that name in Europe before the war and wondered what had become of her.... But somebody else may let them loose any moment. A good many people are interested in her already."

"Well, they can't do anything to her. She's a right to call herself whatever she likes, and she asks no favors. But I'd like to hypnotize Judge Trent and get the truth out of him. He knows, damn him!"

"He's laying up trouble for himself if he's passing off an impostor—letting her get possession of Mary's money. I cannot understand Trent. He's a fool about women, but he's the soul of honor, and has one of the keenest legal minds in the state. That she has fooled him is unthinkable."

"He knows, and is in some way justified. Madame Zattiany *must* have your friend's power of attorney. That's positive. And there is no doubt that Countess Zattiany—Mary Ogden—is in some sanitarium in Vienna, hopelessly ill. She let that out."

"Poor Mary! Is that true?"

"I'm afraid it is ... perhaps ... that *may* be it...."

"What are you talking about?"

"When she was mocking my curiosity she suggested that she might have been an actress and won the confidence of Countess Zattiany owing to the resemblance. It struck me as fantastic, but who knows? ... Still, why should she use the name Zattiany even if your friend did give her the power of attorney ... unless ..." he recalled Gora's suggestion, "she is out for a lark."

"Lark? She hasn't tried to meet people. I can't see any point in your idea. Absurd. And that woman is no actress. She is *grande dame*[1] born and bred."

"I've met some actresses that had very fine manners indeed, and also the *entrée*."

"Well, they don't measure up according to my notion. This girl is the real thing."

"Then why, in heaven's name, doesn't your Countess Loyos know anything about her? If Madame Zattiany is what she says she is, they must have met in Viennese Society a hundred times. In fact she would have been one of the notable figures at court."

"The only explanation I can think of is that Madame Zattiany is all that she claims to be, but that for some reason or other she is not using her own name."

"Ah! That is an explanation. But why—why?"

"There you have me ... unless ... Ah!" The familiar glitter came into his eyes and Clavering waited expectantly. This old bird had a marvellous instinct. "I have it! For some reason she had to get out of Europe. Maybe she's hiding from a man, maybe from the Government. Zattiany may be one of her husband's names—or her mother's. Of course Mary would be interested in her—with that resemblance—and help her out. She knew her well enough

---

1 Grand lady, a respectable upper-class woman.

to trust her, and somebody had to represent her here. Of course Trent knows the truth and naturally would keep her secret."

"Another plot for the movies ... still—it's a plausible enough explanation ... yes ... I shouldn't wonder. But from whom is she hiding?"

"Possibly from her husband."

"Her—her——"

"Like as not. Don't murder me. I think you'd better go to Florida and stay there. Better still, marry Anne Goodrich and take her along——"

Clavering had flung himself out of the room.

XVII

He charged down Madison Avenue, barely escaping disaster at the crossings in the frightful congestion of the hour: he was not only intensely perturbed in mind, but he was in a hurry. His column was unfinished and an article on the "authentic drama" for one of the literary reviews must be delivered on the morrow. In the normal course of events it would have been written a week since.

He was furious with himself. Passionate, impulsive, and often unreasonable, his mind was singularly well-balanced and never before had it succumbed to obsession. He had taken the war as a normal episode in the history of a world dealing mainly in war; not as a strictly personal experience designed by a malignant fate to deprive youth of its illusions, embitter and deidealize[1] it, fill it with a cold and acrid contempt for militarism and governments, convert it to pacificism, and launch it on a confused but strident groping after Truth. It was incredible to him that any one who had read history could be guilty of such jejunity,[2] and he attributed it to their bruised but itching egos. After all, it had been a middle-aged man's war. Not a single military reputation had been made by any one of the millions of young fighters, despite promotions, citations, and medals. Statesmen and military men long past their youth would alone be mentioned in history.

The youth of America was individualism rampant plus the national self-esteem, and the mass of them today had no family traditions behind them—sprung from God knew what. Their

---

1 To subvert the idealizing of something.
2 Lack of sophistication.

ego had been slapped in the face and compressed into a mould; they were subconsciously trying to rebuild it to its original proportions by feeling older than their fathers and showering their awful contempt upon those ancient and despicable loadstones: "loyalty" and "patriotism." Writers who had remained safely at home had taken the cue and become mildly pacifist. It sounded intellectual and it certainly was the fashion.

Clavering, whose ancestors had fought in every war in American history, had enlisted in 1917 with neither sentimentalism, enthusiasm, nor resentment. It was idle to vent one's wrath and contempt upon statesmen who could not settle their quarrels with their brains, for the centuries that stood between the present and utter barbarism were too few to have accomplished more than the initial stages of a true civilization. No doubt a thousand years hence these stages would appear as rudimentary as the age of the Neanderthals had seemed to the twentieth century. And as man made progress so did he rarely outstrip it. So far he had done less for himself than for what passed for progress and the higher civilization. Naturally enough, when the Frankenstein monster heaved itself erect and began to run amok with seven-leagued boots, all the pigmies could do was to revert hysterically to Neanderthal methods and use the limited amount of brains the intervening centuries had given them, to scheme for victory. A thousand years hence the Frankenstein might be buried and man's brain gigantic. Then and then only would civilization be perfected, and the savagery and asininity of war a blot on the history of his race to which no man cared to refer. But that was a long way off. When a man's country was in danger there was nothing to do but fight. Noblesse oblige. And fight without growling and whining. Clavering had liked army discipline, sitting in filthy trenches, wounds, hospitals, and killing his fellow men as little as any decent man; but what had these surly grumblers expected? To fight when they felt like it, sleep in feather beds, and shoot at targets? Disillusionment! Patriotism murdered by Truth! One would think they were fighting the first war in history.

It was not the war they took seriously but themselves.

Like other men of his class and traditions, Clavering had emerged from the war hoping it would be the last of his time, but with his ego unbruised, his point of view of life in general undistorted, and a quick banishment of "hideous memories." (His chief surviving memory was a hideous boredom.) One more war had gone into history. That he had taken an infinitesimal part in it instead of reading an account of it by some accomplished historian was merely the accident of his years. As far as he could see he was precisely the man he was before he was sent to France and he had only unmitigated contempt for these "war reactions" in men sound in limb and with no derangement of the ductless glands.

As for the women, when they began to talk their intellectual pacifism, he told them that their new doctrine of non-resistance became them ill, but as even the most advanced were still women, consistency was not to be expected—nor desired. Their pacifism, however, when not mere affectation—servility to the fashion of the moment—was due to an obscure fear of seeing the world depopulated of men, or of repressed religious instinct, or apology for being females and unable to fight. He was extremely rude.

And now this infernal woman had completely thrown him off his balance. He could think of nothing else. His work had been deplorable—the last week at all events—and although a month since nothing would have given him more exquisite satisfaction than to write a paper on the authentic drama, he would now be quite indifferent if censorship had closed every theatre on Broadway. Such an ass, such a cursed ass had he become in one short month. He had tramped half the nights and a good part of every day trying to interest himself by the wayside and clear his brain. He might as well have sat by his fire and read a piffling[1] novel.

Nevertheless, until Gora Dwight had brought her detached analytical faculty to bear on his case, he had not admitted to himself that he was in love with the woman. He had chosen to believe that, being unique and compact of mystery, she had hypnotized his interest and awakened all the latent chivalry of his nature—something the modern woman called upon precious seldom. He had felt the romantic knight ready to break a lance—a dozen if necessary—in case the world rose against her, denounced her as an impostor. True, she seemed more than able to take care of herself, but she was very beautiful, very blonde, very unprotected, and in that wistful second youth he most admired. He had thought himself the chivalrous son of chivalrous Southerners, excited and not too happy, but convinced, at the height of his restlessness and absorption, that she was but a romantic and passing episode in his life.

When Gora Dwight had ruthlessly led him into those unconsciously guarded secret chambers of his soul and bidden him behold and ponder, he had turned as cold as if ice-water were

---

1 Trivial, foolish.

running in his veins, although he had continued to smile indulgently and had answered with some approach to jocularity. He was floored at last. He'd got the infernal disease in its most virulent form. Not a doubt of it. No wonder he had deluded himself. His ideal woman—whom, preferably, he would have wooed and won in some sequestered spot beautified by nature, not made hideous by man—was not a woman at all, but a girl; twenty-six was an ideal age; who had read and studied and thought, and seen all of the world that a girl decently may. He had dreamed of no man's leavings, certainly not of a woman who had probably had more than one lover, and, no doubt, would not take the trouble to deny it. He hated as much as he loved her and he felt that he would rather kill than possess her.

It was half an hour after he reached his rooms before he finished striding up and down; then, with a final anathema, he flung himself into a chair before his table. At least his brain felt clearer, now that he had faced the truth. Time enough to wrestle with his problem when he had won his leisure. If he couldn't switch her off for one night at least and give his brain its due, he'd despise himself, and that, he vowed, he'd never do. He wrote steadily until two in the morning.

XVIII

He awoke at noon. His first impression was that a large black bat was sitting on his brain. The darkened room seemed to contain a visible presence of disaster. He sprang out of bed and took a hot and cold shower; hobgoblins fled, although he felt no inclination to sing! He called down for his breakfast and opened his hall door. A pile of letters lay on his newspapers, and the topmost one, in a large envelope, addressed in a flowing meticulously fine hand, he knew, without speculation, to be from Madame Zattiany.

He threw back the curtains, settled himself in an armchair, read his other letters deliberately, and glanced at the headlines of the papers, before he carefully slit the envelope that had seemed to press his eyeballs. The time had come for self-discipline, consistently exercised. Moreover, he was afraid of it. What—why had she written to him? Why hadn't she telephoned? Was this a tardy dismissal? His breath was short and his hands shaking as he opened the letter.

It was sufficiently commonplace.

"Dear Mr. Clavering:

"I have been in Atlantic City for a few days getting rid of a cold. I hope you have not called. Will you dine with me tomorrow night at half after eight? I shall not ask any one else.

"Sincerely,

"MARIE ZATTIANY."

So her name was Marie. It had struck him once or twice as humorous that he didn't know the first name of the woman who was demanding his every waking thought. And she had been out of town and unaware that he had deliberately avoided her. Had taken for granted that he had been polite enough to call—and had left his cards at home.

Should he go? He'd have his breakfast first and do his thinking afterward.

He did ample justice to the breakfast which was also lunch, read his newspapers, cursed the printers of his own for two typographical errors he found in his column, then called up her house. Feeling as normal and unromantic as a man generally does when digesting a meal and the news, he concluded that to refuse her invitation, to attempt to avoid her, in short, would not only be futile, as he was bound to respond to that magnet sooner or later, but would be a further confession of cowardice. Whatever his fate, he'd see it through.

He gave his acceptance to the butler, went out and took a brisk walk, returned and wrote his column for the next day, then visited his club and talked with congenial souls until it was time to dress for dinner. No more thinking at present.

Nevertheless, he ascended her steps at exactly half-past eight with the blood pounding in his ears and his heart acting like a schoolboy's in his first attack of calf love. But he managed to compose himself before the footman leisurely answered his ring. If there was one point upon which he was primarily determined it was to keep his head. If he gave her a hint that she had reduced him to a state of imbecility before his moment came—if it ever did!—his chances would be done for—dished. He looked more saturnine than ever as he strode into the hall.

"Dinner will be served in the library, sir," said the footman. "Madame will be down in a moment."

A tête-à-tête by the fire! Worse and worse. He had been fortified by the thought of the butler and footman. An hour under their supercilious eyes would mean the most impersonal kind of small talk. But they'd hardly stand round the library.

However, the small table before the blazing logs looked very cosy and the imposing room was full of mellow light. Two Gothic chairs had been drawn to the table. They, at least, looked uncomfortable enough to avert sentiment. Not that he felt sentimental. He was holding down something a good deal stronger than sentiment, but he flattered himself that he looked as saturnine as Satan himself as he warmed his back at the fire. He hoped she had a cold in her head.

But she had not. As she entered, dressed in a white tea gown of chiffon and lace, she looked like a moonbeam, and as if no mortal indisposition had ever brushed her in passing. Instead of her pearls she wore a long thin necklace of diamonds that seemed to frost her gown. She was smiling and gracious and infinitely remote. The effect was as cold and steadying as his morning's icy shower.

He shook her hand firmly. "Sorry you've been seedy. Hope it didn't lay you up."

"Oh, no. I fancy I merely wanted an excuse to see Atlantic City. It was just a touch of bronchitis and fled at once."

"Like Atlantic City?"

"No. It is merely an interminable line of ostentatiously rich hotels on a *board walk*! None of the grace and dignity of Ostend[1]— poor Ostend as it used to be. The digue[2] was one of the most brilliant sights in Europe—but no doubt you have seen it," she added politely.

"Yes, I spent a week there once, but Bruges[3] interested me more. I was very young at the time."

"You must have been! Don't you like to gamble? The Kursaal[4] could be very exciting."

"Oh, yes, I like to gamble occasionally." (God! What banal talk!) "Gambling with life, however, is a long sight more exciting."

"Yes, is it not? Atlantic City might do you good. You do not look at all well."

"Never felt better in my life. A bit tired. Generally am at this time of the year. May take a run down to Florida."

"I should," she said politely. "Shall you stay long?"

---

1 Belgian city in West Flanders and largest on the Belgium coast. It was occupied and used as a submarine base by the Germans in World War I. In the spring of 1918, the city (held by the Germans) was attacked by the British in several failed raids.
2 Sea wall.
3 Belgian capital and canal city in the northwest.
4 The Casino Kursaal in Ostend (which was known as a resort town).

"That depends." (Presence of servants superfluous!) "Are you fond of the sea?"

"I detest it—that boundless flat gray waste. A wild and rocky coast in a terrific storm, yes—but not that moving gray plain that comes in and falls down, comes in and falls down. It is the mountains I turn to when I can. I often long for the Austrian Alps. The Dolomites! The translucent green lakes like enormous emeralds, sparkling in the sun and set in straight white walls. A glimpse of pine forest beyond. The roar of an avalanche in the night."

"New York and Atlantic City *must* seem prosaic." He had never felt so polite. "I suppose you are eager to return?" (Why in hell don't those servants bring the dinner!)

"I have not seen the Alps since two years before the war. Some day—yes! Oh, yes! Shall we sit down?"

The two men entered with enormous dignity bearing plates of oysters as if offering the Holy Grail[1] and the head of Saint John the Baptist on a charger.[2] Impossible to associate class-consciousness with beings who looked as impersonal as fate, and would have regarded a fork out of alignment as a stain on their private 'scutcheon.[3] They performed the rite of placing the oysters on the table and retired.

Madame Zattiany and Clavering adjusted themselves to the Gothic period. The oysters were succulent. They discussed the weather.

"This was a happy thought," he said. "It feels like a blizzard outside."

"The radiator in the dining-room is out of order."

"Oh!"

---

1 A sacred vessel, understood either as a bowl or a chalice, from which Jesus is said to have drunk at the Last Supper. The Arthurian legends (by various authors) trace the adventures of King Arthur's knights, who undertake a quest to retrieve the Grail, with only the most worthy (Percival) able to discover it.

2 St. John the Baptist, portrayed in Christian literature as having baptized Jesus, was beheaded at the request of King Herod's stepdaughter, Salome, who asked that his head be brought to her on a platter (or charger) because her mother, Herodias, demanded it of her. Herod reluctantly agreed because of his promise to grant Salome anything she desired after she had danced for him.

3 A scutcheon, or finger plate. The pun here calls to mind the alternate meaning of scutcheon (or shield containing a coat of arms) as itself a "stain" on a family's honor when out of place.

She was a woman of the world. Why in thunder didn't she make things easier? Had she asked him here merely because she was too bored to eat alone? He hated small talk. There was nothing he wanted less than the personalities of their previous conversations, but she might have entertained him. She was eating her oysters daintily and giving him the benefit of her dark brown eyelashes. Possibly she was merely in the mood for comfortable silences with an established friend. Well, he was not. Passion had subsided but his nerves jangled.

And inspiration came with the soup and some excellent sherry.

"By the way! Do you remember I asked you—at that last first-night—if you wouldn't like to see something of the Sophisticates?"

"The what?"

"Some of them still like to call themselves Intellectuals, but that title—Intelligentsia—is now claimed by every white collar in Europe who has turned Socialist or Revolutionist. He may have the intellect of a cabbage, but he wants a 'new order.' We still have a few pseudo-socialists among our busy young brains, but youth must have its ideals and they can originate nothing better. I thought I'd coin a new head-line that would embrace all of us."

"It is comprehensive! Well?"

"A friend of mine, Gora Dwight—at present 'foremost woman author of America'—is giving a party next Saturday night. I'd like enormously to take you."

"But I do not know Miss Dwight."

"She will call in due form. I assure you she understands the conventions. Of course, you need not see her, but she will leave a card. Not that it wouldn't be quite proper for me merely to take you."

"I should prefer that she called. Then—yes, I should like to go. Thank you."

The men arrived with the entrée and departed with the soup plates.

Once more he had an inspiration.

"Poor old Dinwiddie's laid up with the gout."

"Really? He called a day or two after the dinner, and I enjoyed hearing him talk about the New York of his youth—and of Mary's. Unfortunately, I was out when he called again. But I have seen Mr. Osborne twice. These are his flowers. He also sent me several books."

"What were they?" growled Clavering. He remembered with dismay that he hadn't even sent her the usual tribute of flowers. There had been no place in his mind for the small amenities.

"A verboten[1] romance called 'Jurgen.'[2] Why verboten? Because it is too good for the American public? 'Main Street.'[3] For me, it might as well have been written in Greek. 'The Domesday Book.'[4] A great story. 'Seed of the Sun.'[5] To enlighten me on the 'Japanese Question.'[6] 'Cytherea.'[7] Wonderful English. Why is it not also verboten?"

"Even censors must sleep. Is that all he sent you?"

"I am waiting for the chocolates—but possibly those are sent only by the very young men to the very young girls."

He glowered at his plate. "Do you like chocolates? I'll send some tomorrow. I've been very remiss, I'm afraid, but I've lost the habit."

"I detest chocolates."

Squabs[8] and green peas displaced the entree. The burgundy was admirable.

Once more he was permitted to gaze at her eyelashes. He plunged desperately. "The name Marie doesn't suit you. If ever I know you well enough I shall call you Mary. It suits your vast repose. That is why ordinary Marys are nicknamed 'Mamie' or 'Mame.'"

---

1 Forbidden, censored.

2 *Jurgen: a Comedy of Justice* (1919), a novel by James Branch Cabel (1879-1958), about a middle-aged man who is able to regain his youth.

3 Sinclair Lewis's 1920 satirical novel about an American middle-western town, Gopher Prairie, Minnesota.

4 A survey of land and property owners in England and Wales commissioned by William the Conqueror in 1085. Its account of property ownership was deemed absolute, so there was no appealing its claims, hence the name of the document.

5 1921 xenophobic novel by Wallace Irwin (1875-1959) set on a Californian prune ranch, which details the nefarious designs of Japanese agricultural workers in California and their hostilities toward (and plans to intermarry with) non-Japanese property owners.

6 A 1920s cultural debate about the potential threat supposedly posed by Japanese immigrants. In 1920, Washington State Congressman Albert Johnson argued for barring Japanese immigration so as to limit the numbers of Japanese on the west coast of the US. Hearings on the "Japanese Question" convened in Seattle in 1920.

7 Another name for Aphrodite, the Greek goddess of love, and the title of a1922 novel by Joseph Hegersheimer, in which a married family man begins an affair with a flapper, only to discover his deeper passion for her married aunt, a woman he compares with his Cytherea doll. The novel was written in florid, descriptive English. A 1924 silent film, based on the novel, was produced by Associated First National.

8 Meat from a pigeon too young to have flown; it is considered a delicacy.

"I was christened Mary." She raised her eyes. They were no longer wise and unfathomable. They looked as young as his own. Probably younger, he reflected. She looked appealing and girlish. Once more he longed to protect her.

"Do you want to call me Mary?" she asked, smiling.

"I hardly know whether I do or not.... There's something else I should tell you. I swore I'd never ask you any more questions— but I—well, Dinwiddie kept on the scent until he was laid up. One of the Thornhills verified your story in so far as he remembered that a cousin had settled in Virginia and then moved on to Paris. There his information stopped.... But ... Dinwiddie met a Countess Loyos at dinner."

"Countess Loyos?"

"Yes—know her?"

"Mathilde Loyos? She is one of my oldest friends."

"No doubt you'd like to see her. I can get her address for you."

"There is nothing I want less than to see her. Nor any one else from Austria—at present."

"I think this could not have been your friend. She emphatically said—I am afraid of being horribly rude——"

"Ah!" For the first time since he had known her the color flooded her face; then it receded, leaving her more pale than white. "I understand."

"Of course, it may be another Countess Loyos. Like the Zattianys, it may be a large family."

"As it happens there is no other."

Silence. He swore to himself. He had no desire to skate within a mile of her confounded mysteries and now like a fool he had precipitated himself into their midst again. But if she wouldn't talk....

"Suppose we talk of something else," he said hurriedly. "I assure you that I have deliberately suppressed all curiosity. I am only too thankful to know you on any terms."

"But you think I am in danger again?"

"Yes, I do. That is, if you wish to keep your identity a secret— for your own good reasons. Of course, no harm can come to you. I assume that you are not a political refugee—in danger of assassination!"

"I am not. What is Mr. Dinwiddie's inference?" She was looking at him eagerly.

"That you really are a friend of Countess Zattiany, but for some motive or other you are using her name instead of your own. That—that—you had your own reasons for escaping from Austria——"

"Escaping?"

"One was that you might have got into some political mess—restoration of Charles, or something——"[1]

She laughed outright.

"The other was—well—that you are hiding from your husband."

"My husband is dead," she said emphatically.

He had never known that clouds, unless charged with thunder, were noisy. But he heard a black and ominous cloud gather itself and roll off his brain. Had that, after all, been ... Nevertheless, he was annoyed to feel that he was smiling boyishly and that he probably looked as saturnine as he felt.

"Whatever your little comedy, it is quite within your rights to play it in your own way."

"It is not a comedy," she said grimly.

"Oh! Not tragedy?" he cried in alarm.

"No—not yet. Not yet! ... I am beginning to wish that I had never come to America."

"Now I *shall* ask you why."

"And I shall not tell you. I have read your Miss Dwight's novel, by the way, and think it quite hideous."

"So do I. But that is the reason of its success." And the conversation meandered along the safe bypaths of American fiction through the ices and coffee.

XIX

They sat beside the fire in chairs that had never felt softer. He smoked a cigar, she cigarettes in a long topaz holder ornamented with a tiny crown in diamonds and the letter Z. She had given it to him to examine when he exclaimed at its beauty.

Z!

But he banished both curiosity and possible confirmation. He was replete and comfortable, and almost happy. The occasional silences were now merely agreeable. She lay back in her deep chair as relaxed as himself, but although she said little her aloofness had mysteriously departed. She looked companionable and serene. Only one narrow foot in its silvery slipper moved

---

1 Charles I, the last ruler of the Austro-Hungarian Empire. Known as Charles I, Emperor of Austria and as King Charles IV, King of Hungary, he reigned from 1916 to 1918. At the conclusion of World War I, he renounced political participation but did not abdicate his royal titles. In 1921 he twice attempted to regain the throne and was exiled to Madeira, where he died in 1922.

occasionally, and her white and beautiful hands, whose suggestion of ruthless power Clavering had appreciated apprehensively from the first, seemed, although they were quiet, subtly to lack the repose of her body.

Once while he was gazing into the fire he felt sure that she was examining his profile. He made no pretensions to handsomeness, but he rather prided himself on his nose, the long fine straight nose of the Claverings. His brow was also good, but although his hair was black, his eyes were blue, and he would have preferred to have black eyes, as he liked consistent types. Otherwise he was one of the "black Claverings." Northumbrian[1] in origin and claiming descent from the Bretwaldes,[2] overlords of Britain, the Claverings were almost as fair as their Anglian[3] ancestors, but once in every two or three generations a completely dark member appeared, resurgence of the ancient Briton;[4] sometimes associated with the high stature of the stronger Nordic[5] race, occasionally—particularly among the women—almost squat. Clavering had been spared the small stature and the small too narrow head, but saving his steel blue eyes—trained to look keen and hard—he was as dark as any Mediterranean. His mouth was well-shaped and closely set, but capable of relaxation and looked as if it might once have been full and sensitive. It too had been severely trained. The long face was narrower than the long admirably proportioned head. It was by no means as disharmonic a type as Gora Dwight's; the blending of the races was far more subtle, and when making one of his brief visits to Europe he was generally taken for an Englishman, never for a member of the Latin peoples; except possibly in the north of France, where his type, among those Norman descendants of Norse[6] and Danes,[7] was not uncommon. Nevertheless, although his northern inheritance predominated, he was conscious at times of a certain affinity with the race that two thousand years ago had met and mingled with his own.

---

1 Medieval kingdom in northern England and southeast Scotland.
2 Anglo-Saxon for "sovereign" or "overlord." This paragraph initiates an interest in Nordicism, or a belief in the innate supremacy of Nordic peoples.
3 Ethnic term for the Germanic-speaking Angles who settled in England, constituting part of Anglo-Saxon England.
4 Ancient Celtic people of Great Britain.
5 Peoples of Northern Europe near the North Atlantic (including Denmark, Norway, Sweden, Finland, Greenland, and Iceland).
6 Scandinavian.
7 Ethnic group from Denmark.

He turned his eyes swiftly and met hers. She colored faintly and dropped her lids. Had she lowered those broad lids over a warm glow?

"Now I know what you look like!" he exclaimed, and was surprised to find that his voice was not quite steady. "A Nordic princess."

"Oh! That is the very most charming compliment ever paid me."

"You look a pretty unadulterated type for this late date. I don't mean in color only, of course; there are millions of blondes."

"My mother was a brunette."

"Oh, yes, you are a case of atavism, no doubt. If I were as good a poet as one of my brother columnists I should have written a poem to you long since. I can see you sweeping northward over the steppes of Russia as the ice-caps retreated ... reëmbodied on the Baltic coast or the shores of the North Sea[1] ... sleeping for ages in one of the Megaliths,[2] to rise again a daughter of the Brythons,[3] or of a Norse Viking ... west into Anglia[4] to appear once more as a Priestess of the Druids chaunting[5] in a sacred grove ... or as Boadicea[6]—who knows! But no prose can regenerate that shadowy time. I see it—prehistory—as a swaying mass of ghostly multitudes, but always pressing on—on ... as we shall appear, no doubt, ten thousand years hence if all histories are destroyed—as no doubt they will be. If I were an epic poet I might possibly find words and rhythm to fit that white vision, but it is wholly beyond the practical vocabulary and mental make-up of a newspaper man of the twentieth century. Some of us write very good poetry indeed, but it is not precisely inspired, and it certainly is not epic. One would have to retire to a cave like Buddha and fast."[7]

"You write singularly pure English, in spite of what seems to me a marked individuality of style, and—ah—your apparent

---

1 Baltic Coast, Northern European land masses surrounding the North Sea (Great Britain, the Scandinavian peninsula, and the Danish islands).
2 Large stone, as in a structure made of extremely large, interlocking stones.
3 Ancient Celtic peoples of England, also known as the Britons.
4 Home of the Angles, now England.
5 Archaic form of "chanting."
6 Queen of the Iceni tribe of Celts in eastern England who led a revolt against the Romans after her husband's death.
7 Reference to the spiritual leader from ancient India, who practiced extreme asceticism (including fasting) before embracing the "Middle Way" as a route to enlightenment.

delight in slang!" Her voice was quite even, although her eyes had glowed and sparkled and melted at his poetic phantasma of her past (as what woman's would not?). "I find a rather painful effort to be—what do you call it? highbrow?—in some of your writers."

"The youngsters. I went through that phase. We all do. But we emerge. I mean, of course, when we have anything to express. Metaphysical verbosity is a friendly refuge. But as a rule years and hard knocks drive us to directness of expression.... But poets must begin young. And New York is not exactly a hot-bed of romance."

"Do you think that romance is impossible in New York?" she asked irresistibly.

"I—oh—well, what is romance? Of course, it is quite possible to fall in love in New York—although anything but the ideal setting. But romance!"

"Surely the sense of mystery between a man and woman irresistibly attracted may be as provocative in a great city as in a feudal castle surrounded by an ancient forest—or on one of my Dolomite lakes.[1] Is it not that which constitutes romance—the breathless trembling on the verge of the unexplored—that isolates two human beings as authentically—I am picking up your vocabulary—as if they were alone on a star in space? Is it not possible to dream here in New York?—and surely dreams play their part in romance." Her fingertips, moving delicately on the surface of her lap, had a curious suggestion of playing with fire.

"One needs leisure for dreams." He stood up suddenly and leaned against the mantelpiece. The atmosphere had become electric. "A good thing, too, as far as some of us are concerned. The last thing for a columnist to indulge in is dreams. Fine hash he'd have for his readers next morning!"

"Do you mean to say that none of you clever young men fall in love?"

"Every day in the week, some of them. They even marry—and tell fatuous yarns about their babies. No doubt some of them have even gloomed through brief periods of unreciprocated passion. But they don't look very romantic to me."

"Romance is impossible without imagination, I should think. Aching for what you cannot have or falling in love reciprocally with a charming girl is hardly romance. That is a gift—like the spark that goes to the making of Art."

---

1   Bodies of clear water in the Italian Alps. In World War I, the front line between the Italian and Austro-Hungarian troops ran through the Dolomites.

"Are you romantic?" he asked harshly. "You look as if born to inspire romance—dreams—like a beautiful statue or painting—but mysterious as you make yourself—and, I believe, are in essence—I should never have associated you with the romantic temperament. Your eyes—as they too often are——Oh, no!"

"It is true that I have never had a romance."

"You married—and very young."

"Oh, what is young love! The urge of the race. A blaze that ends in babies or ashes. Romance!"

"You have—other men have loved you."

"European men—the type my lot was cast with—may be romantic in their extreme youth—I have never been attracted by men in that stage of development, so I may only suppose—but when a man has learned to adjust passion to technique there is not much romance left in him."

"Are you waiting for your romance, then? Have you come to this more primitive civilization to find it?"

She raised her head and looked him full in the eyes. "No, I did not believe in the possibility then."

"May I have a high-ball?"[1]

"Certainly."

He took his drink on the other side of the room. It was several minutes before he returned to the hearth. Then he asked without looking at her: "How do you expect to find romance if you shut yourself up?"

"I wanted nothing less. As little as I wanted it to be known that I was here at all."

"That damnable mystery! Who *are* you?"

"Nothing that you have imagined. It is far stranger—I fancy it would cure you."

"Cure me?"

"Yes. Do you deny that you love me?"

"No, by God! I don't! But you take a devilish advantage. You must know that I had meant to keep my head. Of course, you are playing with me—with your cursed technique! ... Unless ..." He reached her in a stride and stood over her. "Is it possible—do you—*you*——"

She pushed back her chair, and stood behind it. Her cheeks were very pink, her eyes startled, but very soft. "I do not admit that yet—I have been too astounded—I went away to think by

---

1 Mixed drink, with an alcoholic base and a non-alcoholic mixer; most commonly a Scotch and soda.

myself—where I was sure not to see you—but—my mind seemed to revolve in circles. I don't know! I don't know!"

"You do know! You are not the woman to mistake a passing interest for the real thing."

"Oh, does a woman ever—I never wanted to be as young as *that* again! I should have believed it impossible if I had given the matter a thought—It is so long! I had forgotten what love was like. There was nothing I had buried as deep. And there are reasons—reasons!"

"I only follow you vaguely. But I think I understand—worse luck! I've hated you more than once. You must have known that. I believe you are deliberately leading me on to make a fool of myself."

"I am not! Oh, I am not!"

"*Do* you love me?"

"I—I want to be sure. I have dreamed ... I—I have leisure, you see. This old house shuts out the world—Europe—the past. The war might have cut my life in two. If it had not been for that—that long selfless interval ... I'd like you to go now."

"Will you marry me?"

"It may be. I can't tell. Not yet. Are you content to wait?"

"I am not! But I've no intention of taking you by force, although I don't feel particularly civilized at the present moment. But I'll win you and have you if you love me. Make no doubt of that. You may have ten thousand strange reasons—they count for nothing with me. And I intend to see you every day. I'll call you up in the morning. Now I go, and as quickly as I can get out."

XX

He plunged down the steps into a snowstorm. Even during his precipitate retreat he had realized the advisability of telephoning for a taxi, but had been incapable of the anti-climax. He pulled his hat over his eyes, turned up the collar of his coat, and made his way hastily toward Park Avenue. There was not a cab in sight. Nor was there a rumble in the tunnel; no doubt the cars were snow-bound. He hesitated only a moment: it would hardly take him longer to walk to his hotel than to the Grand Central Station, but he crossed over to Madison Avenue at once, for it was bitter walking and there was a bare chance of picking up a cab returning from one of the hotels.

But the narrow street between its high dark walls looked like a deserted mountain pass rapidly filling with snow. The tall street-lamps shed a sad and ghostly beam. They might have been the hooded torches of cave dwellers sheltering from enemies and the storm in those perpendicular fastnesses. Far down, a red sphere glowed dimly, exalting the illusion. He almost fancied he could see the out-posts of primeval forests bending over the cañon and wondered why the "Poet of Manhattan"[1] had never immortalized a scene at once so sinister and so lovely.

And no stillness of a high mountain solitude had ever been more intense. Not even a muffled roar from trains on the distant "L's."[2] Clavering wondered if he really were in New York. The whole evening had been unreal enough. Certainly all that was prosaic and ugly and feverish had been obliterated by what it was no flight of fancy to call white magic. That seething mass of humanity, that so often looked as if rushing hither and thither with no definite purpose, driven merely by the obsession of speed, was as supine in its brief privacy as its dead. In spite of the fever in him he felt curiously uplifted—and glad to be alone. There are moods and solitudes when a man wants no woman, however much he may be wanting one particular woman.... But the mood was ephemeral; he had been too close to her a moment before. Moreover, she was still unpossessed.... She seemed to take shape slowly in the white whirling snow, as white and imponderable.... A Nordic princess drifting northward over her steppes.... God! Would he ever get her? ... If he did not it would be because one of them was qualifying for another incarnation.

He walked down the avenue as rapidly as possible, his hands in his pockets, his head bent to the wind, no longer transported; forcing his mind to dwell on the warmth of his rooms and his bed.... His head ached. He'd go to the office tomorrow and write his column there. Then think things out. How was he to win such a woman? Make her sure of herself? Convert her doubts into a passionate certainty? She, with her highly technical past! Make no mistakes? If he made a precipitate ass of himself—what comparisons! ... His warm bed ... the complete and personal isolation of his rooms ... he had never given even a tea to women ... he gave his dinners in restaurants.... How many more blocks? The snow was

---

1   Walt Whitman (1819-92) frequently wrote about Manhattan, but in chapter 28 Clavering identifies Rollo Landers Todd as the "Poet of Manhattan."
2   New York's rapid transit trains.

thicker. He couldn't even see the arcade of Madison Square Garden, although a faint diffused radiance high in air was no doubt the crown of lights on the Metropolitan Tower.... Had he made a wrong move in bolting——?

His thoughts and counter-thoughts came to an abrupt end. At the corner of Thirtieth Street he collided with a small figure in a fur coat and nearly knocked it over. He was for striding on with a muttered apology, when the girl caught him by the arm with a light laugh.

"Lee Clavering! What luck! Take me home."

He was looking down into the dark naughty little face of Janet Oglethorpe, granddaughter of the redoubtable Jane.

"What on earth are you doing here?" he asked stupidly.

"Perhaps I'll tell you and perhaps I won't. On second thoughts don't take me home. Take me to one of those all-night restaurants. That's just the one thing I haven't seen, and I'm hungry."

He subtly became an uncle. "I'll do nothing of the sort. You ought to be ashamed of yourself—alone in the streets at this hour of the night. It must be one o'clock. I shall take you home. I suppose you have a latch-key, but for two cents I'd ring the bell and hand you over to your mother."

"Mother went to Florida today and dad's duck-hunting in South Carolina. Aunt Mollie's too deaf to hear doorbells and believes anything I tell her."

"I am astonished that your mother left you behind to your own devices."

"I wouldn't go. She's given me up—used to my devices. Besides, I've one or two on her and she doesn't dare give me away to dad. He thinks I'm a darling spoilt child. Not that I'd mind much if he didn't, but it's more convenient."

"You little wretch! I believe you've been drinking."

"So I have! So I have! But I've got an asbestos lining and could stand another tall one. Ah!" Her eyes sparkled. "Suppose you take me to your rooms——"

"I'll take you home——"

"You'll take me to one of those all-nighters——"

"I shall not."

"Then ta! ta! I'll go home by myself. I've had too good a time tonight to bother with old fogies."

She started up the street and Clavering hesitated but a moment. Her home was on East Sixty-fifth Street. Heaven only knew what might happen to her. Moreover, although her mother was one of those women whose insatiable demand for admiration bored him, he had no more devoted friends than her father and her grandmother. Furthermore, his curiosity was roused. What had the little devil been up to?

He overtook the Oglethorpe flapper and seizing her hand drew it through his arm.

"I'll take you where you can get a sandwich," he said. "But I'll not take you to a restaurant. Too likely to meet newspaper men."

"Anything to drink?"

"Ice cream soda."

"Good Lord!"

"You needn't drink it. But you'll get nothing else. Come along or I'll pick you up and carry you to the nearest garage."

She trotted. obediently beside him, a fragile dainty figure; carried limply, however, and little more distinguished than flappers of inferior origin. He led her to a rather luxurious delicatessen not far from his hotel, kept by enterprising Italians who never closed their doors. They seated themselves uncomfortably at the high counter, and the sleepy attendant served them with sandwiches, then retired to the back of the shop. He was settling himself to alert repose when Miss Oglethorpe suddenly changed her mind and ordered a chocolate ice cream soda. Then she ordered another, and she ate six sandwiches, a slice of cake and two bananas.

"Great heaven!" exclaimed Clavering. "You must have the stomach of an ostrich."

"Can eat nails and drink fire water."

"Well, you won't two years hence, and you'll look it, too."

"Oh, no I won't. I'll marry when I'm nineteen and a half and settle down."

"I should say you were heading the other way. Where have you been tonight?"

"Donny Farren gave a party in his rooms and passed out just as he was about to take me home. I loosened his collar and put a pillow under his head, but I couldn't lift him, even to the sofa. Too fat."

"I suppose you pride yourself on being a good sport."

"Rather. If Donny'd been ill I'd have stayed with him all night, but he was dead to the world."

"You say he had a party. Why didn't some of the others take you home?"

"Ever hear about three being a crowd? Donny, naturally, was all for taking me home, and didn't show any signs of collapse till the last minute."

"But I should think that for decency's sake you'd all have gone down together."

"Lord! How old-fashioned you are. I was finishing a cigarette and never thought of it." She opened a little gold mesh bag, took out a cigarette and lit it. Her cheeks were flushed under the rouge and her large black eyes glittered in her fluid little face. She was one of the beauties of the season's débutantes, but scornful of nature. Her olive complexion was thickly powdered and there was a delicate smudge of black under her lower lashes and even on her eyelids. He had never seen her quite so blatantly made up before, but then he had seen little of her since the beginning of her first season. He rarely went to parties, and she was almost as rarely in her own home or her grandmother's. Her short hair curled about her face. In spite of her paint she looked like a child—a greedy child playing with life.

"Look here!" he said. "How far do you go?"

"Wouldn't you like to know?"

"I should. Not for personal reasons, for girls of your age bore me to extinction, but you've a certain sociological interest. I wonder if you are really any worse than your predecessors?"

"I guess girls have always been human enough, but we have more opportunities. We've made 'em. This is our age and we're enjoying it to the limit. God! what stupid times girls must have had—some of them do yet. They're naturally goody-goody, or their parents are too much for them. Not many, though. Parents have taken a back seat."

"I don't quite see what you get out of it—guzzling, and smoking your nerves out by the roots, and making yourselves cheap with men little older than yourselves."

"You don't see, I suppose, why girls should have their fling, or"—her voice wavered curiously—"why youth takes naturally to youth. I suppose you think that is a cruel thing for a girl to say."

"Not in the least," he answered cheerfully. "Don't mind a bit. But what do you get out of it—that's what I'm curious to know."

She tossed her head and blew a perfect ring. "Don't you know that girls never really enjoyed life before?"

"It depends upon the point of view, I should think."

"No, there's a lot more in it than you guess. The girls used to sit round waiting for men to call and wondering if they'd condescend to show up at the next dance; while the men fairly raced after the girls with whom they could have a free and easy time—no company manners, no chaperons, no prudish affectations about kisses and things. No fear of shocking if they wanted to let go—the strain

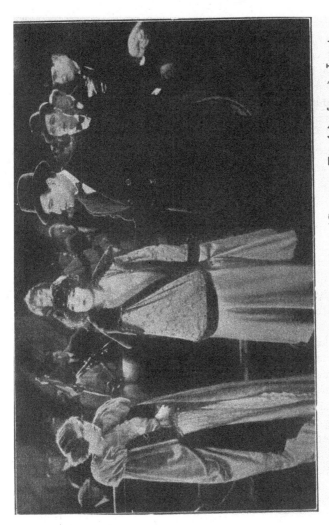

Returning home one night Clavering (Conway Tearle) found Janet Oglethorpe (Clara Bow), daughter of his old friend, in a semi-intoxicated condition.
(*Screen version of "The Black Oxen."*)

must have been awful. You know what men are. They like to call a spade a spade and be damned to it. Our sort didn't have a chance. They couldn't compete. So, we made up our minds to compete in the only way possible. We leave off our corsets at dances so they can get a new thrill out of us, then sit out in an automobile and drink and have little petting parties of two.[1] And we slip out and have an occasional lark like tonight. We're not to be worried about, either."

"Why cryptic after your really admirable frankness? But there's always a point beyond which women never will go when confessing their souls.... I suppose you think you're as hard as nails. Do you really imagine that you will ever be able to fall in love and marry and want children?"

"Don't men?"

"Ancient standards are not annihilated in one generation."

"There's got to be a beginning to everything, hasn't there? One would think the world stood still, to hear you talk. But anything new always makes the fogies sick."

"Nothing makes *me* as sick as your bad manners—you and all your tribe. Men, at least, don't lose their breeding if they choose to sow wild oats. But women go the whole hog or none."

"Other times, other manners. We make our own, and you have to put up with them whether you like it or not. See?"

"I see that you are even sillier than I thought. You need nothing so much as a sound spanking."

"Your own manners are none too good. You've handed me one insult after another."

"I've merely talked to you as your father would if he were not blind. Besides, it would probably make you sick to be 'respected.' Come along. We'll go round to a garage and get a taxi. Why on earth didn't you ring for a taxi from Farren's?"

"I tried to, but it's an apartment house and there was no one downstairs to make the connection. Too late. So I footed it." She yawned prodigiously. "I'm ready at last for my little bunk. Hope you've enjoyed this more than I have. You'd be a scream at a petting party."

Clavering paid his small account and they issued into the storm once more. It was impossible to talk. In the taxi she went to sleep. Thank Heaven! He had had enough of her. Odious brat. More than once he had had a sudden vision of Mary Zattiany during

---

1 Flapper-era parties, notorious for allowing kissing and bodily contact (primarily hugging) among young people.

that astonishing conversation at the counter. The "past" she had suggested to his tormented mind was almost literary by contrast. She, herself, a queen granting favors, beside this little fashionable near-strumpet. They didn't breathe the same air, nor walk on the same plane. Who, even if this little fool were merely demi-vierge,[1] would hesitate between them? One played the game in the grand manner, the other like a glorified gutter-snipe.[2] But he was thankful for the diversion, and when he reached his own bed he fell asleep immediately and did not turn over for seven hours.

XXI

He had informed Madame Zattiany's butler over the telephone that he would call that evening at half-past nine, but he returned to his rooms after a day at the office with lagging steps. He dreaded another evening in that library by the fire. It was beyond his imagination to foresee how she would treat him, what rôle she would choose to play, and although he was grimly determined to play whatever rôle she assigned to him (for the present!), he hated the prospect. He was in no mood for a "game." This wooing was like nothing his imagination had ever prefigured. To be put on trial ... to sit with the woman in the great solitude of the house and the very air vibrating between them ... or frozen ... self-conscious as a schoolboy up for inspection ... afraid of making a false move.... What in God's name would they talk about? Politics? Books? Art? Banalities! ... he'd half a mind to go to Florida after all ... or join Jim Oglethorpe in South Carolina: he had a standing invitation ... he'd return by the next train; he'd felt as if existing in a vacuum all day....

When he reached his rooms he found his problem solved for the moment—possibly. A telephone slip informed him that Madame Zattiany would be at home, and a note from Mrs. Oglethorpe enclosed tickets for her box at the opera that night.

If she would only go!

He called the house. The butler answered and retired to summon Madame Zattiany. Her voice came clear and cool over the telephone. He invited her to go to Sherry's[3] for dinner and to hear

---

1 Provocative young woman who acts promiscuously, but is still a virgin.

2 A child brought up in the streets who behaves in a crude manner.

3 High society New York restaurant located at 5th Avenue and 44th Street, opposite Delmonico's. It closed in 1919 because of Prohibition.

Farrar in *Butterfly*[1] afterward. "I must tell you that we shall sit in a box," he added. "Mrs. Oglethorpe's."

"Oh!" There was a pause that seemed eternal. Then she laughed suddenly, a laugh of intense amusement that ended on a note of recklessness. "Well! Why not? Yes, I will go. Very many thanks."

"Good. It means an early dinner. I'll call for you at a quarter to seven."

"I'm promptness itself. Au 'voir."

So that was that! One night's respite. He'd leave her at her door. He wondered if his voice had been as impersonal as her own: he had almost barked into the telephone and had probably overdone it. But was any man ever in such a ghastly position before? Well, he'd lose the game before he'd make a fool of himself again.... Ass ... he'd had the game in his own hands last night ... could have switched off any moment. He'd let go and delivered himself into hers.

He took a cold shower, and made a meticulous toilet.

When he arrived at the house he was shown into the drawing-room. He had never seen it before and he glanced about him with some curiosity. It was a period room: Louis Quinze.[2] The furniture looked as if made of solid gold and Madame Du Barry herself might have sat on the dainty brocades.[3] The general effect was airy and graceful, gay, frivolous, and subtly vicious. (An emanation to which the chaste Victorian had been impervious.) He understood why Madame Zattiany did not use it. She might be subtly anything, but assuredly she was neither airy nor frivolous.

Then he realized that there was a painting of a girl over the mantel and that the girl was Mary Ogden. He stepped forward eagerly, almost holding his breath. The portrait ended at the tiny waist, and the stiff satin of the cuirass-like bodice was softened with tulle which seemed to float about the sloping shoulders. The soft ashen hair, growing in a deep point on the broad full brow,

---

1 Geraldine Farrar (1882-1967), a popular American soprano associated with the Metropolitan Opera and known for the intimate quality of her voice. She retired in 1922. *Madama Butterfly*, a 1904 opera by Giacomo Puccini (1858-1924).

2 Ornamented French Rococo style, named after Louis XV of France (1710-74). Much of the furniture in this style was gilded.

3 Jeanne Antoinette Bécu (1743-93) was maîtresse-en-titre (chief mistress) to Louis XI of France. Known for her extravagant gowns, hair, and jewels, Du Barry was eventually executed during the Reign of Terror. Two films were made of her life, both entitled, *Madame Du Barry*: a 1917 film starring Theda Bara and a 1919 German film starring Pola Negri and directed by Ernst Lubitsch.

was brushed softly back and coiled low on the long white neck. The mouth was soft and pouting, with a humorous quirk at the corners, and the large dark gray eyes were full of a mocking light that seemed directed straight into the depths of his puzzled brain as he stood gazing at that presentment of a once potent and long vanished beauty.... Extraordinarily like and yet so extraordinarily unlike! But the resemblance may have well been exact when Mary Zattiany was twenty. How had Mary Ogden looked at thirty? That very lift of the strong chin, that long arch of nostril ... something began to beat in the back of his brain....

"What a beauty poor Mary must have been, no?"

He turned, and forgot the portrait. Madame Zattiany wore a gown of that subtle but unmistakable green that no light can turn blue; thin shimmering velvet to the knees, melting into satin embroidered with silver and veiled with tulle. On her head was a small diamond tiara and her breast was a blaze of emeralds and diamonds. She carried a large fan of green feathers.

He had believed he had measured the extent of her beauty, but the crown gave her a new radiance—and she looked as attainable as a queen on her throne.

He went forward and raised her hand to his lips. "I insist," he said gallantly. "Anything else would be out of the picture. I need not tell you how wonderful you look—nor that after tonight you will hardly remain obscure!"

"Why do things halfway? It has never been my method. And Mary told me once that Nile-green had been her favorite color until she lost her complexion. So—as. I am to exhibit myself in a box—*enfin!*[1] ... Besides, I wanted to go." She smiled charmingly. "It was most kind of you to think of me."

"Would that all 'kind' acts were as graciously rewarded. I shall be insufferably conceited for the rest of my life—only it is doubtful if I shall be seen at all. Shall we go?"

When they arrived at Sherry's they found the large restaurant almost deserted. It was barely seven. After he had ordered the dinner—and he thanked his stars that he knew how to order a dinner—she said casually:

"I had a call from your friend, Miss Dwight, today."

"Yes? You did not see her, I suppose?"

"Oh, but I did. We talked for two hours. It was almost comical—the sheer delight in talking to a woman once more. I have never been what is called a woman's woman, but I always had my friends, and I suddenly realized that I had missed my own sex."

---

1 At last; finally.

"I shouldn't fancy that you two would have much in common."

"You forget that we were both nurses. We compared experiences: methods of nursing, operations, doctors, surgeons, shell shock, plastic surgery, the various characteristics of wounded men—all the rest of it."

"It must have been an exciting conversation."

"You never could be brought to believe it, but it was. Afterward, we talked of other things. She seems to me quite a remarkable woman."

"Entirely so. What is it she lacks that prevents men from falling in love with her? Men flock there, and she is more discussed as a mind and a personality than any woman among us; but it is all above the collar. And yet those handsome-ugly women often captivate men."

"You ask one woman why another cannot fascinate men! I should say that it is for want of transmission. The heart and passions are there—I will risk guessing that she has been tragically in love at least once—but there is something wrong with the conduit that carries sexual magnetism; it has been bent upward to the brain instead of directed straight to the sex for which it was designed. Moreover, she is too coldly and obviously analytical and lacks the tact to conceal it. Men do not mind being skewered when they are out for purely intellectual enjoyment, but they do not love it."

Clavering laughed. "I fancy your own mind is quite as coldly analytical, but nature took care of your conduits and you see to the tact. You cannot teach Gora how to redistribute her magnetism, but you might give her a few points."

"They would be wasted. It is merely that I am a woman of the world, something she will never be. And in my hey-day, I can assure you, I was not analytical."

"Your hey-day?"

"I was a good many years younger before the war, remember. Heavens! How rowdy those young people are! A month ago I should have asked if they were ladies and gentlemen, but I have been quite close to their kind in the tea rooms and their accent is unmistakable; although the girls talk and act like *gamines*.[1] One of them seems to know you."

Clavering had been conscious that the restaurant was filling with groups and couples, bound, no doubt, for the opera or theatre. He followed Madame Zattiany's eyes. In the middle of

---

1 Untutored urchins. By the 1920s, the term also suggested a slim, coquettish girl, with boyish mannerisms or clothing.

the room was a large table surrounded by very young men and girls; the latter as fragile and lovely as butterflies: that pathetic and swiftly passing youth of the too pampered American girl. The youth of this generation promised to be briefer than ever!

He gave them a cursory glance, and then his chair turned to pins. Janet Oglethorpe sat at the head of the table. What would the brat do? She had been fond of him as a child, but as he had found her detestable in her flapperhood, and been at no pains to conceal his attitude, she had taken a violent dislike to him. Last night he had deliberately flicked her on the raw.[1]

He was not long in doubt. She had returned his perfunctory bow with a curt nod, and after a brief interval—during which she appeared to be making a communication that was received with joyous hilarity—she left her seat and ran across the room. She might have been in her own house for all the notice she took of the restaurant's other guests.

Clavering rose and grimly awaited the onslaught. Even the waiters were staring, but for the moment only at the flashing little figure whose cheeks matched to a shade the American Beauty rose of her wisp of a gown.

Her big black eyes were sparkling wickedly, her vivid little mouth wore a twist that can only be described as a grin. She had come for her revenge. No doubt of that.

She bore down on him, and shook his unresponsive hand heartily. "I've been telling them how dear and noble you were last night, dear Mr. Clavering, just like a real uncle, or what any one would expect of one of granny's pets. No doubt you saved my life and honor, and I want to tell the world." Her crisp clear voice was pitched in G. It carried from end to end of the silent room.

"Would that I were your uncle! Won't you sit down? I believe that you have not met Madame Zattiany."

Miss Oglethorpe had not cast a glance at her victim's companion, assuming her to be some writing person; although he did once in a while take out Anne Goodrich or Marian Lawrence: old girls—being all of twenty-four—in whom she took no interest whatever.

She half turned her head with a barely perceptible nod. The tail of her eye was arrested. She swung round and stared, her mouth open. For the moment she was abashed; whatever else she may have submerged, her caste instinct remained intact and for a second she had the unpleasant sensation of standing at the bar of her

---

1 To be "flicked on the raw" is to be irritated in the extreme.

entire class. But she recovered immediately. *Grandes dames* were out of date. Even her mother had worn her skirts to her knees a short time since. What fun to "show this left-over." And then her spiteful naughtiness was magnified by anger. Madame Zattiany had inclined her head graciously, but made no attempt to conceal her amusement.

"Yes, I'll sit down. Thanks." She produced a cigarette and lit it. "Granny's got a lot of ancient photographs of her girlhood friends," she remarked with her insolent eyes on Madame Zattiany, "and one of them's enough like you to be you masquerading in the get-up of the eighties. Comes back to me. Just before mother left I heard her discussing you with a bunch of her friends. Isn't there some mystery or other about you?"

"Yes, indeed! Is it not so?" Madame Zattiany addressed her glowering host, her eyes twinkling. It was evident that she regarded this representative of the new order with a scientific interest, as if it were a new sort of bug and herself an entomologist. "Probably," she added indulgently, "the most mysterious woman in New York. What you would call an adventuress if you were not too young to be uncharitable. Mr. Clavering is kind enough to take me on trust."

Miss Oglethorpe's wrath waxed. This creature of an obsolete order had the temerity to laugh at her. Moreover——She flashed a glance from Clavering's angry anxious face to the beautiful woman opposite, and a real color blazed in her cheeks. But she summoned a sneer.

"Noble again! Has he told you of our little adventure last night?"

"Last night?" A flicker crossed the serenity of Madame Zattiany's face. "But no. I do not fancy Mr. Clavering is in the habit of telling his little adventures."

"Oh, he wouldn't. Old standards. Southern chivalry. All the rest of it. That's why he's granny's model young man. Well, I'll tell you——"

"You've been drinking again," hissed Clavering.

"Of course. Cocktail party at Donny's——"

"Well, moderate your voice. It isn't necessary to take the entire room into your confidence. Better still, go back to your own table."

She raised her voice. "You see, Madame Zattiany, I was running round loose at about one o'clock A.M. when whom should I run into but dear old Uncle Lee. He looked all shot to pieces when he saw me. Girls in his day didn't stay out late unless they had a beau. Ten o'clock was the limit, anyhow. But did he take advantage of my unprotected maiden innocence? Not he. He stood there in the snow and delivered a lecture on the error of my ways, then took me to a delicatessen shop—afraid of compromising himself in a restaurant—and stuffed me with sandwiches and bananas. Even there, while we were perched on two high stools, he didn't make love to me as any human man would have done. He just ate sandwiches and lectured. God! Life must have been dull for girls in his day!"

People about them were tittering. One young man burst into a guffaw. Madame Zattiany was calmly eating her dinner. The tirade might have fallen on deaf ears.

Clavering's skin had turned almost black. His eyes looked murderous. But he did not raise his voice. "Go back to your table," he said peremptorily. "You've accomplished your revenge and I've had all I propose to stand.... By God! If you don't get out this minute I'll pick you up and carry you out and straight to your grandmother."

"Yes you would—make a scene."

"The scene could hardly be improved. Will you go?"

He half rose. Even Madame Zattiany glanced at him apprehensively.

Miss Oglethorpe laughed uncertainly. "Oh, very well. At least we never furnish material for your newspapers. That's just one thing we think beneath us." She rose and extended her hand. "Good night, Madame Zattiany," she said with a really comical assumption of the grand manner. "It has been a great pleasure to meet you."

Madame Zattiany took the proffered hand. "Good night," she said sweetly. "Your little comedy has been most amusing. Many thanks."

Miss Oglethorpe jerked her shoulders. "Well, console dear unky. He'd like the floor to open and swallow him. Ta! Ta!" She ran back to her table, and its hilarity was shortly augmented.

Madame Zattiany looked at Clavering aghast. "But it is worse than I supposed!" she exclaimed. "It is really a tragedy. Poor Mrs. Oglethorpe." Then she laughed, silently but with intense amusement. "I wish she had been here! After all! ... Nevertheless, it is a tragedy. An Oglethorpe! A mere child intoxicated ... and truly atrocious manners. Why don't her people put her in a sanitarium?"

"Parents count about as much today as women counted in the cave era. But it is abominable that you should be made conspicuous."

"Oh, that! I have been conspicuous all my life. And you must admit that she had the centre of the stage! If any one is to be commiserated, it is you. But you really behaved admirably; I could only admire your restraint."

Clavering's ferment subsided, and he returned her smile. "I hope I didn't express all I felt. Murder would have been too good for her. But you are an angel. And for all her bravado you must have made her feel like the little vulgarian she is. Heavens, but the civilization varnish is thin!—and when they deliberately rub it off——"

"Tell me of this adventure."

"It was such a welcome adventure after leaving you! She told practically the whole of it. She had been to a party and her host was too drunk to take her home. She couldn't get a taxi, so started to walk. After I had fed the little pig I took her home. Of course I had no intention of mentioning it to any one, but I hardly feel that I am compromising my honor as a gentleman!"

"But will Society permit this state of things to last? New York! It seems incredible."

"Heaven knows. It might as well try to curb the lightning as these little fools. Their own children, if they have any, will probably be worse."

"I wonder. Reformed rakes are not generally indulgent to adventurous youth. There will probably be a violent revulsion to the rigors of the nineteenth century."

"Hope so. Thank Heaven we can get out of this."

They left the table. As he followed her down the long room and noted the many eyes that focussed on the regal and beautiful figure in its long wrap of white velvet and fox he set his lips grimly. Another ordeal before him. For a moment he wished that he had fallen in love with a woman incapable of focussing eyes. He hated being conspicuous as he hated poverty and ugliness and failure and death. Then he gave an impatient sigh. If he could win her he cared little if the entire town followed her every time she appeared on the street. And she had been very sweet after that odious flapper had taken herself off. He had ceased to feel at arm's length.

XXII

They entered the box during the nuptial hymn. Farrar, almost supine in the arms of the seducer, was singing with the voluptuous abandon that makes this scene the most explicit in modern opera. She had sung it a thousand times, but she was still the beautiful young creature exalted by passion, and her voice seemed to have regained its pristine freshness. She had done many things to irritate New Yorkers, but in this scene, whether they forgave her or not, they surrendered; and those to whom love and passion were lost memories felt a dim resurgence under that golden tide.[1]

Clavering had no desire to surrender. In fact he endeavored to close his ears. He had received a cold douche and a hot one in the course of the past hour, and he felt that his equilibrium was satisfactorily established. He had forgotten to warn Madame Zattiany of the step at the front of the box, down which so many novices had stumbled, but she had taken it and settled herself with the nonchalance of custom. Odd. Once more something beat in the back of his brain. But he dismissed it impatiently. No doubt many boxes in Europe were constructed in the same fashion.

He had seated himself a little to the right and behind her. He saw her lids droop and her hands move restlessly. Then, as the curtain went down and Farrar was accepting the customary plaudits, her eyes opened and moved over the rich and beautiful auditorium with a look of hungry yearning. This was too much for Clavering and he demanded abruptly:

"Why do you look like that? Have you ever been here before?"

She turned to him with a smile. "What a question! ... But opera, both the silliest and the most exalting of the arts, is the Youth of Life, its perpetual and final expression. And when the house is dark I always imagine it haunted by the ghosts of dead opera singers, or of those whose fate is sadder still. Does it never affect you in that way?"

"Can't say it does.... But ... I vaguely remember—some ten years ago a young singer with a remarkable voice sang Marguerite once on that stage and then disappeared overnight ... lost her voice, it was said...."[2]

She gave a low choking laugh. "And you think I am she? Really!"

"I think nothing, but that I am here with you—and that in another moment I shall want to sit on the floor—Oh, Lord!"

The house was a blaze of light. It looked like a vast gold and red jewel box, built to exhibit in the fullness of their splendor the most luxurious and extravagant women in the world. And it was filled

---

1 Farrar's affair with conductor Arturo Toscanini resulted in his departure from the Metropolitan Opera in 1915. She was rumored to have been involved with Enrico Caruso, also of the Met. In 1923 she divorced her husband, Lou Tellegen, and his affairs came to light.

2 Character in the opera *Faust* (1859) composed by Charles Gounod (1818-93). Revived throughout the late nineteenth century, its plot traces the consequences of Faust's pact with the devil so as to regain his youth.

tonight from coifed and jewelled orchestra to highest balcony, where plainer people with possibly jewelled souls clung like flies. Not a box was empty. Clavering's glance swept the parterre, hoping it would be occupied for the most part by the youngest set, less likely to be startled by the resemblance of his guest to the girl who had sat among their grandmothers when the opera house was new. But there were few of the very young in the boxes. They found their entertainment where traditions were in the making, and dismissed the opera as an old superstition, far too long-winded and boring for enterprising young radicals.

Against the red backgrounds he saw the austere and homely faces of women who represented all that was oldest and best in New York Society, and they wore their haughty bones unchastened by power. There were many more of the succeeding generation, of course, many more whose ancestry derived from gold not blood, and they made up in style and ritual what they lacked in pulchritude. Lack of beauty in the parterre boxes was as notorious as the "horseshoe" itself,[1] Dame Nature and Dame Fortune, rivals always, having been at each other's throats some century and three-quarters ago, and little more friendly when the newer aristocracy of mere wealth was founded. All the New York Society Beauties were historical, the few who had survived the mere prettiness of youth entering a private Hall of Fame while still alive.

It had begun! Clavering fell back, folded his arms and set his teeth. First one pair of opera glasses in the parterre, then another, then practically all were levelled at Mrs. Oglethorpe's box. Young men and old in the omnibus box remained in their seats. Very soon white shoulders and black in the orchestra chairs began to change their angle, attracted by the stir in the boxes. That comment was flowing freely, he made no doubt. In the boxes on either side of him the occupants were staring less openly, but with frequent amazed side glances and much whispering. Madame Zattiany sat like an idol. She neither sought to relieve what embarrassment she may have felt—if she felt any! thought Clavering—by talking to her escort nor by gazing idly about the house comparing other women's gowns and crowns with her own. She might have been a masterpiece in a museum.

A diversion occurred for which Clavering at least was grateful. The door opened and Mr. Dinwiddie entered, limping and leaning on a cane. He looked pale and worried. Clavering resigned

---

1 In New York's Metropolitan Opera House, the first tier of box seats was known as the "Diamond Horseshoe."

his seat and took one still further in the rear. But the low-pitched dialogue came to him distinctly.

"Is this prudent?" murmured Dinwiddie, as he sat himself heavily beside her. "There will be nothing else talked of in New York tomorrow. So far there have only been rumors. But here! You look like Mary Ogden risen from the dead. There's a rumor, by the way, that she is dead."

"She was alive the last time I heard from Vienna. But why imprudent? Mr. Clavering told me of your kind concern, but I assure you that I am neither a political nor a marital refugee."

"But you have a secret you wish to keep. Believe me, you can do so no longer. The Sophisticates are generous and casual. They take you on your face value and their curiosity is merely human and good-natured. But this! In Jane Oglethorpe's box! It is in the nature of an invasion. You hardly could have done more if you had forced yourself into a drawing-room uninvited. You must either come out tomorrow and tell them who you are, establish yourself ... or ... or——"

"Well?" Madame Zattiany was smiling, and, probably, the most serene person in the house.

"I—I—think you had better go back to Europe. I must be frank. Anything less would be cowardly. You interest me too much.... But I can only suppose that your secret is of the sort that if discovered—and they will discover it!—would cause you grave embarrassment."

"You mean if I am Mary Zattiany's illegitimate daughter?"

"I don't think they would have minded that if you had brought letters to them from Mary asking them to be kind to you—and if you had made a good marriage. But to have it flung in their faces like this—they will never forgive you."

"And you think I am Mary Zattiany's daughter?"

"I—yes—I think I have gone back to my original theory. But there must be something behind. She never would have let you come over here with a letter only to Trent. She knew that she could rely on many of her old friends. No people in the world are more loyal to their own than these old New Yorkers."

"And suppose she did give me letters—and that I have not been interested enough to present them?"

"I knew it! But I am afraid it's too late now. They not only will resent your indifference, but they are extremely averse to anything like sensational drama in private life. And your appearance here tonight is extremely dramatic! They'll never forgive you," he reiterated solemnly.

"Really? Well, let us enjoy the next act," she added indulgently. "I hope you will remain here."

The curtain had gone up. The audience, balked of the private drama, in which they had manifested no aversion whatever from playing their own rôle, transferred their attention to the stage, although Clavering saw more than one glance wander across the house, and those in the adjoining boxes felt themselves free to peer persistently.

Farrar had not finished bowing and kissing her hands before the next curtain when the door of the box opened once more and Mr. Osborne entered. After a few words with Madame Zattiany he went out and returned almost immediately with three other men, two of his own generation, and a tall, dark, extremely good-looking young man, whose easy negligent air was set askew by the eager expression of his eyes. Clavering, not waiting to be introduced, fled to the smoking-room and took a seat in a corner with his back to the other occupants lest some one recognize and speak to him. A hideous fear had invaded his soul. If this world, so indisputably her own, did accept her—as he had not a doubt it would if she demanded it; he made light of Dinwiddie's fears, knowing her as he did—where would he come in? Sheer luck, supplemented by his own initiative, had given him a clear field for a few weeks, but what chance would he have, not only if her house were overrun with people, but if she were pursued by men with so much more to offer, with whom she must have so much more in common? He might be the equal of the best of them in blood and the superior of many, but his life had not been of the order to equip him with those minor but essential and armorial arts, that assured ease and distinction, possessed by men not only born into the best society but bred in it, and who had lived on their background, not on their nerves. To be "born" is not enough. It is long association that counts, and the "air" may be acquired by men of inferior birth but the supreme opportunity. He had managed to interest her because he had no rival, and he was young and his mind in tune with hers. That alone, no doubt, was the secret of her imaginative flight in his direction. For the first time in his life he felt a sense of inferiority, and for the moment he made no attempt to shake it off. He was in the depths of despair. He did not even light a cigarette.... He could hear a group of young men discussing her ... as one of their own kind ... with no lack of respect ... some new friend of Mrs. Oglethorpe's—they were too young to remember Mary Ogden.... She would have many "knights" on the morrow ... he felt on the far side of a rapidly widening gulf ... and he had once sought to dig a gulf! Disapproved! Questioned! Tried to forget her! He wished he had abducted her.

A bell rang. The men moved toward the foyer. In a few moments he followed. The attendant opened the Oglethorpe door and as he entered the ante-room he saw that the box was still filled with men. They had evidently taken root. He was possessed by a dull anger, and as it spread upward his sense of inferiority took flight. He'd rout them all, damn them. After all he had more brains than any man in the house and his manners could be as good and as bad as their own. Moreover, he was probably more strongly endowed in other ways than the youngest of them. The wise thing for him to do was to let her find it out the next time they were alone.

XXIII

But it was some time before he saw her alone again, and meanwhile many things happened.

She took Mr. Dinwiddie home in her car for supper, Clavering following with Osborne in a taxi, and as the abundant repast was spread in the dining-room it was patent that she had gone to the opera with the intention of bringing back willing guests. She knew that both Dinwiddie and Osborne subscribed to the omnibus box, and no doubt if they had failed to put in an appearance she would have dropped—with one of her infernally ready excuses—himself at his own door. She might as well have announced, without bothering to feed these damned old bores, that she did not intend to see him alone again until she had made up her royal mind.

He ground his teeth, but he was master of himself again and had no intention to make the mistake of sulking. The situation put him on his mettle. He led the conversation and did practically all the talking: as if the vital youth in him, stimulated by music and champagne (which the older men were forced to imbibe sparingly), must needs pour forth irresistibly—and impersonally. He was not jealous of Dinwiddie or Osborne (although the black frown on the latter's brow was sufficient evidence of a deeply personal resentment), and although he did not flash Madame Zattiany a meaning glance, might indeed have sat at her board for the first time, he knew that he had never made a better impression. Her eyes, which had been heavy and troubled as they took their seats at the table, and as old as eyes could be in that perfect setting, began to look like a gray landscape illumined by distant flashes of lightning. Before long they were full of life, and response, and laughter. And pride? There was something very like pride in those expressive orbs (not always as subject to her will as she fancied), as they dwelt on the brilliant young journalist whose mind darted hither and thither on every subject he could summon that would afford the opportunity of witty comment. He even quoted himself—skipping the past two months—and what had been evolved with much deliberation and rewriting sounded spontaneous and pertinent. But in truth he was so genuinely stimulated before the brief hour was over that when he returned to his rooms he wrote his column before turning in. He felt as if fiery swords were playing about his mind, flashing out words and phrases that would make his brother columnists, no sluggards in words and phrases themselves, green on the morrow. For the moment he was quite happy, as he always was when his mind was abnormally quickened, and he dismissed women and their infernal whims to limbo.

When he awoke at two o'clock in the afternoon his brain felt like the ashes of a bonfire and his spirits were a leaden weight. He knew what was to be expected of reaction, however, and after his punch bag and showers he felt better. He'd see her today and force some sort of understanding.

But when he opened his door and saw a letter in her handwriting, and evidently delivered by a servant, as it was unstamped, his hand shook and his half-recovered confidence fled. This time he made no attempt at the farce of self-discipline; he opened it at once. When he saw that it began without formality he drew a longer breath.

"I am not going to see you until Saturday," it read, "when I hope you will take me to Miss Dwight's party. Meanwhile I shall ask you not to see Mr. Dinwiddie nor any one else likely to discuss me. I shall not care to stay long at the party and if you will return here with me I will tell you my secret, such as it is. I shall only say here that I had no intention of making a mystery of myself, for I did not expect to exchange a word with any one in America but Judge Trent and his business associates. I came to America for one purpose only, to settle my affairs, which would have dragged on interminably if I had not been here to receive my alienated properties in person. I know many people in New York, but I had no idea of seeing any of them, although tempted on account of the money they might help me to collect for the children of Austria. But I had decided to leave that until the last minute. I not only was no longer interested in these old friends of mine, but I disliked the explanations I should be forced to give them, the comments, the curiosity, the endless questions. What I mean by this you will know on Saturday night.

"But it is not the first time in my life that I have discovered the futility of making plans. My meeting with you and the profound interest you have awakened has upset all calculations. I expected nothing less! If I had I should have told you the truth the night we met. But it never occurred to me for an instant that I could love any man again. I had done with all that years ago, and my intention was to give my life and my fortune to certain problems in Europe which I shall not bore you with here.

"Possibly if I had met you casually with Judge Trent, or if I had not chosen to avoid my old friends and met you at one of their houses, as I might easily have done, I should have made no mystery of myself; if indeed you did not know the truth already.

"But not only the curious circumstances of our meeting after your weeks of silent devotion, but your own personality, quickened to life a flicker of youthful romance so long moribund that I had forgotten it had ever been one of my lost inheritances. I was also both amused and interested, and to play a little comedy with you was irresistible. It did not occur to me for a moment that you would fall in love with me.

"It was not until the second time you came here after the theatre that I realized what was happening in those submerged cells of mine. But I could not make up my mind to tell you that night— nor the next. By that time I was frightened. I feared there could be only one result. I suppose all women are cowards when in love. But I knew that this could not last, and when you asked me to sit in Mrs. Oglethorpe's box I thought the time had come to precipitate matters. After a decisive step like that I could not retreat. But I wish to tell you myself, and for that reason I have asked you to discuss me with no one until we meet. It will probably be the last time I shall see you, but I am prepared for that.

"I shall see Jane Oglethorpe today. She has been very loyal and I think she will forgive me. It would not matter much if she did not, and possibly would save me a good deal of boredom, but after last night an explanation is due her.

"And after Saturday night, *mon ami*,[1] matters will be entirely in your hands. You will realize whether you have merely been dazzled and fascinated or whether there is really between us that mysterious bond that no circumstances can alter. Such things have happened to men and women if we may believe history, but I have had

---

1 My friend.

too good reason to believe that it is not for me. However—at least for a brief time you have given me back something of the hopes and illusions of youth. This in itself is so astonishing that whatever the result I shall never be able to forget you.

"Until Saturday.

"M."

Clavering's immediate act was to dash off a love-letter more impassioned than any he had ever dreamed himself capable of writing, vowing that he was dazzled and fascinated, God knew, but that he loved her with the love of his life and would marry her if she would have him, no matter what her revelations. And with what patience he could muster and with no grace whatever he would make no attempt to see her until Saturday night. But she must believe that he loved her and she must write at once and tell him so. He could not exist throughout that interminable interval unless she wrote him at once that she believed in the existence and the indissolubility of that bond, and that he had given her the highest and deepest and most passionate love of which man was capable, and which no woman but she could inspire, for no woman like her had ever lived.

He dared not read it over. He had never let himself go before, and he had written too much for print not to be self-conscious and critical of even a love-letter intended only for concordant eyes. Nevertheless, he was aware even in his excitement that the more reckless it was the surer its effect. No edited love-letter ever yet hit its mark. (He remembered Parnell's love-letters, however, and devoutly hoped his own would never see the light.)[1] The waiter entered at the moment, and he gave him the missive, hastily addressed and sealed, and asked him to tell the "desk" to send it immediately and give the boy orders to wait for an answer.

He drank his coffee, but ate nothing. Nor did he open his newspapers. He strode up and down his rooms or stood at the window watching the hurrying throngs, the lumbering green busses, the thousand automobiles and taxis over on Fifth Avenue. They were as unreal as a cinema. He had the delusion, common to lovers, that Earth was inhabited by two people only—that brief extension of the soul which in its common acceptance of eternal loneliness

---

1 The eloquent love letters of legendary Irish nationalist leader Charles Stewart Parnell (1846-91) were first published in 1914 in a biography of Parnell written by Katherine O'Shea Parnell, the woman who was his lover for over a decade and, after her divorce, his wife.

looks out upon the world as upon a projected vision in which no reality exists, for man the dreamer is but a dream himself. Phantasmagoria![1]

He glanced at the clock every time he passed it. It seemed incredible that mere minutes were passing. But she was merciful. She kept him in suspense but thirty-five minutes. The messenger boy stared at the celebrated journalist, with whose appearance he was reasonably familiar, as if regarding a phase of masculine aberration with which he was even more familiar. He grinned sympathetically, and Clavering was not too distraught to detect the point of view of the young philosopher. He had been running his hands through his hair and no doubt his eyes were injected with blood. He told him to wait, and went into his bedroom. But the note was brief and required no answer. "I believe you." That was all, and it was enough. He gave the astonished philosopher a five-dollar bill: an automatic American reaction.

Then he sat down to puzzle over those parts of her letter which he had barely skimmed; faded into insignificance for the moment before the outstanding confession that she really loved him. But they loomed larger and larger, more and more puzzling and ominous, as he read and reread them. Finally he thrust the pages into his desk and went out for a tramp.

XXIV

It was a cold bright day. The ice on the trees of Central Park was a diamond iridescence. Nursemaids were leading children, bits of muffled wealth, along the alleys. Horses pounded on the bridle paths. Automobiles and taxis, that must have looked to the airman above like aimless black planes drifting in a crystal sea, were carrying people to a thousand destinies. Towering on all sides was the irregular concrete mass of New York. As dusk fell, lights in those high buildings began to appear, first intermittently, then as long necklaces of brilliants strung against the sky. Silence fell on the Park.

Clavering walked until he could walk no farther, then took a bus at One Hundred and Tenth Street for Claremont. When he reached the restaurant he could think of only three men whose companionship would be endurable, and failing to get any of them on the telephone resigned himself to a solitary dinner. But still

---

1 Fantastical vision with a magical quality.

restless, he wandered over to a window and stared out across the Hudson at the dark Palisades on the opposite shore. Battleships were at anchor, for there had been no ice in the Hudson this winter, and a steamboat with its double chain of lights swam gracefully up the river. The cold winter stars winked down indifferently upon seething human hearts.

He still refused to admit that the source of his uneasiness was that revelation set for Saturday night. Nothing but death itself could halt his marriage with this woman, for she herself had unequivocally stated that after Saturday night the future would be in his hands. *His!* ... Her secret? Not that she had had lovers, for he had accepted that fact already, and for him the past had ceased to exist. Her husband was dead. Nothing else mattered. Nevertheless, the vague prescient chill he had experienced the night he first met her eyes, and once or twice since, accompanied as it was by a curious sense that just below his consciousness lay the key to the mystery, rattling now and again, but sinking deeper every time he made a dart at it, had defied further evasion since the receipt of her cryptic letter. He was the more uneasy as she seemed far more certain of Mrs. Oglethorpe than of himself.

Once more he heard the key rattle, but higher ... almost in his consciousness ... for the first time it seemed to sound a double note of warning ... he had a sudden vision of a locked door—and not a door locked on a mere secret.

He swung about impatiently. The explanation of his mood was this hideous interval to be got through, Heaven alone knew how. No wonder he had felt a sensation of terror. When a man is in the unsatisfied stages of love he must expect occasional attacks of greensickness, sullen passions intensified by unreasoning fear. And he was luckier than most. He had been the confidant of men in love, with hope deferred or blasted, and although he had been sympathetic enough, and convinced that men had a far deeper capacity for suffering than women, still had his pity been tempered by a certain contempt. Those had been the times when he had flouted the idea that he was basically romantic; and that he had never made a jackass of himself over any woman had induced a feeling of superiority that had expanded his ego. Now he was convinced that his capacity for love put theirs to shame, and he was filled with pride at the thought. Still—he wished it were Saturday night.

He was crossing the room to his solitary table when he saw Jim Oglethorpe enter. His first impulse was to avoid him. The restaurant was well-filled and he could easily take a table in a corner with his back to the room. But dining alone was a melancholy business at best—and tonight! If Oglethorpe brought up Madame Zattiany's name he could change the subject or state bluntly that he had his reasons for not wishing to discuss her. As he stood hesitating, Oglethorpe caught sight of him and almost ran across the room, his face, which had looked heavy and worried, glowing with pleasure.

"Jove, this is luck!" he exclaimed. "Alone? So am I. Got in this morning and found Janet had a dinner on for those infernally noisy friends of hers. Got something to think over, so thought I'd come out here. This is really luck as I was going to hunt you up tomorrow. Let's sit here. I want to talk."

He had led the way to a table in a remote corner, secluded, so far. He beckoned the head waiter, who agreed that it should remain secluded. Then he asked Clavering to order the dinner, and, folding his arms, stared out of the window, his face sagging once more. He was still a young man, not more than forty-five, but in spite of his love of outdoor sport he showed a more consistent love of eating and drinking in flabby muscles and pouches under the eyes. It was an amiable, rather weak but stubborn face that had been handsome in youth when his eyes were bright and clear skin covered firm muscles, and it would be handsome again when years had compelled him to diet and his already faded hair had turned white; his features were regular and his figure well-knit under its premature accumulations.

He produced a flask from his pocket when the waiter had discreetly turned his back, and their ice-water might have passed for cold tea.

"Think I'll come to the point," he said. "You know me well enough not to mind anything I say."

Clavering glanced up from his oysters in alarm. "There's just one question I won't discuss," he said sharply.

Oglethorpe stared. "You don't mean to say you're interested in her? So much the better! And it strikes me you can't have any objection to discussing her with me. I'm her father, ain't I?"

"Her father—are you talking of Janet?"

"Who else? I'm worried as the devil. Have been ever since I got in this morning. I'd telegraphed I was coming, and when I got to the house Molly told me that mother wanted to see me at once and I posted down there. It was about Janet, and you know more about it than I do."

"I suppose I know what you mean. But it turned out all right. She happened to meet me, not some man who might have annoyed her. Of course she shouldn't have taken such a risk, but;

what can you do with these flappers? They're all in league together and you might as well let them go their little pace. It won't last. They'll soon be older, and I don't suppose you intend to play the heavy father and lock her up."

"No, but I'd like damn well to get her married. Mother told me a pretty tale. It seems she made a row at Sherry's last night, making you and some lady you had with you as conspicuous as herself. Mrs. Vane was there and carried it straight to mother. Mother's no fool and had already got on to this younger generation business and given Janny one or two tongue lashings, but she never dreamed it had gone as far as it looks. Roaming the streets alone at one in the morning! She'd undoubtedly been drinking last night—God! I've a notion to take a switch to her. And I suppose she was pretty well lit the night you picked her up. I've never seen a hint of it. Janny's spoilt enough. Her mother never had the slightest control over her and she could always get round me. But she won't in the future. I'll get top-hand somehow. God! My daughter! Tell me your side of it, will you?"

Clavering, who was genuinely fond of Oglethorpe, and relieved, moreover, that he had not yet heard of Madame Zattiany, gave a cautious and colorless account of the adventure.

"It is possible that she had had a cocktail or two," he concluded. "But you must expect that. If the flapper should adopt a coat of arms no doubt it would be a cocktail rampant with three cigarettes argent on a field de rouge. However, it wouldn't be a bad idea if you took her in hand. That is, if you can."

"I'll do it all right. D'you mean to tell me she was at Farren's without a chaperon?"

"There may have been a chaperon to each couple for all I know."

"You know damn well there wasn't. No chaperon would have left her alone."

"But surely, Jim, you know that chaperons are practically obsolete. They don't gee with cocktails and petting parties. The New Freedom! The Reign of Youth!"[1]

"Damn nonsense. No, I didn't know it. I supposed she was properly chaperoned, as girls of her class always have been. You know how much I care for Society, and I haven't got to the chicken stage either. Took it for granted that certain cast-iron conventions were still observed, in our set at least. Of course I've seen her drink cocktails at home and thought it rather cute, and I've

---

1 "Gee" was a command for animals to turn right; here used to describe the incongruity between chaperons and the young generation.

rubbed the paint off her cheeks and lips once or twice. Girls are making up nowadays as if they were strumpets, but some little fool started it, and you know the old saying: 'What one monkey does the other monkey must do.' It never worried me. Of course I've heard more or less about these young idiots; they're always being discussed and written up; but somehow you never think those things can happen in your own family.... I went straight home and blew up Molly—haven't had a sight of Janet yet—and of course she bawled. Always does. When I told her that Janet had been at Farren's alone she protested that Janet had told her she was going to bed early that night. Even last night, when she had a theatre party, she understood that some young married woman was along. But Molly's a fool. What on earth am I to do with Janet? There were no such girls in my young days. Some of them were bad uns, but as discreet as you make 'em. Didn't disgrace their families. Some of them used to drink, right enough, but they were as smooth as silk in public, and went to a sanitarium to sober up when it got the best of 'em. But these girls appear to be about as discreet as street-walkers. You don't think they kick over the traces,[1] do you?"

"I'm dead sure that Janet hasn't. She puts on the cap and bells partly because it's the fashion, partly because she thinks girls are alive and having their fun for the first time. But she's no fool. She nearly floored me once or twice. She'll take care of herself."

"Girls don't take care of themselves when they're drunk. But I've an idea there's something else the matter with her. At least mother has?"

"Something else?"

"In love."

"Well, there's your chance to marry her off. The sooner the better. But why should it drive her to drink? If she's fixed her affections on any of those chaps that dance at her beck——"

"She hasn't. She's in love with you."

"What!" Clavering dropped his fork. When the waiter had rushed to present him with another and retired, he still stared at Oglethorpe as if he had been stunned by a blow between the eyes. "Whatever—what on earth put such an idea into Mrs. Oglethorpe's head? The child can't endure me. She pretty well proved it last night, and I've always known she disliked me—since she grew up, that is. To be perfectly frank, aside from the fact that I don't care for young girls, she always irritates me like the deuce,

---

1 To rebel entirely, in this case sexually. The idiom refers to a horse who steps over the straps that connect its bridle to a cart or wagon.

and I've never made any secret of it. Night before last I couldn't well have made myself more disagreeable if I'd rehearsed for the part."

Oglethorpe grinned. "Lot you know about girls. Just the way to make 'em crazy about you. Like all idealists, you don't know a thing about women. Being a rank materialist myself, I know 'em like a book. The emancipated flapper is just plain female under her paint and outside her cocktails. More so for she's more stimulated. Where girls used to be merely romantic, she's romantic—callow romance of youth, perhaps, but still romantic—plus sex-instinct rampant. At least that's the way I size 'em up, and its logic. There's no virginity of mind left, mauled as they must be and half-stewed all the time, and they're wild to get rid of the other. But they're too young yet to be promiscuous, at least those of Janet's sort, and they want to fall in love and get him quick. See the point?"

"No doubt you're right. But I'm not the object of Janet's young affections. She's either led your mother to believe it for purposes of her own, or Mrs. Oglethorpe has merely jumped at that conclusion—well, Heaven only knows why."

"You know why. Because she'd like it. So would I."

"Good Lord, Jim! I'm nearly old enough to be her father. Barely ten years younger than yourself."

"You'll never be as old as I am this minute, and I'd give my eyes to see you married to her. Moreover, I'm convinced mother's right. Janny let out something—broke down, I fancy, although mother wouldn't give her away any further. And you used to be fond of her when she was a child. She's sat on your lap a hundred times."

"My dear Jim," said Clavering drily. "You've just pronounced yourself a man of consummate experience. Need I remind you that when a man has held a girl on his lap as a child, she is generally the last girl he wants on his lap later on? Man love's the shock of novelty, the spice of surprise. It's hard to get that out of a girl you have spanked—as I did Janet on two different occasions. She was a fascinating youngster, but a little devil if there ever was one."

"She's full of fascination yet. I can see that, if I am her father. A year or two from now, when she comes to her senses——"

"Oh, cut it out, Jim! I won't listen. Even it were true—and I'd stake my life it isn't—I—well——"

"D'you mean there's some other woman?"

"I don't care to talk about it—but—let it go at that."

"Sorry. I'd have liked it. You could have made a fine woman out of Janny. She has it in her."

Clavering did not express his doubts on this point aloud. He was in truth horribly embarrassed and hardly knew what to say. Not for a moment did he believe that the minx was in love with him, nor would he have taken the trouble to find out, even to please Jim Oglethorpe and his mother, had Mary Zattiany never crossed his horizon. But he felt sorry for his friend and would have liked to banish his brooding distress.

"Look here!" he exclaimed. "You'll have to buck up and take her in hand. After all, you're her father and she respects you. No girl respects her mother these days, apparently, but the father has the advantage of being male. Give her a talking to. Tell her how cut up you are. She's too young to be as hard as she likes to think. Don't preach. That would make matters worse. Appeal to her. Tell her she's making you miserable. If that doesn't work—well, your idea of taking a switch to her isn't bad. A sound spanking is what they all need, and it certainly would take the starch out of them. Make them feel so damned young they'd forget just how blasé they're trying to be."

"She might run away," rumbled Oglethorpe. "I believe I'll try it, though, if worse comes to worst. I'll have no filthy scandals in my family."

"Why not collect all the fathers and plan a regular campaign? Without their allowances they'd soon be helpless. It would be a battle royal and might make history! Might also get hold of the fathers of these young chaps. Few have independent incomes."

Oglethorpe laughed for the first time. "Not a bad idea for a bachelor, Lee. Maybe I'll try it. Let's get out of this. How about the Follies?"[1]

XXV

When a man has cultivated a practical and methodical habit of mind and body he pursues the accustomed tenor of his way, whatever the ferment of his spirit. Clavering's spirit was mercurial, but long since subject to his will, and it would no more have occurred to him to neglect his regular work because he was in love and [in] a state of suspense than to put on petticoats and walk up Fifth Avenue. It might be better or worse under foreign impact, but it would be done, and all else banished for the hour.

---

1   Elaborate musical revues on Broadway, in existence through the early 1930s, the Ziegfeld Follies were known for their beautiful chorus girls.

There were times when he wrote better surrounded by the stimulations of the office; when he was neither fagged nor disturbed he worked at home. During this week of incertitudes he rose late, lunched with friends at the Sign of the Indian Chief,[1] a restaurant where the cleverest of them—and those who were so excitedly sure of their cleverness that for the moment they convinced others as well as themselves—foregathered daily. Then he went to the office and wrote or talked to other men until it was time to dine. He could always be sure of companionship for the evening. On his "day off" he took a train out into the country and walked for hours.

There was a great deal of scintillating talk in his group on the significant books and tendencies of the day, and if the talk of French youth in their clubs before the Revolution may possibly have been profounder and more far-reaching in its philosophy, more formulative in its plan of action, owing to a still deeper necessity for change in the social order, the very fact that these brilliant young Americans had no personal grievance but merely sharpened their wits on matters in which they were intelligent enough to take an interest, saved their cleverness from becoming mordant or distorted by passion. It was an excellent forcing-house for ideas and vocabulary.

But their most solemn causeries were upon the vital theme of The American Reputation in Letters. Past. Present. Future. This was the age of Youth. Should any of the old reputations be permitted to live on—save in the favor of the negligible public? If so, which? All the recent reputations they would have liked to pronounce equally great, merely on account of their commendable newness, but they were too conscientious for that. They appraised, debated, rejected, finally placed the seal of their august approval upon a favored few. Claques were arranged if the public were obtuse. The future? A few, a very few, were selected from the older group, many more from the younger, and ordained to survive and shed their undying beams for posterity. From these judicial pronouncements there was no appeal, and the pleasant spaces of the Sign of the Indian Chief, so innocuous to the uninitiated eye, was a veritable charnel house[2] that stank in the nostrils of the rejected;

---

1 The Algonquin Hotel, East 44th Street in Manhattan, had a sign with an Indian chief on it. A group of writers, editors, and entertainers met there daily for lunch.

2 Structure for holding unearthed human bones, sometimes situated near churches, for remains that have been disturbed. In areas where grave sites

but, inconsistent even as life itself, those melancholy graves were danced over by the sprightly young feet of the elect. Sometimes there was a terrifying upheaval in one of those graves. A dismal figure fought his way out, tore off his cerements,[1] and stalked forth, muttering: "'But I stride on, austere. No hope I have, no fear,'" leaving a puzzled uneasiness behind him.

But for good or ill, it was a matter for congratulation that criticism was at last being taken seriously in the United States.

There was a jazz party at the studio of a hospitable girl artist where Clavering danced with several of the prettiest young actresses of recent Broadway fame until dawn, and drank enough to make him as wild as the rest of the party had it not been for the seasoned apparatus inherited from hard-drinking Southern ancestors. Altogether, he gave himself little time for thought, and if he felt at times an inclination to dream he thrust it from him with an almost superstitious fear. He would speculate no longer, but neither would he run the risk of invoking the laughter of cynical gods. If unimaginable disaster awaited him, at least he would not weaken his defences by a sojourn in the paradise of fools.

He avoided Oglethorpe and Dinwiddie, and although he had engaged himself to dine at the Goodriches on Thursday night he sent an excuse.

On Thursday morning, as he was turning over the pages of one of the newspapers his eye was arrested by the name Zattiany. He never read Society paragraphs, but that name would leap to his eyes anywhere. The announcement was as brief as "social notes" always are in the daily editions of the morning papers: "Mrs. Oglethorpe gives a luncheon tomorrow at her house in Gramercy Park to the Countess Zattiany of Vienna."

So! She had satisfied Mrs. Oglethorpe. That was one on Dinwiddie.

On the following night he bought himself an admission ticket to the Metropolitan Opera House and entered at the close of the second act. As he had half expected, she was in Mrs. Oglethorpe's box, and it was crowded with men. He fancied that his older friend looked both glum and amused. As for Dinwiddie, his expression was half-witted.

---

were scarce, bodies would first decompose in a holding area for a number of years, then the remains would be transferred to their final destination in a common ossuary or charnel house, in which bones were sometimes arranged in patterns.

1 Burial clothing.

He went home and took a bromide. Sleep, being a function, is outside the domain of the will, and he had had little of it since Tuesday. And sleep he must if he was to be in alert command of his faculties on the following night.

XXVI

Madame Zattiany stood before the long old-fashioned pier glass in her bedroom, a large cheerful room recently done over in white chintz sprayed with violets. The bright winter sun streamed in on a scene of confusion. Gowns were thrown over every chair and hats covered the bed. They all had the air of being tossed aside impatiently, as indeed they had been, and the maid with a last comprehensive look at her mistress began to gather them up and carry them to the large wardrobes in the dressing-room.

Mary regarded herself critically. She had wished (not without malice!) to emphasize her youthful appearance, but not at the expense of dignity, and she felt that she had achieved the subtle combination in the frock of soft black velvet cut with long, sweeping lines and of an excessive simplicity; and a black velvet hat of medium size with a drooping brim that almost covered one eye. The long white gloves disappeared into her sleeves somewhere above the elbow and she wore a single string of pearls. She looked very Parisian, very elegant, as Mrs. Oglethorpe would have expressed it, and very assured. In spite of the mocking gleam in the one visible eye her face was serene and proud.

She had felt some trepidation on Tuesday when she had sought out Mrs. Oglethorpe and made her explanations, but she felt none whatever at the prospect of meeting these other twelve old friends. Whether they approved or resented, were indulgent or elevated their respectable noses and intimated, "You are no longer one of *us*," was a matter of profound indifference to Mary Zattiany. She would have avoided them all if it had been possible, but since she had deliberately permitted her hand to be forced she would take the situation humorously and amuse herself with whatever drama it might afford.

Elinor Goodrich. Mabel Lawrence. Polly Vane. Isabel Ruyler. Ellen de Lacey. Louise Prevost. She had been so intimate with all of them, not only in the schoolroom but when they were all in Society together. Now only her somewhat cynical sense of anticipation mitigated utter boredom at the thought of meeting them again. Of the other six she had still vaguer memories, although she recalled having heard that the beauty of her own last season, Lily Armstrong, had married one of the Tracys. She also was to be at the luncheon.

What on earth was she to talk to them about at the table? She could hardly tell them the story they expected before the servants. That would be for the later hour in the drawing-room—or would it be in that absurd old room of Jane's upstairs?

She recalled Elinor Tracy (Goodrich) and her enthusiastic admiration, which she had accepted as a matter-of-course, and given little beyond amiable tolerance in return. As she had told Clavering, she was not a woman's woman. She hoped Nelly had outgrown "gush." For some ten years after her marriage she had met her from time to time abroad, but she had not seen her for so long that she doubted if she would recognize her if they passed on the street. The only one of her old friends for whom she retained either interest or affection was Jane Oglethorpe, who, ten years older than herself, with a commanding personality unfolding rapidly at the dawn of their intimacy, had attracted deeply but subtly her own untried force of character and ruthless will. Embarrassment over, she had enjoyed their long hour together, and was glad to renew the intimacy, to find that her old friend's warm affection had lost nothing with the years. And she had found her more interesting than in her youth.

She sighed a little as she looked back on her long hours of almost unbroken solitude in this old house. She had been comparatively happy at first—a blessed interval of rest and peace in this marvellously wealthy and prosperous city where the poor were kept out of sight, at least, where all the men were whole and where one never saw a gaunt woman's appealing eyes, or emaciated ragged children. Those untroubled hours had fled for ever and astonishment, impotent fury, and dire mental conflict had followed, but nevertheless she had dreamed—dreamed—and been glad of her freedom from social and all other duties. Now, probably these women and many more would swarm here.

Her mouth twisted as her maid helped her into the soft gray coat trimmed with blue fox. Ordeal! That would come on Saturday night. No wonder she was merely amused and totally indifferent today!

When she arrived at the house in Gramercy Park, purposely late, to give her entrance the effect Mrs. Oglethorpe had commanded, she heard an excited buzz of voices in the drawing-room as she was being relieved of her wrap. As she entered it ceased abruptly and she heard several hardly perceptible gasps. But the pause, before they all crowded about her, was too brief to be noticeable, and they shook her hand heartily or kissed her warmly. If their eyes were perhaps too studiously expressionless, their words and manner might have been those of old friends welcoming back one who had been long absent and nothing more. Conflicting emotions, born of undying femininity, were not evident for the moment. Mrs. Goodrich cried out at once how wonderfully well she looked, Mrs. Lawrence asked if she had stopped in Paris for her clothes, and Mrs. Vane if she found New York much changed. Nothing could have gone off better.

Mrs. Oglethorpe, in old-pile black velvet as usual, with a front and high-boned collar of yellow rose-point lace, stood in the background watching the comedy with a frank sardonic grin. If her guests had been faithless to the traditions in which they had been bred, she would have felt angry and ashamed, but the automatic manner in which they rose to the occasion and took the blow standing (Mrs. Oglethorpe often indulged in the vernacular of her son, her Janet, and her Lee) made her rock with silent mirth. She knew exactly how they felt!

They were a fine-looking set of women and handsomely dressed, but they indisputably belonged to the old régime, and even Mrs. Tracy, the youngest of them, had something of what Mary Zattiany called that built-up look. They were fashionable but not smart. They carried themselves with a certain conscious rigidity and aloofness which even their daughters had abandoned and was a source of disrespectful amusement to their iniquitous granddaughters. Although Mrs. Goodrich, Mrs. Lawrence and Mrs. Tracy were more up to date in their general appearance, wearing slightly larger hats and fewer feathers, with narrow dog collars instead of whaleboned net, they were as disdainful as the others of every art that aims to preserve something of the effect of youth; although they were spickingly groomed. They accepted life as it was, and they had accepted it at every successive stage, serene in the knowledge that in this as in other things they were above the necessity of compromise and subterfuge. They were the fixed quantities in a world of shifting values.

In age they ranged from fifty-six to sixty-two, with the exception of Mrs. Tracy, who was a mere fifty-two. A few were stout, the others bony and gaunt. Their hair was white or gray. Only Mrs. Tracy, with her fresh complexion and soft brown hair, her plump little figure encased in modern corsets, had got on the blind side of nature, as Mrs. Oglethorpe had told Mary. The others were frankly elderly women, but of great dignity and distinction, some charm, and considerable honesty and simplicity. And their loyalty never failed them.

The luncheon was by no means easy and informal. Mary, by racking her memory, recalled the first names of most of them and never in all her varied life had she been more sweetly amiable, made so determined an effort to please. She might not care what they thought of her, but she was sorry for them, they had behaved very decently, and for Jane Oglethorpe's sake alone the occasion must be a success. She was ably seconded by Mrs. Goodrich, who stared at her in wide-eyed admiration and rattled off the gossip of New York, and by Mrs. Tracy, who had an insatiable interest in diplomatic society. When she had satisfied the latter's curiosity she led the conversation by a straight path to the sufferings of the children of Austria and begged them to join her in forming a relief committee. They received this philanthropic suggestion with no apparent fervor, but it served to relieve the stiffness and tension until they retired to the drawing-room for coffee.

They stood about for a few moments, Mary looking up at the portrait of Jane Oglethorpe in her flaming youth. But the hostess ordered them all to sit down and exclaimed peremptorily: "Now, Mary, tell them all about it or I'll have a lot of fainting hysterical women on my hands. We're still human if we are old and ugly. Go to it, as Janet would say. I believe you have met that estimable exponent of the later New York manner. You are no more extraordinary yourself than some of the changes here at home, but you're more picturesque, and that's harder to swallow. Put them out of their misery."

The ladies smiled or frowned, according to what humor the Almighty, niggardly in his bestowal of humor, had allotted them. At all events they were used to "Jane." Mrs. Goodrich, who had led Mary to a sofa and seated herself beside her, took her hand and pressed it affectionately, as if she were encouraging her on the way to the operating room. "Yes, tell us the story, darling. It is all too wonderful!"

"Do you really mean that you have never heard of this treatment?" asked Madame Zattiany, who knew quite well that they had not. "Few things are better known in Europe."

"We have never heard of it," said Mrs. Vane austerely. "We were totally unprepared."

Madame Zattiany shrugged her graceful shoulders. "I have been told that America never takes up anything new in science until it has become stale in Europe. But women as well as men have been flocking to Vienna. Russian princesses have pledged their jewels——"

"How romantic!" exclaimed Mrs. Goodrich, who was one of those women in whom a certain spurious sense of romance increases with age. But Mrs. Vane mumbled something less complimentary. She had never been romantic in her life; and she was beginning to feel the strain.

"Well," said Madame Zattiany, "I suppose I must begin at the beginning. I dislike holding forth, but if you will have it——"

"Don't leave out a word!" exclaimed Mrs. Tracy. "We want every detail. You've made us feel both as young as yourself and as old as Methuselah."

Madame Zattiany smiled amiably at the one woman in the room who had lingered in the pleasant spaces of middle age. "Very well. I'll be as little technical as possible.... As you know, I ran a hospital in Buda Pesth during the war. After the revolution broke out I was forced to leave in secret to escape being murdered. I was on Bela Kun's[1] list——"

There was a sympathetic rustle in the group. This at least they could grasp on the wing. Mrs. de Lacey interrupted to beg for exciting details, but Mrs. Goodrich and Mrs. Tracy cried simultaneously:

"No! No! Go on—please!"

"Quite right," said Mrs. Oglethorpe, who was prepared to enjoy herself. "We can have that later."

"I naturally went to Vienna, not only because I had some money invested there, but because I could live in the Zattiany Palace. The old house was difficult to keep warm, and as I was too tired and nervous to struggle with any new problems I went at a friend's suggestion into a sanitarium.

"The doctor in charge soon began to pay me something more than perfunctory visits when he found that intelligent conversation after my long dearth did me more good than harm. Finally he told me of a method of treatment that might restore my youth, and begged me to undertake it——"

"Ah!" There were sharp indrawn breaths. Mrs. Vane drew herself up—figuratively, for she could hardly be more perpendicular, with her unyielding spine, her long neck encased in whaleboned net and her lofty head topped off with feathers. A look of hostility dawned

---

1 When the Austro-Hungarian Empire dissolved, Béla Kun (1886-1938), a Bolshevik revolutionary and communist leader, headed the Hungarian Soviet Republic, beginning in 1919. Kun enforced his ideals with the "Red Terror," or atrocities enacted by his secret police; the government was overthrown within the year.

in several pairs of eyes, while frank distaste overspread Mrs. Ruyler's mahogany visage. Madame Zattiany went on unperturbed.

"It may relieve your minds to hear that I was at first as indifferent as all of you no doubt would have been. The war—and many other things—had made me profoundly tired of life—something of course that I do not expect you to understand. And now that the war was over and my usefulness at an end, I had nothing to look forward to but the alleviation of poverty by means of my wealth when it was restored, and this could be done by trustees. Life had seemed to me to consist mainly of repetitions. I had run the gamut. But I began to be interested, at first by the fact that science might be able to accomplish a miracle where centuries of woman's wit had failed——"

"Wit?" snorted Mrs. Vane. "Ignoble vanity."

"Well, call it that if you like, but the desire to be young again or to achieve its simulacrum, in both men and women, has something of the dignity which the centuries give to all antiques. However, at the time, you will also be glad to know, I was far more interested in the prospect of reënergizing my worn out mind and body. I was so mortally tired! And if I had to live on, and no doubt with still much work to do in distracted Europe——"

"But what did they *do* to you?" cried Mrs. Tracy. "I'd have done it in your place—yes, I would!" she said defiantly as she met the august disgusted eye of Mrs. Vane. "I think Countess Zattiany was quite right. What is science for, anyhow?"

"Go on! Go on!" murmured Mrs. Goodrich. She was too fat and comfortable to have any desire to return to youth with its tiresome activities, but all her old romantic affection for Mary Ogden had revived and she was even more interested than curious.

"I am trying to! Well, I must tell you that the explanation of my condition, as of others of my age, was that the endocrines——"

"The what?" The demand was simultaneous.

"The ductless glands."

"Oh," said Mrs. Prevost vaguely, "I've seen something——"

"It is all Greek to me," said Mrs. Vane, who felt that unreasoning resentment common to the minor-informed for the major-informed. "You promised to avoid technical terms."

Madame Zattiany explained in the simplest language she could command the meaning and the function of the ductless glands. The more intelligent among them looked gratified, for the painless achievement of fresh knowledge is a pleasant thing. Madame Zattiany went on patiently: "These glands in my case had undergone a natural process of exhaustion. In women the slower functioning of the endocrines is coincident with the climacteric,[1] as they have been dependent for stimulation upon certain ovarian cells. The idea involved is that the stimulation of these exhausted cells would cause the other glands to function once more at full strength and a certain rejuvenation ensue as a matter of course; unless, of course, they had withered beyond the power of science. I was a promising subject, for examination proved that my organs were healthy, my arteries soft; and I was not yet sixty. Only experimentation could reveal whether or not there was still any life left in the cells, although I responded favorably to the preliminary tests. The upshot was that I consented to the treatment——"

"Yes? Yes?" Every woman in the room now sat forward, no longer old friends or rivals, affectionate or resentful, nor the victims of convention solidified into sharp black and white by the years. They were composite female.

"It consisted of the concentration of powerful Röntgen—what you call X-Rays—on that portion of the body covering the ovaries——"[2]

"How horrible!" "Did you feel as if you were being electrocuted?" "Are you terribly scarred?"

"Not at all. I felt nothing whatever, and there was nothing to cause scars——"

"But I thought that the X-Rays——"

"Oh, do be quiet, Louisa," exclaimed Mrs. Tracy impatiently. "Please go on, Countess Zattiany."

"As I said, the application was painless, and if no benefit results, neither will any harm be done when the Rays are administered by a conscientious expert. My final consent, as I told you, was due to the desire to regain my old will power and vitality. I was extremely skeptical about any effect on my personal appearance. During the first month I felt so heavy and dull that, in spite of assurances that these were favorable symptoms, I was secretly convinced that I had forfeited what little mental health I had retained; but was consoled by the fact that I slept all night and a part of the day: I had suffered from insomnia since my duties at the hospital had ended——"

"But surely you must have been nervous and terrified?" All of these women had seen and suffered illness, but all from time-honored visitations, even if under new and technical names, and they had suffered in common with millions of others, which, if it

---

1 Menopause.
2 The X Ray, originally named for its discoverer, Wilhelm Conrad Röntgen (1845-1923).

offended their sense of exclusiveness, at least held the safeguard of normalcy. They felt a chill of terror, in some cases of revulsion, as Madame Zattiany went on to picture this abnormal renaissance going on in the body unseen and unfelt; in the body of one who had been cast in the common mould, subject to the common fate, and whom they had visioned—when they thought about her at all—as growing old with themselves; as any natural Christian woman would. It was not only mysterious and terrifying but subtly indecent. Mrs. Vane drew back from her eager poise. Almost it seemed to the amused Mrs. Oglethorpe that she withdrew her skirts. Drama was for the stage or the movies; at all events drama in private life, among the elect, was objective, external, and, however offensive, particularly when screamed in the divorce court, it was, at least, like the old diseases, remarkably normal. But an interior drama; not to put too fine a point on it, a drama of one's insides, and especially one that dealt with the raising from the dead of that section which refined women ceased to discuss after they had got rid of it—it was positively ghoulish. Drama of any sort in this respectable old drawing-room, which might have been photographed as the sarcophagus of all the Respectabilities, was extremely offensive. And what a drama! Never had these old walls listened to such a tale. Mrs. Vane and others like her had long since outgrown the prudery of their mothers, who had alluded in the most distant manner to the most decent of their internal organs, and called a leg a limb; but the commonplace was their rock, and they had a sense of sinking foundations.

Madame Zattiany, who knew exactly what was passing in their minds, continued placidly: "Almost suddenly at the end of the fourth or fifth week, it seemed to me that an actual physical weight that had depressed my brain lifted, and I experienced a decided activity of mind and body, foreign to both for many years. Nevertheless, the complete reënergizing of both was very slow, the rejuvenation of appearance slower still. Worn-out cells do not expand rapidly. The mental change was pronounced long before the physical, except that I rarely felt fatigue, although I spent many hours a day at the relief stations."

She paused and let her cool ironic glance wander over the intent faces before her. "Not only," she went on with a slow emphasis, which made them prick up their ears, "was the renewed power manifest in mental activity, in concentration, in memory, but that distaste for new ideas, for reorientation, had entirely disappeared. People growing old are condemned for prejudice, smugness, hostility to progress, to the purposes and enthusiasms of youth; but this attitude is due to aging glands alone, all things being equal. They *cannot* dig up the sunken tracks from the ruts in their brain and lay them elsewhere; and they instinctively protect themselves by an affectation of calm and scornful superiority, of righteous conservatism, which deceives themselves; much as I had assumed—and learned to feel—an attitude of profound indifference to my vanished youth, and refused to attempt any transparent disguise with cosmetics."

Intentness relaxed once more. Twelve pairs of eyes expressed at least half as many sentiments. Mrs. Vane gazed at Mary Ogden, whose insolence she had never forgotten, with indignant hostility; Mrs. Poole, who always dressed as if she had a tumor, but whose remnant of a once lovely complexion indicated perfect health, maintained her slight tolerant smile; its effect somewhat abridged by the fact that the small turban of bright blue feathers topping her large face had slipped to one side. Mrs. Goodrich looked startled and gazed deprecatingly at her friends. Mrs. Lawrence's eyes snapped, and Mrs. de Lacey looked thoughtful. Only Mrs. Tracy spoke.

"Wonderful! I feel more like Methuselah than ever. But it certainly is a relief to know what is the matter with me. Do go on, Mary—I may call you Mary? I only came out the year you were married—and you cannot imagine what a satisfaction it is to know that I am younger than you—were once. I've never done any of those things one reads about to keep looking young except cold cream my face at night, but I've often felt as if I'd like to——"

"Do stop babbling, Lily Tracy!" exclaimed Mrs. Vane, who, however disgusted, was quite as curious as the others to hear the rest of the tale. And Mrs. Goodrich said softly:

"Yes, go on, Mary, darling. I am sure the most thrilling part is yet to come. You see how interested your old friends all are."

Madame Zattiany moved her cool insolent eyes to Mrs. Vane's set visage. "The time came when I knew that youth was returning to my face as well as to the hidden processes of my body; and I can assure you that it excited me far more than the renewed functioning of my brain. The treatment induces flesh, and as I had been excessively thin, my skin, as flesh accumulated, grew taut and lines disappeared. My eyes, which had long been dull, had regained something of their old brilliancy under the renaissance of brain and blood, and that was accentuated. My hair——"

"Do you mean to say that it restores hair to its natural color?" demanded Mrs. Tracy, who had been plucking out bleached hairs for the past year. "That would——"

"It does not.[1] But my hair is the shade that never turns gray; and of course my teeth had always been kept in perfect order. I should never in any circumstances be a fat woman, but the active functioning of the glands gave me just enough flesh to complete the outer renovation. My complexion, after so many years of neglect, naturally needed scientific treatment of another sort, but that was still to be had in Vienna."

"Ah!" The exclamation was sharp. Here, at least, was something they knew all about and systematically discountenanced. "Do you mean that you had your skin ripped off?" asked Mrs. Ruyler.

"Certainly not. The skin was simply softened and reinvigorated by massage and the proper applications."

They were too proud to ask for details, and Mrs. de Lacey, who was stout, glanced triumphantly at Mrs. Ruyler, who was stouter. "You mean, Mary, that one has to be thin for this treatment to be a success?"

"That I cannot say. I really do not know what the treatment would do to a stout woman of middle or old age. The internal change would be the same, but, although additional flesh can be kept down by medicaments and diet, I doubt if there would be a complete restoration of the outlines of face and neck. A woman of sixty, with sagging flesh and distended skin, might once more look forty, if the treatment were successful, but hardly as young as I do. I was particularly fortunate in having withered. Still, I cannot say. As I told you, many women of all ages and sizes took the treatment while I was in Vienna. But they are too scattered for me at least to obtain any data on the results. I knew none of them personally and I was too busy to seek them out and compare notes.... But with me——" She leaned back and lit a cigarette, looking over her audience with mischievous eyes. "With me it has been a complete success—mentally, physically——"

"Yes, and how long will it last?" shot out Mrs. Ruyler. She was as strong as a horse and as alert mentally as she had ever been, and her complete indifference to rejuvenation in any of its forms gave her a feeling of superior contempt for all those European women who had swarmed to Vienna like greedy flies at the scent of molasses—no doubt to undergo terrible torments that Mary Zattiany would not admit. But her objective curiosity on the subject of youth was insatiable and she read everything that appeared

---

1 Newspapers of the 1920 debate the effects of the Steinach treatment, including claims regarding the restoration of an individual's original hair color after it had grayed.

in the newspapers and magazines about it, not neglecting the advertisements. If she had sent for a facial masseuse she would have felt that she had planted a worm at the root of the family tree, but the subject was unaccountably interesting.

Mary Zattiany, who understood her complex perfectly, shrugged her graceful shoulders. "It is too soon to reply with assurance. The method was only discovered some six years ago. But the eminent biologists who have given profound study to the subject estimate that it will last for ten years at least, when it can be renewed once at all events. Of course the end must come. It was not intended that man should live for ever. And who would wish it?"

"Not I, certainly," said Mrs. Ruyler sententiously. "Well, I must admit it has been a complete success in your case. That is not saying I approve of what you have done. You know how we have always regarded such things. If you had lived your life in New York instead of in Europe—notoriously loose in such matters—I feel convinced that you would never have done such a thing—exhausted or not. Moreover, I am a religious woman and I do not believe in interfering with the will of the Almighty."

"Then why have a doctor when you are ill? Are not illnesses the act of God? They certainly are processes of nature."

"I have always believed in letting nature take her course," said Mrs. Ruyler firmly. "But of course when one is ill, that is another matter——"

"Is it?" Madame Zattiany's eye showed a militant spark. "Or is it merely that you are so accustomed to the convention of calling in a doctor that you have never wasted thought on the subject? But is not medicine a science? When you are ill you invoke the aid of science in the old way precisely as I did in the new one. The time will come when this treatment I have undergone will be so much a matter of course that it will cause no more discussion than going under the knife for cancer—or for far less serious ailments. I understand that you, Polly, had an operation two years ago for gastric ulcer, an operation called by the very long and very unfamiliar name, gastroenterostomy. Did you feel—for I assume that you agree with Isabel in most things—that you were flying in the face of the Almighty? Or were you only too glad to take advantage of the progress of science?"

Mrs. Vane merely grunted. Mrs. Ruyler exclaimed crossly, "Oh, no one ever could argue with you, Mary Ogden. The truth is," she added, in a sudden burst of enlightenment that astonished herself, "I don't suppose any of us would mind if you didn't look younger than our daughters. That sticks in our craw. Why not admit it?"

Mrs. Oglethorpe chuckled. She and Isabel Ruyler snapped at each other like two belligerent old cats every time they crossed each other's path, but, with the exception of Mary Ogden, whom she loved, she liked her better than any of her old friends.

But once more Mrs. Vane drew herself up (figuratively). "Speak for yourself. It may be that I am too old to accept new ideas, but this one certainly seems to me downright immoral and indecent. This is not intended to reflect on you personally, Mary, and of course you were more or less demoralized by your close contact with the war. I mean the idea—the thing—itself. We may call in doctors and surgeons when we are in bodily discomfort, and be thankful that they are more advanced than in our mothers' time, when people died of appendicitis every day in the week and called it inflammation of the bowels. But no one can tell me that rejuvenation is not against the laws of nature. What are you going to do with this new youth—I never saw any one look less indifferent to life!—make fools of men again—of our sons?"

"Who can tell?" asked Mary maliciously. "Could anything be more amusing than to come back to New York after thirty-four years and be a belle again, with the sons and grandsons of my old friends proposing to me?"

"Do you really mean that?" Mrs. Vane almost rose. She recalled that her youngest son had met Madame Zattiany in Mrs. Oglethorpe's box on Monday night and had been mooning about the house ever since. "If I thought that——"

"Well, what would you do, Polly?" Mary laughed outright. "Your son—Harry is his name, is it not?—is remarkably good-looking and very charming. After all, where could you find a safer and more understanding wife for him than a woman who has had not only the opportunity to know the world and men like the primer, but looks—is—so young that he is bound to forget it and be led like a lamb? Girls, those uncharted seas, are always a risk——"

"Stop tormenting Polly," exclaimed Mrs. Oglethorpe. "Mary has no intention of marrying any one. She's only waiting for her estate to be settled in order to return to Europe and devote herself to certain plans of reconstruction——"

"Is that true?"

"Quite true," said Madame Zattiany, smiling. "Don't worry, Polly. If I marry it will be some one you are not interested in too personally, and it is doubtful if I ever marry at all. There's a tremendous work to be done in Europe, and so far as lies in my power I shall do my share. If I marry it will be some one who can help me. I can assure you I long since ceased to be susceptible, particularly to young men. Remember that while my *brain* has been rejuvenated with the rest of my physical structure, my *mind* is as old as it was before the treatment." She gave a slight unnoticed shiver. "My memory, that for years before the war was dull and inactive, is now as vigorous as ever."

Several of the women recalled those old stories of Countess Zattiany's youth, and looked at her sharply. There was a general atmosphere of uneasiness in the large respectable room. But whether or not they gave her the benefit of the doubt, they had always given her due credit for neither being found out nor embarrassing her virtuous friends with confidences.

Mrs. Tracy was the first to break the silence. "But you will come to all of us as long as you do stay, will you not? I do so want to give you a dinner next week."

"Yes, yes, indeed." The chorus was eager, and sincere enough. After all, nothing could alter the fact that she was one of them.

"Oh, I have enjoyed meeting you all again, and I am hoping to see more of you." Madame Zattiany felt that she could do no less than be gracious. "I have become a very quiet person, but I will go with pleasure."

"You must let us see you daily while you are with us," cried Mrs. Goodrich, her spirits soaring at the prospect. As Mary stood up and adjusted her hat before the mirror she felt that she had successfully distracted their attention from a quick sigh of utter boredom. "You are too kind, Nelly," she murmured, "but then you always were."

"Yes, go, Mary," said Mrs. Oglethorpe peremptorily, and rising also. "Clear out and let them talk you over. They'll burst if you don't. Human nature can stand just so much and no more."

Madame Zattiany took her leave amid much laughter, more or less perfunctory, and one and all, whatever their reactions, insisted that she must give her old friends the pleasure of entertaining her, and of seeing her as often as possible as long as she remained in New York.

She escaped at last. That was over. But tomorrow night! Tomorrow night. Every wheel and tire seemed to be revolving out the words. Well, if he were repelled and revolted, no doubt it would be for the best. She had made up her mind to spare him nothing. He would hear far more than she had told those women. Certainly he should be given full opportunity to come to his senses. If he refused to take it, on his head be the consequences. She would have done her part.

XXVII

On Saturday afternoon as Clavering was walking up Forty-fourth Street he met Anne Goodrich coming out of the Belasco Theatre.[1] He saw her first and tried to avoid her, for her family and the Oglethorpes were as one, but she caught sight of him and held out her hand.

"I shouldn't speak to you after your base desertion the other night," she said, smiling. "But you do look rather seedy and I prefer to flatter myself that you really were ill."

"Was sure I was coming down with the flu," Clavering mumbled. "Of course you know that nothing else——"

"Oh, hostesses are too canny these days to take offence. All we are still haughty enough to demand is a decent excuse. But you really owe me something, and besides I've been wanting to talk to you. Take me to Pierre's for tea."

She spoke in a light tone of command. There had been a time when issuing commands to Clavering had been her habit and he had responded with a certain palpitation, convinced for nearly a month that Anne Goodrich was the Clavering woman. He had known her as an awkward schoolgirl and then as one of the prettiest and most light-hearted of the season's débutantes, but she had never interested him until after her return from France, where she had done admirable work in the canteens. Then, sitting next to her at a dinner, and later for two hours in the conservatory, he had thought her the finest girl he had ever met. He thought so still; but although she stimulated his mind and they had many tastes in common, he had soon realized that when apart he forgot her and that only novelty had inspired his brief desire. She might have everything for another man as exacting as himself, but that unanalyzable something his own peculiar essence demanded no woman had ever possessed until he met Mary Zattiany.

He had begun too ardently to cease his visits abruptly and, moreover, he still found her more companionable than any woman he knew; he continued to show her a frank and friendly devotion until an attack of influenza sent him to the hospital for a month; when he accepted the friendly intervention of fate and thereafter timed his occasional calls to coincide with the hour of tea, when she was never alone. There were no more long morning walks, no more long rides in her car, no more hastily arranged luncheons at

---

1 An elaborate Manhattan theater that ran well-publicized theatrical productions.

the Bohemian restaurants that interested her, no more "dropping in" and long telephone conversations. He still enjoyed a talk with her at a dinner, and she was always a pleasure to the eye with her calm and regular features softened by a cloud of bright chestnut hair that matched her eyes to a shade, her serene brow and her exquisite clothes. She did not carry herself well according to his standard; "well" when she came out six years ago had meant laxity of shoulders and pride of stomach, and in spite of her devotion to outdoor sports she had fallen a prey to fashion. She so far disapproved of the new fashion in girls, however, that she was making an effort to stand erect and she had even banished powder from her clear warm skin. Today she was becomingly dressed in taupe velvet, with stole and muff and turban of sable; but Clavering had fancied that her fine face wore a weary discontented expression until she saw him, when it changed swiftly to a sort of imperious gladness. It made him vaguely uncomfortable. He had never flattered himself that she loved him, but he had believed in the possibility of winning her. He had later chosen to believe that she had grown as indifferent as himself, and he wondered, as he stood plunging about in his mind for an excuse to avoid a tête-à-tête, why she had not married.

"Well—you see——"

"Come now! You don't go to teas, men never call these days, and you surely have done your column for tomorrow. Here is the car. You can spare me an hour."

He had always avoided any appearance of rudeness and in his mind at least he had treated her badly; he followed her without further hesitation, trusting to his agile mind to keep her off the subject of Madame Zattiany. This he would do at the cost of rudeness itself, for he would not permit fiasco at the last moment.

The street was packed with automobiles and taxis, and after a slow progress toward Fifth Avenue they arrived in time to see the traffic towers flash on the yellow light and were forced to halt for another three minutes. He had started an immediate discussion of the play she had just witnessed, knowing her love of argument, but she suddenly broke off and laid her hand on his arm.

"Look!" she exclaimed. "The famous Countess Zattiany in that car with mother. Of course you know her; you were with her at the opera on the historic night, weren't you? Tell me! What is she like? Did you ever hear of anything so extraordinary?"

"Never. I really know her very slightly. But as I had met her and she had kindly asked me to dinner, I was glad to return the compliment when Mrs. Oglethorpe sent me her box, as she always does once or twice during the season, you know. But go on. What you said interested me immensely, although I don't agree with you. I have certain fixed standards when it comes to the drama."

She picked him up and the argument lasted until they were seated in Pierre's and had ordered tea.

"I might have taken you home," she said then. "We could have had tea in my den. No doubt Countess Zattiany was returning with mother, who, it seems, has always adored her——"

"This is ever so much nicer, for we are far less likely to be interrupted. I haven't had a real talk with you for months."

And he gave her a look of boyish pleasure, wholly insincere, but so well done that she flushed slightly.

"Is that my fault? There was a time when you came almost every day. And then you never came in the same way again." It evidently cost her something to say this, for her flush deepened, but she managed a glance of dignified archness.

"Oh, remember I had a villainous attack of the flu, and after that there were arrears of work to make up. Moreover, the dramatic critic came down with an even longer attack and they piled his work on me. I don't know what it is to 'drop in' these days."

"Well—are you always to be driven to death? I read your column religiously and it runs so smoothly and spontaneously that it doesn't seem possible it can take you more than an hour to write it."

"An hour! Little you know. And subjects don't drop out of the clouds, dear Anne. I have to go through all the newspapers, read an endless number of books—not all fiction by a long sight—glance through the magazines, reviews, weekly publications and foreign newspapers, read my rivals' columns, go about among the Sophisticates, attend first-nights, prize-fights, and even see the best of the movies. I assure you it's a dog's life."

"It sounds tremendously interesting. Far, far more so than my own. I am so tired of that! I—that is one thing I wanted to talk to you about—I meant to bring it up at my dinner—I wish you would introduce me to some of your Sophisticates. Uncle Din says they are the most interesting people in New York and that he always feels young again when he is at one of their parties. Will you take me to one?"

"Of course I will. The novelty might amuse you——"

"It's not only novelty I want. I want really to know people whose minds are constantly at work, who are doing the things we get the benefit of when we are intelligent enough to appreciate them. I cannot go on in the old way any longer. I paint more or less and read a great deal—still on the lines you laid down. But one cannot paint and read and walk and motor and dance all the time. Even if I had not gone to France I should have become as bored and disgusted as I am now. You know that I have a mind. What has it to feed on? I don't mean, of course, that all the women I know are fools. Some of them no doubt are cleverer than I am. But all the girls of my set—except Marian Lawrence, and we don't get on very well—are married; and some have babies, some have lovers, some are mad about bridge, a few have gone in for politics, which don't interest me, and those that the war made permanently serious devote themselves to charities and reform movements. The war spoilt me for mere charity work—although I give a charity I founded one afternoon a week—and mother does enough for one family anyhow. I see no prospect of marrying—I don't know a young man who wants to talk anything but sport and prohibition—you are an oasis. There you are! The Sophisticates are an inspiration. I am sure they will save my life."

"But have you reflected——" Clavering was embarrassed. She had controlled her tones and spoken with her usual crisp deliberateness, but he knew that the words came from some profound emotional reaction. For Anne Goodrich it was an outburst. "You see—it is quite possible that when the novelty wore thin you would not be much better off than you are now. All these people are intensely interested in their particular jobs. They are specialists. You——"

"You mean, what have I to give them?"

"Not exactly. You could give them a good deal. To say nothing of your own high intelligence, they are by no means averse from taking an occasional flyer into the realm of fashion. Curiosity partly, natural human snobbishness, perhaps. They will go to your house if you invite them, no doubt of that; and they may conceive an enthusiastic liking for you. But after all, you would not be one of them. Even though they genuinely appreciated your accomplishments, still you would be little more than an interesting incident. They are workers, engaged in doing the things they think most worth while—which are worth while because they furnish what the intelligent public is demanding just now, and upon which the current market places a high value. And you are merely an intellectual young woman of leisure. They might think it a pity you didn't have to work, but secretly, no matter what their regard, they'd consider you negligible because you belong to a class that is content to be, not to do. I assure you they consider themselves the most important group in New York—in America—at present: the life-giving group of suns round which far-off planets humbly revolve."

"I see. You mean that my novelty would wear thin long before theirs. Heaven knows I have little to give them. I should feel rather ashamed sitting at the head of my table offering nothing but terrapin and Gobelins.[1] But don't you think I could make real friends of some of them? Surely we would find much in common to talk about—and they certainly take time to play, according to Uncle Din."

"I think there would always be a barrier.... Ah! I have an idea. Why don't you set up a studio and take your painting seriously? Cut yourself off from the old life and join the ranks of the real workers? Then, by degrees, they would accept you as a matter of course. You could return their hospitality in your studio, which could be one of the largest—there is no danger of overwhelming them; they are too successful themselves. Think it over."

Miss Goodrich's face, which had looked melancholy, almost hopeless, lit up again. Her red mouth lifted at the corners, light seemed to pour into her hazel eyes. "I'll do it!" she exclaimed. "I did a portrait of father last month and it really is good. He is delighted with it, and you know how easy he is to please! I wonder I never thought of it before. You certainly are the most resourceful man in the world, Lee—by the way, I hear there is a party at that wonderful Gora Dwight's tonight. Do take me."

"Oh! ... I'm so sorry ... it's quite impossible, Anne. I wish I could.... I'll take you to one next week. And meanwhile get to work. Be ready to meet them in the outer court at least. You'll find it an immense advantage—rob your advent of any suggestion of curiosity."

"I'll look for a studio tomorrow. That is the way I do things—my father's daughter, you see."

She spoke with gay determination, but her face had fallen again. In a moment she began to draw on her gloves. "Now I'll have to run if I'm to dress and get over to Old Westbury for dinner at eight. Thank you so much, Lee; you've been a godsend. If I were a writer instead of a mere dabbler in paints I'd dedicate my first book to you. I'm so sorry I haven't time to drive you down to Madison Square."

Clavering, drawing a long breath as if he had escaped from imminent danger, saw her into her car and then walked briskly home. He intended to dine alone tonight. And in a moment he had forgotten Anne Goodrich as completely as he had forgotten Janet Oglethorpe.

---

1 Turtle soup and ornate tapestry.

XXVIII

He called for Madame Zattiany at ten o'clock. This time she was standing in the hall as the man opened the door, and she came out immediately. A lace scarf almost concealed her face.

"I didn't order the car," she said. "It is such a fine night, and she lives so near. Do you mind?"

"I much prefer to walk, but your slippers——"

"They are dark and the heels not too high."

"I'm not going to make the slightest preliminary attempt at indifference tonight, nor wait for one of your leads. How long do you intend to stay at this party?"

"Oh, an hour, possibly. One must not be rude." Her own tones were not even, but he could not see her face.

"But you'll keep your word and tell me everything tonight?"

She gave a deep sigh. "Yes, I'll keep my word. No more now—please! ... Tell me, what do they do at these parties besides talk—dance?"

"Not always. They have charades, spelling matches, pick a word out of a hat and make impromptu speeches——"[1]

"But *Mon dieu!*" She stopped short and pushed back her scarf. Whatever expression she may have wished to conceal there was nothing now in her face but dismay. "But you did not tell me this or I should not have accepted. I never bore myself. I understood these were your intellectuals. Charades! Spelling matches! Words in the hat! It sounds like a small town moved to New York."

"Well, a good many of them are from small towns and they rather pride themselves on preserving some of the simplicities of rural life and juvenescence, while leading an exaggerated mental life for which nature designed no man. Perhaps it is merely owing to an obscure warning to preserve the balance. Or an innocent arrogance akin to Mrs. Oglethorpe's when she is looking her dowdiest.... But Gora often has good music ... still, if you don't want to go on I'm sure I do not."

"No," she said hurriedly. "I shall go. But—I am still astonished. I do not know what I expected. But brilliant conversation, probably, such as one hears in a European salon. Don't they relax their great minds at outdoor sports? I understand there are golf links and tennis courts near the city."

---

1   These activities were forms of nineteenth-century parlor games and appear shockingly banal to the Countess Zattiany.

"A good many of them do. But they like to relax still further at night. You see we are not Europeans. Americans are as serious as children, but like children they also love to play. Remember, we are a young nation—and a very healthy one. And you will have conversation if you want it. The men, you may be sure, will be ready to give you anything you demand."

"I had rather hoped to listen. Is this the house?"

Several taxis were arriving and there were many cars parked along the block. When they entered the house they were directed to dressing-rooms on the second floor, and Clavering met Madame Zattiany at the head of the staircase. She wore a gown of emerald green velvet, cut to reveal the sloping line of her shoulders, and an emerald comb thrust sideways in the low coil of her soft ashen hair. On the dazzling fairness of her neck lay a single unset emerald depending from a fine gold chain. Clavering stared at her helplessly.... It was evident she had not made her toilette with an eye to softening a blow!

"Am I overdressed?" she murmured. "I did not know.... I thought I would dress as if—well, as if I had been invited by one of my own friends——"

"Quite right. To 'dress down' would have been fatal. And Gora must spend a small fortune on her clothes.... But you ... you ... I have never seen you——"

"I am fond of green," she said lightly. "*Couleur d'espérance.*[1] Shall we go down?"

He followed her down the stairs and before they reached the crowded room below he had managed to set his face; but his heart was pounding. He gave Gora, who came forward to meet them, a ferocious scowl, but she was too much engaged with Madame Zattiany to notice him; and so, for that matter, was the rest of the company. Miss Dwight's gown was of black satin painted with flaming poinsettias, and Clavering saw Madame Zattiany give it a swift approving glance. Around her thin shoulders was a scarf of red tulle that warmed her brown cheeks. She looked remarkably well, almost handsome, and her strange pale eyes were very bright. It was evident that she was enjoying her triumphs; this no doubt was the crowning one, and she led Madame Zattiany into the room, leaving Clavering to his own devices.

It was certainly the "distinguished party" he had promised. There were some eight or ten of the best-known novelists and story-writers in the country, two dramatists, several of the younger

---

1 French for "the color of hope."

publishers, most of the young editors, critics, columnists, and illustrators, famous in New York, at least; a few poets, artists; the more serious contributors to the magazines and reviews; an architect, an essayist, a sculptress, a famous girl librarian of a great private library, three correspondents of foreign newspapers, and two visiting British authors. The men wore evening dress. The women, if not all patrons of the ranking "houses" and dressmakers, were correct. Even the artistic gowns stopped short of delirium. And if many of the women wore their hair short, so did all of the men. Everybody in the room was reasonably young or had managed to preserve the appearance and spirit of youth. Clavering noticed at once that Mr. Dinwiddie was not present. No doubt he had been ordered to keep out of the way!

Miss Dwight led Madame Zattiany to the head of the room and enthroned her, but made no introductions at the moment; a young man stood by the piano, violin in hand, evidently waiting for the stir over the guest of honor to subside. The hostess gave the signal and the guests were polite if restless. However, the playing was admirable; and Madame Zattiany, at least, gave it her undivided attention. She was, as ever, apparently unconscious of glances veiled and open, but Clavering laid a bet with himself that before the end of the encore—politely demanded—she knew what every woman in the room had on.

The violinist retired. Cocktails were passed. There was a surge toward the head of the room.

Clavering had dropped into a chair beside the wife of De Witt Turner, eminent novelist, who, however, called herself in print and out, Suzan Forbes. She was one of the founders of the Lucy Stone League,[1] stern advocates of the inalienable individuality of woman. Whether you had one adored husband or many, never should that individuality (presumably derived from the male parent) be sunk in any man's. When Suzan's husband took his little family travelling the astonished hotel register read: De Witt Turner, Suzan Forbes, child and nurse. Sometimes explanations were wearisome; and when travelling in Europe they found it expedient to bow to prejudice. Several of the Lucy Stoners, however, had renounced Europe for the present, a reactionary government refusing to issue separate passports. You took your husband's name at

---

1 An organization founded in 1921 to promote married women's retention of their maiden or birth names; its founder was journalist Ruth Hale, whose husband, columnist Heywood Broun, was one of the founding members of the Algonquin Round Table.

the altar, didn't you? You are legally married? You are? Then you're no more miss than mister. You go to Europe as a respectable married woman or you stay at home. So they stayed. But they would win in the end. They always did. As for the husbands, they were amenable. Whether they really approved of feministics in extenso, or were merely good-natured and indulgent after the fashion of American husbands, they were at some pains to conceal. All the bright young married women who were "doing things," however, were not Lucy Stoners, advanced as they might be in thought. They were mildly sympathetic, but rather liked the matronly, and possessive, prefix. And, after all, what did it matter? There were enough tiresome barriers to scale, Heaven knew. This was the age of woman, but man, heretofore predominant by right of brute strength and hallowed custom, was cultivating subtlety, and if he feminized while they masculinized there would be the devil to pay before long.

Miss Forbes was a tiny creature, wholly feminine in appearance, and in spite of her public activities, her really brilliant and initiative mind, was notoriously dependent upon her big burly husband for guidance and advice in all practical matters. When they took a holiday the younger of his children gave him the least trouble, for she had a nurse: he dared not give his wife her ticket in a crowd lest she lose it, far less trust her to relieve his burdened mind of any of the details of travel; nor even to order a meal. Nevertheless, he invariably, and with complete gravity, introduced her and alluded to her as Suzan Forbes (she even tabued the Miss), and he sent a cheque to the League when it was founded. His novels had a quality of delicate irony, but he avowed that his motto was live and let live.

Miss Forbes was not pretty, but she had an expressive original little face and her manners were charming. Janet Oglethorpe was a boor beside her. It was doubtful if she had ever been aggressive in manner or rude in her life; although she never hesitated to give utterance to the extremest of her opinions or to maintain them to the bitter end (when she sometimes sped home to have hysterics on her husband's broad chest). She was one of Clavering's favorites and the heroine of the comedy he so far rejected.

She lit a cigarette as the music finished and pinched it into a holder nearly as long as her face. But even smoking never interfered with her pleasant, rather deprecatory, smile.

"It must be wonderful to be an authentic beauty," she said wistfully, glancing at the solid phalanx of black backs and sleek heads at the other end of the room. "And she's ravishing, of course. The men are sleepless about her already. Do assure me that she is stupid! Nature would never treat the rest of us so unfairly as to spare brains for that enchanting skull when she hasn't enough to go round as it is. I believe I'd give mine to look like that."

"She's anything and everything but stupid. Ask Gora. They've met already."

"Well, there's *something*," she said wisely. "Law of compensation. Although any woman who can look like that should have a special dispensation of Providence. Are you interested in her, Clavey?"

"Immensely. But I want to talk to you about another friend of mine." And he told her something of Anne Goodrich, her ambitions, her talents, and her admiration of the new aristocracy.

Suzan Forbes listened with smiling interest and bobbed her brown little head emphatically. "Splendid! I'm having a party on Thursday night. Be sure to bring her. She'll need encouragement at first, poor thing, and I'll be only too glad to advise her. I'll tell Tommy Treadwell to find a studio for her. I've an idea there's one vacant in The Gainsborough,[1] and she'd love the outlook on the Park. Witt can help her furnish; he's a wonder at picking up things. Mother can furnish the kitchenette. Do you think she'd join the Lucy Stone League?"

"No doubt, as she was brought up in the most conservative atmosphere in America, she'll leap most of the fences after she takes the first. But I don't think she's the marrying kind."

"I shall advise her to marry. Husbands are almost indispensable in a busy woman's life; and there are so many new ways of bringing up a baby. D'you like my gown?"

It was a charming but not extravagant slip of bright green chiffon and suited her elfishness admirably, as he told her.

"I paid for it myself. I pay for all my gowns, as I think it consistent, but I can't afford the expensive dressmakers yet. At least I think I've paid for it. Witt says I haven't and that he expects a collector any day. But I must have, because I told her to send the bill at once so that it wouldn't get lost among all the other bills on the first of the month. Your column's been simply spiffing lately. Full of fire and go, but rather—what shall I call it—explosive? What's happened, Clavey?"

"Good of you to encourage me, Suzanna. I'd thought it rotten. What are you working at?"

---

1 The Gainsborough, a building of studio apartments, was completed in 1908 at 222 Central Park South.

"I've just finished a paper on John Dewey[1] for the *Atlantic*. I was so proud when Witt said he hadn't a criticism to make. I'm on a review for the *Yale* now; and the new *Century* has asked me for a psychological analysis of the Younger Generation.[2] I'm going to compare our post-war product with all that is known of young people and their manifestations straight back to the Stone Age. I've made a specialty of the subject. Witt has helped me a lot in research. D'you think he's gone off?"

"Gone off? Certainly not. Every columnist in town had something to say about that last installment of his novel. Best thing he's ever done, and that's saying all. He's strong as an ox, too. Why in heaven's name should he go off?"

"Well, baby's teething and won't let any one else hold her when she gets a fretting spell. He's been up a lot lately."

Clavering burst into a loud delighted laugh. He had forgotten his personal affairs completely, as he always did when talking to this remarkable little paradox. "Gad! That's good! And his public visualizes him as a sort of Buddha, brooding cross-legged in his library, receiving direct advice from the god of fiction.... But I wouldn't have you otherwise. The nineteenth century bluestocking[3] with twentieth century trimmings.... What now?"

Rollo Landers Todd, the "Poet of Manhattan," had stalked in with a Prussian helmet on his head, his girth draped in a rich blue shawl embroidered and fringed with white, a bitter frown on his jovial round face; and in his hand a long rod with a large blue bow on the metal point designed to shut refractory windows. Helen Vane Baker, a contribution from Society to the art of fiction, with flowing hair and arrayed in a long nightgown over her dress, fortunately white, was assisted to the top of the bookcase on the west wall. Henry Church, a famous satirist, muffled in a fur cloak, a small black silk handkerchief pinned about his lively face, stumped heavily into the room, fell in a heap on the floor against the opposite wall, and in a magnificent bass growled out the re-

---

1 John Dewey (1859-1952), an educational and social reformer and proponent of populism, was also a prolific author. From 1904 to 1930, he taught philosophy at Columbia University and Columbia University's Teacher's College, in New York City.

2 The *Yale* refers to the *Yale Review*, a literary journal affiliated with the university, published under that name since 1892. *Century*, a journal in publication between 1880 and 1930, later known as one of the four "quality" journals.

3 An educated or literary individual, usually a woman.

sentment of Ortrud,[1] while a rising but not yet prosilient[2] pianist, with a long blonde wig from Miss Dwight's property chest, threw his head back, shook his hands, adjusted a cigarette in the corner of his mouth, and banged out the prelude to *Lohengrin* with amazing variations.[3] Elsa,[4] with her profile against the wall and her hands folded across her breast, sang what of Elsa's prayer she could remember and with no apparent effort improvised the rest. Lohengrin pranced up and down the room barking out German phonetics (he did not know a word of the language, but his accent was as Teutonic as his helmet), demanding vengeance and threatening annihilation. He brandished his pole in the face of Ortrud, stamping and roaring, then, bending his knees, waddled across the room and prodded Elsa, who winced perceptibly but continued to mingle her light soprano with the rolling bass of Mr. Church and the vociferations of the poet. Finally, at the staccato command of Mr. Todd's hoarsening voice, she toppled over into his arms and they both fell on Ortrud. The nonsense was over.

No one applauded more spontaneously than Madame Zattiany, and she even drank a cocktail. By this time every one in the room had been introduced to her and she was chatting as if she hadn't a care in the world. As far as Clavering could see, she had every intention of making a Sophisticate night of it.

The pianist, after a brief interval for recuperation, played with deafening vehemence and then with excruciating sweetness. Once more cocktails were passed, and then there was a charade by Todd, Suzan Forbes and the handsome young English sculptress, which Madame Zattiany followed with puzzled interest; and was so delighted with herself for guessing the word before the climax that she clapped her hands and laughed like a child.

More music, more cocktails, a brief impromptu play full of witty nonsense, caricaturing several of the distinguished company, whose appreciation was somewhat dubious, and Miss Dwight led the way down to supper. Clavering watched Madame Zattiany go

---

1 A witch character from Richard Wagner's opera *Lohengrin* (1848), Ortrud transforms a young duke into a swan in order to accuse the opera's heroine, Elsa, of the murder of her young brother, the duke. Ortrud plots with her husband, Telramund, against Elsa. The opera also begins with a German king expelling Hungarians from their lands.
2 Conspicuous or standing forth.
3 The characters are performing an impromptu and largely satiric performance of the opera and of Elsa, Ortrud, and Lohengrin's parts.
4 The heroine figure in *Lohengrin* who is falsely accused by Ortrud; Lohengrin is the hero and a knight of the Grail.

out with the good-looking young editor of one of the staid old fiction magazines which he had recently levered out of its rut by the wayside, cranked up and driven with a magnificent gesture into the front rank of Youth. She was talking with the greatest animation. He hardly recognized her and it was apparent that she had entered into the spirit of the evening, quite reconciled to any dearth of intellectual refreshment.

The supper of hot oysters, chicken salad, every known variety of sandwich, ices and cakes was taken standing for the most part, Madame Zattiany, however, once more enthroned at the head of the room, women as well as men dancing attendance upon her. Prohibition, a dead letter[1] to all who could afford to patronize the underground mart, had but added to the spice of life, and it was patent that Miss Dwight had a cellar. More cocktails, highballs, sherry, were passed continuously, and two enthusiastic guests made a punch. Fashionable young actors and actresses began to arrive. Hilarity waxed, impromptu speeches were made, songs rose on every key. Then suddenly some one ran up to the victrola and turned on the jazz; and in a twinkling the dining-room was deserted, furniture in the large room upstairs was pushed to the wall and the night entered on its last phase.

Then only did Madame Zattiany signify her intention of retiring, and Clavering, to whom such entertainments were too familiar to banish for more than a moment his heavy disquiet, hastened to her side with a sigh of relief and a sinking sensation behind his ribs. Madame Zattiany made her farewells not only with graciousness but with unmistakable sincerity in her protestations of having passed her "most interesting evening in New York."

Miss Dwight went up to the dressing-room with her, and Clavering, retrieving hat and top-coat, waited for her at the front door. She came down radiant and talking animatedly to her hostess; but when they had parted and she was alone with Clavering her face seemed suddenly to turn to stone and her lids drooped. As she was about to pass him she shrank back, and then raised her eyes to his. In that fleeting moment they looked as when he had met them first: inconceivably old, wise, disillusioned.

"Now for it," he thought grimly as he closed the door and followed her out to the pavement. "The Lord have mercy——" And then he made a sudden resolution.

---

1 Mail that cannot be delivered because of a confusion over its delivery address.

XXIX

Madame Zattiany did not utter a word during the short walk to her house. It was evident that she had dismissed the merry evening from her mind and was brooding on the coming hour. At the top of the steps she handed him the latchkey, but still lingered outside for a moment. As he took her hand and drew her gently into the house he felt that she was trembling.

"Come," he said, his own voice shaking. "Remember that you need tell me nothing unless you wish. This idea of confession before marriage is infernal rot. I have not the least intention of making one of my own."

"Oh!" She gave a short harsh laugh. "I should never dream of asking for any man's confession. They are all alike. And I must tell you. I cannot leave you to hear it from others."

He helped her out of her wrap and she threw the lace scarf on a chair and preceded him slowly down the hall.

"I am a coward. A coward," she thought heavily. "Have I ever felt moral cowardice before? I don't remember. Not toward any other man who loved me. But——Oh, God! And I shall never see him again. How shall I begin?"

She was totally unprepared for the beginning. She heard him shut the library door, and then it seemed to her that her entire body was encircled by flexible hot bars of iron and her face, her mouth, were being flagellated.[1] If he hadn't held her in that vise-like grip she would have fallen. She lay back on his arm as he kissed her and for the moment she forgot the past and the future and was happy, although she felt dimly that life was being drained out of her. She was passive in that fierce possessive embrace. She had lost all sense of separateness.

"I won't listen to your story," he muttered. "This is no time for talk."

His voice, hoarse and shaking as it was, broke the spell; with a sudden lithe movement she twisted herself out of his arms. Before he realized what was happening she had run across the room, snatched the key from the door and locked it on the other side. He heard her run up the stairs.

Clavering did and said most of the things men do and say when balked in mid-flight, but in a moment he took the little key from the drawer in the table and poured himself out a whiskey and soda—he had taken almost nothing at the party—lit a cigarette

---

1 Whipped.

and threw himself into a chair. He had no desire to stride up and down; he felt as if all the strength had gone out of him. But he felt no apprehension that she had left him for the night. Nor should he take possession of her again until she had told her story: he reflected with what humor was left in him that when a woman had something to say and was determined to say it, the only thing to do was to let her talk. Words to a woman were as steam to a boiler, and no man could control her mind until she had talked off the lid.

She was giving him time to cool off, he reflected grimly, as he glanced at the clock. Well, he felt heavy and inert enough—hideous reaction! He was in a condition to listen to anything. If she was determined to work her will on him, at least he had worked his on her for a brief moment. She knew now that in the future she might as well try to resist death itself. Let her have her last fling.

He rose as she entered, and for the moment his heart failed him. He had never seen even her look more like marble, and she did not meet his eyes as she crossed the room and seated herself so that her profile would be toward him as she talked. As she had chosen the large high-backed chair, Clavering, knowing her love of comfort, hoped that her discourse was to be brief.

"When I finish," she said in her low vital voice, "I shall leave the room immediately and I must have your word that you will make no attempt to detain me, and that you will go at once and not return until Monday afternoon. I shall not wish to see you again until you have had time to deliberate calmly on what I shall tell you. I do not want any embarrassed protests from a gallant gentleman—whose confusion of mind is second only to his chivalrous dismay. Have I your word?"

"It never takes me long to make up my mind——"

"That may be, but I intend to save you from an embarrassing situation. You need not come on Monday unless you wish. You may write—or, for that matter, if I do not hear from you on Monday by four I shall understand——"

"I—for God's sake, Mary——"

"You must do as I say—this time. And—and—you could not overcome me again tonight. I can turn myself to stone when I choose."

"Oh!" He ground his teeth. His own nerves might be lulled for the moment, but he had anticipated reaction when she finished her story. "Very well—but it is for the last time, my dear. And why Monday? Why not this afternoon?"

"You must sleep and write your column, is it not so? Moreover—and deliberately—I am lunching with Mrs. Ruyler and dining at the Lawrences'."

"Very well. Monday, then. You have set the stage. If I must be a puppet for once in my life, so be it. But, I repeat, it's for the last time. Now, for heaven's sake, go ahead and get it off your chest."

"And you will let me go without a word? Otherwise I shall not speak—and I'll leave the room again and not return."

"Very well. I promise."

"I told part of it the other day at Mrs. Oglethorpe's luncheon—I had told her before. But there's so much else. I hardly know how to begin with you, and I have not the habit of talking about myself. But I suppose I should begin at the beginning."

"It is one of the formulae."

"It is the most difficult of all—that beginning." And although she had announced the torpidity of her nerves, her hands clenched and her voice shook slightly.

"Let me remind you that to begin anywhere you've got to begin somewhere." And then as she continued silent, he burst out: "For God's sake, say it!"

"Is—is—it possible that the suspicion has never crossed your mind that I am Mary Ogden?"

"Wh-a-at!"

"Mary Ogden, who married Count Zattiany thirty-four years ago. I was twenty-four at the time. You may do your own arithmetic."

But Clavering made no answer. His cigarette was burning a hole in the carpet. He mechanically set his foot on it, but his faculties felt suspended, his body immersed in ice-water. And yet something in his unconscious rose and laughed ... and tossed up a key ... if he had not fallen in love with her he would have found that key long since. His news sense rarely failed him.

"I've told a good many lies, I'm afraid," she went on, and her voice was even and cool. The worst was over. "You'll have to forgive me that at least. I dislike downright lying, if only because concessions are foreign to my nature, and I quibbled when it was possible; but when cornered there was no other way out. I had no intention of being forced to tell you or any one the truth until I chose to tell it."

"Well, you had your little comedy!"

"It did amuse me for a time, but I think I explained all that in my letter. I also explained why I came to America, and that if I had not met you I should probably have come and gone and no one but Judge Trent been the wiser. I had prepared him by letter, and to him, I suppose, it has been a huge comedy—with no tragic sequel. Be sure that I never entertained the thought that I could ever love any man again. But I have made up my mind to disenchant you as far as possible, not only for your sake but my own. I wish you to know exactly whom you have fallen in love with."

"You grow more interesting every moment," said Clavering politely, "and I have never been one-half as interested in my life."

"Perhaps you have heard—Mrs. Oglethorpe, I should think, would be very much disposed to talk about old times—that I was a great belle in New York—belles were fashionable in those days of more marked individuality. I suppose no girl ever had more proposals. Naturally I grew to understand my power over men perfectly. I had that white and regular beauty combined with animation and great sex-magnetism which always convinces men that under the snow volcanic fires are burning. I was experienced, under the frankest exterior, in all the subtle arts of the coquette. Men to me were a sort of musical instrument from which I could evoke any harmony or cacophony I chose.

"What held the men I played with and rejected was my real gift for good-fellowship, my loyalty in friendship, and some natural sweetness of disposition. But such power makes a woman, particularly while young, somewhat heartless and callous, and I was convinced that I had no capacity for love myself; especially as I found all men rather ridiculous. I met Otto Zattiany in Paris, where he was attached to the Embassy of the Dual Empire.[1] He was an impetuous wooer and very handsome. I did not love him, but I was fascinated. Moreover, I was tired of American men and American life. Diplomacy appealed to my ambition, my love of power and intrigue. He was also a nobleman with great estates; there could be no suspicion that he was influenced by my fortune. He followed me back to New York, and although my parents were opposed to all foreigners, I had my way; there was the usual wedding in Saint Thomas's, and we sailed immediately for Europe.[2]

"I hated him at once. I shall not go into the details of that marriage. Fortunately he soon tired of me and returned to his mistresses. To him I was the Galatea[3] that no man could bring to

---

1 The Austro-Hungarian Empire.

2 Episcopalian church located at 5th Avenue and 53rd Street in New York; it was completed in 1914.

3 The common name of the female statue carved by Pygmalion (from Greek mythology), which comes to life; the figure was said to be as white as milk.

life. But he was very proud of me and keenly aware of my value as the wife of an ambitious diplomatist. He treated me with courtesy, and concerned himself not at all with my private life. He knew my pride, and believed that where he had failed no man could succeed; in short, that I would never consider divorce nor elopement, nor even run the risk of less public scandals.

"I was not unhappy. I was rid of him. I had a great position and there was everything to distract my mind. I was not so interested in the inner workings of diplomacy as I was later, but the comedy of jealousy and intrigue in the diplomatic set was amusing from the first. I was very beautiful, I entertained magnificently, I was called the best-dressed woman in Paris, I was besieged by men— men who were a good deal more difficult to manage than chivalrous Americans, particularly as I was now married and the natural prey of the hunter. But it was several years before I could think of men without a shudder, little as I permitted them to suspect it. I learned to play the subtle and absorbing game of men and women as it is played to perfection in the bolder civilizations. It was all that gave vitality to the general game of society. I had no children; my establishment was run by a major domo;[1] it bore little resemblance to a home. It was the brilliant artificial existence of a great lady, young, beautiful, and wealthy, in Europe before nineteen-fourteen. Of course that phase of life was suspended in Europe during the war. All the women I knew or heard of worked as hard as I did. Whether that terrible interregnum left its indelible seal on them, or whether they have rebounded to the old life, where conditions are less agonizing than in Vienna, I do not know."

She paused a moment, and Clavering unconsciously braced himself. Her initial revelation had left the deeper and more personal part of him stunned, and he was listening to her with a certain detachment. So far she had revealed little that Dinwiddie had not told him already, and as he knew that this brief recapitulation of her earlier life was not prompted by vanity, he could only wonder if it were the suggestive preface to that secret volume at which Dinwiddie had hinted more than once.

As she continued silent, he got suddenly to his feet. "I'll walk up and down a bit, if you don't mind," he muttered. "I'm rather— ah—getting rather cramped."

"Do," she said indifferently.

"Please go on. I am deeply interested."

She continued in a particularly level voice while he strode unevenly up and down: "Of course the time came when ugly

---

1 Concierge.

memories faded, my buoyant youth asserted itself and I wanted love. And when a woman feels a crying need to love as well as to be loved, her whole being a peremptory demand, unsatisfied romance quickening, she is not long finding the man. I had many to choose from. I made my choice and was happy for a time. Although I had been brought up in the severest respectability—just recall Jane Oglethorpe, Mrs. Vane, Mrs. Ruyler, and you will be able to reconstruct the atmosphere—several of the women I had known as a girl had lovers, it seemed to me that American women came to Europe for no other purpose, and I was now living at the fountain-head of polite license. Not that I made any apologies to myself. I should have taken a lover if I had wanted one had virtue been the fashion. And the contract with my husband had been dissolved by mutual consent. The only thing that rebelled was my pride. I hated stepping down from my pedestal."

Clavering gave a short barking laugh. "Your arrogance is the most magnificent thing about you, and that is saying more than I could otherwise express. I'll fortify myself before you proceed further, if you will permit." He poured himself out a drink, and returned to his chair with the glass in his hand. "Pray go on."

She had not turned her head and continued to look into the fire. She might have been posing to a sculptor for a bust that would hardly look more like marble when finished.

"I soon discovered that I had not found happiness. Men want. They rarely love. I realized that I had demanded in love far more than passion, and I received nothing else.

"I am not going to tell you how many lovers I have had. It is none of your business——"

"Ah!" Clavering, staring at her, had forgotten his first shock, everything but her living presence; forgotten also that he had once apprehended something of the sort, then dismissed it from his mind. He spilt the whiskey over the arm of the chair, then sprang to his feet and began to pace the room once more.

She went on calmly: "Disappointment does not mean the end of seeking.... They gave me little that I wanted. They were clever and adroit enough in the prelude. They knew how to create the illusion that in them alone could be found the fulfillment of all aspiration and desire. No doubt they satisfied many women, but they could not satisfy me. They gave me little I did not find in the mere society of the many brilliant and accomplished men with whom I was surrounded. I had a rapacious mind, and there was ample satisfaction for it in the men who haunted my salon and were constantly to be met elsewhere. European men are *instruits*.[1] They are interested in every vital subject, intellectual and political, despite the itch of amor, their deliberate cult of sex. They like to talk. Conversation is an art. My mind was never uncompanioned. But that deeper spiritual rapacity, one offspring of passion as it may be, they could not satisfy; for love with them is always too confused with animalism and is desiccated in the art of love-making. Fidelity is a virtue relegated to the bourgeois——"

"What about Englishmen?" demanded Clavering sarcastically. "I thought they were bad artists but real lovers."

"I know little of Englishmen. Zattiany was never appointed to St. James's,[2] and although, of course, I met many of them in the service on the continent, and even visited London several times, it must have happened that I was interested in some one else or in a state of profound reaction from love at the time—at least so I infer. It is a long while ago. I remember only the fact.

"Those whom I tried to love would soon have tired of me had I not played the game as adroitly as themselves, and if I had permitted them to feel sure of me. The last thing any of them wanted was depth of feeling, tragic passion.... My most desperate affair was my last—after a long interval.... I was in my early forties. I had thought myself too utterly disillusioned ever to imagine myself in love again. Men are gross and ridiculous creatures in the main, and aside from my personal disappointments, I thought it was time for that chapter of my life to finish; I was amusing myself with diplomatic intrigue. I was in the Balkans at the time, that breeding ground of war microbes, and I was interested in a very delicate situation in which I played a certain part.[3]

"The awakening was violent. He was an Austrian, with an important place in the Government; he came to Belgrade on a private mission. He was a very great person in many ways, and I think I really loved him, for he seemed to me entirely worthy of it. He certainly was mad enough about me for a time—for a year, to be exact. When he returned to Vienna it was not difficult for me to find an excuse to go also. Although Zattiany was a Hungarian, he never visited his Hungarian estates except for the boar hunting, and spent his time when on leave, or between appointments, in

---

1 French for "educated," implying "knowledgeable."

2 I.e., was never accredited with ambassadorial status in the United Kingdom by appointment to the Court of Saint James's (named after the most senior royal palace in the United Kingdom).

3 The term "microbes" was used to refer to microorganisms.

Vienna, where he had inherited a palace—I must tell you that the city residence of a nobleman in the Dual Empire was always called a palace, however much it might look like a house.

"I shall always remember this man with a certain pleasure and respect, for he is the only man who ever made me suffer. A woman forgets the lovers she has dismissed as quickly as possible. Their memory is hateful to her, like the memory of all mistakes. But this man made me suffer horribly. (He married a young girl, out of duty to his House, and unexpectedly fell in love with her.) Therefore, although I recovered, and completely, still do I sometimes dwell with a certain cynical pleasure on the memory of him——"

"Have you never seen him since?" asked Clavering sharply. He had returned to his chair. "How long ago was that?"

"Quite sixteen years ago. I did not visit Vienna again for several years; in fact, not until after my husband's death, when I returned there to live. But by that time I had lost both youth and beauty. His wife had died, but left him an heir, and he showed no disposition to marry again; certainly he was as indifferent to me as I to him. We often met, and as he respected my mind and my knowledge of European affairs, we talked politics together, and he sometimes asked my advice.

"But to go back. After that was over I determined to put love definitely out of my life. I believed then and finally that I had not the gift of inspiring love; nor would I ever risk humiliation and suffering again. I played the great game of life and politics. I was still beautiful—for a few years—I had an increasingly great position, all the advantages, obvious and subtle, that money could procure. My maid was very clever. My gowns, as time went on, were of a magnificent simplicity; all frou-frous were renounced. I had no mind to invite the valuation I heard applied to certain American women in Paris: 'elderly and dressy.'"

Clavering laughed for the first time. "I wonder you ever made a mistake of any sort. I also wonder if you are a type as well as an individual? I have, I think, followed intelligently your psychological involutions and convolutions so far. I am only hoping you will not get beyond my depth. What was your attitude toward your past mistakes—beyond what you have told me? Did you suffer remorse, as I am told women do when they either voluntarily renounce or are permitted to sin no more?"

"I neither regarded them as mistakes nor did I suffer remorse. Every human being makes what are called mistakes and those happened to be mine. Therefore I dismissed them to the limbo of the inevitable.... As your world, I am told, looks upon you as the coming dramatist, it may appeal to your imagination to visualize that secret and vital and dramatic undercurrent of what was on the surface a proud and splendid life.... Or, if there are regrets, it is for the weight of memories, the completeness of disillusion, the slaying of mental youth—which cannot survive brutal facts.

"I think that for women of my type—what may be called the intellectual siren—the lover phase is inevitable. We are goaded not only by the imperious demands of womanhood and the hope of the perfect companion, but by curiosity, love of adventure, ennui; possibly some more obscure complex—vengeance on the husband who has wrecked our first illusions—on Life itself. Bringing-up, family and social traditions, have nothing to do with it. Only opportunity counts. Moreover, we are not the product of our immediate forebears, but of a thousand thousand unknown ancestors...."

"God! True enough!"

"Unfortunately, these women who have wasted so much time on love never realize the tragic futility until Time himself disposes of temptation, and then it is too late for anything but regrets of another sort. The war may have solved the problem for many a desperate spirit.

"My own case has assumed an entirely different complexion. With my youth restored I have the world at my feet once more, but safeguarded by the wisdom of experience—in so far as a mortal ever may be. The bare idea of that old game of prowling sex fills me with ennui and disgust. The body may be young again, but my mind, reënergized though it is, is packed with memories, a very Book of Life. When I found that my beauty was restored I thought of nothing less than returning to the conquest of men in the old manner, although quite aware of its powerful aid in the work I have made up my mind to do in Austria. Of late, of course, I have thought of little else but what this recrudescence of my youth means to you and to myself. But—please do not interrupt—this I shall not discuss with you again until Monday—if then.

"But once more I wish to impress you with the fact that I indulge in nothing so futile as regrets for my 'past.' 'Sack-cloth and ashes' provokes nothing but a smile from women of my type and class. Moreover, I believe that my education would not be complete without that experience—*mine*, understand. I am not speaking for women of other temperaments, opportunities, of less intellect, of humbler character, weaker will.... And if I had persisted in virtue at that time I should probably make a fool of myself today, an even more complete fool than women do when they feel youth slipping but still are able with the aid of art and arts to fascinate younger men.

"That almost standardized chapter I renounced peremptorily. My pride was too great to permit me to be foolish even in the privacy of my mind over men half my age. Nor did I make any of the usual frantic attempts to keep looking young. I had seen too much of that, laughed at it too often. Nevertheless, I hated the approach of age, the decay of beauty, the death of magnetism, as bitterly as the silliest woman I had ever met.

"Some women merely fade: lose their complexions, the brightness of their eyes and hair. Others grow heavy, solid; stout or flabby; the muscles of the face and neck loosen and sag, the features alter. I seemed slowly to dry up—wither. There was no flesh to hang or loose skin to wrinkle, but it seemed to me that I had ten thousand lines. I thought it a horrid fate. I could not know that Nature, meaning to be cruel, had given me the best chance for the renewal of the appearance as well as the fact of youth.

"I suppose all this seems trivial to you—this mourning over lost youth——"

"Not at all. It must have been hell to a woman like you. As for women in general—they may make more fuss about it, but I fancy they hate it less than men."

"Yes, men are vainer than women," said Madame Zattiany indifferently. "But I have yet to waste any sympathy on men....

"I suppose I only fully realized that my youth, my beauty, my magnetic charm, had gone when men ceased to make violent love to me. They still paid court, for I was a very important person, my great prestige was a sort of halo, and I had never neglected my mind. There was nothing of significance I had not read during all these years. I was as profoundly interested in the great political currents of Europe, seen and unseen, as any man—or as any intelligent woman of European society. Moreover, I had the art of life down to a fine point, and I had not forgotten that even in friendship men are drawn to the subtle woman who knows how to envelop herself in a certain mystery. And European men are always eager to talk with an accomplished woman, even if she has no longer the power to stir their facile passions.

"When I realized that my sex power had left me I adopted an entirely new set of tactics—never would I provoke a cynical smile on the faces I once had the power to distort! With no evidence of regret for my lost enchantment I remained merely the alert and always interested woman of the world, to whom men, if sufficiently entertaining, were welcome companions for the moment, nothing more. I cemented many friendships, I cultivated a cynical philosophy—for my own private succor—and although, for a time, there were moments of bewildered groping and of intense rebellion, or a sudden and hideous sense of inferiority, I twisted the necks of those noxious weeds thrusting themselves upward into my consciousness and threatening to strangle it, and trampled them under the heel of my will. It was by no means the least happy interval of my life, for I was very healthy, I took a great deal of outdoor exercise, and there was a sense of freedom I never had experienced before. Love is slavery, and I was no longer a slave.

"After my husband's death, as I told you, I opened the Zattiany palace in Vienna once more (my nephew and his wife preferred Paris, and I leased it from them), expecting to follow the life I had mapped out, until I was too old for interests of any sort. I had a brilliant salon and I was something of a political power. Of course, I knew that the war was coming long before hatreds and ambitions reached their climax, and advised this man of whom I have spoken, Mathilde Loyos, and other friends, to invest large sums of money in the United States. Judge Trent arranged the trusteeship in each case——"

"Where is this man?"

"I do not know. He went down with the old régime, of course, and would be a pauper but for these American investments and a small amount in Switzerland. He has occupied no position in the new Government, although he was a Liberal in politics. What he is doing I have no idea. I have not seen him for years."

"Well—go on."

"It was only when I became aware of a growing mental lassitude, a constant sense of effort in talking everlastingly on subjects that called for constant alertness and often reorientation, that I was really aghast and began to look toward the future not only with a sense of helplessness but of intolerable weariness. I used to feel an inclination to turn my head away with an actual physical gesture when concentration was imperative. I thought that my condition was psychological, that I had lived too much and too hard, that my memory was over-burdened and my sense of the futility and meaninglessness of life too overwhelming. But I know now that the condition was physical, the result of the degeneration of certain cells.

"I spent the summer alone on my estate in Hungary, and when it was over I determined to close the palace in Vienna and remain in the country. I could not go back to that restless high-pitched life, with its ceaseless gaiety on the one hand and its feverish politics and portentous rumblings on the other. My tired mind rebelled. And the long strain had told on my health.

"I lived an almost completely outdoor life, riding, walking, swimming in the lake, hunting, but careful not to overtax my returning strength. I was not in love with life, far from it! But I had no intention of adding invalidism to my other disintegrations. In the evening I played cards with my secretary or practised at the piano, with some revival of my old interest in music. I read little, even in the newspapers. I was become, save perhaps for my music, an automaton. But, although I did not improve in appearance, my health was completely restored, and when the war came I was in perfect condition for the arduous task I immediately undertook. Moreover, my mind, torpid for a year, was free and refreshed for those practical details it must grapple with at once. I turned the Zattiany palace in Buda Pesth into a hospital. And then for four years I was again an automaton, but this time a necessary and useful one. When I thought about myself at all, it seemed to me that this selfless and strenuous interval was the final severance from my old life. If Society in Europe today were miraculously restored to its pre-war brilliancy—indifferent to little but excitement and pleasure—there would be nothing in it for me.

"Now I come to the miracle." And while she recapitulated what she had told the women at Mrs. Oglethorpe's luncheon, Clavering listened without chaos in his accompanying thoughts. "Certainly, man's span is too brief now," she concluded. "He withers and dies at an age when, if he has lived sanely—and when a man abuses his natural functions he generally dies before old age, anyhow—he is beginning to see life as a whole, with that detachment that comes when his personal hold on life and affairs is relaxing, when he has realized his mistakes, and has attained a mental and moral orientation which could be of inestimable service to his fellow men, and to civilization in general. What you call crankiness in old people, so trying to the younger generations, does not arise from natural hatefulness of disposition and a released congenital selfishness, but from atrophying glands, and, no doubt, a subtle rebellion against nature for consigning men to ineptitude when they should be entering upon their best period of usefulness, and philosophical as well as active enjoyment of life.

"Science has defeated nature at many points. The isolation of germs, the discovery of toxins and serums, the triumph over diseases that once wasted whole nations and brought about the fall of empires, the arrest of infant mortality, the marvels of vivisection and surgery—the list is endless. It is entirely logical, and no more marvellous, that science should be able to arrest senescence, put back the clock. The wonder is that it has not been done before."

She rose, still looking down at the fire, which Clavering had replenished twice. "I am going now. And I have no fear that you will not keep your promise! But remember this when thinking it over: I do not merely *look* young again, *I am* young. I am not the years I have passed in this world, I am the age of the rejuvenated glands in my body. Some day we shall have the proverb: 'A man is as old as his endocrines.' Of course I cannot have children. The treatment is identical with that for sterilization. This consideration may influence you. I shall use no arguments nor seductions. You will have decided upon all that before we meet again. Good night." And she was gone.

XXX

It seemed to Clavering that he had run the gamut of the emotions while listening to that brief biography, so sterilely told, but there had also been times when he had felt as if suspended in a void even while visited by flashes of acute consciousness that he was being called upon to know himself for the first time in his life. And in such fashion as no man had ever been called upon to know himself before.

There was no precedent in life or in fiction to guide him, and he had realized with a sensation of panic even while she talked that it was doubtful if any one had ever understood himself since the dawn of time. Man had certain standards, fixed beliefs, ideals, above all, habits—how often they scattered to the winds under some unheralded or teratogenic[1] stress. He had seen it more than once, and not only in war. Every man had at least two personalities that he was aware of, and he dimly guessed at others. Some were frank enough to admit that they had not an idea what they would do in a totally unfamiliar situation. Clavering had sometimes emblemized man and his personalities with the old game of the ivory egg. A twist and the outer egg revealed an inner. Another and one beheld a third. And so on to the inner unmanipulatable sphere, which might stand for the always inscrutable soul. Like all intelligent men, he had a fair knowledge of these two outer layers of personality, and he had sometimes had a flashing glimpse of others, too elusive to seize and put under the microscopic eye of the mind.

---

1   Substance that is disruptive to the growth of an embryo.

What did he know of himself? He asked the question again as he sat in his own deep chair in the early morning hours. The heat in the hotel had been turned off and he had lit the gas logs in the grate—symbol of the artificialities of civilization that had played their insidious rôle in man's outer and more familiar personality. Perhaps they struck deeper. Habit more often than not dominated original impulse.

His own room, where he was nearly always alone, with its warm red curtains and rug, the low bookcases built under his direction and filled with his favorite books, the refectory table and other pieces of dark old English oak that he had brought from home, and several family portraits on the wall, restored his equilibrium and his brain was abnormally clear. He wondered if he ever would sleep again. Better think it over now.

Mary Zattiany as she talked had never changed her expression. She might have been some ancient oracle reciting her credo, and she seemed to have narcotized that magnetic current that had always vibrated between them. Nevertheless, he had been fully aware that she felt like nothing less than an oracle or the marble bust she looked, and that her soul was racked and possibly fainting, but mastered by her formidable will.

Formidable. Did that word best express her? Was she one of the superwomen who could find no mate on earth and must look for her god on another star? He certainly was no superman himself to breathe on her plane and mate that incarnate will. Had she any human weakness? Even that subterranean sex-life in her past had not been due to weakness. She was far too arrogant for that. Life had been her foot-stool. She had kicked it about contemptuously. Even her readjustments had been the dictates of her imperious will. And her pride! She was a female Lucifer in pride.

No doubt the men she had dismissed had been secretly relieved; stung for the only time in their lives perhaps, with a sense of inferiority. It must have been like receiving the casual favors of a queen on her throne. Well, she had got it in the neck once; there was some satisfaction in that. He wished he knew the man's name. He'd hunt him up and thank him in behalf of his sex.

For an hour he excoriated her, hated her, feared her, dissociating her from the vast army of womanhood, but congratulating himself upon having known her. She was a unique if crucifying study.

With restored youth superimposed upon that exhaustive knowledge of life—every phase of it that counted in her calculations—the rejuvenation of all her great natural endowments, she'd probably go back and rule Europe! What use could she possibly have for any man?

He made himself a cup of coffee over his electric stove, turned off the malodorous gas, which affected his head, stood out on his balcony for a moment, then lit his pipe and felt in a more mellow mood.

After all, she had suffered as only a woman so liberally endowed could suffer, and over a long period of years. She had known despair and humiliation and bewilderment, lethargic hopelessness, and finally a complete sacrifice of self. His imagination, in spite of his rebellious soul, had furnished the background for that bald recital.

And she must have an indomitable soul, some inner super-fine spiritual essence, with which arrogance and even pride had less to do than she imagined. Otherwise, after the life she had led, she would either have become an imperious uncomfortable old woman or one of those faltering non-entities crowded into the backwaters of life by a generation which inspires them with nothing but timidity and disapproval. Towering individualities often go down to defeat in old age.

And nothing could alter the fact that she was the most beautiful and the most wholly desirable woman he had ever known, the one woman who had focussed every aspiration of his mind, his soul, and his body. He knew he must ask himself the inevitable question and face it without blinking. Was he appalled by her real age; could he ever get away from the indubious fact that whatever miracle science may have effected, her literal age was verging on sixty? If she were not an old woman she had been one. That beautiful body had withered, undesired of all men, that perfect face had been the battered mirror of an aged ego. He did not ask himself if the metamorphosis would last, if the shell might not wither again tomorrow. He was abreast of the important scientific discoveries of his day and was not at all astonished that the problem of senescence should be solved. It was no more remarkable than wireless, the Röntgen Ray, the properties of radium, or any one of the beneficent contributions of science to the well-being of mankind that were now too familiar for discussion. He had heard a good deal of this particular discovery as applied to men. No doubt Dinwiddie and Osborne would soon be appearing as gay young sparks[1] on her doorstep. It might be the greatest discovery of all time, but it certainly would work both ways. While its economic value might

---

1 Suitors.

be indisputable, and even, as she had suggested, its spiritual, it would be hard on the merely young. The mutual hatreds of capital and labor would sink into insignificance before the antagonism between authentic youth and age inverted. On the other hand it might mean the millennium. The threat of overpopulation—for man's architectonic[1] powers were restored if not woman's; to say nothing of his prolonged sojourn—would at last rouse the lawmakers to the imperious necessity of eugenics, birth control, sterilization of the unfit, and the expulsion of undesirable races.[2] It might even stimulate youth to a higher level than satisfied it at present. Human nature might attain perfection.

However, he was in no mood for abstract speculation. His own problem was absorbing enough.

He might as well itemize the questions he had to face and examine them one by one, and dispassionately. He would never feel more emotionless than now; and that mental state was very rare that enabled a man to think clearly and see further than a yard ahead of him.

Her real age? Could he ever forget it? Should he not always see the old face under the new mask, as the X-Rays revealed man's hideous interior under its merciful covering of flesh? But he knew that one of the most beneficent gifts bestowed upon mankind is the talent for forgetting. Particularly when one object has been displaced by another. Reiteration dulls the memory. He might say to himself every hour in the day that she was sixty not thirty and the phrase would soon become as meaningless as absent-minded replies to remarks about the weather.

And he doubted if any man could look at Mary Zattiany for three consecutive minutes and recall that she had ever been old, or imagine that she ever could be old again. However prone man may be to dream, he is, unless one of the visionaries, dominated by the present. What he wants he wants now and he wants what he sees, not what may be lurking in the future. That is the secret of the early and often imprudent marriage—the urge of the race. And if a man is not deterred by mere financial considerations, still less is he troubled by visions of what his inamorata[3] will look like thirty years hence or what she might have looked like had disease pre-

---

1 Generative.

2 These arguments suggest why eugenicists embraced rejuvenation treatments, for they saw them as allowing the "best" examples of the human race to work for a longer and more productive swath of time.

3 Female lover.

maturely withered her. He sees what he sees and if he is satisfied at all he is as completely satisfied as a man may be.

He made no doubt that Mary Zattiany would have, if she chose, as many suitors among men of his own age as among her former contemporaries. They would discuss the phenomenon furiously, joke about it, try to imagine her as she had been, back water, return out of curiosity, hesitate, speculate—and then forget it.

No one would forget it sooner than himself. He had no doubt whatever that when he went to her house tomorrow afternoon he would remember as long as she kept him waiting and no longer. So that was that.

Did he want children? They charmed him—sometimes—but he had never been conscious of any desire for a brood of his own. He knew that many men felt an even profounder need of offspring than women. Man's ego is more strident, the desire to perpetuate itself more insistent, his foresight is more extended. Moreover, however subconsciously, his sense of duty to the race is stronger.... But he doubted if any man would weigh the repetition of his ego against his ego's demand to mate with a woman like Mary Zattiany. He certainly would not. That was final.

What was it she demanded in love, that she had sought so ardently and ever missed? Could he give it to her? Was she merely glamored once more, caught up again in the delusions of youth, with her revivified brain and reawakened senses, and this time only because the man was of a type novel in her cognizance of men? Useless to plead the urge of the race in her case.... Nevertheless, many women, denied the power of reproduction fell as mistakenly in love as the most fertile of their sisters. But hardly a woman of Mary Zattiany's exhaustive experience! She certainly should know her own mind. Her instincts by this time must be compounded of technical knowledge, not the groping inherited flashes playing about the shallow soil of youth.... If her instincts had centred on him there must be some deeper meaning than passion or even intellectual homology. After all, their conversations, if vital, had been few in number.

Perhaps she had found, with her mind's trained antennae, some one of those hidden layers of personality which she alone could reveal to himself. What was it? She wanted far more than love-making and mental correspondence. What was it? He wished he knew. Tenderness? He could give her that in full measure. Sentiment? He was no sentimentalist, but he believed that he possessed the finer quality. Fidelity? That was not worth consideration. Appreciation of the deepest and best in her, sympathetic understanding of all her mistakes and of all that she had suffered? She knew the answer as well as he did. The ability to meet her in many moods, never to weary her with monotony? He was a man of many moods himself. What had saved him from early matrimony was a certain monotony in women, the cleverest of them.

But there must be something beyond, some subtle spiritual demand, developed throughout nearly twice as many years as he had dwelt on earth; born not only of an aspiring soul and terrible disenchantments, but of a wisdom that only years of deep and living experience, no mere intelligence, however brilliant, could hope to assemble. He was thirty-four. There was no possible question that at fifty-eight, if he lived sanely, and his intellectual faculties had progressed unimpaired, he would look back upon thirty-four as the nonage[1] of life—when the future was a misty abyss of wisdom whose brink he had barely trod. She herself was an abyss of wisdom. How in God's name could he ever cross it? Her body might be young again, but never her mind. Never her mind! And then he had a flash of insight. Perhaps he alone could rejuvenate that mind.

Certainly he could make her forget. Men and women would be aged at thirty, but for this beneficent gift of forgetting.... He could make the present vivid enough.

He explored every nook of those personalities of his, determined to discover if he felt any sense of inferiority to this woman who knew so much more, had lived and thought and felt so much more, than himself—whom he still visioned on a plane above and apart. No woman was ever more erudite in the most brilliant and informing declensions of life, whatever the disenchantments, and for thirty years she had known in varying degrees of intimacy the ablest and most distinguished men in Europe. She had been at no pains to conceal her opinion of their intellectual superiority over American men....

He concluded dispassionately that he never could feel inferior to any woman. Women might arrest the attention of the world with their talents, change laws and wring a better deal out of life than man had accorded them in the past, but whatever their gifts and whatever their achievements they always had been and always would be, through their physical disabilities, their lack of ratiocination,[2] of constructive ability on the grand scale, the inferiors of men. The rare exceptions but proved the rule, and no doubt they had been cast in one mould and finished in another.

---

1 Period of immaturity.
2 Process of logical thinking.

In sheer masculine arrogance he was more than her match. Moreover, there were other ways of keeping a woman subject.

Did he love her? Comprehensively and utterly? Clear thinking fled with the last of his doubts.... And when a man detaches himself from the gross material surface of life and wings to the realm of the imagination, where he glimpses immortality, what matter the penalty? Any penalty? Few had the thrice blessed opportunity. If he were one of the chosen, the very demi-gods, jeering at mortals, would hate him.

And then abruptly he fell asleep.

XXXI

He went direct from the office that evening to Mrs. Oglethorpe's house in Gramercy Park. During the morning he had received the following note from her, and he had puzzled over it at intervals ever since.

"Dear Lee:

"Will you dine alone with an old woman tonight—a rather bewildered and upset old woman? I suppose to the young nothing is too new and strange for readjustment, but I have hardly known where I am these last few days. You are the only friend I care to talk to on the subject, for you always understand. I am probably older than your mother and I look old enough to be your grandmother, but you are the only person living with whom I ever feel inclined to lay aside all reserve. Old men are fossils and young men regard me as an ancient wreck preserved by family traditions. As for women I hate them and always did. Do come and dine with a lonely puzzled old woman unless you have an engagement impossible to break. Don't bother to dress.

"Your affectionate old friend,
"JANE OGLETHORPE."

"What's up?" Clavering had thought as he finished it. "Mary or Janet?"

It was an extraordinary letter to receive from Mrs. Oglethorpe, the most fearsome old woman in New York. To Clavering she had always shown the softer side of her nature and he knew her perhaps better, or at all events more intimately, than any of her old friends, for she had not treated him as a negligible junior even when he arrived in New York at the tender age of twenty-two. His ingenuous precocity had amused her and she had discovered a keen interest in the newspaper world of whose existence she had hardly been aware; no interviewer had ever dared approach her; and as he grew older, developing rapidly and more and more unlike her sons and her sons' friends, they had fallen into an easy pallish[1] intimacy, were frank to rudeness, quarrelled furiously, but fed each other's wisdom and were deeply attached. During the war she had knitted him enough socks and sweaters to supply half his regiment; and when he had left the hospital after a serious attack of influenza it had been for the house in Gramercy Park, where he could have remained indefinitely had he wished.

But in all the years of their intimacy never before had she "broken," given a hint that she felt the long generation between them. He found her more interesting in talk than any girl, except when he was briefly in love, and her absence of vanity, her contempt for sentiment in any of its forms, filled him with a blessed sense of security as he spent hours stretched out on the sofa in her upstairs sitting-room, smoking and discussing the universe. She was not an intellectual woman, but she was sharp and shrewd, a monument of common sense and worldly wisdom. It would be as easy to hoodwink her as the disembodied Minerva, and it was doubtful if any one made even a tentative attempt. Clavering wondered which of those inner secret personalities was to be revealed tonight.

As he stood in the drawing-room waiting for her to come down he examined for the first time in many years the full-length picture of her painted shortly before her marriage to James Oglethorpe. She was even taller than Mary Zattiany and in the portrait her waist was round and disconcertingly small to the modern therapeutic eye. But the whole effect of the figure was superb and dashing, the poise of the head was almost defiant, and the hands were long, slender, and very white against the crimson satin of her gown. She looked as if about to lead a charge of cavalry, although, oddly enough, her full sensuous mouth with its slightly protruding lower lip was pouting. Beautiful she had never been; the large bony structure of her face was too uncoverable, her eyes too sharp and sardonic; but handsome certainly, and, no doubt, for many years after she had stood for this portrait in the full insolence of her young womanhood. She retained not a trace of that handsomeness today. Her hands were skinny, large-veined, discolored by moth patches, and her large aquiline nose rose from her sunken cheeks like the beak of an old eagle—an indomitable old eagle.

---

1 Chummy.

Many women of sixty-eight had worn far better, but looks need care, spurred by vanity, and she had a profound contempt for both. No doubt if she had made a few of the well-known feminine concessions [she] would have looked at least ten years younger than her age, for she had never had a day's illness: eight lyings-in were not, in her case, to be counted as exceptions.[1] No doubt, thought Clavering, as he turned to greet her, she had thought it quite enough to be imposing.

She certainly looked imposing tonight in spite of her old-fashioned corsets and her iron-gray hair arranged in flat rolls and puffs on the precise top of her head, for although flesh had accumulated lumpily on her back, her shoulders were still unbowed, her head as haughtily poised as in her youth, and the long black velvet gown with yellow old point about the square neck (the neck itself covered, like the throat, with net), and falling over her hands, became her style if not the times.

"Well, Lee!" she said drily. "I suppose when you got my note you thought I had gone bug-house, as my fastidious granddaughter Janet would express it. But that is the way I felt and that is the way I feel at the present moment."

"Dear Lady Jane! Whatever it is, here I am to command, as you see. There is no engagement I wouldn't have broken——"

"You are a perfect dear, and if I were forty years younger I should marry you. However, we'll come to that later. I want to talk to you about that damnable little Janet first—we'll have to go in now."

When they were seated at a small table at one end of the immense dining-room she turned to the butler and said sharply:

"Get out, Hawkins, and stay out except when we can't get on without you." And Hawkins, whom a cataclysm would not have ruffled after forty-five years in Mrs. Oglethorpe's service, vanished.

"Jim said he had a talk with you about Janet, and that you advised him to spank her," she said. "Well, he did."

"What?" Clavering gave a delighted grin. "I never believed he'd do it."

"Nor I. Thought his will had grown as flabby as his body. But when she stood up to him and with a cool insolence, which she may or may not have inherited from me, or which may be merely part and parcel of the new manner, and flung in his face a good deal more than he knew already, and asked him what he was going

---

1 A woman's "lying in" was a period (between two weeks and two months) of bed rest for pregnant women who were about to deliver babies.

to do about it, he turned her over his knee and took a hair-brush to her."

"It must have been a tussle. I suppose she kicked and scratched?"

"She was so astonished that at first she merely ejaculated: 'Oh, by Jimminy!' Then she fought to get away and when she found she couldn't she began to blubber, exactly as she did when she was not so very much younger and was spanked about once a day. That hurt his feelings, for he's as soft as mush, and he let her go; but he locked her up in her room and there she stays until she promises to behave herself as girls did in his time. I'm afraid it won't work. She hasn't promised yet, but merely hisses at him through the keyhole. D'you understand this new breed? I'm afraid none of the rest of us do."

"I can't say I've been interested enough to try. Janet informed me that they were going the pace because they couldn't hold the men any other way. But I fancy it's merely a part of the general unrest which is the usual aftermath of war. This was a very long war, and the young seem to have made up their minds that the old who permitted it are bunglers and criminals and idiots and that it is up to them to demonstrate their contempt."

"And what good do they think that will do them?" Mrs. Oglethorpe's face and inflection betrayed no sympathy with the Younger Generation.

"You don't suppose they worry their little heads with analysis, do you? Somebody started the idea and the rest followed like sheep. No doubt it had its real origin in the young men who did the fighting and saw their comrades do the dying, and all the kudus carried off by the old men who ran no risks.[1] They are very bitter. And women generally take their cues from men, little as they suspect it. However, whatever the cause, here it is, and what to do about it I've no more idea than you; but I should think it would be a good idea for Jim to take her abroad for a year."

"I don't see Jim giving up his clubs and sports, and tagging round the world after a flapper. He never took himself very seriously as a parent ... still, he is really alarmed.... Are you going to marry Marian Lawrence?"

"Do you think I'd engage myself to any one without telling you first of all?"

"Better not. Are you in love with her?"

"No."

"I'm told you were devoted to her at one time. That was one of the times when I saw little or nothing of you."

---

1 The Greek term "kudos": deserving of praise and glory.

"I've been devoted to quite a number of girls, first and last, but there's really been nothing in it on either side. I know what you're driving at. Shoot."

"Yes, Jim said he told you. Well, I've changed my mind. Janet's a little fool, perhaps worse. Not half good enough for you and would devil the life out of you before you got rid of her in self-defence. Let her hoe her own row. How about that writing person, Gora Dwight, you and Din are always talking about?"

"Never been the ghost of a flirtation. She's all intellect and ambition. I enjoy going there for I'm almost as much at home with her as I am with you."

"Ha! Harmless. I hope she's as flattered as I am. There remains Anne Goodrich. She's handsome, true to her traditions in every way—Marian Lawrence is a hussy unless I'm mistaken and I usually am not—she has talent and she has cultivated her mind. She will have a fortune and would make an admirable wife in every way for an ambitious and gifted man. More pliable than Marian, too. You're as tyrannical and conceited as all your sex and would never get along with any woman who wasn't clever enough to pretend to be submissive while twisting you round her little finger. I rather favor Anne."

Clavering was beginning to feel uneasy. What was she leading up to? Who next? But he replied with a humorous smile:

"Dearest Lady Jane! Why are you suddenly determined to marry me off? Are you anxious to get rid of me? Marriage plays the very devil with friendships."

"Only for a year or so. And I really think it is time you were settling yourself. To tell you the truth I worry about you a good deal. You're a sentimental boy at heart and chivalrous and impressionable, although I know you think you're a seasoned old rounder. Men are children, the cleverest of them, in a scheming woman's hands."

"But I don't know any scheming women and I'm really not as irresistible as you seem to think. Besides, I assure you, I have fairly keen intuitions and should run from any unprincipled female who thought it worth while to cast her nets in my direction."

"Intuitions be damned. They haven't a chance against beauty and finesse. Don't men as clever as yourself make fools of themselves over the wrong woman every day in the week? The cleverer a man is the less chance he has, for there's that much more to play on by a cleverer woman. It would be just like you to fall in love with a woman older than yourself and marry her——"

"For God's sake, Jane, cut out my fascinating self! It's a subject that bores me to tears. Fire away about Janet. How long's she been shut up? What will Jim do next? I'll do my best to persuade him to take her round the world. He'd enjoy it himself for there are clubs in every port and some kind of sport. I'll look him up tomorrow."

Mrs. Oglethorpe gave him a sharp look but surrendered. When he shouted "Jane" at her in precisely the same tone as he often exploded "Jim" to her son, she found herself suddenly in a mood to deny him nothing.

XXXII

They went up to her sitting-room to spend the rest of the evening. It was a large high room overlooking the park and furnished in massive walnut and blood-red brocade: a room as old-fashioned and ugly as its mistress but comfortable withal. On a table in one corner was an immense family Bible, very old, and recording the births, marriages, and deaths of the Van den Poeles from the time they began their American adventures in the seventeenth century. On another small table in another corner was a pile of albums, the lowest containing the first presentments of Mrs. Oglethorpe's family after the invention of calotype photography.[1] These albums recorded fashion in all its stages from 1841 down to the sport suit, exposed legs and rolled stockings of Janet Oglethorpe; a photograph her grandmother had sworn at but admitted as a curiosity.

One of the albums was devoted to the friends of Mrs. Oglethorpe's youth, and Mary Ogden occupied the place of honor. Clavering had once derived much amusement looking over these old albums and listening to Mrs. Oglethorpe's running and often sarcastic comment; but although he had recalled to mind this photograph the night Mr. Dinwiddie had been so perturbed by the stranger's resemblance to the flame of his youth, he had, himself, been so little interested in Mary Ogden that it had not occurred to him to disinter that old photograph of the eighties and examine it in detail. He turned his back squarely on it tonight, although he had a misgiving that it was not Janet who had inspired Mrs. Oglethorpe's singular note.

---

1 Early photographic process involving silver iodide, invented in 1841 by William Talbot.

On one wall was a group of daguerreotypes,[1] hideous but rare and valuable. An oil painting of James Oglethorpe, long dead, hung over the fireplace; an amiable looking gentleman with long side-whiskers sprouting out of plump cheeks, a florid complexion, and the expression of a New Yorker who never shirked his civic obligations, his chairmanships of benevolent institutions, nor his port. Opposite was another oil painting of young James taken at the age of twelve, wearing a sailor suit and the surly expression of an active boy detained within walls while other boys were shouting in the park. Beside it was a water color of Janet at the age of two, even then startlingly like her grandmother. She had been Mrs. Oglethorpe's favorite descendant until the resemblance had become too accentuated by modern divagations.

Clavering did not extend himself on the sofa tonight but drew a leather chair (built for Mr. Oglethorpe) to the small coal grate, which inadequately warmed the large room. Mrs. Oglethorpe, like many women of her generation, never indulged her backbone save in bed, and she seated herself in her own massive upright chair not too close to the fire. She had made a concession to time in the rest of the house, which was lighted by electricity, but the gas remained in her own suite, and the room was lit by faint yellow flames struggling through the ground-glass globes of four-side brackets. The light from the coals was stronger, and as it fell on her bony austere old face with its projecting beak, Clavering reflected that she needed only a broomstick. He really loved her, but a trained faculty works as impersonally as a camera.

He smoked in silence and Mrs. Oglethorpe stared into the fire. She, too, was fond of her cigar, but tonight she had shaken her head as Hawkins had offered the box, after passing the coffee. Her face no longer looked sardonic, but relaxed and sad. Clavering regarded her with uneasy sympathy. Would it be possible to divert her mind?

"Lady Jane," he began.

"I wish you would call me Jane tonight. I wouldn't feel so intolerably old."

"Of course I'll call you Jane, but you'll never be old. What skeleton have you been exhuming?" He was in for it and might as well give her a lead.

"It's Mary Ogden," she said abruptly and harshly.

---

1 Early photographs made with a process that involved mercury and silver, developed in France in 1839 by Louis Daguerre.

"Oh—I wondered how you felt about it. You certainly have been splendid——"

"What else could I do? She was the most intimate friend of my youth, the only woman I ever had any real affection for. I had already seen her and recognized her. I suppose she has told you that I went there and that she treated me like an intruding stranger. But I knew she must have some good reason for it—possibly that she was here on some secret political mission and had sworn to preserve her incognito. I knew she had been mixed up in politics more than once. I thought I was going mad when I saw her, but I never suspected the truth. The light was dim and I took for granted that some one of those beauty experts had made a mask for her, or ripped her skin off—I hardly knew what to think, so I concluded not to think about it at all, and succeeded fairly well in dismissing it from my mind. I was deeply hurt at her lack of confidence in me, but I dismissed that, too. After all it was her right. I do as I choose, why shouldn't she? And I remembered that she always did."

Here Clavering stirred uneasily.

"When she came to me here last Tuesday and told me the whole truth I felt as if I were listening to a new chapter out of the Bible, but on the whole I was rather pleased than otherwise. I had never been jealous of her when we were young, for I was married before she came out, and she was so lovely to look at that I was rather grateful to her than otherwise. After her marriage I used to meet her every few years in Europe up to some three or four years before the outbreak of the war, and it often made me feel melancholy as I saw her beauty going ... until there was nothing left but her style and her hair. But nothing else was to be expected. Time is a brute to all women.... So, while she sat here in this room so radiantly beautiful and so exquisitely and becomingly dressed, and leaning toward me with that old pleading expression I remembered so well; when she wanted something and knew exactly how to go to work to get it; and looking not a day over thirty—well, while she was here I felt young again myself and I loved her as much as ever and felt it a privilege to look at her. I arranged a luncheon promptly to meet several of her old friends and put a stop to the clacking that was going on—I had been called up eight times that morning.... I could have boxed your ears, but of course it was a natural enough thing to do, and you had no suspicion.... Well, as soon as she had gone I wrote to twelve women, giving them a bare sketch of the truth, and sent the notes off in the motor. And then—I went and looked at myself in the glass."

She paused, and Clavering rose involuntarily and put his hand on her shoulder.

"Never mind, Jane," he said awkwardly. "What does it matter? You are you and there's only one of the kind. After all it's only one more miracle of Science. You could do it yourself if you liked."

"I? Ha! With twenty-three grandchildren. I may be a fool but I'm not a damn fool, as James used to say. What good would it do me to look forty? I had some looks left at that age but with no use for them as women go. I'd have less now. But Mary was always lucky—a daughter of the gods. It's just like her damned luck to have that discovery made in her time and while she is still young enough to profit by it, besides being as free as when she was Mary Ogden. Now, God knows what devilment she'll be up to. What she wants she'll have and the devil take the consequences." She patted his hand. "Go and sit down, Lee. I've a good deal more to say."

Clavering returned to his seat with no sense of the old chair's comfort, and she went on in a moment.

"The unfairness of it as I looked at that old witch in the glass that had reflected my magnificent youth, seemed to me unendurable. I had lived a virtuous and upright life. I knew damned well she hadn't. I had done my duty by the race and my own and my husband's people, and I had brought up my sons to be honorable and self-respecting men, whatever their failings, and my daughters in the best traditions of American womanhood. They are model wives and mothers, and they have made no weak-kneed concessions to these degenerate times. They bore me but I'd rather they did that than disgrace me. Mary never had even one child, although her husband must have wanted an heir. I have lived a life of duty—duty to my family traditions, my husband, my children, my country, and to Society: she one of self-indulgence and pleasure and excitement, although I'm not belittling the work she did during the war. But noblesse oblige. What else could she do? And now, she'll be at it again. She'll have the pick of our young men—I don't know whether it's all tragic or grotesque. She'll waste no time on those men who loved her in her youth—small blame to her. Who wants to coddle old men? They've all got something the matter with 'em.... But she'll have love—love—if not here—and thank God, she's not remaining long—then elsewhere and wherever she chooses. Love! I too once took a fierce delight in making men love me. It seems a thousand years ago. What if I should try to make a man fall in love with me today? I'd be rushed off by my terrified family to a padded cell."

"Well—Jane——"

"Don't 'well Jane' me! You'd jump out of the window if I suddenly began to make eyes at you. I could rely on your manners. You wouldn't laugh until you struck the grass and then you'd be arrested for disturbing the peace. Well—don't worry. I'm not an old ass. But I'm a terribly bewildered old woman. It seems to me there has been a crashing in the air ever since she sat in that chair.... Growing old always seemed to me a natural process that no arts or dodges could interrupt, and any attempt to arrest the processes of nature was an irreverent gesture in the face of Almighty God. It was immoral and irreverent, and above all it showed a lack of humor and of sound common sense. The world, my candid grandchild tells me, laughs at the women of my generation for their old-fashioned 'cut.' But we have our code and we have the courage to live up to it. That is one reason, perhaps, why growing old has never meant anything to me but reading-spectacles, two false teeth, and weak ankles. It had seemed to me that my life had been pretty full—I never had much imagination—what with being as good a wife as ever lived—although James was a pompous bore if there ever was one—bringing eight children into the world and not making a failure of one of them, never neglecting my charities or my social duties or my establishments. As I have grown older I have often reflected upon a life well-spent, and looked forward to dying when my time came with no qualms whatever, particularly as there was precious little left for me to do except give parties for my grandchildren and blow them up occasionally. I never labored under the delusion that I had an angelic disposition or a perfect character, but I had always had, and maintained, certain standards; and, according to my lights, it seemed to me that when I arrived at the foot of the throne the Lord would say to me 'Well done, thou good and faithful servant.' The only thing I ever regretted was that I wasn't a man."

She paused and then went on in a voice that grew more raucous every moment. "That was later. It's a long time since I've admitted even to myself that there was a period—after my husband's death—when I hated growing old with the best of them. I was fifty and I found myself with complete liberty for the first time in my life; for the elder children were all married, and the younger in Europe at school. I had already begun to look upon myself as an old woman.... But I soon made the terrible discovery that the heart never grows old. I fell in love four times. They were all years younger than myself and I'd have opened one of my veins before I'd have let them find it out. Even then I had as little use for old men as old men have for old women. Whatever it may be in men, it's the young heart in women. I had no illusions. Fifty is fifty. My complexion was gone, my stomach high, and I had the face of an old war horse. But—and here is the damned trick that nature plays on us—I hoped—hoped—I dreamed—and as ardently as I ever had dreamed in my youth, when I was on the look-out for the perfect knight and before I compromised on James Oglethorpe, who was handsome before he grew those whiskers and got fat— yes, as ardently as in my youth I dreamed that these clever intelligent men would look through the old husk and see only the young heart and the wise brain—I knew that I could give them more than many a younger woman. But if beauty is only skin deep the skin is all any man wants, the best of 'em. They treated me with the most impeccable respect—for the first time in my life I hated the word—and liked my society because I was an amusing caustic old woman. Of course they drifted off, either to marry, or because I terrified them with my sharp tongue: when I loved them most and felt as if I had poison in my veins. Well, I saved my pride, at all events.

"By the time you came along I had sworn at myself once for all as an old fool, and, in any case, I would hardly have been equal to falling in love with a brat of twenty-two."

She seized the stick that always rested against her chair and thumped the floor with it. "Nevertheless," she exclaimed with savage contempt, "my heart is as young today as Mary Ogden's. That is the appalling discovery I have made this week. I'd give my immortal soul to be thirty again—or look it. Why in heaven's name did nature play us this appalling dirty trick?"

"But Jane!" He felt like tearing his hair. What was Mary Zattiany's tragedy to this? Banalities were the only refuge. "Remember that at thirty you were in love with your husband and bent on having a family——"

"I meant thirty and all I know now.... I'm not so damn sure I'd have tried to make myself think I was in love with James—who had about as much imagination as a grasshopper and the most infernal mannerisms. I'd have found out what love and life meant, that's what! And when I did I'd have sent codes and traditions to the devil."

"Oh, no, you would not. If you'd had it in you you'd have done it, anyhow. All women of your day were not virtuous—not by a long sight. I'll admit that your best possibilities have been wasted; I've always thought that. You have a terrific personality and if you were at your maturity in this traditionless era you'd be a great national figure, not a mere social power. But nature in a fit of spite launched you too soon and the cast-iron traditions were too strong for you. It was the epoch of the submerged woman."

"Mary Ogden was brought up in those same cast-iron traditions."

"Yes, but Madame Zattiany belongs to a class of women that derive less from immediate ancestors than from a legendary race of sirens—not so merely legendary, perhaps, as we think. Convention is only a flexible harness for such women and plays no part whatever in their secret lives."

"You're in love with Mary."

"*Don't* come back to me. I won't have it. For the moment I don't feel as if I had an atom of personality left, I'm so utterly absorbed in you; and I'd give my immortal soul to help you."

"Yes, I know that. I wouldn't be turning myself inside out if I didn't. I've never talked to a living soul as I've talked to you tonight and I never shall again."

She stared at him for a moment, and then she burst into a loud laugh. It was awe-inspiring, that laugh. Lucifer in hell, holding his sides at the futilities of mankind, could not have surpassed it. "What a mess! What a mess! Life! Begins nowhere, ends nowhere." She went on muttering to herself, and then, abruptly, she broke into the sarcastic speech which her friends knew best.

"Lord, Lee, I wish you could have been behind a screen at that luncheon. Thirteen old tombstones in feathers and net collars—seven or eight of 'em, anyhow—colonial profiles and lorgnettes, and all looking as if they'd been hit in the stomach. I at one end of the table looking like the Witch of Endor,[1] Mary at the other looking like one of our granddaughters and trying to be animated and intimate. I forgot my own tragedy and haw-hawed three times. She looked almost apologetic when she called us by our first names, especially when she used the diminutive. Polly Vane, who's got a head like a billiard ball and has to wear a wig for decency's sake, drew herself up twice and then relaxed with a sickly grin.... All the same I don't think Mary felt any more comfortable or liked it much better than the rest of us. Too much like reading your own epitaph on a tombstone. I thought I saw her squirm."

"How did they take it individually?" Clavering hoped she was finally diverted. "Were they jealous and resentful?"

"Some. Elinor Goodrich had always been too besottedly fond of her to mind. Others, who had been merely admirers and liked

---

1 A woman mentioned in the First Book of Samuel, 28:3, who summoned the ghost of the prophet Samuel.

her, were—well, it's too much to say they were enchanted to see Mary looking not a day over thirty, but they were able to endure it. Isabel Lawrence thought it downright immoral, and Polly Vane looked as if she had fallen into a stinking morass and only refrained from holding her nose out of consideration for her hostess. I think she feels that Mary's return is an insult to New York. Lily Tracy was painfully excited. No doubt she'll begin collecting for the Vienna poor at once and finding it necessary to go over and distribute the funds in person. Mary lost no time getting in her fine work for Vienna relief."

"But they'll all stand by her?"

"Oh, yes, she's Mary Ogden. We'd be as likely to desert New York itself because we didn't like the mayor. And she'll need us. It's the young women she'll have to look out for. My God! How they'll hate her. As for Anne Goodrich and Marian Lawrence——"

Clavering sprang to his feet. "Who's that? Jim?"

A man was running up the stairs.

"Janet," said Mrs. Oglethorpe grimly. "She's out."

XXXIII

"Don't be a flat tyre,
   Don't be a dumb-bell;
   Run from the dumb ducks,
   Run from the plumbers.
   Ha! Ha! Ha! Ha! Ha! Ha! Ha!"

Oglethorpe pounded on the door with his stick. There was a sudden hush in the room, then a wild scurry and a slamming door. He rattled the knob and, to his surprise, for he had assumed that these wild parties of his young friends were soundly barricaded, the door opened.

There were only four young men standing about a table covered with the remains of a chafing dish supper and many champagne bottles, but an excited whispering came through the partition. Young Farren was leaning against the table, his large moon-face pallid with fright. As he recognized Oglethorpe and Clavering fright was wiped out by astonishment and relief.

"Thought you were the police," he muttered. "Though they've got no business here——"

"I've come for Janet. Go into that room and bring her out at once."

"Janet ain't here. Haven't seen Janet for a week. Tried to get her on the 'phone early this afternoon and couldn't——"

"If you don't go into that room and fetch her, I will." As he started for the inner door, Farren with drunken dignity opposed his broad bulk.

"Now, Mr. Oglethorpe, you wouldn't do that. Ladies in there. Chorus girls——"

"That's a lie. Stand aside."

Farren, who was very young and very drunk, but who had a rudimentary sense of responsibility where girls of his own class were concerned, burst into tears. "You wouldn't, Mr. Oglethorpe! I swear to God Janet's not there. But—but—some of her friends are. They wouldn't want you to see them." His mood changed to righteous indignation. "What right you got breaking into a gentleman's rooms like a damned policeman? It's an outrage and if I had a gun I'd shoot you. I'd—I'd——" And then he collapsed on a chair and was very sick.

Oglethorpe turned to Clavering, who had thought it best to remain in the hall and watch other exits. "Just stay there, will you?" He turned to the three gaping youngsters. "You dare make a move and I'll knock your heads together. Just remember that you're drunk and I'm sober."

He went into the next room, and immediately saw several forms under the bed. He reached down and jerked them out by their legs. They rolled over, covering their faces and sobbing with fright. Emancipated as they were and disdainful of pre-war parents, when it came to late parties in a bachelor's rooms they exercised strategy to slip out, not defiance.

"Oh, Mr. Oglethorpe," gasped one convulsively. "Don't tell on us, p-l-e-a-s-e."

"I've no intention of telling on you. You can go to the devil in your own way for all I care. I'm after Janet——"

"She's not here——"

"That's what I'm going to find out." He opened the door of a wardrobe and another girl tumbled into his arms, shrieked, and flung herself face downward on the bed. But it was not Janet. He investigated every corner of the apartment and then returned to Clavering, slamming the door behind him.

"She's not there, Lee," he said, leaning heavily against the wall. "Where in God's name is she? I don't know where to look next. This is her particular gang. She has no other intimates that I know of. But what do I know about her, anyway?"

"You're sure she isn't hiding anywhere at home?"

"Searched the house from top to bottom."

"I suppose it isn't likely that she's gone to any of her aunts."

"Good Lord, no. She'd take a chance on mother, but never with any of the rest of the family, and she's got no money. I saw to that. D'you suppose she's roaming the streets?"

"Well, she can't roam long; legs will give out. Perhaps she's home by now or at Mrs. Oglethorpe's. Better telephone."

They went out and found a public telephone. Janet had not been seen nor heard from.

"You don't think it's going to be another Dorothy Arnold[1] case?" gasped Oglethorpe, who seemed completely unnerved.

"Good Heavens no, Jim! And she's able to take care of herself. Nobody better. She'll give you a scare and then turn up—with her thumb at her nose, likely. Better come up to my rooms and have a drink."

"Orright. I can't go home and I don't want to be alone anywhere. I'd go out of my senses. Anything might happen to her, and I shan't call in the police until the last minute. Filthy scandal."

"Police? Certainly not. And as Janet is cold sober, be sure she'll come to no harm."

A few moments later they were in the lift ascending to Clavering's rooms. "Hullo!" he said, as he opened the door of his little hall. "The fool maid has left the light on," and, as they entered the living-room, "what the devil—" Cigarette smoke hung in the air.

There was a wild shriek from a corner of the room, a slim girl leapt across the intervening space like a panther, and flinging herself upon Oglethorpe, beat his chest with her fists.

"You damned old plumber, you old dumb-duck!" shrieked his little daughter. "What did you come here and spoil everything for? He'd have had to marry me tomorrow if you'd minded your own business. I'll claw your eyes out." But her hands were imprisoned in her father's hard fists, and she turned and spat at the petrified Clavering. "I hate you! I hate you! But I'm going to marry you all the same. One way or another I'll get you. I meant to wait awhile; for I hadn't had fun enough yet, and I'd have precious little with you, you old flat tyre. But when I heard that old Zattiany

---

1 A fashionable young woman who disappeared in New York City in 1910 and was never found. On the day of her disappearance, she bought candy and met a friend at a bookstore, then planned to walk home through Central Park. Arnold's parents did not contact the police for six weeks, fearing that their daughter had eloped (which she had done once before). There were many supposed sightings of Dorothy Arnold through the 1920s.

It took a lot of self possession and grit for Zattiany (Corinne Griffith) and Clavering (Conway Tearle) to hide their feelings when she alighted to go to the ship which was to return her to Europe.

(Screen version of "The Black Oxen.")

woman'd got hold of you—and then locked up and not able to do a thing—I thought I'd go mad. I dropped my diamond bracelet out of the window and one of the servants let me out—I won't tell which. You've been seen coming out of her house at all hours, but she's a thousand years old and nobody cares what she does, but I intended to rouse this whole house and I'd have been so compromised you'd have had to marry me. You're a gentleman if you are a damned old left-over, and you're a friend of granny's and dad's. I'd have had you tied up so tight you'd have toddled straight down to the City Hall."

Clavering stared at her, wondering how women felt when they were going to have hysterics. What a night! And this girl's resemblance to her grandmother was uncanny. He could see the Jane Oglethorpe of the portrait in just such a tantrum. And he had thought he knew both of them. He wanted to burst into wild laughter, but the girl was tragic in spite of her silly plot and he merely continued to regard her stonily.

"How did you get in?" he asked. "That's not easy in this house."

"I just got in the lift and told the boy I was your sister just arrived from the South and he let me in with the pass key. He took me for sixteen and said that as you weren't one for chickens he'd chance it."

"He'll get the sack in the morning."

"I don't care what happens to him." Suddenly she burst into tears, her face working like a baby's, and flung herself into her father's arms.

"Make him marry me, daddy. Make him! I want him. I want him."

Oglethorpe put his arms about her, but his sympathies were equally divided, and he understood men far better than he did young girls. "You wouldn't want to marry a man who doesn't love you," he said soothingly. "Where's your pride?"

"Who cares a damn about pride? I want him and that's all there is to it." She whirled round again. "Do you think you're in love with that rejuvenated old dame who's granny's age if she's a day? She's hypnotized you, that's what. It isn't natural. It isn't. It isn't."

"I certainly shall marry Madame Zattiany if she will have me."

"O-h-h." Tears dried. She showed her teeth like a treed cat. Her eyes blazed again and she would have precipitated herself upon him, but her father held her fast. "Oh! Oh! Oh! It can't be. It can't be. It's as unnatural as if you married granny. It isn't fair. How dare she come here with her whitewash and sneak young girls' lovers away from them?"

"Really, Janet."

"Oh, I know, you thought you didn't care for me, but you always did, and I'd have got you in time. I knew there was no chance for Marian and Anne; they're old maids, and I'm young—young. If I'd cut out the fun and concentrated on you I'd have got you. I wish I had! I wish I had! But you were such an old flat tyre I thought you were safe."

"What in heaven's name makes you think you're in love with me?" exploded Clavering. "Your opinion of me is anything but complimentary, and I'm everything your chosen companions are not. You don't want me any more than I want you. You've simply been playing some fool game with yourself——"

"It's not! It's not! It's the real thing. I've been in love with you since I was six. Ask daddy. Daddy, didn't I always say I was going to marry him?"

"Yes, when you were little more of a baby than you are now. Can't you imagine how ashamed you'll be of such an undignified performance as this?"

"I ashamed? Not much. I always intend to do just as I please and damn the consequences."

"A fine wife you'd make for Lee or any other man."

"I'd make him the best wife in the world. I'd do everything he told me. No, I wouldn't. Yes, I would." Sheer femaleness and the spirit of the age seesawed inconclusively. "Anyhow, I'd make you happy, because I'd be happy myself," she added naïvely. "Much happier than your grand-mother——"

"Perhaps you will oblige me by making no further allusion to Madame Zattiany."

"No, I won't. And the first time I see her when there's a lot of people round I'll tell her just what she is to her face."

"If you dare!" Clavering advanced threateningly and she swung herself behind her father, who, however, took her firmly by the arm and marched her to the door.

"Enough of this," he said. "You come home and pack your trunk and tomorrow we take the first steamer out of New York. If there isn't one, we'll take the train for Canada——"

"I won't go."

"It's either that or a sanitarium for neurotics. I'll have you strapped down and carried there in an ambulance. You may take your choice. Good night, Lee. Forget it, if you can."

As Clavering slammed the door behind them he envied men who could tear their hair. He had wanted to spend a long evening alone thinking of Mary Zattiany, dreaming of those vital hours before him, and he had been treated to a double nightmare. For the moment he hated everything in petticoats that walked, and he felt like taking a steamer to the ends of the earth himself. But he was more worn out than he knew and was sound asleep fifteen minutes later.

XXXIV

Janet had her revenge. Words have a terrible power. And Janet's vocabulary might be as primitive as lightning, but unlike lightning it never failed to strike.

"That old Zattiany woman." "She's a thousand years old and nobody cares what she does." "That rejuvenated old dame who's granny's age if she's a day." "Much happier than your grandmother." The phrases flashed into his mind when he awoke and echoed in his ears all day. No doubt similar phrases, less crude, but equally scorching, were being tossed from one end of New York Society to the other. If Janet knew of his devotion to Madame Zattiany others must, for it could only have come to her on the wings of gossip. He was being ridiculed by people who grasped nothing beyond the fact that the woman was fifty-eight and the man thirty-four. Of course it would be but a nine days' wonder and like all other social phenomena grow too stale for comment, but meanwhile he should feel as if he were frying on a gridiron. Anne Goodrich would merely exclaim: "Abominable." Marian Lawrence would draw in her nostrils and purr: "Lee was always an erratic and impressionable boy. Just like him to fall in love with an old woman. And she's really a beautiful blonde—once more. Poor Lee." As for Gora and Suzan Forbes—well, Gora would understand, and impale them sympathetically in her next novel, and Suzan would read up on endocrines, blend them adroitly with psychology, and write an article for the *Yale Review*.

He avoided the office and wrote his column at home. Luckily a favorite old comedian had died recently. He could fill up with reminiscence and anecdote. But it was soon done and he was back in his chair with his thoughts again.

It had been his intention when he awakened on Sunday after a few hours of unrefreshing sleep to dispatch his work as quickly as possible, take a long walk, and then return to his rooms and keep the hours that must intervene until Monday afternoon, sacred to Mary Zattiany. But if man wishes to regulate his life, and more particularly his meditations, to suit himself he would be wise to retire to a mountain top. Civilized life is a vast woof and the shuttle pursues its weaving and counter-weaving with no regard for the plans of men. It was impossible to ignore Mrs. Oglethorpe's appeal, and it was equally impossible to refuse to aid in the hunt for that damnable Janet when her distracted father and his own intimate friend took his coöperation as a matter of course. And even if he had remained at home, no doubt she would have wiggled her way in before he could shut the door in her face. Then there *would* have been the devil to pay, for she would have seen to it that he was hopelessly compromised. No doubt she would have run out on the balcony and screamed for help. Her failure was the one saving grace in the whole wretched night.

But she had planted her stings.

He was in a fine frame of mind to make love to a woman. He had pictured that scene as one of the great moments of life, so subtly beautiful and dramatic, so exalted and exulting, so perfect in its very incompleteness, that not a lifetime of suffering and disappointment could blur it. And he felt exactly like the flat tyre of Janet's distinguished vernacular. Even his body was worn out, for he had had but nine hours' sleep in two nights. What a dead cinch the playwrights had. A man might as well try to breathe without oxygen on Mount Everest as attempt to give his own life the proper dramatic values. He was a cursed puppet and Life itself was a curse.

He excoriated himself for his susceptibility to mere words; he who juggled in words, and often quite insincerely when it suited his purpose. But "that rejuvenated old dame," and "that old Zattiany woman" crawled like reeking vapors across some fair landscape a man had spent his life seeking, blotting out its loveliness, turning it to a noisome morass.

He had used equally caustic phrases when some young man he knew had married a woman only ten years older than himself, and when old men had taken to themselves young wives. And meant them, for he was fundamentally as conventional and conservative as all men.... But he cared less that he would be the laughing stock of New York than that his own soul felt like boiling pitch and that he was ashamed of himself.

He looked at the clock. It was twenty minutes to four. There was neither love nor desire in him and he would have liked to throw himself on the divan and sleep. But he set his teeth and got to his feet. He would go through it, play up, somehow.

He felt better in the nipping air and soon began to walk briskly. And then as he crossed Park Avenue and entered her street he saw two men coming down her steps. They were Mr. Dinwiddie, and the extremely good-looking young man whom Osborne had brought to the box on Monday night. The young man was smiling fatuously.

A wave of rage and jealousy swept Clavering from head to foot. She, at least, could have kept these hours sacred, and she had not only received this grinning ape, but evidently given him a delectable morsel to chew on. He could have knocked both men down but he was not even permitted to pass them by with a scowling nod. Another contretemps.[1]

Dinwiddie hailed him delightedly.

"Good old Lee! Haven't seen you in an age. Where've you kept yourself? Know Vane? Mother's an old friend of Mary's. He's head over like the rest of us. Who says we don't live in the age of miracles?"

"Yeh, ain't life wonderful?" Clavering's jocular faculty was enfeebled, but it came to the rescue. He was staring at Vane. Evidently this young man was unimpressed by searing phrases and he must have heard several, for, if he remembered aright, "Polly Vane" with "her head like a billiard ball," who "wore a wig for decency's sake," had been one of the most resentful women at the luncheon. For a moment he had a queer impression that his stature had diminished until the top of his head stood level with this glowing young man's waistcoat. And then he shot up to seven feet. Something had turned over inside him and vomited forth the pitch and its vapors. But he still felt angry and jealous. He managed to reply, however:

"Well, I must be getting on. Have an engagement at four. See you in a day or two, Din." He nodded to young Vane and in another moment he was taking Madame Zattiany's front steps three at a time.

XXXV

When Mary Zattiany had reached her bedroom on Sunday morning she had leaned heavily on her dressing-table for a few moments, staring into the mirror. Then she curled her lip and shrugged her shoulders. Well, it was done. She had been as bald and uncompromising as she knew how to be. A picturesque softening of details, pleas to understand, and appeals to the man's

---

1   An inopportune event.

sympathy, might be for other women but not for her. Life had given her a respect for hard facts and an utter contempt for the prevalent dodging of them.

She had told him that she was determined to relate her story in full as much for his sake as her own. But she had told it far more for her own. Before going any farther she was determined to know this man, who may only have intoxicated her, as thoroughly as it was possible for a woman to know any man she had not lived with. If he met the test she could be reasonably sure that for once she had made no mistake. If he did not—well, perhaps, so much the better. Surely she had had more than her share of love, and she had something to do in the world of vastly greater importance than wasting time in a man's arms. And did she really want passion in her life again? She with her young body and her old mind! Did she?

She recalled those brief moments of complete and ecstatic sur-render. Or tried to recall them. She was very tired. Perhaps she might dream about them, but at the moment they seemed as far away as her first youth.

She awoke the next day only in time to dress and go to Mrs. Ruyler's for luncheon. She attended a concert in the afternoon, and she did not return from the Lawrences' until midnight. On Monday she lunched with Mrs. Vane and brought "Harry" and Mr. Dinwiddie home with her. She would give herself no time to think and brood. She was too wise to harden her heart against him by bitter fancies that might be as bitterly unjust, and assuredly she had no intention of meeting disaster weakened by romantic castle-building. Not she. Let events take their course. Whatever came, she had the strength to meet it.

As Clavering entered the library she was standing by the hearth, one hand on the mantelshelf. Her repose was absolute as she turned her head. In her eyes was an insolent expression, a little mocking, a little challenging. There was no trace of apprehension. As she saw Clavering's angry face her brows lifted.

"What did you let those fellows in for?" he demanded, glaring at her from the door. "You set this hour for our meeting and I just missed finding them in this room. I should have thought you would have wanted to be alone before I came——"

And then for a moment Mary Zattiany's mind felt as young as her body. It seemed to her that she heard ruins tumbling behind her, down and out of sight. Her head felt light and she grasped the mantel for support; but she was not too dazed to realize that Clavering was in anything but a love-making mood, and she man-aged to steady her voice and reply lightly:

"I lunched with Polly Vane, and her devoted son was hanging 'round. Mr. Dinwiddie was also at the luncheon, and as they both walked home with me I could do no less than ask them in for a moment. But I never have the least difficulty getting rid of people."

"Ah!" He continued to stand staring at her, and, as he had anticipated, he saw only Mary Zattiany. As far as he was concerned Mary Ogden had never existed. But he still felt no immediate desire to touch her. He came over and stood opposite her on the hearthrug, his hands in his pockets.

"What have you been through?" he asked abruptly. "I've been through hell."

"So I imagined," she said drily. "I can't say I've been through hell. I've grown too philosophical for that! I have thought as little as possible. I left it on the knees of the gods."

There certainly was neither despair nor doubt in that vital voice of hers as she looked at him, and she was smiling. He twitched his shoulders under those understanding eyes and turned his own to the fire with a frown.

"I don't believe you had a moment of misgiving. You were too sure of me."

"Oh, no, I was not! I know life too well to be sure of anything, mon ami.[1] Unlike that nice Vane boy, you have imagination and I gave you some hard swallowing. Poor boy, I'm afraid you've been choking ever since——"

"Don't 'poor boy' me. I won't have it. I feel a thousand years old." He glared at her once more. "You are sure of me now—and quite right ... but I don't feel in the least like kissing you.... I've barely slept and I feel like the devil."

For the first time in many days she felt an inclination to throw back her head and give vent to a joyous laugh—joyous but amused, for she would always be Mary Zattiany. But she merely said: "My dear Lee, I could not stand being made love to at four in the afternoon. It is not aesthetic. Suppose we sit down. Tell me all about it."

"I'll not tell you a thing." But he took the chair and lit a cigarette. "I'm more in love with you than ever, if you want to know. When will you marry me?"

"Shall we say two months from today?"

"Two months! Why not tomorrow?"

"Oh, hardly. In the first place I'd like it all to be quite perfect, and I'd dreamed of spending our honeymoon in the Dolomites.

---

1 My friend.

I've a shooting box[1] there on the shore of a wonderful lake. I used to stay there quite alone after my guests had left…. And then—well, it would hardly be fair to give New York two shocks in succession. They all take for granted I'll marry some one—I am already engaged to Mr. Osborne, although I have heard you alluded to meaningly—but better let them talk the first sensation to rags…. They will be angry enough with me for marrying a young man, but perhaps too relieved that I have not carried off one of their own sons…. Polly is in agonies at the present moment … we'll have to live in New York more or less—I suppose?"

"More or less? Altogether. My work is here."

"I believe there is more work for both of us in Europe."

"And do you imagine I'd live on your money? I've nothing but what I make."

"I could pull wires and get you into one of the embassies——"

"I'm no diplomat, and don't want to be. Rotten lazy job."

"Couldn't you be foreign correspondent for your newspaper?"

"We've good men in every European capital now. They've no use for more, and no excuse for displacing any of them. Besides, I've every intention of being a playwright."

"But playwrighting isn't—not really—quite as important as poor Europe. And I know of several ways in which we could be of the greatest possible use. Not only Austria——"

"Perhaps. But you'll have to wait until I've made money on at least one play. I'll be only too glad to spend the honeymoon in the Dolomites, but then I return and go to work. You'll have to make up your mind to live here for a year or two at least. And the sooner you marry me, the sooner we can go to Europe to live—for a time. I've no intention of living my life in Europe. But I'm only too willing to help you. So—better marry me tomorrow."

"I can't get away for at least two months—possibly not then. Ask Judge Trent. And a honeymoon in New York would be too flat—not?"

"Better than nothing … however—here's an idea. I'll get to work on my play at once and maybe I can finish it before I leave. If it went over big I could stay longer. Besides, it'll be something to boil over into; I don't suppose I shall see any too much of you. What's your idea? To set all the young men off their heads and imagine you are Mary Ogden once more? It *would* be a triumph. I've an idea that's what you are up to."

---

1 Hunting lodge.

"Certainly not," she said angrily. "How trivial you must think me. I've not the least intention of going to dancing parties. I should be bored to death. I hardly knew what young Vane was talking about today. He seems to speak a different language from the men of my time. But it is only decent that I bore myself at luncheons and dinners, for my old friends have behaved with the utmost loyalty and generosity. Jane Oglethorpe would have been quite justified in never speaking to me again, and I have violated the most sacred traditions of the others. But it has not made the least difference. Besides, I must keep them up to the mark. I have their promise to form a committee for the children of Austria."

"Well, that's that. We'll marry two months from today. I can finish my play in that time, and I won't wait a day longer."

"Very well.... I met Marian Lawrence the other day. I'm told you were expected to marry her at one time. She is very beautiful and has more subtlety than most American women. Why didn't you?"

"Because she wasn't you, I suppose. Did she stick a little bejewelled gold pin into you?"

"Only with her eyes. She made me feel quite the age I had left behind me in Vienna." And then she asked irresistibly, "Do you think you would have fallen in love with me, after a much longer and better opportunity to know me, if you—if we had met in Vienna before that time?"

"No, I should not. What a question! I should have loved you in one way as I do now—with that part of me that worships you. But men are men, and never will be demi-gods."

This time she did laugh, and until tears were in her eyes. "Oh, Lee! No wonder I fell in love with you. Any other man—well, I couldn't have loved you. My soul was too old." And then her eyes widened as she stared before her. "Perhaps——"

He sprang to his feet and pulled her up from her chair. "None of that. None of that. And now I do want to kiss you."

And as Mary Zattiany never did anything by halves she was completely happy, and completely young.

XXXVI

He left her at ten o'clock, and the next morning rose at seven and went to work at once on his play. He chose the one that had the greatest emotional possibilities. Gora Dwight had told him that he must learn to "externalize his emotions," and he felt that here was the supreme opportunity. Never would he have more turgid, pent-up, tearing emotions to get rid of than now. He wrote until one o'clock, then, after lunch and two hours on his column, went out and took a long walk; but lighter of heart than since he had met Mary Zattiany. He also reflected with no little satisfaction that when writing on the play he had barely thought of her. All the fire in him had flown to his head and transported him to another plane; he wondered if any woman, save in brief moments, could rival the ecstasy of mental creation. That rotten spot in the brain, dislocation of particles, whatever it was that enabled a few men to do what the countless millions never dreamed of attempting, or attempt only to fail, was, through its very abnormality, productive of a higher and more sustained delight, a more complete annihilation of prosaic life, than any mere function bestowed on all men alike. It might bring suffering, disappointment, mortification, even despair in its train, but the agitation of that uncharted tract in the brain compensated for any revenge that nature, through her by-product, human nature, might visit on those who departed from her beloved formulae.

Nevertheless, and before his walk was finished and he had returned home to dress for dinner with her, the play was on one plane and he on another, visioning himself alone with her in the Austrian agapemone.[1] And cursing the interminable weeks between. He anathematized himself for consenting to the delay, and vowed she'd had her own way for the last time. He foresaw many not unagreeable tussles of will. She was far too accustomed to having her own way. Well, so was he.

For two weeks he left his rooms only to walk, or dine or spend an hour with her in the afternoon when she was alone. He rebelled less than he had expected. If he could not have her wholly, the less he saw of her the better.

Dinners, luncheons, theatre parties, receptions, were being given for her not only by her old friends—who seemed to her to grow more numerous daily—but by their daughters and by many others who made up for lack of tradition by that admirable sense of rightness which makes fashionable society in America such a waste of efficiency and force. And whether the younger women privately hated her or had fallen victims to that famous charm was of little public consequence. It was as if she had appeared in their midst, waved a sceptre and announced: "I am the fashion. Always have I been the fashion. That is my *métier*.[2] Bow down." At all

---

1 Greek for "abode of love."
2 Vocation, trade, calling.

events the fashion she became, and it was quite as patent that she took it as a matter of course. The radiant happiness that possessed her, refusing as she did to look into the future with its menace to those high duties of her former dedication—clear, sharp, ruthless children of her brain—not only enhanced both her beauty and magnetism, but enabled her to endure this social ordeal she had dreaded, without ennui. She was too happy to be bored. She even plunged into it with youthful relish. For the first time in her life she was at peace with herself. She was not at peace when Clavering made love to her, far from it; but she enjoyed with all the zest of a woman with her first lover, and something of the timidity, this tantalizing preliminary to fruition. How could she ever have believed that her mind was old? She turned her imagination away from that lodge in the Dolomites, and believed it was because the present with its happiness and its excitements sufficed her.

Moreover, she was having one novel experience that afforded her much diversion. The newspapers were full of her. It took exactly five days after Mrs. Oglethorpe's luncheon for the story she had told there to filter down to Park Row, and although she would not consent to be interviewed, there were double-page stories in the Sunday issues, embellished with snapshots and a photograph of the Mary Ogden of the eighties: a photographer who had had the honor to "take" her was still in existence and exhumed the plates.

Doctors, biologists, endocrinologists, were interviewed. Civil war threatened: the medical fraternity, upheld by a few doubting Thomases among the more abstract followers of the science, on one side of the field, by far the greater number of those who peer into the human mechanism with mere scientific acumen on the other. Doctors, notoriously as conservative as kings and as jealous as opera singers, found themselves threatened with the loss of elderly patients whose steady degeneration was a source of respectable income. When it was discovered that New York actually held a practicing physician who had studied with the great endocrinologists of Vienna, the street in front of his house looked as if some ambitious hostess were holding a continual reception.

Finally Madame Zattiany consented to give a brief statement to the press through her lawyers. It was as impersonal as water, but technical enough to satisfy the *Medical Journal*. At the theatre and opera people waited in solid phalanxes to see her pass. Her utter immobility on these occasions but heightened the feverish interest.

Women of thirty, dreaming of becoming flappers overnight, and formidable rivals, with the subtlety of experience behind the mask of seventeen, were desolated to learn that they must submit to the claws and teeth of Time until they had reached the last mile-post of their maturity. Beauty doctors gnashed their teeth, and plastic surgeons looked forward to the day when they must play upon some other form of human credulity. As a subject for the press it rivalled strikes, prohibition, German reparations, Lenin, prize-fights, censorship and scandalous divorces in high life.

"Why isn't your head turned?" Clavering asked her one day when the sensation was about a month old and was beginning to expire journalistically for want of fresh fuel. (Not a woman in New York could be induced to admit that she was taking the treatment.) "You are the most famous woman in America and the pioneer of a revolution that may have lasting and momentous consequences on which we can only speculate vaguely today. I don't believe you are as unmoved as you look. It's not in woman's nature—in human nature. Publicity goes to the head and then descends to the marrow of the bones."

"I'm not unmoved. I've been tremendously interested and excited. I find that newspaper notoriety is the author of a distinctly new sensation." And then she felt a disposition to play with fire. Clavering was in one of his rare detached moods, and had evidently come for an hour of agreeable companionship. "I am beginning to get a little bored and tired. If it were not for this Vienna Fund—and to the newspapers for their assistance I am eternally grateful—I believe I'd suggest that we leave for Austria tomorrow."

"And I wouldn't go." Clavering stood on the hearthrug smiling down at her with humorous defiance. "You switched me on to that play, and there I stick until it is finished. No chance for it in a honeymoon, and no chance for undiluted happiness with that crashing round inside my head."

She shrank and turned cold, but recovered herself sharply and dismissed the pang. It was her first experience, in her exhaustive knowledge of men, of the writing temperament; and after all it was part of the novelty of the man who had obliterated every other from her mind. Nor had she any intention of letting him see that he could hurt her. She smiled sweetly and asked:

"How is it coming on? Are you satisfied with it?"

"Yes, I am. And so is Gora Dwight. I've finished two acts and I read them to her last night."

"Ah? Your Egeria?"[1]

---

1 Name of a mythological water nymph who was the consort of King Numa Pompilius of Rome. Her name became synonymous with wisdom based on the counsel she provided.

"Not a bit of it. But she's a wise cold-blooded critic. You can't blame me for not even talking about it to you. I see so little of you that I've no intention of wasting any of the precious time."

"But you might let me read it."

"I'd rather wait until it's finished and as polished and perfect as I can make it. I always want you to know me at my best."

"Oh, my dear! You forget that we are to be made one and remain twain. Do you really believe that we shall either of us always be at our best?"

"Well, to tell you the truth, I don't care a hang whether we are or not. I'll have you, and all to myself. And I won't say 'for a while, at least.' Do you imagine that when we return to New York I'm going to let Society take possession of you again? Not only shall I work harder than I've ever worked before, but I'd see little more of you than I do now. And that I'll never submit to again. I'll write my next play inside this house, and you'll be here when I want you, not gadding about."

She felt a sudden pang of dismay, apprehension. New York? She realized that not for a moment had she given up her original purpose. But why disturb the serenity of the present? When she had him in the Dolomites ... She answered him in the same light tone.

"I'm having my last fling at New York Society. When we return we'll give our spare time to the Sophisticates. I see far less of them now than I like." Then, with a further desire to investigate the literary temperament, even if she were stabbed again in the process, she looked at him with provocative eyes and said: "I've sometimes wondered why you haven't insisted upon a secret marriage. I'm told it can be done with a reasonable prospect of success in certain states."

"Don't imagine I didn't think of it ... but—well—I think the play would go fluey ... you see...."

"I see! And what about your next?"

"The next will be a comedy. I'll never be able to write a tremendously emotional play again."

"And meanwhile you will not deny that the artist has submerged the lover."

"I admit nothing of the sort. But you yourself let the artist loose—and what in God's name should I be doing these cursed weeks if you hadn't? You know you never would have consented to a secret marriage. You've set your heart on the Dolomites.... How about that interval of travel, by the way? Liners and trains are not particularly conducive to illusions."

"I thought I'd told you. My plan is to be married there. I should go on a preceding steamer and see that the Lodge was in proper condition. I want everything to be quite perfect, and Heaven only knows what has happened to it."

"Oh! This is a new one you've sprung. But—yes—I like the idea. I'd rather dreaded the prelude." And then he made one of those abrupt vaultings out of one mood into another which had fascinated her from the first. "God! I wish we were there now. When I'm not writing——! How many men have you got in love with you already? But no. I don't care. When I'm here—*like this, Mary, like this*—I don't care a hang if I never write another line."

XXXVII

During the following week she gave a dinner and insisted upon his attendance. She had given others to that increasing throng that had been young with her in the eighties and to others who had stormed and conquered that once impregnable citadel, but, she informed him, it was now time to entertain some of the younger women, and he must help her.

He consented readily enough, for he was curious to see her surrounded by a generation into which she had coolly stepped with no disadvantage to herself and, from all he heard, considerable to them. He knew that not only Vane but other men in their late twenties and early thirties were paying her devoted attentions. Dinwiddie, who met him in the Park one day and dined with him in the Casino, had spoken with modified enthusiasm of these conquests, but added that it was yet to be demonstrated whether the young men were egged by novelty or genuine coveting. When he hinted that she may have appealed to that secret lust for the macabre that exists somewhere in all men, Clavering had scowled at him so ferociously that he had plunged into rhapsody and bewailed his own lost youth.

And then he had endeavored to sound the young man in whom he was most interested, but of whose present relations with Mary Zattiany he had no inkling; he had not seen them together nor heard any fresh gossip since her second début. But he was told to shut up and talk about the weather.

Clavering, who knew that he would not have a moment alone with her, went to the dinner in much the same mood as he went to a first-night at which he was reasonably sure of entertainment. It certainly would be good comedy to the detached observer, and this he was quite capable of being with nothing better in prospect. Nevertheless, he was utterly unprepared for the presence of Anne Goodrich and Marian Lawrence, for he understood that the dinner was given to the more important of the young married women. But they were the first persons he saw when he entered the drawing-room. They were standing together—shoulder to shoulder, he reflected cynically—and he knew that they privately detested each other, and not on his account only.

How like Mary Zattiany, with her superb confidence in herself, to ask these beautiful girls who she had heard wanted to marry him themselves. Well, he understood women well enough to be indulgent to their little vanities.

He was almost the last of the guests, but he had time to observe the two girls before dinner was announced, in spite of the fact that he was claimed by other acquaintances before he could reach them.

Anne looked regally handsome in gold-colored tissue and paillettes[1] that gave a tawny light to her eyes and hair, and to her skin an amber glow. She held her head very high, and in spite of her mere five feet five, looked little less stately than Madame Zattiany, who wore a marvellous velvet gown the exact shade of her hair. Marian Lawrence was small but so perfectly made that her figure was always alluded to as her body, and she carried her head, not regally, but with an insolent assurance that became her. She was very beautiful, with a gleaming white skin that she never powdered nor colored, and hair like gold leaf, parted and worn in smooth bands over her ears and knotted loosely on her neck in the fashion known as à la vierge. Her large grayish-green eyes were set far apart and her brows and lashes were black. She had a straight innocent-looking nose with very thin nostrils, into which she was capable of compressing the entire expression of a face. She generally wore the fashionable colors of the moment, but tonight her soft shimmering gown was of palest green, and Clavering wondered if this were a secret declaration of war. She, too, was of the siren class, and it was possible that she and Mary Zattiany derived from some common ancestress who had combed her hair on a rock or floated northward over the steppes of Russia. But there were abysmal differences between the two women, as Clavering well knew. Marian Lawrence, with great natural intelligence, never read anything more serious than a novel and preferred those that were not translated into English. She took no interest whatever

---

1 A spangle or sequin.

in anything outside her inherited circumference, and had prided herself during the war upon ignoring its existence. She was as luxurious and as dainty as a cat and one of the most ardent sportswomen in America. She looked as if she had just stepped out of a stained-glass window, and she was a hard, subtle, predatory flirt; too much in love with her beautiful body to give it wholly to any man. She had never really fallen in love with Clavering until she had lost him, and he, his brief enthusiasm for her unique beauty and somewhat demoniac charm having subsided, had avoided her ever since; although they danced together at the few fashionable parties he attended. He knew her better now than when he had seen her daily, almost hourly, at a house party in the White Mountains, and almost as often for several weeks after his return. This was shortly after his mistake with Anne, and her attraction had consisted largely in her complete difference from a really fine character toward whom he felt a certain resentment for having so much and still lacking the undefined essential. He had not deluded himself that he would find it in Marian Lawrence, but her paradoxes diverted him and he was quite willing to go as far as her technique permitted. It had never occurred to him for a moment that she was seriously in love with him, but he had had more than one glimpse of her claws and he regarded her uneasily tonight. And what were she and Anne whispering about?

"You will take in Miss Goodrich," Madame Zattiany had said to him, her eyes twinkling, and he had merely shrugged his shoulders. He did not care in the least whom he talked to; it was the ensemble that interested him. Anne and Marian were the only girls present. The other women were between twenty-five and thirty-five or -six. Madame Zattiany would seem to have chosen them all for their good looks, and she looked younger than several of them.

Mauve was the fashionable color of the season. There were three mauve gowns and the table was lit by very long, very thin mauve candles above a low bank of orchids. Mrs. Ruyler had disinterred the family amethysts, but Mrs. de Lacey and Mrs. Vane, "Polly's" daughter-in-law, wore their pearls. There were several tiaras, for they were going on to the opera and later to a ball. The company numbered twenty in all and there were three unmarried men besides Clavering, and including Harry Vane. Clavering found Marian Lawrence on his left, and once more he caught a twinkle in Madame Zattiany's eyes as the guests surrounded the table.

He had not seen Anne since the night of Suzan's party, when they had varied the program by sitting on the floor in front of the fire, roasting chestnuts and discussing philosophy; then playing poker until two o'clock in the morning. He asked her if she were comfortable and happy in her new life.

"Rather!" She smiled with all her old serene brightness and her eyes dwelt on him in complete friendliness. "I'd even sleep in the studio, but have made one concession to my poor family. They're not reconciled, but, after all, I am twenty-four—and spent two years in France. I have had three orders for portraits—friends of the family, of course. I must be content with 'pull' until I am taken seriously as an artist. If I can only exhibit at the next Academy I shall feel full-fledged."

"And what of your new circle?"

"I've been to several parties and enjoyed myself hugely. Some of them get pretty tight, but I've seen people tighter at house parties and not nearly so amusing. And then Gora and Suzan! I've never liked any women as well.... This is the first dinner of the old sort I've been to since I started."

"Ah?" asked Clavering absently. "Why the exception?"

"Well, you see, I am tremendously *intriguée*, like every one else. I'd met her several times at home, and she came one day to my studio, where the Sophisticates made the most tremendous fuss over her. But I was curious to see her in her own old home, where she had reigned so long ago as Mary Ogden. Mother told me that everything was unchanged except the stair carpet and her bedroom." Her tone was lightly impersonal, and still more so as she added: "Why don't you write a novel about her, Lee? She must be the most remarkable psychological study of the age. Fancy living two lifetimes in the same body. It puts reincarnation to the blush. I suppose she'll bury us all."

Clavering shot her a sharp investigating glance, but replied suavely: "Not necessarily. The same road is open to all of you."

Miss Goodrich had never looked more the fine and dignified representative of her class as she lifted her candid eyes with an expression of disdain.

"My dear Lee! Really! There *are* some women above that sort of thing."

"Above? I don't think I follow you. But of course she's given hide-bound conservatism a pretty hard jolt."

"It's not that—really. But all women growing old and trying to be or to look young again are rather undignified—according to our standards at least, and I have been brought up in the belief that they are the highest in the world. And then, one's sense of humor——!"

"Humor? Is that what you call it?" (Damn all women for cats, the best of them. Anne!)

"Why, yes, isn't it rather absurd—for more reasons than one? To my mind it is the complete farce. She has regained the appearance—and—*possibly*—the real feeling of youth, with all its capacity for enthusiasm and unworn emotions—it seems rather ludicrous, but still it may be; certainly the interior should be in some degree a match for that marvellously restored face and body—but the whole thing is made farcical by the fact that she never can have children. And what else does youth in women really mean?"

"Experience has taught me that it means quite a number of other things. And painting portraits is not fulfilling the first and highest duty of womanhood, dear Anne."

Miss Goodrich flushed, but accepted his score calmly. "Oh, I shall marry, of course. But then, you see, I am young—really young."

"What are you two quarrelling about?" broke in Miss Lawrence's husky voice. She had smoked steadily since taking her seat at the table, not so much because she had an irresistible passion for tobacco as because it destroyed her appetite and preserved her figure. "I haven't seen Anne blush like that since she got back from France."

"I was just telling her how beautiful she looked tonight." And angry as he was, it amused him to hear Anne's little gasp of pleasure.

"Yes, doesn't she?" Miss Lawrence blew a ring and smiled sweetly. "I've always been jealous of Anne. She's such a beautiful height. I'm so glad the giraffes of the last generation seem to have died out. Too bad, when Madame Zattiany rejuvenated herself, she didn't slice off a few inches. She dwarfs even men of your height, although, of course, you are really taller. But then tall women——" She shrugged her shoulders, her crisp voice softened and she went on as if thinking aloud. "Do you know ... to me she does not look young at all. I have a fancy she's hypnotized every one but myself. I seem to see an old woman with a colossal will.... But I'd like to know the name of that whitewash she uses. It may come in handy some day. Not for another ten years, though. Oh, Lee! it's good to be really young and not have to be flattened out on a table under broiling X-Rays and have your poor old feminine department cranked up.... I wonder just how adventurous men are?"'

But Clavering, although seething, merely smiled. He knew himself to be like the man who has had a virulent attack of smallpox and is immune for the rest of his life. Nevertheless, he would cheerfully have twisted her neck. She was holding that slim lily-like throat up for his inspection, a cigarette between her thin scarlet lips as she looked at him over her shoulder. At sixteen she could not have been more outwardly unblemished, and she emanated a heady essence. Her long green eyes met his keen satiric ones with melting languor. But she said unexpectedly:

"I hear she's going to marry Mr. Osborne, mother's old beau—or is that Mr. Dinwiddie? How can one straighten out those old-timers? But it would be quite appropriate, if she must marry—and I suppose she's dying to; but I notice she hasn't asked either of them tonight. I suppose it makes her feel younger to surround herself with young people. It certainly makes me feel frightfully young——I mean she does."

"Do you think it good manners to discuss your hostess at her own table?"

"Oh, manners! You'll always be a Southerner, Lee. New York has always prided itself on its bad manners. That is the real source of our strength."

"Pretty poor prop. It seems to me a sign of congenital weakness."

"Oh, we never defend ourselves. By the way, I hear Jim Oglethorpe rushed poor little Janet off to Egypt because he found her in your rooms and you refused to marry her. You're not such a gallant Southerner, after all——"

"What a lie! Who on earth started such a yarn?" But he turned cold and his hand shook a little as he raised his wine glass.

"It's all over town, and people think you really ought to marry her. Of course those ridiculous little flappers don't care whether they are talked about or not, but their families do. I hear that old Mrs. Oglethorpe is quite ill over the scandal, and she always swore by you."

"Mrs. Oglethorpe, I happen to know, as I dined there last night, was never better and is delighted with the idea that Jim has taken Janet abroad to get her away from that rotten crowd."

She looked nonplussed, but returned to the charge. "How stories do get about! They even say that he horsewhipped you——"

"Pray don't overtax your powers of invention. You know there's no such story going about or everybody here would have cut me dead. Try another tack."

"Well, I'll confess I made that up just to get a rise out of you." She looked at him speculatively. "But about Janet—well, you see, I know you for a gay deceiver—mother is always using those old expressions that were the fashion in her—and Mary Ogden's—day.[1] I hear you even made love to our fair hostess until you found

---

1 A "gay deceiver" or lothario, a seducer of women.

out the truth and then you dropped her like a hot potato—or a cold fish. I was surprised when she told me you were coming here tonight, and asked her at once to seat us three together so that Anne and I could save you from feeling embarrassed—not that I told her that, of course. I merely said we were such old friends we would naturally have a thousand things to talk about. She didn't turn a hair; I'll say that much for her. But perhaps she thinks she's playing you on a long string. She's playing several poor fish who are here tonight."

Should he tell her? He really could stand no more. He hadn't a doubt that the same rumor that had driven Janet to her crude attempt, to compromise him and then blast her rival with naked words, had reached these two older and cleverer, but hardly subtler girls, and they had joined forces to disenchant him and make him feel the misguided young man they no doubt believed him to be. He hated them both. They had that for their pains. He'd never willingly see one of them again.

He longed to blurt out the truth. But his was not the right. He glanced over at Madame Zattiany, who sat in the middle of the table's length, receiving the intent homage of the men on either side of her and looking more placid than any other woman in the room.... It occurred to him that the rest were animated to excess, even the wives of those two men, to whom, it was patent, they were non-existent. He would have given his play at that moment to be able to stand up and ask the company to drink his health and hers.

For a few moments he was left to himself, both Marian and Anne being occupied with their neighbors, and during those moments he sensed an atmosphere of hostility, of impending danger. He caught more than one malicious glance directed at Mary, and once a man, in response to a whispered remark, burst into uncontrollable laughter. Had these women come here—but that was impossible. Even New York had its limits. They might be icily rude to a pushing outsider, as indeed they had every right to be, but never to one of their own. Still—to this alarmed generation possibly Madame Zattiany was nothing more than a foreign woman who had stormed the gates and reduced them to a mere background. The fact that she had belonged to their mothers' generation and had abruptly descended to theirs was enough to arouse every instinct of self-defence. He quite understood they must hate her, but in spite of that common enmity his sensitive mind apprehended, they'd surely commit no overt act of hostility. Like all their kind, they were adepts in the art of "freezing out." He had no doubt they had come here from mere curiosity and that he would shortly hear they had ceased to entertain or receive her. But he wished the dinner were over.

He was soon enlightened.

Marian Lawrence leaned across the table. "Oh, Madame Zattiany! Will you settle a dispute? Harry and I have been arguing about Disraeli. Your husband was an ambassador, wasn't he? Did you happen to be at the Berlin What-d'you-call-it?"[1]

"Oh, no," replied Madame Zattiany, with open amusement. "I was still Mary Ogden in eighteen-seventy-eight."

"Oh! The seventies and eighties are all one to me, I'm afraid. I'm shockingly ignorant. But we've all been saying that you ought to write your memoirs. Thirty-four years of diplomatic life in Europe! You must have met every one worth knowing and it would be such a delightful way for us youngsters to learn history."

"Oh, I kept a diary," said Madame Zattiany lightly. "I may publish it some day." And she turned pointedly to the man on her right. Why had she invited the little cat?

"Oh, but Madame Zattiany!" exclaimed young Mrs. Ruyler, whose black eyes were sparkling. "Please don't wait. I'm so interested in German history since the war. You must have known four generations of Hohenzollerns[2] ... too thrilling! And Bismarck.[3] And the Empress Elizabeth.[4] And Crown Prince Rudolf[5]—do tell us the truth of that mysterious tragedy. Did you ever see Marie

---

1 Benjamin Disraeli (1804-81), prime minister of England in 1868 and 1874-80, is remembered for his influential negotiations at the Congress of Berlin (June-July 1878), at which the Balkans were reorganized. Represented were delegates from the Ottoman Empire, Britain, Russia, and Austria-Hungary. Disraeli was instrumental in limiting Russia's power in the Balkans.

2 German Imperial family dating from the eleventh century and aligned most closely with Prussia by the late nineteenth century; the 1918 German Revolution and formation of the Weimar Republic forced the Hohenzollerns to abdicate.

3 Otto von Bismarck (1815-98), Chancellor of Germany and leading diplomat of his age; he engineered the unification of Germany and, by the 1920s, would have represented the stability of old Europe.

4 Spouse of Franz Joseph I, the beautiful and beloved Empress of Austria and Queen of Hungary during the Dual Empire. She was assassinated in 1898 by an anarchist.

5 Archduke and Crown Prince of Austria, son and heir of Franz Joseph I and Empress Elisabeth. In 1889 at the age of 30, Rudolf was found dead with his mistress, Baroness Mary Vetsera, in what was believed to have been a murder-suicide. The discovery of their deaths at his hunting lodge was termed the "Mayerling Incident" or "Mayerling Tragedy."

Vetsera? I never heard of it until the other day when some of mother's friends raked it up, and I've been excited ever since."

"Unfortunately my husband was an attaché in Paris at the time, and I never saw her. I am afraid your curiosity will never be satisfied. There was a general impression that if Vienna ever became the capital of a Republic the archives would be opened and the truth of the Meyerling tragedy given to the world. But all documents relating to private scandals must have been destroyed." She spoke with the utmost suavity, the patient hostess with rather tiresome guests. "People in Vienna, I assure you, take very little interest in that old scandal. They are too busy and too uncomfortable making history of their own."

"Yes, it must be a hideously uncomfortable place to live in." Mrs. Leonard, another daughter-in-law of one of Mary's old friends, gave a little shudder. "No wonder you got out. I was so glad to subscribe to your noble charity, dear Madame Zattiany. But"—and she smiled winsomely—"I think we should get up a subscription for those wonderful scientists in Vienna. Every once in a while you hear the most harrowing stories of the starving scientists of Europe, and it would be too awful if those miracle men in Vienna should pass away from malnutrition before it is our turn to need them."

"Ah, dear Mrs. Ruyler!" exclaimed Madame Zattiany with a smile as winsome as her own. "You forget they will probably all be dead by that time and that their pupils will be equally eminent and even more expert. For that matter there will be experts in every city in the world."

But Clavering, watching her anxiously, had seen an expression of wonder dawn in her eyes, quickly as she had banished it. It was evident that whatever the secret spite of these women, this was the first time they had given it open expression. He glanced about the table. Young Vane's face was crimson and he had turned his back pointedly on Marian Lawrence, who was smoking and grinning. She had started the ball and was too indolent to take it out of hands that seemed to be equally efficient.

Clavering leaned forward and caught Mary's eye with a peremptory expression, but she shook her head, although too imperceptibly for any one else to catch the fleeting movement, and he sank back with a humiliating sense of impotence. He wished she were not so well able to take care of herself.

"But this is abominable," murmured Anne Goodrich. It was possible that she was not in on the baiting. "Abominable. What must she think of us? Or, perhaps they don't really mean to be horrid. They look innocent enough. After all, she could tell us many interesting things."

"Oh, they mean it," said Clavering bitterly. "They mean it all right and she knows it."

"You speak as if you were even more interested in her than poor Harry Vane." The indignation had faded from Miss Goodrich's lofty countenance. "Are you?"

"Yes, I am, if you want the truth. I'd marry her tomorrow if she'd have me." This was as far as he could go.

"Oh!" Her mouth trembled, but she did not look wholly unprepared for the statement. "But——Lee——You know how interested I have always been in you—how interested we all are in you——"

"What has that to do with it? If you are so interested in me I should think I'd have your best wishes to carry off such a prize. Have you ever seen a more remarkable woman?"

"Oh, remarkable, yes. But—well——" And then she burst out: "It seems to me unspeakably horrid. I can't say *all* I'd like to——"

"Pray, don't. And suppose we change the subject——They're at it again, damn them."

The men were looking very uncomfortable. The women were gazing at their hostess with round apologetic eyes. Mrs. de Lacey, the youngest and prettiest of the married women, had clasped her hands as if worshipping at a shrine.

"It seems too terrible when we look back upon it!" she exclaimed, and she infused her tones with the tragic ring of truth, "*dear* Madame Zattiany, that for even a little while we thought the most awful things about you. We'd heard of the wonderful things surgeons had done to mutilated faces during the war, and we were sure that some one of them had taken one of your old photographs—how could we even guess the truth? How you must have hated us!"

"How could I hate you?" Madame Zattiany smiled charmingly. "I had not the faintest idea you were discussing me."

"But why—why—did you shut yourself up so long after you came when you must have known how mother and all your old friends longed to see you again?"

"I was tired and resting." She frowned slightly. Such a question was a distinct liberty and she had never either taken or permitted liberties. But she banished the frown and met her tormentor's eyes blandly. She had no intention of losing her poise for a moment.

"Ah! I said it!" cried Mrs. de Lacey. "I knew it was not because you felt a natural hesitation in showing yourself. To me you seem brave enough for anything, but it *must* have taken a lot of courage."

"Courage?"

"Why, yes! Fancy—well, you see, I'm such a coward about what people say—especially if I thought they'd laugh at me—that if I'd done it I should have run off and hidden somewhere."

"Then what object in invoking the aid of science to defeat nature at one more point? And I can assure you, dear Mrs. de Lacey, that when you are fifty-eight, if you have not developed courage to face the world on every count it will merely be because you have indulged too frequently in unbridled passions."

"Ah—yes—but you didn't have any qualms at all?"

"Certainly not. I confess I am surprised at your rather strained view of what is really a very simple matter."

"*Simple?* Why, it's the most extraordinary thing that ever happened."

"The world is equally astonished—and resentful—at every new discovery, but in a short time accepts it as a commonplace. The layman resents all new ideas, but the adjustment of the human mind to the inevitable is common even among savages." Her slight affectation of pedantry was very well done and Clavering could not detect the flicker of a lash as her eyes rested indulgently upon her tormentor.

"Well, I don't see what that has to do with it. Anyhow, it must make you feel terribly isolated."

Madame Zattiany shrugged her shoulders. She could make this common gesture foreign, and her accent was a trifle more marked as she answered, "Here, possibly, but not in Europe, where the treatment has been known and practised for several years. It may interest you to hear that only yesterday I had a letter from a friend in Vienna telling me that an elderly countess, a great beauty some forty years ago, had announced triumphantly that once more men were following her on the street."

Mrs. de Lacey burst into a peal of girlish laughter. "Pardon me, dear Madame Zattiany. We are used to it in your case, now that we have got over the shock, but it does seem too funny. And Europe almost manless. What—what will the poor girls do?"

"Scratch their eyes out," said Clavering, who could contain himself no longer.

Mrs. de Lacey made no attempt to conceal the wicked sparkle in her eyes as she turned to him. "How crude! I suppose it was you who set those dreadful newspapers on poor Madame Zattiany." She turned back to her hostess. "That has been a shocking ordeal for you. You know how we always avoid that sort of thing. We've felt for you—I wanted to come and tell you—you don't mind my telling you now?"

"Your sympathy is very sweet. But I really have enjoyed it! You see, my dear child, when one has lived as long as I have, a new sensation is something to be grateful for."

"Oh, but——" Mrs. de Lacey's bright eyes were now charged with ingenuous curiosity. "You don't really mean—we've had the most furious arguments—*couldn't* you fall in love again? I don't mean like silly old women with boys, but *really*—like a young woman? Please let me have my little triumph. I've sworn you could. And then the poor men——"

"Upon my word!" Madame Zattiany laughed outright. "This has gone far enough. I refuse to be the exclusive topic of conversation any longer. I am immensely flattered, but you are making me feel the rude hostess." And this time she turned with an air of finality to the apologetic, almost purple, man at her side and asked him to continue to enlighten her on municipal politics.

One or two women shrugged their shoulders. A few looked crestfallen, others, like Marian Lawrence, malignant. She had marched off with the flag, no use blinking the fact, and it had been small satisfaction to make her admit what she had already told the world. The "rubbing in" had evidently missed its mark. And the men, instead of looking cheap, were either infuriated or disgusted. Only Clavering, who managed to look bored and remote, was attending strictly to his salad.

One thing more they could do, however, and that was to make the dinner a failure. They barely replied to the efforts of the men to "make things go" and gloom settled over the table. Madame Zattiany continued to talk with placidity or animation to the men beside her, and Clavering started a running fire with Anne Goodrich, who, almost as angry as himself, loyally helped him, on censorship, the latest books and plays, even the situation in Washington; and they continued their painful efforts until the signal was given to leave the table.

XXXVIII

The men did not linger in the dining-room. The women, protesting that they were later than usual for the opera, left immediately after they returned to the drawing-room. There was a cool insolence in their "good-byes" and there was no doubt that they meant them to be final. Only Anne Goodrich shook the imperturbable hostess's hand warmly and asked if she might come some day to tea.

The husbands perforce went with their wives, after farewells that sounded more like au revoirs, and so did the younger men, except Clavering and Harry Vane. Clavering planted himself on the hearthrug, and Vane, scowling at him, lingered uncertainly.

He plunged his hands into his pockets, and, very red, stood in front of Madame Zattiany, who was leaning back in her chair and fanning herself leisurely. "I feel like apologizing for those beastly women," he blurted out.

"Apologize?" Madame Zattiany raised her eyebrows.

"Yes. Can't you see they came here tonight with the deliberate intention of making New York too hot to hold you? So that you'd clear out? They'd made up their minds that you'd changed yours about returning to Europe. They hate you. They're used to being jealous of one another, but this has knocked them silly and they can't get used to it. It's—it's—oh, it's too awful! I almost died of shame."

"I really do not understand. Do you mean to tell me they meant to be rude? I thought they were rather naïve and charming."

"Damned hypocrites. They hoped to make you simply expire with embarrassment. But you were splendid. They must feel like naughty children that have been stood in a corner."

Madame Zattiany laughed. "Then I have unwittingly been playing my part in a little comedy. How stupid they must have thought me! But I really hope for their sakes that you are mistaken." She rose and held out her hand. "I am going to ask you to excuse me, Mr. Vane. I have a small commission for Mr. Clavering, who has kindly waited. And I am very tired."

Vane's face fell and he looked resentfully at Clavering, in whom he instantly recognized a rival. But there was nothing to do but go and he went.

When Madame Zattiany heard the front door close she told the footman on duty in the hall to put out the lights and go to bed.

Then she walked down the room to the library door. "Will you put out these lights?" she asked Clavering. "I believe we still have a fire in here."

Clavering, expecting to find her dissolved in tears, and, violent as his sympathy for her was, rejoicing that his was the part to comfort her, followed her precipitately. But she was standing by the table with scornful lips and eyes.

"I thought you'd be all broken up," he stammered. Tears of disappointment almost rose to his own eyes.

She laughed shortly. "I? Do you suppose I would pay them so great a compliment? But what a ridiculous exhibition they made of themselves. It seems incredible."

"But surely you must have been hurt—and stabbed. It isn't possible that you weren't!"

"Oh, yes, I was stabbed, but I think I was even more amused. I felt sorry for the poor things. I certainly never saw a more comically naked exhibition of human nature. It was worth coming to America for. Nor do I blame them. No doubt I should have felt the same at their age—although I hope I should even then have expressed myself in a fashion a trifle more subtle, a little less primeval."

"Good God! Are you always so—so rational?"

She smiled slightly. "If I deliberately unlearned the more valuable things a long life taught me there would be no object beyond vanity in being young again. And don't you suppose I was grateful tonight for my years—those years so crowded with training and experience? Who better prepared than I to hold my own against a lot of raw Americans?"

"That is the first human thing you've said. Raw? Wasn't it Darwin who said that we are all such a short distance, in time, removed from our common savage ancestors that it is a wonder we don't revert oftener than we do? They were plain unadulterated females. I believe men are more civilized than women."

"Oh, no, but they revert on the grand scale.... I cannot say I was totally unprepared—not for such a concerted and shocking exhibition, of course; but I've felt their antagonism and expected to be dropped gradually from their set. Of course, this is the end, definitely. However," she shrugged her shoulders again, "I have enjoyed the New York which seems to have changed in so many ways since my day, and all dramas should have a proper 'curtain,' should they not? Is your own play finished, by the way?"

"Oh!" He turned his back on her and leaned on the mantelpiece, dropping his head on his arms. He had never felt as far away from her when he had been unable to learn even her name. What need had she of him or any man?

Mary gave him a quick comprehending glance, and came out of her isolation. She went over to him, turned him around, and took his face between her hands.

"Can't you imagine what it meant to me to have you there?" she asked softly. "It seemed to me that nothing else mattered. We two are in a world of our own. How could they seem more to me than the buzzing of so many brainless insects? Forget it, and I shall."

But although he was consoled, he wondered, as he left the house, if he would ever feel more depressed in his life. She might love him, but what else could he ever be to her but a lover? His manhood rebelled. If she had only flung herself weeping into his arms. If for once he could have felt himself stronger than she—indispensable.

XXXIX

The dinner was on Monday. On Wednesday morning she met him at the Fort Lee Ferry at seven o'clock for one of their rare tramps. She wore high-laced boots of soft leather, a short skirt and jersey and a soft hat; and if she had met any of her guests of that memorable dinner they would have looked profoundly thoughtful, and renounced whatever hope of having seared her to the bone they may have cherished. She strode through the woods above the Palisades beside Clavering with high head and sparkling eyes, her arms swinging like a schoolboy's. It was evident even to him, who had waited for her anxiously, that she had rubbed a sponge over her memory. She was in high spirits and looked as if she had not a care in the world.

There was a soft mist of green on the trees of the wood, a few birds had already migrated northward, their own world-old wireless having warned them of the early awakening of spring after an unusually mild winter, and they were singing their matins.

She did not seem inclined for more than desultory conversation, but she had the gift of making silence eloquent, and Clavering, his fears banished, although by no means at peace, gave himself up to the pleasure of the moment. They walked briskly for several miles, then had their breakfast at a roadside inn; and both were so hungry that they talked even less than before. But there was little need for words between them; the current was too strong, and both were merely vital beings to whom companionship and healthy exercise were the highest good at the moment.

During the long walk back to the ferry she talked with a certain excitement. But it was all of the woods of Austria, the carefully tended woods with their leaping stags, their winding paths where no trolley-cars over-laden with commuters rushed shrieking by, their enchanting vistas with a green lake at the end, or a monastery, or a castle on a lofty rock. She told him of the river Inn roaring through its gorges, with its solitary mills, its clustered old villages huddled at the foot of the heavy silent woods and forgotten by the world. The millers were all old men now, no doubt, and the poor villages inhabited only by women and children. Or blinded and broken men who had dragged themselves back from the war to exist where they once had given life and energy to that quiet valley of the Inn. If this made her sad for a moment it was purely an impersonal sadness, and when they parted on the New York side of the ferry Clavering had forgotten his doubts and went back to his work with a light heart and an untroubled mind.

The play was almost finished, and its chances for swift production were far greater than is usually the case with the new adventurer into the most inhospitable of all fields of artistic endeavor. Adrian Hogarth, who had a play on Broadway every year, and Edwin Scores, who had recently exchanged the esteem of the few for the enthusiasm of The Public, had read it act by act and given him the practical advice he needed. A dramatic critic always believes he knows more about plays than any one else until he attempts to write one, but Clavering, at least, if not unduly modest, was too anxious to succeed not to welcome all the help he could get.

They even "sat in" with him during the final revision, and the dispute was hot over the last act, an act so daring in technique they were loath to believe that even Clavering, whose striking gifts they had always recognized, could "put it over." Moreover, there was only one woman on the American stage who could act it and that was Margaret Anglin. If it didn't appeal to her he might as well dock it. The younger actresses, clever as some of them were, had so far given no evidence of sustained emotional power. During the entire act no one was on the stage but the woman and she sat at a telephone talking with the man who controlled her destiny. Not only must that one-sided dialogue give as sharp and clear an idea of what the man was saying as if he had been present, with the vivid personality, the gestures and the mobile face he must have for the part, but the conversation, beginning in happy confidence, ran the gamut of the emotions, portraying a war of wills and souls, and rising to inexorable spiritual tragedy. It was a scene whose like had never before been attempted without both protagonists on the stage, and it lasted twenty-five minutes; a scene as difficult to write as to act; but the two playwrights admitted that in the deft use of words which, without repetitions by the woman, left the audience in no doubt what the man was saying, made it almost possible to see him, and in the rising scale of emotion, the act was a surpassingly brilliant piece of work. Clavering rewrote it fourteen times, and Hogarth and Scores were finally almost as excited as himself, although it was the last sort of thing either would have "tackled." Whatever the originality of their own ideas they were careful to stick to the orthodox in treatment, knowing the striking lack of originality in audiences.

Gora Dwight was more enthusiastic than he had ever known her to be over anything, and one night he read the play to a select few at her house. Abbott was there and two other critics, as well as Suzan Forbes and her distinguished consort, De Witt Turner.

The critics preserved their ferocious and frozen demeanor common to first-nights and less common where cocktails were plentiful. Not for them to encourage a tyro and a confrère,[1] as if they were mere friends and well-wishers. They left that to the others, but after the last act had been discussed with fury, Abbott arose and said with a yawn:

"Oh, well, what's the use? It's about the hardest play for actors ever written and the audience will either crack on that last act or pass away of their own emotions. It would be the former if any one else had written the damn thing, but it'll go because it isn't time yet for the Clavering luck to break. You'll get it in the neck, old man, one of these days, and when you least expect it. You're one of Fate's pets, her pampered pup, and she'll purr over you until she has you besotted, and then she'll give you such a skinning that you'll wish you were little Jimmy Jones, cub reporter, with a snub nose and freckles. I only hope to be in at the death to gloat." Then he shot out his hand. "Good stuff, Clavey. Congratulate you. Count on me."

And he drank a highball and waddled out.

The others, expressing their congratulations in various keys, soon followed, and Clavering was left alone with Gora. He was flushed and restless, but he doubted if he would feel happier on the first-night with the entire Sophisticate body howling for "author." He had been more afraid of Abbott and the two other critics than he, a hardened critic himself, had dared admit.

Gora watched him from her ottoman, where she sat stark upright, as usual, and smoking calmly. But her cold gray eyes were softer than usual. She knew exactly how he felt and rejoiced with him, but her expression in the long silence grew more and more thoughtful. Finally she threw away her cigarette and said abruptly:

"Clavey."

"Yes, Gora." He had been wandering about the room, but he halted in front of her, smiling.

She smiled also. "You do look so happy. But you're such a mercurial creature that you'll probably wake up tomorrow morning with your soul steeped in indigo."

"Oh, no, I won't. It isn't as if I had nothing else in my life." Gora alone knew of his engagement to Mary Zattiany.

"That is it. I want to say something. I know you'll be angry with me, but just remember that I am not speaking as a friend, merely as an artist."

---

1 Colleague or fellow professional.

"What are you driving at?" Some of the exultation faded from Clavering's face.

"This. I no longer want you to marry Madame Zattiany. She's served her purpose."

Clavering stared, then laughed. "Little you know about it."

"I know more about it than you think. Remember it is my business to know people's mental insides down to the roots——"

"Not such a good metaphor, that."

"Let it pass. I'm not to be diverted. I've seen her several times alone, you know. She lunched here the other day, and I purposely asked no one else. I believe I know her well enough to put her in a book, complex, both naturally and artificially, as she is. Maybe I shall some day. You once told me that she had a character of formidable strength and the 'will to power'—something like that. Well, I agree with you, and I don't think you'd stand a chance of becoming a great artist if you married her."

"You're talking utter rot."

"Am I? Tell me that a year hence—if you marry her."

"If? I'd tear the artist in me out by the roots before I'd give her up."

"You think so. I don't doubt it. But have you really projected your imagination into the future? I mean beyond the honeymoon? She tells me that she intends to live in Europe—that she has a great work to accomplish——"

"Yes, and she needs my help."

"She doesn't need your help, nor anybody's help. For that matter she'd be better off alone, for I don't doubt she would be in love with you longer than might be convenient. She has formidable powers of concentration.... But you—what would become of your own career? You'd be absorbed, devoured, annihilated by that woman. You're no weakling, but you're an artist and an artist's strength is not like the ordinary male's. It's too messed up with temperament and imagination. You are strong enough to impress your personality on her, win her, make her love you to the exclusion of everything else for the moment, and possibly hold her for a time. But you never could dominate her. What she needs is a statesman, if she must have marital partnership at all. Possibly not even a great executive brain could dominate her either, but at least it could force upon her a certain equality in personality, and that you never could do. Not only would your own career be wrecked, but you'd end by being wretched and resentful—quite apart from your forfeited right to express your genius in your own way—because you've been accustomed all your life yourself to the dominating act. You've always been a star of some sort, and you've never discouraged yourself—except when in the dumps—out of the belief that a fixed position was waiting for you in the stellar firmament. To vary the metaphor, you've always been in the crack regiment, even when the regiment was composed of cub reporters.... And you'd find yourself shrinking—shrinking—nothing but a famous woman's husband—lover, would be perhaps more like it——"

Here Clavering swore and started down the room again. That interview in the library two weeks ago tonight came back to him. He had banished its memory and she had been feminine and exquisite, and *young*, ever since. But that sudden vision of her standing by the table as he had rushed to her succor, calm and contemptuous in her indomitable powers, weakened his muscles and he walked unsteadily.

Miss Dwight went on calmly. "For she's going to be a very famous woman, make no doubt about that. It's quite on the cards that she may have a niche in history. You might be useful to her in many ways, with that brain of yours, but it was given to you for another purpose, and you'd end by leaving her. You'd come home like a sick dog to its kennel—and become a hack. Your genius would have shrivelled to the roots. If you give her up now your very unhappiness and baffled longings will make you do greater and greater things. Talent needs the pleasant pastures of content to browse on but they sicken genius. If you married her you wouldn't even have the pastures after the first dream was over and you certainly would have neither the independence of action nor the background of tragedy so necessary to your genius. That needs stones to bite on, not husks.... Believe me, I know what I am talking about. I have been through worse. If personal happiness were brought to me on a gold platter with Divine assurance that it would last—which it never does—remember that, Clavey— I should laugh in its face. And if you let her go now you will one day say the same thing yourself."

But Clavering had made a violent rebound. He threw himself into a chair and lit a cigarette, smiling at her indulgently. "The trouble with you, Gora," he said, "is that you are—and probably always were—artist first and woman last. If you'd got the man you thought you wanted you'd have chucked him in about six months. But I happen to be a man first and artist next."

Miss Dwight shrugged her shoulders. "Will you deny that you have been completely happy while writing that play? So happy and absorbed that you forgot everything else on earth—and everybody?"

"That's true enough. But if it's a mere question of happiness, that's not the sort that lasts, and the reaction is frightful. I am beginning to feel a hideous sense of loss and wish I had it to do all over again."

"You can go to work on another."

"I'll never feel to another play as I have to this."

"That's what every artist has said to himself since the gods plucked out a rib and invented the breed. Even if you do your comedy next your submergence will be precisely the same. It's the creative pot boiling that does the business."

"I don't believe it."

"Well, don't, then. And don't wake up as blue as paint tomorrow morning. Reaction is the price we all have to pay for keeping the brain too long at a pitch so high above the normal. It's the downwash of blood from the organ it has kept at fever heat. And it's a long sight less commonplace than reaction from too much love-making. Especially when love-making has begun to pall—which it does sooner in artists than in ordinary men....Writers begin life all over again with each new release of the creative faculty; and each new work is as enthralling as the last. But love!" She sighed. "You don't look as if I had made the slightest impression on you."

"You haven't. A man can combine both if a woman cannot. You forget that we return here after two or three months in Austria, and here we remain for at least two years."

"Why are you so sure of that? Have you her actual promise?"

"It is understood. I told her we should return and she knew that I meant what I said."

"It is quite likely that she knew you meant it! But I'd like you to promise me that you will ask her to tell you exactly what she does intend to do—when the honeymoon is over."

"What do you mean?" Clavering asked sharply.

"I mean, that although she told me nothing of her plans, it was perfectly evident from her conversation that she intends to live her life in Europe and play a great rôle there. I infer that she is in constant correspondence with political friends in Austria. Do you mean that she has never told you this?"

Clavering sat forward, frowning. "No. We—have had little time together and have not wasted it on politics. Did she tell you this?"

"Not she. But I 'got' it. I can't tell you just how, but my intuitions are pretty good."

"Intuitions be hanged. Your creative tract is prepared for action and has been doing a little stunt all by itself. Better get to work on it and plough up a new book. I don't doubt Mary has politi-cal friends in Austria, and corresponds with them. Why shouldn't she? But she's not committed to any definite date or action. I'll swear to that. She'd have told me so honestly."

"Very well. I've said my say. But I wish——" She fell silent and sat very still for several moments regarding the point of her slipper. Then she looked up and said brightly: "Don't you think it's time to let the rest of them know what's going to happen? It's hardly fair to your other friends—and they are your friends, Clavey. Of course they are practically certain of it."

"I don't think she'll mind, particularly as the first sensation has pretty well run its course—she thought she'd spare her own friends two shocks at once. But I fancy she intends to go out among them less and less. I'll ask her, and if she agrees, suppose you announce it?"

Miss Dwight bent down and removed a pinch of ashes from her slipper. "Do—persuade her. It would be a tremendous feather in my cap. I'll give you both a dinner and announce it then."

"Settled. Well, I'm off. Got my column to write." He gathered up his manuscript, and she went to the door with him. As he held her hand, he felt one of those subtle whispers along his nerves that had warned him of danger before. He dropped her hand with a frown.

"Look here, Gora," he said. "You haven't any mistaken idea of appealing to her, have you?"

"What do you take me for?" demanded Miss Dwight angrily. "The father in *Camille*?"[1]

"Well, keep off the grass, that's all. Ta, ta."

XL

When Mary Zattiany returned home at twelve o'clock after a tire-some morning in Judge Trent's office she told the butler to send her luncheon upstairs, and ascended to the seclusion of her room, delighted with the prospect of a few hours she could call her own. These hours had been increasing during the past fortnight but

---

[1] French 1852 melodramatic play adapted from Alexandre Dumas's 1848 novel *La dame aux camélias* which focused on the tubercular death of a courtesan, abandoned by her lover despite the purity of their love. The role was made famous by several actresses, including Sarah Bernhardt, Lillian Gish, and Theda Bara (in a 1917 film). The 1921 film, *Camille*, featured Rudolph Valentino.

were no less welcome. Not a word of that dinner was known to any but those who had attended it. People do not foul their own nest unless they are ready to desert it and sometimes not then. Moreover, the women were too ashamed or too humiliated with their failure to invite the criticism of their friends, and although they avoided the subject among themselves, their agreement to bury it was no less final for being tacit. The men, with something of the deliberation of male guests at a diplomatic dinner where there has been an unfortunate incident involving dangerous possibilities if known, called one another up on the telephone the next day and agreed to "forget it." Even Dinwiddie never heard of it. As for Madame Zattiany, she could be trusted to dismiss it from her contemptuous mind. Nevertheless, these young women, who had entertained her almost constantly, pointedly omitted her from their luncheons and dinners and parties—in her new lightheartedness she had been induced to attend several parties during the past six weeks. And they had little difficulty in persuading others to follow their example. The more amiable of the younger women might have looked upon their attack that night with horror if they had heard of it, as, indeed, several at the dinner had done, but they were no more enthusiastic over the "foreign invasion" than their militant sisters. The remonstrances of the men were unheeded, and when one or two tried to arrange theatre parties or dinners in Madame Zattiany's honor they received graceful regrets.

Even the attitude of her older friends had changed, now that the dramatic novelty of her return to them, and their first determined enthusiasm, had worn off. They were betraying more and more their disapproval of what she had done, the more so perhaps, as the majority of them, being excessively thin, might have accomplished a like result had not their standards protected them. This naturally inspired them with a full realization of their superiority, which increased daily.

If she had made the attempt and failed it would have been bad enough, for such violations of the law of orthodoxy insulted the code in which she had been born and reared: but triumphantly to have succeeded in making herself young again while the rest of them were pursuing their unruffled way to the grave was a deliberate insult both to themselves and to God.

Moreover, they hardly knew what to talk to her about, and although this might still have been the case had she returned to them carrying aloft the crinkled and spotted flag of time, so far apart their lines had run, her scientific victory added an ever-increasing irritant. Also, she had never been a "woman's woman," and it was patent that, as ever, she was far more animated in the company of men. Inevitably, old scandals were raked up. They had been frowned upon in the days when she was protected by her husband and the great position he gave her, and the rumors had been dismissed for more interesting scandals, both public and private, at home. They no doubt would have remained in the limbo of history had she returned looking no better than themselves, but her ridiculous defiance of nature revived them, and these ladies discovered that their memories were more lively than might have been expected of their years.

It would be too much, as Mary told Clavering, to ask a violent contradiction of human nature from worn out glands, and she bore them no malice. She only wondered that Jane Oglethorpe, Elinor Goodrich, and Lily Tracy were still faithful in private—to the world all of them preserved a united front; they would not even discuss her with their children, much less their grandchildren; but they made up their minds that it would be for the good of her soul to let her see, with no flaw in their politeness, just what uncompromisingly sensible women of high moral and social responsibilities thought of her.

Mary, being human, felt the pin-pricks, but was glad on the whole to be rid of them. Those first weeks of almost girlish pleasure in what was to her a novel society, had vanished for ever on the night of her dinner. Scornful and indifferent she might be, but although they could not kill her youth, they drove home to her what she had guessed in the beginning, that the society and the companionship of young people—fashionable young people, at least—were not for her. Their conversations, interests, shallow mental attitude to life, bored her. That curious brief period of mental rejuvenescence had been due to the novelty and excitement of being in love again, after long and arid years.

And now, Judge Trent had told her that she would be free to leave in a fortnight. She had walked the three miles from Broad Street with a buoyant step, and she had vowed that never, not for any consideration whatever, would she set foot in America again. Vienna was the city of her heart as well as of her future exploits. She would buy the old Zattiany palace from her widowed niece-in-law and make it the most famous rendezvous in Europe. But of all this nothing to Clavering until they were in the Dolomites.

She rang for her maid and exchanged her tweed walking suit for a tea gown of violet velvet and snow white chiffon, with stockings and slippers to match. She expected no one but it was always a delight to her to be exquisitely and becomingly dressed. Even in the seclusion of her Hungarian estate she had arrayed herself as appropriately for outdoors, and as fastidiously for the house, as if she had been under the critical eye of her world, for daintiness and luxury were as ingrained as ordinary cleanliness and refinement. During the war she had not rebelled at her hard and unremitting labors, but she had often indulged in a fleeting regret for the frequent luxury of the bath, the soft caress of delicate underwear, for charming toilettes; and she had sometimes scowled at her white cotton stockings with a feeling of positive hatred.

Judge Trent, while she was still in Austria, had sent her a cheque for forty thousand dollars. She had given half of it to relief organizations in Vienna, and then gone to Paris and indulged in an orgy of clothes. She looked back upon that wholly feminine reversion, when she had avoided every one she had ever known, as one of the completely satisfactory episodes of her life. Even with unrestored youth and beauty, and a soberer choice of costumes, she would still have experienced a certain degree of excited pleasure in adorning herself.

She had always liked the light freshness of chintz in her bedroom, leaving luxury to her boudoir; but here she had furnished no boudoir; her stay was to be short, and her bedroom was as large as two ordinary rooms. She spent many hours in it, when its violet and white simplicities appealed to her mood. Today it was redolent of the lilacs Clavering had sent her, and through the open windows came the singing of birds in the few trees still left in the old street.

She loved comfort as much as she loved exercise, and after her careful toilette was finished and her maid had gone, she settled herself luxuriously in a deep chair before her desk and opened one of the drawers. The European mail had arrived yesterday and she had only glanced through half of it. But she must read all of those letters today and answer some of them before the sailings on Saturday.

The telephone on a little stand at her elbow rang, and she took the receiver from its spreading violet skirts and raised it to her ear. As she had expected, it was Clavering. He told her that he had promised Gora Dwight the evening before to ask her permission to announce their engagement.

For a moment she stared into the instrument. Then she said hurriedly, almost breathlessly: "No—I'd rather not. I hate the vulgarity of congratulations—publicity of my private affairs. I've always said that when one marries a second time the decent thing to do is to marry first and tell afterward."

"But they guess it, you know."

"That is quite different." It was Madame Zattiany who spoke now and her tones were deliberate and final. "Quite a different thing from being congratulated, and tormented by newspapers." She dismissed the subject. "I shall be free two weeks from today. What do you think of that?" Her voice was both gay and tender. "Judge Trent will see at once about engaging my stateroom. Don't tell me that that play of yours will prevent you from following shortly after."

"Not a bit of it. We shall only be gone two months, and even if Hogarth succeeds in placing it with his manager as he expects, it might be several months before rehearsals."

"Then it all fits in quite charmingly. You are coming to dinner tonight?"

"Well, rather."

"Mind you come early. I have many things to tell you."

"It'll not be for that I'll come early."

Mary smiled and hung up the receiver. She would have to let him return to New York for a time—possibly. But herself, she would go on to Vienna. No doubt about that.

She returned to her letters. Those that required answers she placed in a separate heap with a pencilled note on the back, for she was neat and methodical; she even slit the envelopes with a paper-knife that was always at hand for the purpose, and the envelopes were dropped at once into the waste basket.

The contents for the most part were expected, and related to her work in Vienna, the disposition of moneys she had sent over, and the usual clamoring for more. But when she had read halfway through a long letter from Baroness Tauersperg, in whose capable hands she had left the most important of her charities, she involuntarily stiffened and sat forward a little.

Several pages of her friend's letters were always devoted to business, the rest to gossip. In return Mary enlivened her own letters with many of her American adventures, although she had made no mention of Clavering.

"I need not ask if you remember Hohenhauer," continued Frau von Tauersperg, "although, I suppose, like the rest of us, you saw nothing of him after the war. He was, as you know, not in bad standing with the new Government, like the reactionary nobles, as he had always been a liberal in politics, and had a good record as a generous and just landlord. But they did not have intelligence enough to ask him to be a member of the Cabinet, or to send him to the Peace Conference, where he alone, of all Austrians, perhaps, might have won some advantage for this wretched country.[1]

"The present Government seems to have appreciated that initial mistake of ignoring him, for they have invited him to return from his estate in Switzerland, where he has been staying, and to act in some advisory capacity. That means, we think here, that he will soon have the whole thing in his hands. The first step he took was to pay a visit to Bavaria and have a conference with Count L., and no doubt you will surmise what that means. He went incognito, however, and few people even here in Vienna know of that visit, much less the rest of Europe. Very shortly he goes to America, whether for reasons connected with his sudden interest in Bavaria, I have no means of knowing, but ostensibly because his New York lawyers demand his presence in regard to the large sum of money he invested in the United States. The Government makes no objection to this journey, as you may imagine, for they know they can depend on him to spend it in the cause of Austria—under his leadership! Imagine what it will mean to have the income of several million American dollars rolling in to be exchanged for Austrian kronen![2] Or the capital, if he thinks the end justifies it.

"No doubt you will see him, for he always had the greatest respect for your opinion—was it not you who advised him to sell out practically everything he possessed, except the land in Galicia, and invest it in America? I have no doubt he will confide in you and ask your advice. You have a wonderful flair for politics, dear Marie, and you know what we all expect of you. Hurry, hurry and come back to us. We need you in a thousand ways. But what a rest that sojourn in the gay and brilliant and *rich* city of New York must have given you. It is both wonderful and saddening to read of the almost unbelievable contrast to our poor Vienna. But they are generous. The second cheque from your Vienna Fund came yesterday. Do leave the *oeuvre* in reliable and sympathetic hands, dear Marie, so that it may go on until—well, God only knows when."

Mary read this portion of the letter over twice, the serenity of her face routed by a frown. Of course she had expected to meet this man in the future, indeed had had a very definite idea of playing his cards immediately upon her return to Vienna. But that he should come here! Now. That was another matter. She had succeeded in dismissing the past, and she resented this dark reminder.

---

1 The 1919 Paris Peace Conference that ended World War I resulted in the Treaty of Versailles and the creation of the League of Nations.
2 Austrian currency between 1919 and 1925.

Well, she could refuse to see him, and possibly he would not arrive until after her departure. And then she sighed again. The futility of attempting to travel through even one brief cross-section of life on a straight line!

Her luncheon was brought up to her and when it was finished she answered her letters and settled down to the latest novel of one of her new friends. But Gora Dwight was announced and she put the book aside with a sensation of pleasant anticipation. She liked no one better, of her new American acquaintances, and had made no objection when Clavering had asked her to let him confide his engagement to Gora Dwight alone. He felt that he owed her the compliment (how he was to obtain the forgiveness of Mrs. Oglethorpe was a thought he dared not dwell on), and Mary, little disposed as she was to intimacies, had felt a certain release in speaking of her engagement to another woman.

XLI

Gora was looking her best in a smart spring frock of brown tweed with a drooping red feather on her hat, whose pointed brim almost but not quite obscured one eye. The two women greeted each other with something like affection, and after the usual feminine preliminaries were over, Gora exclaimed with enthusiasm:

"I have come to tell you how really wonderful Lee's play is, and to say that I could have shaken him for not letting you hear it, but he seems determined that it shall burst upon you in the unmitigated glory of a first-night performance."

Madame Zattiany smiled, very slightly. "Yes, he made a great point of that. I could only let him have his way. He is very fond of having his way, is he not?"

"Well, we've spoiled him, you see. And those of us who have heard the play are more excited than we have been over anything for a long time. Those that haven't are not far behind. I believe there is a dinner or a party in his honor projected for every night for weeks to come."

Madame Zattiany raised her eyebrows in genuine surprise. "Isn't it rather unusual, that—to fête an author before he has made his début?"

"It is, rather. But in this case it's different. We've waited so long for Clavey to do the big thing that we must let off steam at once."

"He certainly seems to be a tremendous favorite among you. Several of his friends were here at dinner the other night—I was so sorry you were unable to come—and really they seemed to be able to talk of nothing else. They are all very charming to me now, but I am wondering if they will be more than amiably interested in me when I am merely the wife of a famous playwright?"

"Oh, you must do something yourself," said Miss Dwight emphatically. "I am sure you could write. And equally sure that you will try, for you could not live constantly with such workers as we are without being stung by the same busy little bee. You have suggested genius to me from the first, and I am convinced it is not merely the genius of personality. Your life has stifled your talents, but now is the time to discover them and take your place in American letters."

"I had thought such talents as I possessed should be used in the attempt to play a humble part in the reconstruction of Europe," murmured Madame Zattiany; and one of her beautiful white hands moved toward the cigarette box with a curious tensing of the muscles that seemed to rob it subtly of its likeness to flesh. Nothing escaped Miss Dwight's observing eye, and she replied casually: "Oh, Europe isn't worth the effort, dear Madame Zattiany. It's too far gone. The future of the world lies here in the United States. New York is the brain and soul of the United States. Moreover, if you want to help Europe, you can write about it here, be the one to give us all a clearer understanding of that miserable chaos."

"But I detest writing," said Madame Zattiany, who was lying back and watching her smoke rings. "I like the activity of doing, and I have had an experience that particularly fits me for political intrigue. If this were Washington, now——"

"Oh, Washington! Washington is merely one of the islands outside of New York. So is Chicago, Boston, the rest of them.... And don't imagine you would not become fascinated with writing as soon as you were in your stride. Here is a simple recipe to begin with. Get up every morning with the set intention of writing and go to your desk and sit there for three hours, whether you accomplish anything or not. Before long you will find that you are writing madly, not waiting for inspiration. And you will have Clavey to criticize you. The rest is only stern self-discipline. Here is another suggestion: when you have brain fag go to bed for two days and starve. The result is miraculous."

"So, that is the way American writers are made. There are so many of them—I had often wondered——"

"Oh, not at all!" Miss Dwight rushed to the defence of native American genius. "But all writers, no matter what their gifts, often go through a period of torture while forming habits of regular work."

"It sounds like torture!" She gave Gora a glance of lazy amuse-ment. "Really, Miss Dwight! Are you trying to frighten me off?"

But Gora did not blush. If she chose to concentrate her agile mind on acting, the accomplished actress opposite could give her few points. She replied with convincing emphasis: "Certainly not. What an odd idea. I have the most enormous respect for your abilities, and you should be famous for something besides beau-ty—and I should like to see you live down mere notoriety."

"I've loved the notoriety, and rather regret that it seems to have lost flavor with time. But I'll never make a writer, Miss Dwight, and have not the least intention of trying."

"But surely you'll not be content to be just Lee's wife? Why, practically every woman in our crowd does something. There used to be a superstition that two brain-workers could not live comfort-ably under the same roof, but as a matter of fact we've proved that a woman keeps her husband far longer if her brain is as productive as his. Each inspires and interests the other. Another old *cliché* gone to the dust bin. Our sort of men want something more from a woman than good housekeeping. Not that men no longer want to be comfortable, but the clever women of today have learned to combine both."

"Marvellous age and marvellous America! Don't you think I could keep Lee interested without grinding away at my desk for three hours every morning and lying in hungry misery for days at a time?"

"You could keep any man interested. I wasn't thinking of him, but of you. He has more than a man's entitled to already. Men are selfish brutes, and I waste no sympathy on them. It's women who have the rotten deal in this world, the best of them. And men are as vain as they are selfish. It's an enormous advantage for a woman to have her own reputation and her own separate life. No man should be able to feel that he possesses a woman wholly. He simply can't stand it."

"Quite right. Discarding modesty, I may add that I am an old hand at that game."

Gora regarded her with frank admiration, wholly unassumed. "Oh, you couldn't lose Clavey if you tried. He is mad about you. We can all see that, and I knew it before he did himself. It's only—really—that I'm afraid you'll be bored to death with so much shop if you don't set up one for yourself."

"Oh, I never intend to be bored again as long as I live." Mary Zattiany was a very shrewd woman and she determined on a bold stroke. Her suspicion lingered but had lost its edge. Gora Dwight was deep and subtle but there was no doubt that she was honorable. "I shall tell you something," she said, "but you must give me your word that you will not betray me—not even to Lee."

Miss Dwight's mind, not her body, gave a slight stir of uneasiness. But she answered warmly: "Of course I promise."

"Very well, then. It is this. I shall never return to America. I sail in a fortnight. Lee follows soon after, and we shall be married in Austria."

"But—but—his play!" Miss Dwight was too startled to act. "He must be here for rehearsals. Some one has said that plays are not written, they're rewritten, and it's pretty close to the truth."

"I shall consent to his returning in time for rehearsals. Prolonged honeymoons are indiscreet. It is better to divide them into a series. I fancy the series might hold out indefinitely if adroitly spaced. Moreover, being a modern myself, I like new methods. And he will be too busy to miss me. I shall be equally busy in Vienna."

"But will he consent? Lee? He's not used to having his plans made for him. He's about the most dominating male I know."

"I feel sure he will when the time comes. It is woman's peculiar gift, you know, to convince the dominating male that he wants what she wants."

Gora laughed. But she also could turn mental somersaults. "I think it a splendid arrangement. Then we should not lose Lee altogether, for we really are devoted to him. He is an adorable creature for all his absurdities. But I can't endure the thought of losing you."

"You must pay me a long visit in Vienna. Many visits. I can assure you that you will find material there, under my guidance, for a really great novel."

Gora's eyes sparkled. She was all artist at once. "I should like that! How kind of you. And what a setting!"

"Yes, Austria is the most interesting country in Europe, and the most beautiful to look at—and describe."

"It will be heavenly." Gora made up her mind at once that she would waste no more ingenuity to stop this marriage. Its modernity appealed to her, and she foresaw new impulses to creation. "The American Scene," conceivably, might grow monotonous with time; and with these daily recruits bent upon describing its minutiae with the relentless efficiency of the camera. And with all her soul she loved beauty. With the possible exception of Bavaria she knew Austria to be the darling of nature.

Once more she chose to believe this woman would manage Clavering to his own good, and to the satisfaction of his friends, who, as she well knew, were alarmed and alert. They were too polite to show it, but much of their enthusiasm for Madame Zattiany had dimmed with the knowledge that she was a scientific phenomenon. Fundamentally the brilliant creative mind is quite as conservative as the worldly, or the inarticulate millions between, for they have common ancestors and common traditions. They feared not only to lose him, moreover, but had begun to ask one another if his career would not be wrecked.

Miss Dwight concluded that such an uncommon and romantic marriage might be a spur to Clavering's genius, which might weaken in a conventional marital drama set in the city of New York.

She rose and for the first time kissed Madame Zattiany. "It will be too perfect!" she said. "Let me visit you in summer when he is rehearsing. He can arrange to have his first-nights in September, and then write his next play in Austria, filling his time while you are absorbed in politics. Heavens, what a theme! Some day I'll use it. Perfectly disguised, of course."

"And I'll give you points," said Mary, laughing. She returned the other's embrace; but when she was alone she sighed and sank back in her chair, without picking up her book. Miss Gora Dwight had given her something to think of! The last thing she wanted was a serial honeymoon. She wanted this man's companionship and his help. But she had slowly been forced to the conclusion that Clavering's was a mind whose enthusiasms could only be inspired by some form of creative art; politics would never appeal to it. In her comparative ignorance of the denaturalized brain, she had believed that a brilliant gifted mind could concentrate itself upon any object with equal fertility and power, but she had seen too much of the Sophisticates of late, and studied Clavering in too many of his moods to cherish the illusion any longer. Playwrighting seemed to her a contemptible pastime compared with the hideous facts of Life as exemplified in Europe, and she had restrained herself from an angry outburst more than once. But she was too philosophical, possibly too fatalistic, not to have dismissed this attitude eventually. Clavering could not be changed, but neither could she. There would be the usual compromises. After all, of what was life made up but of compromise? But the early glow of the wondrous dream had faded. The mistress was evidently the rôle nature had cast her to play. The vision of home, the complete matehood, had gone the way of all dreams.

XLII

She was not sorry to forego the doubtful luxury of meditation on the sadness of life. When Miss Trevor's card was brought to her she told the servant to show her up and bring tea immediately. She was not interested in Agnes Trevor, a younger sister of Polly Vane, but at all events she would talk about her settlement work and give a comfortably commonplace atmosphere to the room in which tragic clouds were rising. As it had happened, Mary, during these past weeks, had seen little of New York women between the relics of her old set and their lively Society-loving daughters. The women between forty and fifty, whether devoted to fashion, politics, husbands, children, or good works, had so far escaped her, and Agnes Trevor, who lived with Mrs. Vane, was practically the only representative of the intermediate age with whom she had exchanged a dozen words. But the admirable spinster had taken up the cause of the Vienna children with enthusiasm and raised a good deal of money, besides contributing liberally herself. She was forty-two, and, although she was said to have been a beautiful girl, was now merely patrician in appearance, very tall and thin and spinsterish, with a clean but faded complexion, and hair-colored [sic] hair beginning to turn gray. She had left Society in her early twenties and devoted herself to moralizing the East Side.

She came in with a light step and an air of subdued bright energy, very smartly but plainly dressed in dark blue tweed, with a large black hat in which a wing had been accurately placed by the best milliner in New York. Her clothes were so well-worn, and her grooming was so meticulous, her accent so clean and crisp, her manner so devoid of patronage, yet subtly remote, her controlled heart so kind that she perennially fascinated the buxom, rather sloppy, preternaturally acute, and wholly unaristocratic young ladies of the East Side.

Mary, who had a dangerous habit of characterizing people in her Day Book, had written when she met Agnes Trevor: "She radiates intelligence, good will, cheeriness, innate superiority and uncompromising virginity."

"Dear Mary!" she exclaimed in her crisp bright tones as she kissed her amiable hostess. "How delightful to find you alone. I was afraid you would be surrounded as usual."

"Oh, my novelty is wearing off," said Mary drily. "But I will tell them to admit no one else today. I find I enjoy one person at a time. One gets rather tired in New York of the unfinished sentence."

"Oh, do." Mary's quick eye took note of a certain repressed excitement in the fine eyes of her guest, who had taken an upright chair. Lounging did not accord with that spare ascetic figure. "And you are quite right. It is seldom one has anything like real conversation. One has to go for that to those of our older women who have given up Society to cultivate the intellects God gave them."

"Are there any?" murmured Mary.

"Oh, my dear, yes. But, of course, you've had no time to meet them in your mad whirl. Now that things have slowed down a bit you *must* meet them."

"I'm afraid it's too late. I sail in a fortnight."

"Oh!" Miss Trevor's voice shook oddly, and the slow color crept up her cheeks. But at that moment the tea was brought in.

"Will you pour it out?" asked Mary. "I'm feeling rather lazy."

"Of course." Miss Trevor was brightly acquiescent. She seated herself before the table. The man retired with instructions that Madame was not at home to other callers.

Mary watched her closely as she stirred the tea with a little business-like air, warmed the cups, distributed the lemon and then poured out the clear brown fluid.

"Formosa Oolong," she said, sniffing daintily. "The only tea. I hate people who drink scented teas, don't you? I'm going to have a very strong cup, so I'll wait a minute or two. I'm—rather tired."

"You? You look as if you never relaxed in your sleep. How do you keep it up?"

"Oh, think of the life the younger women lead. Mine is a quiet amble along a country road by comparison.... But ... monotonous!"

The last word came out with the effect of a tiny explosion. It evidently surprised Miss Trevor herself, for she frowned, poured out a cup of tea that was almost black, and began sipping it with a somewhat elaborate concentration for one so simple and direct of method.

"I'm afraid good works are apt to grow monotonous. A sad commentary on the triumphs of civilization over undiluted nature." Mary continued to watch the torch bearer of the East Side. "Don't you sometimes hate it?"

She asked the question idly, interested for the moment in probing under another shell hardened in the mould of time, and half-hoping that Agnes would be natural and human for once, cease to be the bright well-oiled machine. She was by no means prepared for what she got.

Miss Trevor gulped down the scalding tea in an almost unladylike manner, and put the cup down with a shaking hand.

"That's what I've come to see you about," she said in a low intense voice, and her teeth set for a moment as if she had taken a bit between them. "Mary, you've upset my life."

"I? What next!"

"I suppose you have troubles of your own, dear, and I hate to bother you with mine——"

"Oh, mine amount to nothing at present. And if I can help you——" She felt no enthusiasm at the prospect, but she saw that the woman was laboring under excitement of some sort, and if she could not give her sympathy at least she might help her with sound practical advice. Moreover, she was in for it. "Better tell me all about it."

"It is terribly hard. I'm so humiliated—and—and I suppose no more reticent woman ever lived."

"Oh, reticence! Why not emulate the younger generation? I'm not sure—although I prefer the happy medium myself—that they are not wiser than their grandmothers and their maiden aunts. On the principle that confession is good for the soul, I don't believe that women will be so obsessed by—well, let us say, sex, in the future."

Miss Trevor flushed darkly. "It is possible.... That's what I am—a maiden aunt. Just that and nothing more."

"Nothing more? I thought you were accounted one of the most useful women in serious New York. A sort of mother to the East Side."

"Mother? How could I be a mother? I'm only a maiden aunt even down there. Not that I want to be a mother——"

"I was going to ask you why you did not marry even now. It is not too late to have children of your own——"

"Oh, yes, it is. That's all over—or nearly. But I can't say that I ever did long for children of my own, although I get on beautifully with them."

"Well?" asked Mary patiently, "what is it you do want?"

"A husband!" This time there was no doubt about the explosion.

Mary felt a faint sensation of distaste, and wondered if she were reverting to type as a result of this recent association with the generation that still clung to the distastes and the disclaimers of the nineteenth century. "Why didn't you marry when you were a girl? I am told that you were quite lovely."

"I hated the thought. I was in love twice; but I had a sort of cold purity that I was proud of. The bare idea of—of that nauseated me."

"Pity you hadn't done settlement work first. That must have knocked prudishness out of you, I should think."

"It horrified me so that for several years I hardly could go on with it, and I have always refused to mix the sexes in my house down there, but, of course, I could not help hearing things—seeing things—and after a while I did get hardened—and ceased to be revolted. I learned to look upon all that sort of thing as a matter of course. But it was too late then. I had lost what little looks I had ever possessed. I grew to look like an old maid long before I was thirty. Why is nature so cruel, Mary?"

"I fancy a good many American women develop very slowly sexually. You were merely one of them. I wonder you had the climacteric so early. But nature is very fond of taking her little revenges. You defied her and she smote you."

"Oh, yes, she smote me! But I never fully realized it until you came."

"I hardly follow you."

"Oh, *don't* you see? You have shown us that women can begin life over again, undo their awful mistakes. And yet I don't dare—don't dare——"

"Why not, pray? Better come with me to Vienna if you haven't the courage to face the music here."

"Oh, I haven't the courage. I couldn't carry things off with such a high hand as you do. You were always high and mighty, they say, and have done as you pleased all your life. You don't care a pin whether we approve of what you've done or not. It's the way you're made. But I—couldn't stand it. The admission of vanity, of—of—after the life I've led. The young women would say, in their nasty slang, that I was probably man-crazy."

"And aren't you?" asked Mary coolly. "Isn't that just what is the matter? The sex-imagination often outlives the withering of the sex-glands. Come now, admit it. Forget that you are a pastel-tinted remnant of the old order and call a spade a spade."

"There's something terrifying about you, Mary." Miss Trevor had flushed a dark purple, but she had very honest eyes, and they did not falter. "But I respect you more than any woman I have ever known. And although you are not very sympathetic you are the only person on earth to whom I could even mention such a subject."

"Well, go ahead," said Mary resignedly. "If you want my advice, take your courage in your hands and do it. However people may carp, there is nothing they so much admire as courage."

"Yes, but they make you suffer tortures just because they do admire it—or to keep themselves from admitting it."

"True enough. But after all, they don't matter. Life would be so much simpler if we'd all make up our minds that what other people think about us does not signify in the least. It's only permitting it to signify that permits it to exist."

"That's all very well for you, but it's really a question of temperament. Do you think I'd dare come back here looking like a girl again—and I suppose I should. I'm sixteen years younger than you.... You must know how many of the women hate you."

"That sort of hate may be very stimulating, my dear Agnes," said Madame Zattiany drily.

"I can understand that. But I should return to what it is hardly an exaggeration to call a life of a thousand intimacies. The ridicule! The contempt! The merciless criticism! I don't want to live anywhere else. I can't face it! But, oh, I do so want it! I do so want it!"

"But just think of the compensations. No doubt you would marry immediately. If you were happy, and with a man to protect you, how much would you care?"

"Oh!" Once more the thin ascetic face was dyed with an unbecoming flush. "Oh!" And then the barriers fell with a crash and she hurried on, the words tumbling over one another, as her memory, its inhibitions shattered, swept back into the dark vortex of her secret past. "Oh, Mary! You don't know! You don't know! You, who've had all the men you ever wanted. Who, they say, have a young man now. The nights of horror I've passed. I've never slept a wink the nights our girls married. I could have killed them. I could have killed every man I've met for asking nothing of *me*. It seems to me that I've thought of nothing else for twenty years. When I've been teaching, counselling good thoughts, virtue, good conduct, to those girls down there, it's been in the background of my mind every minute like a terrible obsession. I wonder I haven't gone mad. Some of us old maids do go mad. And no one knew until they raved what was the matter with them. When Hannah de Lacey lost her mind three years ago I heard one of the doctors telling Peter Vane that her talk was the most libidinous he had ever listened to. And she was the most forbidding old maid in New York. I know if I lose my mind it will be the same, and that alone is enough to drive any decent woman mad.... I thought I'd get over it in time—I used to pray—and fight with my will—but when the time came when I should have been released I was afraid I would, and then I deliberately did everything I could to keep it alive. I couldn't lose my right——It was my right. I couldn't tell you all the things I've——Oh, I tell you that unless I can be young again and have some man—any man—I don't care whether he'll marry me or not—I'll go mad—mad!"

Her voice had risen to a shriek. She would be in hysterics in another moment. Mary, who was on the point of nausea, went hastily into her dressing-room and poured out a dose of sal-volatile.[1] "Here!" she said peremptorily. "Drink this. I'll not listen to another word. And I don't wish to be obliged to call an ambulance."

Miss Trevor gulped it down, and then permitted herself to be led to a sofa, where she lay sprawled, her immaculate hat on one side, giving her the look of a debauched gerontic[2] virgin. She lay panting for a few moments, while Madame Zattiany paced up and down the room.

She turned as she heard a groan. Miss Trevor was sitting up, straightening her hat. "Feel better?" she asked unsympathetically.

"Oh, yes—my nerves feel better! But what have I said? What must you think of me? I never expected to give way like that when I came. I thought I could put it all to you in a few delicate hints, knowing that you would understand. What have I said? I can hardly remember."

"Better not try! I'll promise to forget it myself." She sat down beside the sofa. "Now, listen to me. It would not be wise for you to go to Vienna. They would suspect, if not at once, then certainly when you returned. It can be done here. The rejuvenescence is so gradual that it would hardly be noticed. Fully a year. You do not have to go into a hospital, nor even to bed. You are not spied on, so no one would suspect that you were taking the treatment. At your age success is practically assured. Take it, and don't be a fool. If you don't it's only a question of time when that superb self-control you have practised for so many years will go again. And, too possibly, in the wrong place.... It is quite likely that you will never be suspected, because women often bloom out in their forties, take on a new lease of life. Begin to put on a little make-up——"

Miss Trevor interrupted with a horrified exclamation.

"It would be judicious. If they criticize you, remember that nothing they can say will be as bad—from your point of view— as their finding out the truth. They will lay it to that, and to the fact that you have grown a little stouter. And let me tell you, you won't care in the least, even if conservatism attacks you in solid

---

1 A smelling salt made of ammonium carbonate.
2 Elderly.

battalions, for your mental attitude to life will be entirely changed. Remember that you will be young again, and too gay and happy to mind what people think of you. Now, promise me that you will take my advice, and then go home and to bed."

Miss Trevor got up and went to the mirror. "Yes, I'll do it." And then she said, no doubt for the first time in her life: "And I'll not give a damn, no matter what happens."

When she had left Mary Zattiany stood for a few moments striking her hands together, her face distorted. A wave of nausea overwhelmed her. She felt as if there had been an earthquake in her own soul and its muck were riding the surface. She loathed herself and all women and all men. She knew that the violence of the revulsion must be temporary, but for the moment it was beyond her control. She went to the telephone and called up Clavering and told him that she had a severe headache and was going to bed. And she cut short both his protests and his expression of sympathy by hanging up the receiver. And then she picked up a vase and hurled it to the floor and smashed it.

XLIII

Clavering stood on his high balcony and looked down upon Madison Square. Spring had come. The Square looked like an oasis in a rocky gorge. The trees were covered with the tender greens of the new birth, and even President Arthur and Roscoe Conkling,[1] less green than in winter, looked reconciled to their lot. A few people were sunning themselves on the benches, many more were on top of the busses over on Fifth Avenue, and even the hurrying throngs, preoccupied with crass business, seemed to walk with a lighter step, their heads up, instead of sullenly defying winds and sleet. The eight streets that surrounded or debouched into the Square poured forth continuous streams of figures, constantly augmented by throngs rising out of the earth itself. There was a vivid color running like ribbons through the crowds, for it was nearly nine o'clock and the doors of offices and shops and business houses were open to women as to men. Overhead a yellow sun shone in

---

1 Roscoe Conkling (1829-88), a representative and Senator from New York. Chester A. Arthur (1829-86), a one-time protégée of Conkling's, cut ties with his old associates once he became US president (succeeding James Garfield, who was assassinated in office). Monuments to both stand in Madison Square, Manhattan.

a pale filmy sky and the air was both warm and sharp. The doves were circling and settling.

The prize-fighters had taken their prowess elsewhere, and a circus had come to Madison Square Garden. Clavering had heard the roar of lions in the night. A far different crowd would stand under the arcade in a few hours, but the peanut venders would ply their trade, and a little booth for candies and innocuous juices had been erected in an alcove in the front wall, presided over by a plump pretty blonde. She alternated "jollying" and selling with quiet intervals of beading a bag, undisturbed either by ogling or the hideous noises of Twenty-sixth Street.[1]

In spite of his disappointment two nights before he found it impossible to feel depressed in that gay spring sunshine. He did not believe in the headache, but she had written him a charming note and he supposed that a man must get accustomed to the caprices of women if he intended to live with one. And a month from now they would be in the Dolomites, and she would be his. Let her have her caprices. He had his own. There were times when he didn't want to see her.

Moreover, he was still too jubilant over his play to feel depressed for long over anything; the warm and constantly manifested enthusiasm of his friends had kept his spirits from suffering any natural reaction. Their demand for his companionship was almost peremptory, and his thoughts turned to them as he stood on his balcony looking down on the waning throngs: the great stone buildings were humming like hives, and figures were passing busily to and fro behind the open windows. It astonished him a little. True, it was his first play and he was very popular. But he had a vague uneasy idea they were overdoing it. They talked of nothing else: his play, his brilliant future, his sure place in the crack regiment "if he hung on"; and they insisted that he must also express himself at least once through the medium of the novel. The great New York novel had yet to be written. They fairly dinned his gifts into his ears, until he was almost sick of them, and wondered if Mary were not also. She had seen a good deal of the Sophisticates lately, and from what she had let drop he inferred that even when he had not been present they had talked of little else. They had by no means waited for his play to be finished and read to a select few. Hogarth and Scores had assured them long before it was finished that it would be a great play.

---

1 Site of the B&O Railroad yard, where freight was loaded and unloaded.

Once or twice there was a rustling in the back of his mind. They were not given to wild enthusiasms of this sort. They thought too highly of themselves. He realized how genuinely fond they were of him, but he had not hoped for more than critical appreciation, from the men, at least. Could it be possible ...

But he was still in the first flush of his triumph, his brain hummed with pleasant memories of those hours at Gora Dwight's, three nights ago. He had cleared the base of the pedestal on whose narrow and unaccommodating top he was soon to have his foothold, and it was not in human nature, at this stage of his progress, to suspect the sincerity of the adulation so generously poured at his feet.

And Mary, during this past fortnight (when he had been present, at least) had seemed to bask contentedly in reflected glory, and smiled sympathetically while they talked of the many Clavering first-nights they would attend in the sure anticipation of that class of entertainment up to which the Little Theatres and the Theatre Guild were striving to educate the public. They took it as a matter of course that he was to abide in the stimulating atmosphere of New York for the rest of his days. And they invariably insisted that "Madame Zattiany" must always sit in a stage box and be a part of the entertainment. They were too well-bred (and too astute) to hint at the engagement they were positive existed, but "hoped" she would be willing to add to the prestige of one who was now as much her friend as theirs. It was a curious position in which to place a woman like Mary Zattiany, but Sophisticate New York was not Diplomatic Europe, and he thought he saw her smile deepen into humor once or twice; no doubt she was reflecting that she had lived long enough to take people as she found them.

His reverie was interrupted by a buzzing at the end of his hall and he went to the door quickly, wondering who could have sent him a special delivery letter or a note at this hour. It proved to be a cablegram. He read it when he returned to his living-room. It was dated Rome, Italy, and read:

"I'll have you yet: Janet."

Clavering swore, then laughed. He tore the message into strips and sat down to read his newspapers; he had merely glanced at the headlines and his column. His eye was arrested by the picture of a man at the top of the first page of his own newspaper. Although smooth-shaven and very regular of feature, with no pronounced racial characteristics, it was, nevertheless, a foreign face, although difficult to place. From its distinction it might be Austrian, but the name below, "Prince Hohenhauer," might as easily be German.

Still, it was not a German face, and Clavering studied it for a moment before reading the news text, wondering faintly at his interest.

It was unmistakably the face of a statesman, and reminded him a little of a picture of Prince Schwarzenberg,[1] prime minister when Franz Josef ascended the throne, he had seen lately in a history of Austria. There was the same broad placidity of brow, the long oval face, the thin long slightly curved nose, the heavy lids, the slim erectness, the same suave repose. But this man's large beautifully cut mouth was more firmly set, had a faintly satiric expression, and the eyes a powerful and penetrating gaze. It was the face of a man who was complete master of himself and accustomed to the mastery of men.

Clavering read the story under the headlines:

PRINCE HOHENHAUER ARRIVES IN NEW YORK
GOES AT ONCE TO WASHINGTON

"Prince Hohenhauer, a distinguished political factor under the old Austrian Empire, arrived yesterday morning on the Noordam. He refused to be interviewed, but it is understood he has a large amount of money invested in the United States and has come to New York at the request of his lawyers to attend to certain necessary formalities. He was, in fact, met at Quarantine by Judge Trent, one of the most distinguished members of the New York Bar since his retirement from the Bench, and they went at once to the Prince's stateroom and remained there until it was time to leave the ship. It is significant, however, that the Prince, after engaging a suite at the Ritz-Carlton, and lunching there with Judge Trent, took the afternoon train for Washington. As he recently left his estate in Switzerland to return to Vienna and accept a position in the Cabinet, and as it is well known that Austria desires the backing of the American Government to enable her to overcome the opposition of France to her alliance with Germany, or, it is whispered, with a kingdom farther south, it is not unreasonable to infer that he has come to the United States on a special, if secret, mission.

"The Prince was the subject of lively interest on the boat and of much speculation, but he took his meals in his suite and walked the deck only in the company of his secretary.

---

1 Prince Felix of Schwarzenberg (1800-52), minister-president who helped reestablish Austria's monarchy, thus securing the throne for Franz Joseph.

"He is a man of striking appearance, quite six feet in height, with a spare erect figure, fine features, and hardly looks his sixty years, in spite of his white hair."

Then followed a brief biography, which illustrated the efficiency of the newspaper "morgue," for the statesman's reputation was, so far, wholly European.

"Prince Moritz Franz Ernst Felix von Hohenhauer was born October 6th, 1862, on his ancestral estate in what was then known as Galicia. His mother was a princess of the House of Schwarzenberg. He has been the head of his own historic house for the last forty years, and has one son and two daughters. His wife, a member of the Kalnóky family, died several years ago. "Hohenhauer" was one of those almost unbelievably vast estates of sixteen million acres possessed by a few of the Austrian noblemen under the old régime. In spite of the fact that Prince Hohenhauer was one of the greatest landlords in all Christendom he was a liberal in politics from the first and the author of several of the reform laws in behalf of the people which from time to time were forced upon the most conservative monarch in Europe. He was in sympathy with the revolution and offered his services at once to the new Government. They were declined, and he retired to Switzerland, where he has an estate near St. Moritz, and, it is understood, considerable money invested. His vast estates in what is now Poland were confiscated, but he was one of the wealthiest men in the Empire and is said to have transferred immense sums to the United States before the war."

Clavering dropped the newspaper. Liberal in politics. Immense sums invested in the United States. Judge Trent. There could be no possible doubt as to who the man was. The floor seemed unsteady for a moment.

And yet there was as little doubt that Mary Zattiany had long since ceased to care for him. That was over fifteen or sixteen years ago. *They* had known each other in later years, both equally indifferent to the other and to the past.... Yes ... but she had then completely lost the beauty and the charm that had enthralled him, while he was still a man in his prime, who, with that appearance, no doubt had other young and beautiful women in his life.

He may or may not have heard of the metamorphosis. At all events they had been political allies. He would call on her as a matter of course. And possibly out of more than politeness: he may have brought her an important message. Or he might find it expedient to confer with her on his present mission. That he had come on an important mission did not admit of a doubt; but at least he had not gone to her at once. His interest in her, so far, was still impersonal.

Clavering had too much of the arrogance of youth and he was too sure of Mary Zattiany's love for himself, to be apprehensive of the charms of a man of sixty, but he was invaded by a nameless and almost sickening fear. He had very swift and often very sure intuitions, and he was shaken by a premonition that in some manner, which, in his ignorance of the facts he was unable to define, this man's presence in America boded no good to himself.

But Clavering was also a man of swift decisions and resource, and he knew this was no time to lose his head, nor even to play a waiting game. And he must tread warily. Impulsive as he was by nature he could be as wary as a Red Indian when wariness would serve his purpose. He called up Mr. Dinwiddie on the telephone and asked if he might see him at once. It was only half past nine and Mr. Dinwiddie was just finishing his breakfast in bed, but he told his favorite cordially to "come along."

XLIV

"What is it?" asked Mr. Dinwiddie, as Clavering entered his bedroom fifteen minutes later. "This is an early call. Thought you didn't get up till noon."

"Went to bed early last night for a change. I've come to ask a favor. I'll smoke, if you don't mind."

He took a chair beside the bed, where Mr. Dinwiddie, in skull cap and decorous pyjamas, leaned against high pillows, happily digesting his breakfast, with the newspapers beside him. Clavering smoked for a few moments in silence, while his host watched him keenly. He had never seen his young friend in quite this mood. There was a curious deadly stillness about him.

"What is it, Lee?" he asked when curiosity finally got the better of him. "Nothing wrong between you and Mary, I hope? Of course you know it's all over town that you're engaged to her. Don't mind my saying this, do you? And you know you can trust me. Nothing like an old gossip for keeping a confidence sacred."

"Well, I am. But she chooses not to announce it and that is her right. And here is where you can help me. I want you to open your camp in the Adirondacks and give Mary a house party. I suppose Larsing and his wife are still there?"

"Yes, but it's too early——"

"Spring is early this year. The ice must have gone out. And the house is always comfortable; we've often had fires there when people were having sunstroke in New York. I want you to get busy, so that we can leave tomorrow morning——"

"Tomorrow morning? You young dynamo. It can't be done."

"It can. I'll call up the people I want in a few minutes—from here. You can telephone to the camp. Provisions can go tonight. I'll see to that also——"

"But can you get away yourself?"

"I'd get away if I had to resign, but I shan't. I shall break away for two months later anyhow. We have planned to marry in Austria in about a month from now."

"Then why in thunder do you want to run off to the woods with her now? I never heard of anything so unreasonable. She has friends here who'd like to see her until the last minute, you selfish young beggar——"

"It's the most reasonable thing I ever did. Don't insist upon an explanation, Din. Just accept my word that it's a vital matter to me."

"Ah! But I know!" Mr. Dinwiddie's eyes glittered. "Hohenhauer is here. That's the milk in the cocoanut."

Clavering scowled. "What do you mean by that?"

"I—I—well—there was a good deal of talk at the time—but then you know, Lee, I told you the very first time we both saw her that there had been stories about Mary."

"Well, as it happens, she told me about this man, although not his name. Enough, however, for me to know at once this morning who he was. I don't intend she shall see him."

"You don't mean to tell me that you are jealous of Hohenhauer. Why, that was nearly twenty years ago, and he is almost as old as I am."

"I'm not jealous, but I've got a hunch." He scowled again, for he fancied he could see that old story unrolling itself in Dinwiddie's mind. It is one thing to dismiss the past with a lordly gesture and another to see it rise from the dead and peer from old eyes. He went on calmly, however. "I've no faith, myself, in the making of bonfires out of dead ashes, but all the same I scent danger and I intend to get her away and keep her away until the day before she sails; and I'll marry her the morning she does. I'll take no chances of their travelling on the same steamer."

"I see. Perhaps you are right. He's a damn good-looking chap, too, and has that princely distinction peculiar to Austrians. Some European princes look like successful businessmen of the Middle-West. I was once stranded at Abbazia, Austria's Riviera, during a rainy spell, and as there were only two other people in the vast dining-room I thought I'd speak to them. I took for granted they were Americans. He was a big heavy man, with one of those large, round, fat, shrewd, weary faces you see by the hundreds in the lobbies of Chicago hotels. She looked like a New England school-marm, and wore a red plaid waist. Well—he was the reigning prince of Carlstadt-Rudolfstein, one of those two-by-six German principalities, and she was an Austrian archduchess. She was the only Austrian I ever saw that didn't look like one, but her manners were charming and we became great friends and they took me home with them to their beautiful old castle.... Ah, those wonderful old German castles! Profiteers living in them today, I suppose. But Hohenhauer is a perfect specimen of his class—and then some. I met him once in Paris. Intensely reserved, but opened up one night at a small dinner. I never met a more charming man in my life. And unquestionably one of the ablest men in Europe.... However, he's sixty and you're thirty-four. If he has any influence over her it's political, and in European politics one never knows what dark business is going on under the surface. Good idea to get Mary away. I'll get some fun out of it, too. Who'll you ask?"

"None of your crowd. How many bedrooms have you? I don't remember."

"Ten. If you want a large party you can turn in with me. There are twin beds in every room. I don't know how Mary'll like it; she's a luxurious creature, you know, and we don't go to the woods to be comfortable——"

"You forget she got pretty well used to worse while she was running that hospital. And hardy people never do mind."

"True. I'll give her a room to herself, for I don't see her doubling-up, at all events. That would leave eight good-sized rooms. Don't ask all married couples, Lee, for heaven's sake. Let's have two girls, at least. But the season is still on. Sure you can get anybody?"

"Of course. They're not all pinned down to regular jobs, and will be only too glad to get out of New York after a grinding winter. The novelty of a house party in the mountains at this season will appeal to them. I'll call up Gora first."

He was crossing the room to the telephone when Mr. Dinwiddie said hesitatingly: "And so—so—you're really going to marry Mary? Have you thought what it means? I mean your own career. She'll never live here—she's out of the picture and knows it."

Clavering took down the receiver and called Miss Dwight's number. Mr. Dinwiddie sighed and shrugged his shoulders. But his eyes were bright. He would have a love drama under his very nose.

XLV

Mary's "headache" had continued for two days, but Clavering came to her house by appointment that same afternoon at five o'clock. She kept him waiting fully ten minutes, and wandered back and forth in her room upstairs with none of her usual eagerness to welcome him after even a brief separation. The violence of her revulsion had passed, but she was filled with a vast depression, apathetic, tired, in no mood for love-making. Nor did she feel up to acting, and Clavering's intuitions were often very inconvenient. He would never suspect the black turmoil of these past two days, nor its cause, but it would be equally disconcerting if he attributed her low spirits to the arrival of Hohenhauer. What a fool she had been to have made more than a glancing reference to that last old love-affair, almost forgotten until that night of stark revelation. She must have enjoyed talking about herself more than she had realized, unable to resist the temptation to indulge in imposing details. Or self-justification? Perhaps. It didn't matter, and he must have "placed" Hohenhauer at once this morning, and would imagine that she was depressed at the thought of meeting him. There was no one on earth she wanted to meet less, although she felt a good deal of curiosity as to the object of his visit to Washington.

She heard the maid in the dressing-room and was visited by an inspiration. She called in the woman, gave her a key and told her to go down to the dining-room and bring her a glass of curaçao[1] from the wine-cupboard.

The liqueur sent a glow of warmth through her veins and raised her spirits. Then, reflecting that Clavering never rushed at her in the fashion of most lovers, nor even greeted her with a perfunctory kiss, but waited until the mood for love-making attacked him suddenly, she took a last look at her new tea-gown of corn-flower blue chiffon and went down stairs with a light step.

"Shocking to keep you waiting," she said as they shook hands, "but I came in late. You'll stay to dinner, of course. I had an engagement but broke it, as I'm still feeling a little out of sorts."

---

1 Orange-flavored liqueur.

"Never saw you look better. Nor in blue before. You look like a lily in a blue vase, or a snow maiden rising from a blue mist. Not that I'm feeling poetic today, but you do look ripping. What gave you a headache? I thought you scorned the ills of the flesh."

"So I do, but I had spent three hours in Judge Trent's office that morning, and you know what these American men are. They keep the heat on no matter what the temperature outside, and every window closed. On Tuesday the sun was blazing in besides, and Judge Trent and the two other men I was obliged to confer with smoked cigars incessantly. It gave me the first headache I'd had for twenty years. I felt as if I'd been poisoned."

She looked up at him, smilingly, from her deep chair as he stood above her on the hearthrug. He didn't believe a word of it: he was convinced she had been advised of Hohenhauer's coming, and that for some reason the news had upset her; but he had no intention of betraying himself. Moreover, he didn't care. He was too intent on his own plans.

"The rest has done you good," he said, smiling also. "But as you were looking rather fagged before you came down with that two-days' headache, I made up my mind that you needed a change and dropped Din a hint to open his camp in the Adirondacks and give you a farewell house-party. He jumped at the idea and it's all arranged. You'll have eight days of outdoor life and some sport, as well as a good rest. He's got a big comfortable camp on a beautiful lake, where we can boat and fish——"

"But Lee——" She was almost gasping.

"No buts. Not only do you need a rest before that long journey but I want these last days with you in the mountains where I can have you almost to myself. It seems to me sometimes that I do not know you at all—nor you me. And to roam with you in the woods during the day and float about that lake at night—it came to me suddenly like a foretaste of heaven. I couldn't stand the thought of the separation otherwise. Besides, here you'd be given a farewell luncheon or dinner every day until you sailed. I'd see nothing of you. And you'd be worn out. You must come, Mary dear."

Mary felt dimly suspicious, but it was possible that he had read his morning papers hastily, or that in his mental turmoil that night she had told him her story he had paid little attention to details, or forgotten them later. He certainly had never alluded to the man since. And this sudden impetuous plan was so like him that he needed no foreign impulse.

But she answered with some hesitation: "I'd like it, of course. And Judge Trent has nothing more for me to sign until the last minute. But—a woman always has a thousand things to do before going on a journey——"

"Your maid can do all that. And pack your trunks. She goes with you, doesn't she? And you'll only need warm sweaters and skirts up there. We never dress. You'll not need a maid."

"Well—but—do you mean to tell me that the whole thing is settled?"

"To the last detail. There'll be twelve of us, including Din."

"Really, Lee, you *are* high-handed. You might have consulted me first."

"No time to waste on argument. We'll only have a little over a week there as it is. It takes a day to go and another to return, and you'll need one day here in New York before you sail. I made up my mind you should go if I had to take you by force. I *will* have those last days in the Adirondacks."

Her faint resentment vanished and she felt a languid sense of well-being in this enveloping atmosphere of the tactless imperious male, so foreign to her experience; of freedom from the necessity for independent action; and the prospect was certainly enchanting. Moreover, she would be able to avoid seeing Hohenhauer in surroundings where this strange love-affair of hers had obliterated the past (for the most part!), and she had found, for a time at least, happiness and peace. She would see him in Vienna, of course, and she had no wish to avoid him there; no doubt they would work together and as impersonally as they had sometimes done in the past; but to see him here, even in the drawing-room, which held no sacred memories, would be but another and uglier blot on her already dimming idyl; and a subtle infidelity to this man whose every thought seemed to be of her in spite of all he had to inflame and excite his ego.

And if she remained and Hohenhauer wished to see her she could hardly keep on making excuses for nearly a fortnight. So she merely smiled up at Clavering, who was gazing down at her intently, and said softly: "Of course I'll go. I always have sport things in my wardrobe and I think it a wonderful idea. Now tell me who is going. Miss Dwight, I suppose—and hope. And the De Witt Turners?" Madame Zattiany had no respect whatever for the Lucy Stone League, and invariably forgot the paternal names of the emancipated young wives of the men she found interesting.

"They can't get away. Gora, yes; and Rolly Todd, the Boltons, the Minors, Eva Darling, Babette Gold, Gerald Scores."

"Miss Darling is rather a nuisance. She flung her arms round me the other night at the Minors' and left a pink kiss on my neck. She was very tight. Still, she is amusing, and a favorite of Din's."

"I would have submitted the list to you in the first place, darling, but I knew I should have to take what I could get on such short notice. The only two I really care about are Gora and Todd. But there wasn't a moment to lose. I wish to heaven I'd thought of it before, but that play had to be finished, and it looked as if the date of your sailing might be postponed, after all."

He had no intention of letting her suspect that the wonderful plan was just eight hours old.

"I understand," she said. "When do we start?"

"Tomorrow morning. Eight-thirty. Grand Central."

"Tomorrow morning!" She looked almost as dismayed as Mr. Dinwiddie had done, then laughed and shrugged her shoulders. "Of course it can be done—but——"

"Anything can be done," he said darkly. And then, having got his way, he suddenly felt happy and irresponsible, and made one of his abrupt wild dives at her.

XLVI

The "camp," a large log house, with a great living-room, a small room for guns and fishing-tackle, two bedrooms, besides the servants' wing, downstairs, and eight bedrooms above, stood in a clearing on the western shore of a lake nearly two miles long, and about three-quarters of a mile wide in the centre of its fine oval sweep. The lake itself was in a cup of the mountains, whose slopes in the distance looked as if covered with fur, so dense were the woods. Only one high peak, burnt bare by fire, was still covered with snow.

The camp was in a grove of pines, but the trees that crowded one another almost out into the lake among the lily pads were spruce and balsam and maple.

The party arrived at half-past nine in the evening, and crossed the lake in a motor launch. It was very dark and the forest surrounding the calm expanse of water looked like an impenetrable wall, an unscalable rampart. There was not a sound but the faint chugging of the motor. The members of the party, tired after their long trip on the train and two hours' drive up the rough road from the station to the lake, surrendered to the high mountain stillness, and even Rollo Todd, who had been in his best spirits all day, fell silent and forgot that he was a jolly good fellow, remembered only that he was a poet. Eva Darling, who had flirted shamelessly with Mr. Dinwiddie from New York to Huntersville, forgot to hold his hand, and he forgot her altogether.

Mary had a sudden and complete sense of isolation. Memory had played her a trick. These were the mountains of her girlhood, and she was Mary Ogden once more. Even the future that had been so hard of outline in her practical mind, that unescapable future just beyond a brief interval in an Austrian mountain solitude, seemed to sink beyond a horizon infinitely remote. Europe was as unreal as New York. She vowed, if it were necessary to vow, that she would give neither a thought while she was here in the wilderness. And as she was a thorough-going person she knew she would succeed.

She took her first step when Mr. Dinwiddie was showing them to their rooms. She drew Gora into her own room and shut the door.

"I want you to do me a favor—if you will, dear Miss Dwight," she said.

"Of course." Gora wondered what was coming.

"I want you to ask the others to abandon their subtle game while we are up here and ignore the subjects of Lee's play, his future, his genius, which will wither outside of New York, and cease to attempt to strike terror into my soul. You may tell them that we are to be married in a month or two from now—in Austria—but that I shall do nothing to interfere with his career; nor protest against his passing a part of each year in the United States. Ask them kindly to refrain from congratulations, or any allusion to the subject whatever. We have only eight days here, and I should like it to be as nearly perfect as possible."

Gora had had the grace to blush. "They *have* been worried, and I'm afraid they hatched a rather naughty plot. But they'll be delighted to have their apprehensions banished—and of course they'll ignore the entire matter. They won't say a word to Clavey, either."

"They've not made the slightest impression on him, so it really doesn't matter whether they do or not. But—when it dawned on me what they were up to, and the sound reasoning beneath it, I will confess that I had some bad half-hours. Of course, Lee has a right to his own life. I had hoped he would help me in my own field, but he could not if he would. I have come to see that plainly. I do not mean to say that these amiable machinations of your friends caused me for a moment to consider giving him up. I have survived worse——" She shuddered as she recalled that hideous hour with Agnes Trevor, but promptly whipped the memory back to cover. "But it made me very uncomfortable, and I realized there was nothing to do but compromise. We must take what we can get in this world, my dear Miss Dwight, and be thankful for a candle when we cannot have the sun."

And Gora, feeling unaccountably saddened, summoned the others to her room and told them of Madame Zattiany's announcement and request. Some gasped with astonishment and delight, others were darkly suspicious, but all gave their word unhesitatingly to "forget it" while they were in camp. Those that regarded Madame Zattiany as the most fascinating woman they had ever known, but also as an intrigante[1] of dark and winding ways, made a mental reservation to "say a few things to Clavey" before he had time to buy his ticket for the Dolomites.

Mary, having accomplished her purpose, swept the whole thing from her mind and looked about her room with pleasure. The walls were ceiled with a wood that gleamed like gold in the candle-light, and gave out a faint scent of the forest. On the bare floor were two or three small blue rugs, there were pretty blue counterpanes on the beds, and blue curtains on the small windows. It looked like a young girl's room and was indescribably sweet and fresh. Her own room at her father's camp, on another lake many miles away, had been not unlike it. Moreover, it was pleasantly warm, for the caretaker had made a fire in the furnace the day before. A window was open and she could hear the soft lap of the water among the lily pads, but there was no moon and she could see nothing but a dim black wall on the opposite shore. And the silence! It might not have been broken since the glacial era, when mighty masses of ice ground these mountains into permanent form, and the air was filled with the roaring horrors of desolation. But they had gone, and left infinite peace behind them. That peace had endured for many thousands of years and it was unimaginable that any but the puny sounds of man would disturb that vast repose for thousands of years to come. The peaks of those old Adirondacks, their quiet lakes, their massive forests, looked as deathless as time itself. "The Great North Woods" could not have been more remote from, more scornful of the swarming cities called civilization, if they had been on another star.

Luxury in camp did not extend to hot water in the bedrooms, particularly as Mr. Dinwiddie had had no time to assemble a

---

1 Someone who schemes or intrigues.

corps of servants, and as Mary washed her face and hands in what felt like melted ice, the shock made her tingle and she would have liked to sing.

A deep bell sounded. Doors flew open up and down the corridor, which was immediately filled with an eager chatter. Rollo Todd stamped down the stair singing "Oh, Hunger, Sweet Hunger!" The others took it up in various keys, and when Mary went down a moment later they were all swarming about the dining-table at the end of the living-room.

This room, which was fully fifty feet long and half as wide, was lit by lamps suspended from the ceiling and heated by an immense fireplace in which logs, that looked like half-sections of trees, were blazing in a pile as high as a small bonfire. The walls were ceiled and decorated with antlered deerheads, woven bright Indian blankets, snap-shots of Mr. Dinwiddie's many guests, and old Indian weapons. In one corner, above a divan covered with gay cushions, were bookshelves filled with old novels. A shelf had been built along one side of the room for fine specimens of Indian pottery and basket weaving. The comfortable chairs were innumerable, and there was another divan, and a victrola. The guide had filled the vases with balsam, whose pungent odor blended with the resinous fumes of the burning logs; and through the open door came the scents of the forest.

"Ideal place for everything but spooning," cried Todd. "The woods and the lake are all right in fine weather, but what do you expect us to do if it rains, mine host? D'you mean to say you haven't any little retiring rooms?"

"Not a thing unless you retire to the gun-room, but who comes up to the woods to spoon in the house?"

"Rolly never spoons, anyhow," announced Eva Darling, whose blue eyes, however, were languishing toward the table. "But it makes him unhappy to think he can't burst in on somebody——"

"Hold your tongue, Evy. You don't know what you're talking about. Because I'm quite insensible to your charms, don't fool yourself that I'm an anchorite. I merely prefer brunettes."

"Come, come, children!" Mr. Dinwiddie was rubbing his hands at the end of the table covered with blue china and mounds of home-made cake. "Stop quarrelling and sit down. Anywhere. No ceremony here."

Some of the guests were in their seats. The others fairly swooped into theirs, entirely regardless of anything so uneatable as neighbors. Mrs. Larsing, a tall, red-haired, raw-boned New England woman, had entered, bearing an enormous platter of fried trout, fresh from the lake. Larsing, burnt almost as dark as an Indian, followed with a plate of potatoes boiled in their jackets balanced on one hand, and a small mountain of johnny cake[1] on the other. He returned in a moment with two large platters of sliced ham and cold boiled beef, and the guests were left to wait on themselves.

The dinner was the gayest Mary had ever attended, for even the Sophisticates, however lively, preserved a certain formality in town; when she was present, at all events. Rollo Todd, broke into periodical war whoops, to Mr. Dinwiddie's manifest delight. The others burst into song, while waiting for the travelling platters. Eva Darling got up twice and danced by herself, her pale bobbed head and little white face eerily suspended in the dark shadows of the great room. Other feet moved irresistibly under the table. Good stories multiplied, and they laughed uncontrollably at the worst of the jokes.

They drank little, for the supply was limited, but the altitude was four thousand feet and the thin light air went to their heads. They were New Yorkers suddenly snatched from the most feverish pitch of modern civilization, but no less primitive in soul than woodsmen who had never seen a city, and the men would have liked to put on war paint and run through the forest with tomahawks.

Todd, when the dinner was over, did seize a tomahawk from the wall, drape himself in an Indian blanket, and march up and down the room roaring out terrific battle-cries. Three minutes later, Minor and Bolton had followed his example, and marched solemnly behind him, brandishing their weapons and making unearthly noises. Mary, from her chair by the hearth, watched them curiously. At first it was merely the exuberant spirits of their release and the unaccustomed altitude that inspired them, but their countenances grew more and more sombre, their eyes wilder, their voices more war-like. They were no longer doing a stunt, they were atavistic.[2] Their voices reverberated across the lake.

One by one the other men had joined them, until even Mr. Dinwiddie was in the procession, marching with loud stamping feet round and round the big room. The cries became shorter, menacing, abrupt, imperative. The high lamps cast strange shadows on their lost faces. The voices grew hoarse, dropped to low growls, their faces changed from ferocity to a mournful solemnity

---

1 New England term for cornmeal flatbread; a common food in early America.
2 An example of reversion back to an earlier genetic type.

until they looked even more like primal men than before; but they continued their marching and stamping until Gora, who, with the other women, had begun to fear that the rhythm would bring down the house, had the inspiration to insert a Caruso[1] disk into the victrola; and as those immortal notes flung themselves imperiously across that wild scene, the primitive in the men dropped like a leaden plummet, and they threw themselves on the floor by the fire. But they smoked their pipes in silence. They had had something that no woman could give them nor share, and there was an ungallant wish in every manly heart that they had left the women at home.

Caruso was succeeded by Emma Eames, and the great lost diva by Farrar and Scotti.[2] Then, the concert over, a yawning party stumbled upstairs to bed and not a sound was heard from them until the first bell rang at seven o'clock next morning.

XLVII

"You forgot me last night."

"Yes, I did." Clavering smiled unrepentantly.

"You looked horribly primitive."

"No more so than I felt."

They were in a boat on the lake. The air was crisp and cold although the sun blazed overhead. Clavering was happy in a disreputable old sweater that he kept at the camp, and baggy corduroy trousers tucked into leggins, but Mary wore an angora sweater and skirt of a vivid grass green and a soft sport hat of the same shade, the rim turned down over eyes that might never have looked upon life beyond these woods and mountains. Clavering was hatless and smoked his pipe lazily as he pulled with long slow strokes.

Other boats were on the lake, the women in bright sweaters and hats that looked like floating autumn leaves, and the lake was liquid amber. A breeze blew warm scents out of the woods. The water

---

1 Enrico Caruso (1873-1921), the illustrious Italian tenor and Metropolitan Opera star from 1903 to 1921.

2 Antonio Scotti (1866-1936), an Italian baritone who formed his own company in 1919. Emma Eames (1865-1952), an American opera singer, most popular from the 1890s through the first decade of the twentieth century to the 1910s. The succession here refers to records being played. Scotti and Geraldine Farrar appeared in Puccini's *Tosca*, with Farrar playing the titular role of the celebrated singer (or diva) who is killed before a firing squad at the opera's conclusion.

lilies had opened to the sun and looked oddly artificial in their waxen beauty, at the feet of those ancient trees. Stealthy footsteps behind that wall of trees, or a sudden loud rustling, told of startled deer. The distant peak looked to be enamelled blue and white, and the long slopes of the nearer mountains were dark green under a blue mist, the higher spruce rising like Gothic spires.

Clavering smiled into her dancing eyes. "You look about fourteen," he said tenderly.

"I don't feel much more. I spent a month or two every year in these woods—let us play a game. Make believe that I am Mary Ogden and you have met me here for the first time and are deliberately setting out to woo me. Begin all over again. It—you, perhaps!—was what I always dreamed of up here. I used to row on the lake for hours by myself, or sit alone in the very depths of the woods. Do you think that famous imagination of yours could accomplish a purely personal feat? I haven't nearly as much but I'm quite sure I could. And then—after—we could just go on from here."

He looked at her in smiling sympathy. "Done. We met last night, Miss Ogden, and I went down at the first shot. I'm now out to win you or perish in the attempt. But before we get down to business I'll just inform you of a resolution I took a day or two ago. I shall get a license the day we return and marry you the morning you sail."

"Oh!" And then she realized in a blinding flash what she had fought out of her consciousness: that she had shrunk from the consummation of marriage, visualized a long period of intermittent but superficial love-making and delightful companionship, an exciting but incomplete idyl of mind and soul and senses.... Underneath always an undertone of repulsion and incurable ennui ... the dark residuum of immedicable disillusion ... that what she had really wanted was love with its final expression eliminated.

But she realized it only as a fact, ... a psychological study of another ... buried down there in an artificial civilization she had forgotten ... in that past that belonged to Marie Zattiany ... with which Mary Ogden had nothing to do ... her mind at last was as young as her body, and this man had accomplished the miracle. The present and the future were his.

She looked up into his eyes, anxious but imperious, and answered softly: "Why not?"

"Exactly. I've no desire to take that long journey with you, but I'm not going to take any chances, either.... Ah! Here's an idea that beats the other hollow. When the party breaks up we'll go down to Huntersville with them, marry there, and return to the camp. I don't see how your Dolomites could beat this for a honeymoon. Why in thunder should we trail all the way over to Europe to find seclusion when we must return in two or three months, anyhow? It's a scandalous waste. We can go to the Dolomites for our second honeymoon—we'll have one every year. And this is much more in the picture if you want to be Mary Ogden again. *She* never would have proposed anything so elaborate and unnecessary. Say yes, and don't be more than a minute about it."

Mary drew in her breath sharply. The plan made a violent and irresistible appeal. There would be no long interval for possible reversal, for contacts in which it might be difficult to hold fast to her new faith. But what excuse could she make to leave him later? ... Later? Did Austria really exist? Did she care? Let the future take care of itself. Her horizon, a luminous band, encircled these mountains.... She smiled into his ardent eyes. "Very well. I'll write to Hortense today and tell her to send me up a trousseau of sorts. And now—you are to understand that you have not dared to propose to me yet and are suffering all the qualms of uncertainty, for I am a desperate flirt, and took a long walk in the woods this morning with Mr. Scores."

"Very well, Miss Ogden, I will now do my best to make a fool of myself, and as soon as we return to camp will telegraph to New York for a five-pound box of chocolates."

"Hark! Hark! The Lark!" shouted Todd as he rowed past with Babette Gold. "Only there isn't a lark or any other bird in these woods that I've been able to discover."

"Birds sing one at a time," shouted back Clavering. "Choir of jealous soloists."

He rowed into a little cove and they gazed into the dim green woods, but the maple leaves grew almost to the ground, and it was like peering through the tiny changing spaces of a moving curtain through which one glimpsed green columns flecked with gold.

He beached the boat, and they walked, single file, up a narrow run-way made by the deer. Everywhere was that leafy whispering curtain. Between the rigid spruce and soft maples were fragrant balsams, and ferns, and an occasional pine with its pale green spikes. They passed enormous boulders detached from the glaciers that had ground mountains in their embrace, but today things of mere beauty in their coats of pink and green and golden moss.

Their footsteps made no sound on the mossy path, and they came suddenly upon a deer and his doe drinking at a pool. But the antlered head was flung back instantly, the magnificent buck wheeled on his hind legs, gave a leap and went crashing through the forest snorting his protesting fury. The doe scampered after, her white-lined tail standing up perfectly straight.

They sat down on a log, dried and warmed by the sun in this open space, and talked for two hours. There was no need for careful avoidance of dangerous subjects. Clavering had come to these woods nearly every year since he had made the north his home, and she had forgotten nothing of her woodland lore. When one is "in the woods," as the great Adirondacks are familiarly called, one rarely talks of anything but their manifold offerings. It is easy enough to forget the world. They both had had their long tramps, their rough campings-out, more or less exciting adventures. When a loud bell, hung in a frame outside the camp, summoned them to dinner, they walked out briskly. Once, as the trail widened, he touched her fingers tentatively. She let her own curl for a moment, then gave him a provocative glance over her shoulder and hurried on.

XLVIII

Clavering, when making up his list with Mr. Dinwiddie (by courtesy), had, with the exception of Todd, who was always the life of any party, Gora, whom he always liked to have at hand, and Eva Darling, who was a favorite of "The Ambassador to the Court of the Sophisticates," as Todd had long since dubbed him, chosen his guests at random, taking whom he could get, careful merely to ask those who, so far as he knew, were on speaking terms.

But he hardly could have gathered together a more congenial and lively party, nor one more delighted to leave New York for the woods. Henry Minor, editor of one of the intellectual and faintly radical magazines, whose style was so involved in his efforts to be both "different" and achieve an unremitting glitter, that he had recently received a petition to issue a glossary, was as amiable as a puppy in the society of his friends and when in the woods talked in words of one syllable and discovered a mighty appetite. His wife, who had demonstrated her originality by calling herself Mrs. Minor, was what is known as a spiffing cook and a top-notch dresser. She had, in fact, the most charming assortment of sports clothes in the camp. Eva Darling, who danced for pastime and illustrated for what little bread she was permitted to eat at home, was as lively as a grasshopper and scarcely less devastating. Babette Gold wore her black hair in smooth bands on either side of the perfect oval of her face, and had the sad and yearning gaze of the unforgiven Magdalen,[1] and she had written two novels dealing with the domesticities of the lower middle class, treating with a clinical wealth of detail the irritable monotonies of the nuptial couch and the artless intimacies of the nursery. She smoked incessantly, could walk ten miles at a stretch, and was as passionless as a clam. Gerald Scores, who wore a short pointed beard and looked the complete artist, was one of the chief hopes of the intellectual drama cunningly commercialized; and as capable as Clavering of shutting up his genius in a water-tight compartment, and enjoying himself in the woods. He was mildly flirtatious, but looked upon emotional intensity in the personal life of the artist as a criminal waste of force. Halifax Bolton, who claimed to be the discoverer of the Younger Generation (in fiction) and was just twenty-eight himself, was a critic of formidable severity and the author of at least five claques.[2] The intense concentration of writing routed his sense of humor, but he had as many droll stories in his repertoire as Todd. His wife, the famous "Alberta Jones," fierce Lucy Stoner, was the editor, at a phenomenal salary, of one of the "Woman's Magazines," and wrote short stories of impeccable style and indifferent content for the *Century* and the *Dial*.[3]

They were all intimate friends and argued incessantly and amiably. And they were all devoted to Mr. Dinwiddie, whom they addressed as Excellence, without accent.

When Mary and Clavering arrived at the camp in response to the dinner bell, Eva Darling, who wore very pretty pink silk bloomers under her sport skirt, was turning hand-springs down the living-room, while the rest of the party applauded vociferously, and Mrs. Larsing, who was entering with the fried chicken, nearly dropped the platter.

"Just in time, Madame Zattiany," cried Minor. "This is the sixth round and she is panting——"

But she interrupted him. "'Mary'—from this time on. I insist. You make me feel an outsider. I won't be addressed in that formal manner nor answer to that foreign name again."

---

1 Mary Magdalene, described in the Bible as a follower and caretaker of Jesus, was frequently depicted in paintings as a penitent because of interpretations of her dissolute life; some interpretations cast her as a prostitute.

2 Audience members who are paid to applaud loudly for certain performers.

3 American periodical published from 1840 to 1929. In the 1920s, *The Dial* was an important venue for modernist poetry and prose, publishing T.S. Eliot's *The Waste Land* in 1922.

"Mary! Mary! Mary!" shouted the party with one accord, and Clavering drew a long breath. He had wondered how she would manage to feel Mary Ogden under the constant bombardment of a name that was a title in more ways than one. But he might have trusted her to manage it!

In the afternoon Mrs. Minor suggested having tea in the woods, and they all walked—single file—five miles to drink their tea and eat their cakes (Larsing carrying the paraphernalia) in a pine grove on the summit of a hill, and then walked back again, clamoring for supper. Mary had been monopolized by Scores and Bolton, occasionally vouchsafing Clavering a glance. During the evening they were all too pleasantly tired and replete to dance or to play the charades they had planned, but lay about comfortably, listening to a concert of alternate arias and jazz. Clavering did not have a word alone with Mary. She sat on one of the divans between Gora and Todd, while Scores lay on the floor at her feet, his head on a cushion, one foot waving over a lifted knee, the perfect picture of the contented playwright. They kept up a continuous murmur, punctuated with gales of laughter. Clavering had sulkily taken a chair beside Babette Gold, whose metallic humor sometimes amused him, but she went sound asleep before his eyes, and he could only gaze into the fire and console himself with visions of a week hence, when these cursed people had gone and he was the most fortunate man on earth.

His room was downstairs next to Mr. Dinwiddie's, and he made up his mind to let himself out softly at midnight, throw pebbles at her window and whisper to her as she leaned from her casement. It was a scene that if introduced into a modern play would have driven him from the theatre and tipped his pen with vitriol next morning, but it appealed to him, somehow, as a fitting episode in his own high romance. But he was asleep before his head touched the pillow, and did not lift an eyelash until the first bell roused him at seven o'clock. Then, however, he lay for some time thinking, soberly.

XLIX

The hour between seven and eight was a lively one in the upper corridor. There was only one bathroom on the second floor. Scores and Miss Gold took their morning plunge in the lake, but the rest preferred the less drastic shower, and there was a continual darting to and fro of forms clad in bath-robe or kimono;

the vanquished peeping through door-cracks waiting for the bathroom door to open—signal for another wild rush down the hall, a scuffle at the door, a triumphant slam and hoot, and loud vituperations from the defeated. Mary cannily waited until the last, and came down, clad in a white sweater and heavy white tweed skirt, after the others had cleared the generous platter of ham and eggs, and the mountain of corn bread was a hillock of crumbs.

"Oh, Mary!" said Mr. Dinwiddie, reprovingly, "and you as prompt as royalty. In camp——"

"I've no thought of going without my breakfast," said Mary unrepentantly. "Ring the bell, Din."

The men had risen, but Clavering alone had determination in his eye. He pulled out a chair beside his own, and Mary accepted it gracefully, waving a morning greeting to the others.

"How good of you to keep this chair for me, Mr. Clavering," she murmured. "It is shocking of me to be so lazy."

"I'm sick of this game," growled Clavering. "If you act today——"

"Shh! I am sure you are going to take me out on the lake immediately after breakfast."

His amiability was immediately restored, but his gaiety was somewhat forced. "You are looking charming this morning, Miss Ogden. I wished last night that there was a guitar or even a banjo in the camp, that I might serenade beneath your window."

And Mary actually blushed. She had slept dreamlessly, and between the light mountain air and her new rôle, she felt as light-hearted as Eva Darling, who was holding Mr. Dinwiddie's hand openly.

"Oh, Excellence!" cried Mrs. Minor from the other end of the table. "What do you say to having a picnic lunch? Didn't you tell me that you knew of a lovely gorge about six miles from here? Steak broiled between forked sticks! Potatoes roasted in the ashes! Flapjacks! Heavenly."

"Anything you say," replied Mr. Dinwiddie rather tonelessly. "Want to put it to the vote?"

"Let me answer for the crowd," commanded Todd. "It is our duty when in the woods to eat our meals after as much unnecessary toil, and to enjoy as much discomfort, as is humanly possible. Otherwise we might as well stay in town. We'll hilariously tramp six miles with packs, sit on the damp ground, extract earwigs, eat burnt steak and half-cooked potatoes, and then tramp back again, our spirits gradually rising at the prospect of a decent meal eaten in comfort——"

"Kill-joy!" cried Minor. "Don't we come to the woods to tramp? I want to lose twenty pounds this trip, and if you don't you ought to. I vote we make Rolly carry a sack of potatoes."

"It's agreed then?" asked Mr. Dinwiddie, veiling his hope that it was not. But the assent was general. They were all as excited over the prospect of a picnic as if they were slum children about to enjoy their first charitable outing, and it was settled that they were to start at ten o'clock. Mrs. Minor and Miss Gold went into the kitchen to help Mrs. Larsing make sandwiches and salads, and the others ran down to the lake.

L

Clavering had tied the boat to a tree in a little inlet far down the lake, and they were walking through a wood of spruce trees and balsam. There was no leafy curtain here, although they could see one swaying on either side through open vistas between the rigid columns of the spruce. A trail was hardly necessary for there was no undergrowth, and although the trees were set close together they were easily circumnavigated.

It was some time since they had spoken. His face was graver than she had ever seen it, and she waited for him to speak. She almost could feel those unuttered words beating on the silence of the woods. There was nothing else to break that silence but the faint constant murmur in the tree-tops, and once, beyond that leafy curtain, the sudden trilling of a solitary bird. Again, the tremendousness of this high isolation swept over her. The camp and its gay party might have been on some far distant lake.

He put his arm around her firmly. "I am not going to pretend any further," he said. "It is too big for that. And you have never been anything but Mary Ogden to me, except, perhaps, on that night I have practically dismissed from my mind. I called you Mary Ogden to myself until I learned your new name, and I don't think that name has ever come into my thoughts of you. And although you slipped on another skin with it you were always Mary Ogden underneath. You needed a new name for your new rôle, but, like any actress on the stage, it had nothing to do with your indestructible personality. I say this because I want you to understand that although I cannot play up to your little comedy any longer and go through the forms of wooing you as if you were a girl—I shouldn't like you half as well if you were—I do not think of you or wish you to think of yourself as anything but Mary Ogden."

He paused a moment, and she slipped her arm about him and they walked on through the wood.

"I cannot go on with it because these days up here that we can spend almost altogether alone, if we will, are too sacred to waste on an amusing but futile game. Do you realize that we do not know each other very well? I sometimes wonder if you know me at all. From the time I fell in love with you until you promised to marry me, I was at one sort of fever-pitch, and when I got to work on that play I was at another. No writer while exercising an abnormal faculty is quite sane. His brain is several pitches above normal and his nerves are like hot taut wires—that hum like the devil. If this were not the case he would not be an imaginative writer at all. But he certainly is in no condition to reveal himself to a woman. I have made wild and sporadic love to you—sporadic is the word, for between my work and your friends, we have had little time together—and I don't think I have ever taken you in my arms with the feeling that you were the woman I loved, not merely the woman I desired. And I believe that I love you even more than I desire you. You are all that, but so much—so much—more."

She had fixed her startled eyes on him, but he did not turn his head.

"There has always been a lot of talk about the soul. Sentimentalists wallow in the word, and realists deride it. What it really is I do not pretend to know. Probably as good a word as any—and certainly a very mellifluous word—for some obscure chemical combination of finer essence than the obvious material part of us, that craves a foretaste of immortality while we are still mortal. Perhaps we are descended from the gods after all, and unless we listen when they whisper in this unexplorable part of our being, we find only a miserable substitute for happiness, and love turns to hate. Whatever it is that golden essence demands, I have found it in you, and if circumstances had been different I should have known it long ago. I know now what you meant that night when you told me you had spent many distracted years looking for what no man could give you, and although I doubted at that time I could even guess what your own mysterious essence demanded, I know now—still vaguely, for it is something as far beyond the defining power of words as the faith of the Christian. It can never be seen, nor heard, nor expressed, but it is there. And only once in a lifetime does any one mortal have it to give to another. A man may love many times, but he is a god-man only once."

He held her more closely, for she was trembling, but he continued to walk on, guiding her automatically through the trees, for his eyes were almost vacant, as if their vision had been reversed.

"I have had some hours of utter despair, in spite of the double excitement of these past weeks, for it has seemed to me that I was no nearer to you than I had been in the beginning. There was a sense of unreality about the whole affair. At first it seemed to me the most romantic thing that could happen to any man, and it was incredible that I had been chosen the hero of such an extraordinary romance—intensified, if anything, by the fact that it was set in roaring New York, where you have to talk at the top of your voice to hear yourself think.... But that passed—in a measure. I was beset by the fear—at times, I mean: I was not always in a state to look inward—that you were slipping away. Not that I doubted for a moment you would marry me, but that your innermost inscrutable self had withdrawn, and that you accepted what must have appeared to be my own attitude—that we were merely two vital beings, who saw in each other a prospect of a superior sort of sensual delight——"

"That is not true," she interrupted him fiercely. "But you seemed to me to be in that phase when a man can think of nothing else. If I hadn't hoped—and believed—in you against all I knew of men, I'd never have gone on with it."

"I'm sure that is true. I must have disappointed you horribly. You had felt the bond from the beginning, and I can imagine what you must have dreamed I alone could give you. The trouble was that I didn't realize that I alone was in fault, at the time. That boiling pot in my brain was making too much noise. But I can assure you that I have returned to normal, and if I thought I couldn't satisfy you I'd let you go without a word. But you know that I can, don't you?"

She nodded.

"What is it, I wonder?" He sighed. "I wish I knew. But it is enough to feel.... You must understand that in spite of the erratic creature you have known since you refused to marry me at once and left me with no resource but to let that play boil out, I am man first and a writer incidentally. I also have a stronger ambition to be your husband than to write plays. If I don't strangle what talent I have it is because I must have the money to be independent of newspaper work. Otherwise I should have neither peace of mind nor be able to live abroad with you. I know that you cannot be happy here, and I am not a victim of that ancient myth that two people who love each other can be happy anywhere. Environment is half the battle—for the super-civilized, at all events. But you shall never have another dose of the writer. I'll write my plays in New York and rush production. The greater part of the year I shall spend with you in Europe, and I cannot think of anything I'd like more—why, the very night I first saw you I was longing with all my soul to get out of New York and over to the other side of the world——Why, Mary! You are not crying? You! I never believed you could——"

"I—I—did not believe it either.... But, are you sure? Could you reconcile yourself? You seem so much a part of New York, of this strange high-pitched civilization. If you are not sure—if you are only tired of New York for the moment.... I—yes, I will! I'll give it all up and live here. Of course I love New York itself—was it not my Mary Ogden home? And there are delightful people every-where.... No doubt my dream of doing great things in Europe was mere vanity——"

"Do you believe that?"

"Perhaps not. But, after all, what I tried to do might be so eas-ily frustrated in that cauldron—why should I risk personal happi-ness—the most precious and the rarest thing in life, for what may be a chimera—wasted years and a wasted life. Why are we made as we are, if to coax that hidden spark into a steady flame is not our highest destiny? It certainly is our manifest right.... Dreams of doing great things in this world are nine-tenths personal vanity. I believe that when we leave this planet we go to a higher star, where our incompleteness here will be made complete; and perhaps we are spared a term of probation if we make ourselves as complete here as mortal conditions will permit. And, possibly, once in a great while, two human beings are permitted to effect that com-pleteness together."

They were both in an exalted mood. The wood was very still, its beauty incomparable. And they might already have been on another star.

Across that divine balsam-scented stillness came the deep im-perative notes of a bell.

Clavering twitched his shoulders impatiently.

"Let them go on their screaming picnic," he said. "We stay here. Did you mean that, Mary?"

"Yes, I meant it. We will not go to Europe at all—except to visit my Dolomites some day. When you are writing I'll come up here."

"I don't know that I shall ask that sacrifice of you. A part of your brain is asleep now, but it is a very active and insistent part when awake. In time you might revert—and resentment is a fatal canker; but let's leave it open. It is generally a mistake to settle things off-hand. Let them alone and they settle themselves."

"Very well. At all events, while we are here, I shall not give it another thought. The present at least is perfect."

"Yes, it is perfect!" He put both arms about her. The past was a blank to both. Their pulsing lips met in the wonder and the ecstasy of the first kiss of youth, of profound and perfect and imperishable love. They clung together exalted and exulting and for the moment at least they were one.

LI

They ate their dinner under the amused eyes of Mrs. Larsing, who had served dinners à deux before to couples that had "lost their way." Afterward they sat by the fire and talked desultorily: a great deal about themselves; sometimes wandering to the subjects that had interested them most before they had met each other. Clavering told her of the many plays he had written, and burned; because in his inordinate respect for the drama he had found them, when not wholly bad, too good to be good enough. But the long practice had given him a certain mastery of technique, and when she had set his brain on fire he had had less trouble than most young playwrights in compelling his imagination to adapt itself to the inexorable framework. He had always felt that the imagination, what is called, for want of a better term, the "creative faculty," was there, but it was lethargic; it sometimes roused itself to spurts and flashes during wakeful nights, but slept like a boa-constrictor that had swallowed a pig when he tried to invoke it. No doubt, as Gora had told him, his life had been too easy and agreeable; he made a good deal of money with no particular effort, he was a favorite with the cleverest men and women in New York, and he had no one to think of but himself. His mother was dead and his sisters married. And there was no doubt that if you were on top, a personality, New York was the most enchanting place in the world to live in, just as it must be the most unsatisfactory for the poor and insignificant. To have conquered New York meant more—several thousand times more—than conquering all the rest of the United States put together, with New York left out. Moreover, it was the only place where you could have any real fun, if you wanted your fun with the sort of men who drifted to New York from all parts of the nation as naturally as pilgrims went to Mecca. If it was your fate to be a politician, Washington, of course, was the goal, but that, in his opinion, was merely moving from a little small-town to a big one, and he thanked his stars he did not have to live in a place where there was nothing but politics and society. In New York you had only to help yourself to any phase of life you wanted.

Mary smiled as she remembered the contemptuous remark of another New York convert: "Oh, Washington is merely an island outside of New York," and she fell to wondering what New York would have been like if it had not been fed so persistently by those streams of eager and ambitious brains debouching into it from every part of a by no means unambitious and negligible commonwealth. Another island, probably. Certainly it was the most exhilarating place in the world today, with its atmosphere of invincible security and prosperity, its surging tides of life. No wonder it was impossible for the intensive New Yorker to realize that four thousand miles away a greater world was falling to ruin.

She told him something of the old political life of Vienna, continually agitated by some "Balkan Question";[1] of the general dislike of the "Heir,"[2] whose violent death at Sarajevo had been the death knell of European peace; apprehensions of the day when he should ascend the throne, for he was intensely clerical and reactionary. If he had survived until the old Emperor's death, and there had been no war, it was doubtful if there would not have been a "palace revolution" within six months of his succession. It was also possible that the people would have had their revolution, for they were becoming enlightened and discontented, and powerful men in the highest offices of the Government were in sympathy with them.

"I suppose you mean this Prince Hohenhauer for one," said Clavering.

"Hohenhauer believed that every throne in Europe would be overturned before the middle of the twentieth century, and that it was the part of wise leaders to prepare not only themselves but the people for a republican form of government. He had the greatest admiration for the principles on which this Republic was founded, and said that Europe was to be congratulated that we had made the mistakes for her to avoid. Much as the rest of the world congratulates itself that Bolshevism was tried out in Russia and made a ghastly mess of improving the condition of the underdog before the masses in other countries had time to lose their heads. I've no doubt that he will be the next Chancellor of Austria, and that

---

1 A reference to the long history of alliances among the Balkan nations, including the difficulty of maintaining a balance of power in Eastern Europe, particularly in regard to matters of race, religion, and nationalism. *The Balkan Question* was also the title of a 1905 book.

2 Archduke Franz Ferdinand of Austria, heir to the Austro-Hungarian throne, who was assassinated in Sarajevo on 28 June 1914; responses to his death led directly to the outbreak of World War I.

when he gets the reins of power in his hands, he'll keep a firm hold on them, which is more than any one else has done——"

"What do you suppose has brought him to this country?"

"I fancy he has come to obtain the moral support of the American Government in whatever plan he may have made for putting Austria on her feet again."

"Have you any idea of what that plan may be?" Clavering was watching her intently, his ear attuned to every inflection of her voice. But her tones were as impersonal as if reciting a page out of ancient history, and her gaze was frank and direct.

"I can only guess. Personally I should think his present plan would be an alliance with Bavaria and other South German States—a South German Confederacy. That would make a powerful combination, and as Bavaria has always hated Prussia, she would be the last to lend herself to any schemes of vengeance the north may cherish—particularly if she remains a republic. And, of course, she would assume her share of the Allied debt.[1] ... It would be a wonderful thing if it could be brought off. Vienna"—her eyes sparkled—"Vienna, of course, would be the capital—and again one of the great capitals of Europe. Perhaps the greatest."

"Were you ever closely associated with Hohenhauer in any of his schemes?"

"He had no immediate schemes then. He only awaited events. While the old Emperor lived no move was possible; he was most illogically adored by his people. But Hohenhauer told me more than once that he was only biding his time."

"And what of that preposterous estate of his in the old Galicia—sixteen million acres, wasn't it? Did he expect to hang on to that under a popular form of government?"

"He would have retained the castle and a few hundred acres, for he naturally had a great affection for his birthplace; and divided the rest among the people, whose natural inheritance it was. But he could do nothing until the proper time, for such an act would undoubtedly have resulted in confiscation and banishment. He would have accomplished no good, and lost his immediate power for usefulness besides. Like all those old-world statesmen, he knows how to play a waiting game."

"Sounds like a great man—if there are any such."

---

1 Reparations paid by Germany and its allies to the Americans, French, and British at the conclusion of World War I, as stipulated in the Treaty of Versailles.

"I should certainly call him a great man," said Mary, but still with that note of complete personal indifference in her voice. "He not only has immense brain power and personality, but farsight and a thorough understanding of the people, and sympathy with them. Even the Social-Democrats liked and trusted him. And he has more than the ordinary politician's astuteness in trimming his sails; but coming out, nevertheless, at the end of the course exactly at the point he had aimed for. If he captures the bridge, to change the simile, he'll steer Austria out of her deep waters. No doubt of that."

"Exactly what was the part you intended to play in Austria?" he asked. "You have never told me."

"I thought we were not to talk of that. It is impossible to make deliberate plans, anyhow. Only, there is a part for any one who loves the country and has the brains and the wealth and the political knowledge to help her."

"I have never quite understood why it should be Austria. Why not Hungary? After all——"

"I never cared for anything in Hungary but the castle, which was wonderfully situated in the mountains of Transylvania. The surroundings were wild beyond description and the peasants the most picturesque and interesting in Europe. But even if Buda Pesth had appealed to me socially, which it never did, there were deep personal reasons that made me dislike Hungary—I never spent a night in the Zattiany palace until I turned it into a hospital. But Vienna! I always lived in Vienna when I could, even during my first years in Europe, and later I made it my home. It is the most fascinating city, to me at least, in the world. Besides, Hungary is in the hands of Horthy and Bethlen,[1] who have no more idea of making a republic of it than of permitting any one else to be king. There is no rôle for——"

"Hullo! Hullo! Hullo!"

Clavering sprang to his feet. "Shall we take the bull by the horns and go to meet them?" he asked. "Poor devils! They'll hate us for looking so fresh."

---

1 István Bethlen (1874-1946), Hungarian prime minister, 1921-31, and Admiral Miklós Horthy (1868-1957) were leaders of the "white" Hungarian government, which succeeded the communist Hungarian Soviet Republic. The early years of this government, termed the "White Terror," characterized by roving bands of mercenaries who instigated politically motivated killings; it lasted until 1922.

LII

They were forced to submit to a vast amount of good-natured chaffing, for they had invited it, but it was the sort of chaffing with which this amiable company would have victimized any pair that had recently met, and found each other's society suddenly preferable to that of the crowd.

They were all very tired. Mr. Dinwiddie, after refreshing his guests and himself with highballs, went to his room and to bed. Rollo Todd announced that it was time to go back to New York to rest, and all fell down on the divans or floor for half an hour before going up to revive themselves with a hot and cold shower.

But fatigue passes away quickly in the mountains. They were as lively as ever the next morning, although they unanimously elected to spend the day on the lake or idling in the woods. Clavering and Mary walked to another gorge he knew of and sat for hours among boulders and ferns on the brink of the stream, and surrounded by the maples with their quietly rustling leaves.

When they returned, Miss Darling, attired in ferns, was executing what she called the wood-nymph's dance, and Todd and Minor were capering about her making horrible faces and pretending to be satyrs. The rest were keeping time with hands and feet. All had agreed that not a letter nor a newspaper should be brought to the camp during their eight days' absence from civilization. Freedom should be complete. It seemed to Clavering that the expression of every face had changed. They all wore the somewhat fixed and dreamy look one unconsciously assumes "in the woods." It was only a few moments before the onlookers had joined hands and were dancing around the central figures; chanting softly; closing in on them; retreating; turning suddenly to dance with one another ... but with a curious restraint as if they were reviving some old classic of the forest and were afraid of abandonment. Almost unconsciously Clavering and Mary joined in the dance. Only Mr. Dinwiddie, a smile half-puzzled, half-cynical, in his eyes, remained a spectator. They swayed rhythmically, like tides, the chanting was very low and measured, the faces rapt. Even Todd and Minor looked exalted. Impossible to imagine they had ever been Sophisticates. They were creatures of the woods, renegades for a time, perhaps, but the woods had claimed them.

Then Mr. Dinwiddie did an impish thing. He inserted a disk in the victrola, and at once they began to jazz, hardly conscious of the transition.

LIII

At nine o'clock the moon was on the lake, and several couples, announcing their need of exercise, went out in boats.

Clavering rowed with long swift strokes until the others were far behind. Mary, muffled in a warm white coat and with a scarf twisted round her head like an Oriental turban, lay on a pile of cushions in the bottom of the boat, her head against the seat. She had the sensation of floating in space. From the middle of the lake the forest on every side was a mass of shadows, and nothing was visible but that high vast firmament sprinkled with silver—silver dust scattered by the arrogant moon. The great silver disk, which, Mary murmured, looked like the tomb of dead gods, seemed to challenge mortals as well as planets to deny that he was lord of all, and that even human emotions must dwindle under his splendor.

"The moon is so impersonal," she sighed. "I wonder why the poets have made so much of it? I'm sure it cares nothing about lovers—less about poets—and thinks the old days, when the world was a heaving splitting chaos, and glaciers were tearing what was already made of it to bits, were vastly superior to the finished perfection of form today. Like all old things. If it has the gods in there, no doubt it wakes them up periodically to remind them how much better things were in their time. Myself, I prefer the sun. It is far more glamoring."[1]

"That is because you can't look it in the eye," said Clavering, smiling down on her. "You really don't know it half as well, and endow it with all sorts of mysterious attributes. I think I prefer the moon, because it is inimitable. You can counterfeit the light and warmth and heat of the sun, and even its color. But silver is used to describe the complexion of the moon only for want of a better word. It is neither silver nor white, but is the result of some mysterious alchemy known only to itself. And its temperature does not affect our bodies at all. You cannot deny that it has exercised a most beneficent effect on the spirits of lovers and poets for all the centuries we know of. Every pair of lovers has some cherished memories of moonlight, and poets would probably have starved without its aid. It is a most benevolent old god, and the one thing connected with Earth that doesn't mind working overtime."

"I'm sure it must be frayed at the edges and hollow at the core. And when it is in the three-quarters it looks exactly like a fish that has lost its platter."

---

1 The archaic form of "glamour," suggesting a magical spell.

"If you continue to insult the moon, I shall take you back to camp and ask Minor to teach you how to jazz."

"I love the moon," said Mary contentedly, and pushing a cushion between her head and the sharp edge of the seat, "I'd like to stay out all night."

They continued to talk nonsense for a while and then fell silent. When the boat was almost at the head of the lake Clavering turned it into a long water lane where the maples met overhead and the low soft leaves kept up a continual whispering. It was as dark as a tunnel, but he knew every inch of the way and presently shot out into another lake, small enough for its shores to be sharply outlined under the full light of the moon, which appeared to have poised itself directly overhead.

Here it was less silent than on the larger lake. There was a chorus of frogs among the lily pads, an owl hooted wistfully in the forest, and they heard an angry snort from the underbrush, followed by a trampling retreat.

"I fancy if we had lingered quietly in that passage we should have seen deer drinking from that patch of sward[1] over there," said Clavering. "But I was not thinking of deer."

"What were you thinking of?"

"Why—you—in a way, I suppose. If I was thinking at all. I was merely filled with a vast content. God! I have found more than I ever dreamed any man could imagine he wanted. Vastly more than any man's deserts. It is an astonishing thing for a man to be able to say."

Mary sat up suddenly. "Be careful. A little superstition is a good thing to keep in one's bag of precautions."

"I feel good enough to disdain it. Of course I may be struck by lightning tomorrow, or the car may turn turtle when we go down to be married, but I refuse to contemplate anything of the sort. I feel as arrogant as that moon up there, who may have all the gods inside him, and do not mind proclaiming aloud that earth is heaven."

"Well—it is." She was not superstitious herself, but she was suddenly invaded by a sinister inexplicable fear, and smiled the more brightly to conceal it. But she lowered her eyelids and glanced hastily about her, wondering if an enemy could be hiding in those dark woods. She was not conscious of possessing enemies venomous enough to assassinate her, but she knew little of Clavering's life after all, and he was the sort of man who must inspire

---

1 Grassy area.

hate as well as love ... danger assuredly was lurking somewhere ... it seemed to wash against her brain, carrying its message.... But there were no wild beasts in the Adirondacks, nor even reptiles.... Nor a sound. The owl had given up his attempt to entice his lady out for a rendezvous and the frogs had paused for breath. There was not the faintest rustle in the forest except those eternally whispering leaves and the faint surging tide in the tree-tops. That ugly invading fear was still in her eyes as she met his.

"What is the matter?" he asked. "You look frightened."

"I am a little—I have a curious feeling of uneasiness—as if something were going to happen."

"'Out of the depths of the hollow gloom,
    On her soul's bare sands she heard it boom,
    The measured tide of the sea of doom,'"[1]

he quoted lightly. "I fancy when one is too happy, the jealous gods run the quicksilver of our little spiritual barometers down for a moment, merely to remind us that we are mortals after all."

The shadow on her face lifted, and she smiled into his ardent eyes.

"Ah, Mary!" he whispered. "Mary!"

LIV

As they left the boathouse an hour later and walked up the steep path to the camp, once more that sense of coming disaster drove into her mind and banished the memory of the past hour, when she had forgotten it. What did it mean? She recalled that she had had dark presentiments before in her life, and they had always come in the form of this sudden mental invasion, as if some malignant homeless spirit exulted in being the first to hint at the misfortune to come.

But the camp was silent. Every one, apparently, had gone to bed, and slept the sleep of valiant souls and weary bodies. One lamp burned in the living-room, and Clavering turned it out and they parted lingeringly, and she went up to her room.

She had barely taken off her coat and scarf when she heard a tap on her door. She stared for a moment in panic, then crossed the room swiftly and opened it. Mr. Dinwiddie, wrapped against

---

1 From "Rose Mary," a poem by Dante Gabriel Rossetti (1828–82).

the cold in a padded dressing-gown and with noiseless slippers on his feet, entered and closed the door behind him.

"What has happened?" she demanded sharply. "Something. I know it."

"Don't look so frightened, my dear. I have no bad news for you. Only it's rather annoying, and I knew I shouldn't get a word alone with you in the morning."

"What is it? What is it?"

"I had this telegram an hour ago from Trent." He took a sheet of paper from the pocket of his dressing-gown, covered with handwriting. "Of course those bumpkins down in Huntersville took their time about telephoning it up. Luckily the telephone is over in Larsing's room——"

Mary had snatched the paper from his hand and was reading it aloud.

"Hohenhauer took morning train for Huntersville stop will spend night there and go to camp in morning stop must see M.Z. stop don't let anything prevent stop very important stop he will not ask you to put him up stop thought best to warn you as you might be planning expedition. Trent."

"Hohenhauer!" exclaimed Mary, and now, oddly enough, she felt only astonishment and annoyance. "Why should he come all this way to see me? He could have written if he had anything to say." And then she added passionately, "I won't have him here!"

"I thought perhaps you'd rather go down to Huntersville to see him," said Mr. Dinwiddie, looking out of the window. "Besides, he would make thirteen at table. I can take you down in the morning and telephone him to wait for us at the same time I order the motor to be sent up."

"I don't know that I'll see him at all."

"But you must realize that if you don't go down he'll come here. I don't fancy he's the sort of man to take that long journey and be put off with a rebuff. From what I know of him he not only would drive up here, but, if you had gone off for the day, wait until you returned. I don't see how you can avoid him."

"No, you are right. I shall have to see him—but what excuse can I give Lee? He must never know the truth, and he'll want to go with us."

"I've thought of that. I'll tell him that Trent is sending up some important papers for you to sign, and as some one is obliged to go to Huntersville to check up the provisions that will arrive on the train tomorrow morning, I've told Trent's clerk to wait there, as I prefer to see to the other matter myself. I—I—hate deceiving Lee——"

"So do I, but it cannot be helped. Did he bring me up here to get me away from Hohenhauer?"

Mr. Dinwiddie's complexion suddenly looked darker in the light of the solitary candle. "Well—you see——"

"I suspected it for a moment and then forgot it. No doubt it is the truth. So much the more reason why he should know nothing about that man's following me. Why should he be made uneasy—perhaps unhappy? But what excuse to go off without him?"

"They have a Ford down there. I'll tell them to send that. With the provisions there'll be no room for four people."

"That will answer. And I'll give Hohenhauer a piece of my mind."

"But, Mary, you don't suppose that one of the most important men in Europe, with limited time at his disposal, would take that journey unless he had something very important indeed to say to you? Not even for your *beaux yeux*,[1] I should think, or he'd have asked Trent to get him an invitation to spend several days at the camp. I must say I'm devoured with curiosity——"

Mary shrugged her shoulders. "I'm too sleepy for curiosity. What time must we start?"

"About nine, if the car gets here on time. It takes two hours to come up the mountain, and they'll hardly be induced to start before seven. I'll tell Larsing to telephone at six."

"It's now eleven. We have eight hours for sleep. Good night, and believe that I am immensely grateful. You've arranged it all wonderfully."

She stamped her foot as Mr. Dinwiddie silently closed the door.

"Moritz! *What* does he want? *Why* has he followed me here? But he has no power whatever over my life, so why should I care what he wants? ... But that this—this—should be interrupted!"

She undressed without calm and slept ill.

LV

The flight next morning proved simpler of accomplishment than she had anticipated. The men were going to a neighboring lake to fish, Larsing having excited them with the prospect of abundant

---

1 Beautiful eyes.

trout; and why fish in your own lake when you may take a tramp of several miles through the woods to another? They begged Clavering to go with them, and as man cannot exist for long in the rarefied atmosphere of the empyrean without growing restive,[1] he was feeling rather let down, and cherished a sneaking desire for a long day alone with men.

But he told Mary that he did not want to go out of their woods and down to that hideous village for any such purpose as to watch her sign papers, and he stood on the landing waving his hat as she and Mr. Dinwiddie crossed the lake in the motor boat to the waiting Ford. For once his intuitions failed him, and he tramped off with the other men, his heart as light as the mountain air, and his head empty of woman.

Mary looked back once at the golden-brown lake, set like a jewel in its casket of fragrant trees, and wondered if she would see it again with the same eyes. She was both resentful and uneasy, although she still was unable to guess what harm could come of this interview. If Hohenhauer wanted her to go to Washington she could refuse, and he had long since lost his old magnetic power over her.

But as the Ford bumped down the steep road between the woods she felt less like Mary Ogden every moment ... those mists of illusion to withdraw from her practical brain ... returning to the heights where they belonged ... she wondered how she could have dared to be so unthinkingly happy ... the sport of the cynical gods? ... sentimental folly that she had called exaltation? After all! After all!

Could she recapture that mood when she returned? Certainly, whatever this man wanted of her, it would be hard facts, not illusions, he would invite her to deal with. Even when he had been the most passionate of lovers, his brain had always seemed to stand aloof, luminous and factual. He had not an illusion. He saw life as it was, and although his manners were suave and polished, and his voice the most beautiful she had ever heard, he could be brutally direct when it suited his purpose. For a moment she hated him as ardently as she had for a time after he left her.

They descended into lower and lower altitudes until the air grew intensely hot, physically depressing after the cold wine of the mountains; finally, ten minutes ahead of time, they drove into the doubly depressing village of Huntersville. It was no uglier than

---

1 The empyrean in Christian literature, particularly Dante's *Divine Comedy*, is the highest level of heaven, where God exists.

thousands of other villages and small towns that look as if built to demonstrate the American contempt for beauty, but the fact mitigated nothing to eyes accustomed to the picturesqueness of mountain villages in Europe, where the very roofs are artistic and the peasants have the grace to wear the dress of their ancestors.

There were a few farms in the valley, but if Huntersville had not been a junction of sorts, it is doubtful if it would have consisted of anything but a "general store," now that the saloons were closed. There was one long crooked street, with the hotel at one end, the Store at the other (containing the post office), and a church, shops for automobile supplies, two garages, a drug store, and a candy store; eight or ten cottages filled the interstices. Men were working in the fields, but those in Huntersville proper seemed to be exhausted with loafing. Campers going in and out of the woods needing shelter for a night, and people demanding meals between trains, kept the dismal looking hotel open and reasonably clean.

The situation was very beautiful, for the mountains rose behind and there was a brawling stream.

Mr. Dinwiddie having ascertained that "Mr." Hohenhauer had received his message and gone for a walk, leaving word he would return at ten o'clock, Mary went into the hotel parlor to wait for him. The room was seldom used, patrons, local and otherwise, preferring the Bar of happy memories, and it smelled musty. She opened the windows and glanced about distastefully. The walls were covered with a faded yellow paper, torn in places, and the ceiling was smoked and fly-specked. The worn thin carpet seemed to have been chosen for its resemblance to turtle soup squirming with vermicelli. Over the pine mantel, painted yellow, were the inevitable antlers, and on a marble-topped table were badly executed water lilies under a glass dome. The furniture was horsehair, and she wondered how she and the Austrian statesman were to preserve their dignity on the slippery surface. Then she heard his voice in the hall as he stopped to speak to Mr. Dinwiddie, and she glanced out curiously.

She had not seen him since a year before the war, but he was little changed; improved if anything, for there was more color in his formerly pale face. He was as straight and as thin as ever, his fine head erect, without haughtiness; his dark eyes under their heavy lids had the same eagle glance. He was still, she concluded dispassionately, the handsomest man she had ever seen, even for an Austrian, the handsomest race on earth; he combined high intelligence with a classic regularity of feature, grace, dignity; and when the firm lips relaxed he had a delightful smile. If it had not been for his hair, very thick white hair, he would have passed for little over forty. He wore loose gray travelling clothes, and every detail was as quietly faultless as ever.

She went hastily to the speckled mirror beneath the antlers and surveyed herself anxiously. Her own travelling suit of dark green tweed, with its white silk shirt, was as carelessly perfect as his own, and the little green turban, with its shaded, drooping feather, extremely becoming. No color set off her fairness like green, but she turned away with a sigh. It was not the eyes of the past three days that looked back at her.

And then she remembered that he had not seen her since the renaissance. The moment was not without its excitements.

Their meeting was excessively formal.

"Frau Gräfin."[1]

"Excellenz."

She lifted her hand. He raised it to his lips.

And then he drew back and looked at her with penetrating but smiling eyes.

"I had heard, of course," he said gallantly, "but I hardly was prepared. May I say, Frau Gräfin, that you look younger than when I had the pleasure of meeting you first?"

"I assure you that I feel many years younger," she replied lightly. "May I add that I am delighted to see that you are in the best of health? Your rest in Switzerland has done you good, although it would have been better for Austria had it been shorter. Shall we sit down?"

Two tall dignified bodies adjusted themselves to chairs both slippery and bumpy. He had closed the door behind him.

"Now that the amenities are over, Excellenz," she said with the briskness she had picked up from her American friends, "let us come to the point. I infer you did not take a day's journey and put up with this abominable hotel to tell me that you are forming a Federation of Austria and the South German States. You were sometimes kind enough to ask my help in the past, but I have no influence in Washington."

"No, dear Gräfin. I do not need your assistance in Washington. But I do need it in Austria, and that is why I am here."

"But it is—was—my intention to return to Austria almost immediately. Surely Judge Trent must have told you."

"Yes, dear Gräfin, he told me, but he also told me other things. I shall not waste the little time at our disposal in diplomacy. He

---

1 Gräfin, or "Countess."

told me that you have the intention to marry a young American."
There was the faintest accent on the *young*.

Mary was annoyed to feel herself flushing, but she answered
coldly, "It is quite true that I intend to marry Mr. Clavering."

"And I have come here to ask you to renounce that intention
and to marry me instead."

"You!" Mary almost rose from her chair. "What on earth do
you mean?"

"My dear Marie." He renounced formalities abruptly. "I think
you will be able to recall that whether I wrapped my meaning in
diplomatic phrases or conveyed it by the blunter method, it was
always sufficiently clear to the trained understanding. I have never
known a more trained or acute understanding than yours. I wish
you to marry me, and I beg you to listen to my reasons."

She gave the little foreign shrug she had almost forgotten. "I
will listen, of course. Need I add that I am highly honored? If I
were not so astonished, no doubt I should be more properly appreciative of that honor. Pray let me hear the reasons." Her tone
was satirical, but she was beginning to feel vaguely uneasy.

Neither her words nor her inflections ruffled the calm of that
long immobile face with its half-veiled powerful eyes.

"Let us avert all possible misunderstandings at the beginning,"
he said suavely. "I shall not pretend that I have fallen in love with
you again, for although my gallantry prompts me to such a natural
statement, I have not the faintest hope of deceiving you. What I
felt for you once can never be revived, for I loved you more than I
have ever loved any woman; and when such love burns itself out,
its ashes are no more to be rekindled than the dust of the corpse.
You thought I fell in love with my pretty young wife, but I was
merely fond and appreciative of her. I knew that the end had come
for us, and that if I did not recognize that sad fact, you would. My
marriage, which, as you know, was imperative, afforded a graceful
climax to a unique episode in the lives of both of us. There was no
demoralizing interval of subterfuge and politely repressed ennui.
On the other hand, it did not degenerate into one of those dreary
and loosely knit *liaisons*, lasting on into old age. We left each other
on the heights, although the cliff was beginning to crumble."

"Really, Moritz! I hope you have not come up here to indulge
in sentimental reminiscence. Why rake up that old—episode? I assure you I have practically forgotten it."

"And I can assure you that I never felt less sentimental. I wish
merely to emphasize the fact that it was complete in itself, and
therefore as impossible of resuscitation as the dead. Otherwise,

you might naturally leap to the conclusion that I was an elderly romantic gentleman——"

"Oh, never! It is obvious that you are inclined to be brutally frank. But, as you said, time is short."

"If what I said sounded brutal, it was merely to remind you that love—the intense passionate love I have no doubt you feel for this young man who helps you to realize your renewed youth—never lasts. And when this new love of yours burns itself out—you never had the reputation of being very constant, dear Marie—you will have an alien young man on your hands, while that remarkable brain of yours will be demanding its field of action. You are European, not American—why, even your accent is stronger than mine! That may be due to an uncommonly susceptible ear, but as a matter of fact your mind has a stronger accent still. You became thoroughly Europeanized, one of us, and—I say this quite impartially—the most statesman-like woman in Europe. Your mind was still plastic when you came to us—and your plastic years are long over, *ma chère*.[1] If your mind had become as young as your body, you would have bitterly resented it. You were always very proud of that intellect of yours—and with the best of reasons."

Mary was staring out of the window. She recalled that she had faced the fact of the old mind in the young brain when she first discovered that she loved Clavering. How could she have forgotten ... for a few short weeks—and up there? ... She raised her eyes to the mountain. From where she sat she could not see the top. It looked like an impenetrable rampart, rising to the skies.

"Can you tell me with honesty and candor," he continued in those same gentle tones that had always reminded her of limpid water running over iron, "—and for all your subtlety your mind is too arrogant and fearless to be otherwise than honest *au fond*[2]—that you believe you could remain satisfied with love alone? For more, let us say, than a year?"

She moved restlessly. "Perhaps not. But I had planned to live in Vienna. He would spend only a part of the year there with me. His own interests are here, of course. It would be a perfectly workable arrangement."

"Are you sure? If you are, I must conclude that in the mental confusion love so often induces, you have lost temporarily your remarkable powers of clear and coherent thought. Do you not realize that you would no longer be Gräfin Zattiany, you would

1 My dear.
2 Basically.

be Mrs. Lee Clavering? Do you imagine for a moment that you could play the great rôle in Austrian affairs you have set yourself, handicapped by an American name—and an American husband? Not with all your gifts, your wealth, your genius for playing on that complex instrument called human nature. Austria may be a Republic of sorts, but it is still Austria. You would be an American and an outsider—a presumptuous interloper."

She stared at him aghast. "I—oh!—I had not thought of that. It seems incomprehensible—but I had never thought of myself as Mrs. Clavering. I have been Gräfin Zattiany so long!"

"And your plans were well-defined, and your ambition to play a great rôle on the modern European stage possessed you utterly until you met this young man—is it not so?"

"Oh, yes, but——"

"I understand. It must have been a quite marvellous experience, after those barren years, to feel yourself glowing with all the vitalities of youth once more; to bring young men to your feet with a glance and to fancy yourself in love——"

"Fancy!" She interrupted him passionately. "I am in love—and more—more than I ever was with you. Until I met him I did not even guess that I had the capacity to love again. It was the last thing I wanted. Abhorrent! But ... but ... he has something for me that you—not even you—ever had ... that I had given up hope of finding long before I met you...."

She stopped, coloring and hesitating. She had an intense desire to make this man understand, but she shivered, as if her proud reserve were a visible garment that she had torn off and flung at his feet, leaving her naked to his ironic gaze.

He was leaning forward, regarding her through his veiled eyes. Their light was not ironic, but it was very penetrating.

"And what is that something, Marie?" he asked softly.

"I—you know those things cannot be put into words."

"I fancy they can. It is merely one more delusion of the senses. One of the imagination's most devilish tricks. I had it for you and you for me—for a time! In the intimacies of either a liaison or matrimony that supreme delusion is soon scattered, *ma chère*."

"But I believe it." She spoke obstinately, although that brawling stream seemed to take on a note of derision.

"Do you? Not in the depths of your clear brain. The mist on top is dense and hot—but, alas for those mists!"

"I refuse to discuss it," she said haughtily. "Why do you wish to marry me yourself?"

"Because I need your partnership as much as you need mine. Even if you returned to Austria unencumbered, you could accomplish less alone than with a man of equal endowments and greater power beside you. Two strong brains and characters with similar purpose can always accomplish more together than alone. I intend to rule and to save Austria, and I need you, your help, your advice, your subtlety, your compelling fascination, and your great personality."

"Do you intend to make yourself king?" she asked insolently, although his words had thrilled her.

"You know that is a foolish question. I do not even use my title there. But I intend to make Vienna the capital of a great and powerful Republic, and I therefore ask you to renounce, before it is too late, this commonplace and unworthy dream of young love, and stand beside me. Youth—real youth—and the best years of maturity are the seasons for love. You and I have sterner duties. Do you suppose that I would sacrifice Austria for some brief wild hope of human happiness? And you are only two years younger than I am. Nothing can alter the march of the years. Moreover, you owe to Austria this wonderful rejuvenescence of yours. Steinach is not an American."

She stamped her foot. "You descend to quibbling. And I have more than repaid Austria all that I owe her."

"You have given her money and service, but she expects more, and you pledged yourself to her before you left. And don't forget that she is the country of your deliberate adoption. A far more momentous thing than any mere accident of birth. You did not return to America when Zattiany died. You never even paid her a brief visit after your marriage. You would not be here now but for the imperative necessities of business. You are Austrian to your marrow."

"I had a rôle thrust on me and I played it. My parents came to Europe every year until they died. When Zattiany went, there were no ties to draw me back and habit is strong. But—underneath—I don't believe that I have ever been other than Mary Ogden."

She blushed as she said it, and he looked at her keenly.

"I think I understand. He is a very clever young man—of an outstanding cleverness, I am told. Or it may be that he is merely in love, and love's delusions are infinite—for a time. I doubt if a young man with so brilliant an intellect would, if he faced himself in honest detachment, admit that he believed anything of the sort. Nor do you, my dear Marie, nor do you."

She twisted her hands together, but would not raise her eyes. He bent forward again and said harshly:

"Marie! Glance inward. Do you see nothing that causes you to feel ashamed and foolish? Do you—*you*—fail to recognize the indecency of a woman of your mental age permitting herself to fancy that she is experiencing the authentic passions of youth? Are you capable of creating life? Can you love with unsullied memory? Have you the ideals of youth, the plasticity, the hopes, the illusions? Have you still even that power of desperate mental passion, so often subordinating the merely physical, of the mature woman who seeks for the last time to find in love what love has not? The final delusion. No, Marie. Your revivified glands have restored to you the appearance and the strength of youth, but, although you have played with a rôle that appealed to your vanity, to your histrionic powers—with yourself as chief audience—your natural desire to see if you could not be—to yourself, again—as young as you appear, you have no more illusion in your soul than when you were a withered old woman in Vienna."

She looked at him with hostile but agonized eyes.

"Your calculated brutality does not affect me in the least. And you are merely one more victim of convention—like those old women in New York. It never has been, therefore it never can be. Many women are not able to bear children, even in youth."

"It is your turn to quibble. Tell me: until you were attracted to this young man—attracted, no doubt, because he was so unlike the European of your long experience—had you deviated from the conclusion, arrived at many years before, that you had had enough of love—of sex—to satisfy any woman? You implied as much to me a few moments since. I know the mental part of you so well that I am positive the mere thought would have disgusted you. If you had been starved all your life it would be understandable, but you had experimented and deluded yourself again and again—and you were burnt out when you came to Vienna to live—burnt out, not only physically but spiritually. Your imagination was as arid as a desert without an oasis. If any man had made love to you then, you would merely have turned on him your weary disillusioned eyes, or laughed cynically at him and yourself. Your keen aesthetic sense would have been shocked. You were playing then an important and ambitious rôle, you had the greatest political salon in Vienna—in Europe—and you went away to rest that you might continue to play it, not that you might feel fresh enough once more to have *liaisons* like other foolish old women.... But the part you played then was a bagatelle to the one awaiting you now. With your splendid mental gifts, your political genius, your acquired statecraft, your wealth, and your restored beauty, you could become the most powerful woman in Europe. But only as my wife. Even you are not strong enough to play the part alone. There is too much prejudice against women to permit you to pull more than hidden strings. Masculine jealousy of women is far more irritable in a democracy than in a monarchy, where women of rank are expected to play a decorative—and tactful part in politics. But if they step down and come into conflict with ambitious men of the people, class jealousy aggravates sex jealousy. You might have a salon again and become a power somewhat in the old fashion, but you never would be permitted to play a great public rôle. But as the consort (I think the word will pass) of the President—or Chancellor—you could wield almost sensational power."

"I should probably be quite overshadowed by you," she murmured; but she was hardly conscious of speaking. Her brain was whirling.

"Your position would be too eminent for that, even if I wished it, which I assuredly should not. I value you too highly. Perhaps I am one of the few men in Europe who admit—and believe—that a woman may have as powerful and accomplished an intellect as any man. I did not appreciate your mind as you deserved when I loved you, but I did during those subsequent years in Vienna."

"You did not ask me to marry you then—when you appreciated me so highly. You never seemed to know whether you were talking to a man or a woman when you were with me. And yet I was, possibly, more interesting psychologically than I had ever been."

"No man is interested in an old woman's psychology. I am not interested in your psychology today. And I did not ask you to marry me then for a great many reasons. I was too handicapped to play a great rôle myself, you will remember. Nor could you have been of the same service to me. Even if your fatigued mind had been refreshed, by your stay in Hungary, you had lost the beauty and the energy, the power of ardent interest in the affairs of state, which have now been restored to you. With your rare gifts and your renewed youth, I repeat you have it in your power to be the most famous woman in Europe, and perhaps the most useful. But not with a young alien husband. Not only would you automatically revert to the status of an American, but the dignity which, unlike so many women of your age who had been *dames galantes*,[1] you took care to impress on the world, would be hopelessly sacrificed. Incredible. To

---

1 Gallant ladies.

spend yourself on a love affair, wantonly to throw away an historic career, merely because a young man has hypnotized you into the delusion that you may once more enjoy the passions of youth——"

"Stop! You shall not!" She had sprung to her feet. Her face was drawn and pinched but her eyes were blazing. "Every word you say is for a purpose. If that were all I should have hated him. As much as I hate you. My mind never dwelt on that—not for a moment—I—I never faced it. You don't know what you're talking about."

"Ah, but I do." He had risen also, and he put his hands on her shoulders. They were long thin hands but very powerful, and it seemed to her that they sank slowly through her flesh, until, however painlessly, they gripped the skeleton underneath. "Look at me, Marie. Your Mary Ogden died many, many years ago. She died, I should say, at the first touch of Otto Zattiany. There was nothing in your new life to revive her, assuredly not your first lover. Certainly you were Marie Zattiany, the most subtle, complex, and fascinating woman in Europe when I met you—but abominably disillusioned even then. I revived your youth for a time, but never your girlhood. You have been able to deceive yourself here in the country of that girlhood, for a time, with this interesting young gentleman in love with you, and, no doubt, extremely ardent."

"Oh!" Her head sank. But she could not turn away, for his hands still gripped her shoulders. The roar of the stream sounded to her horrified ears like the crash of falling ruins.

"Listen, Marie," he said more gently. "If I have been brutal, it was merely because there was no other way to fling you head first out of your fool's paradise. If I had not known the common sense that forms the solid lower stratum of your mind, I should not have come here to say anything at all. You would not have been worth it. But remember, Marie, that under this new miracle of science, the body may go back but never the mind. You, your ego, your mind, your *self*, are no younger than your fifty-eight hard-lived years. And what object in being young again for any of us if we are to make the same old mistakes? Remember, that when you were as young as you look now you had no such opportunity offered you as in this terrible period of European history. Nor could you have taken advantage of it if you had, for mere mental brilliancy and ambition cannot take the place of political experience and an intellect educated by the world. It may be that we shall both be destroyed, that our efforts will avail nothing, and we shall all be swallowed up in chaos. But at least we shall have done what we could. And I know you well enough to believe that such an implacable end would give you greater satisfaction than dallying in the arms of a handsome young husband."

He pushed her back into her chair, and resumed his own. "Would you like to smoke?" he asked.

"Yes." She looked at him with bitter eyes, but she had recaptured her threatened composure. He regarded her with admiration but they smoked in silence for several moments. Then he spoke again.

"You remember Elka Zsáky, I suppose? She was several years older than you and one of the *dames galantes* of her day. She has taken the treatment and looks many years younger, at least, than when she was a painted old hag with a red wig. She is still forced to employ artifice, but she has lovers again, and that is all she did it for. Vienna is highly amused. No doubt all women of her sort will take it for no other purpose. But many of the intellectual women of Europe are taking it, too—and with the sole purpose of reinvigorating their mental faculties and recapturing the physical endurance necessary to their work. I happen to know of a woman scientist, Frau Bloch, who is now working sixteen hours a day, and she had had a bitter struggle with her enfeebled forces to work at all. Lorenz[1] is no more remarkable. He seems to be the only disciple besides yourself that this country has heard of, but I could name a hundred men, out of my own knowledge, who are once more working with all the vigor of youth——"

"Yes," she interrupted sarcastically. "And without a thought of women, of course."

"Probably not." He waved his hand negligently. "But incidentally. That is where men have the supreme advantage of women. The woman is an incident in their lives, even when sincerely in love. And if these men indulge occasionally in the pleasures of youth, or even marry young wives, the world will not be interested. But with women, who renew their youth and return to its follies, it will be quite another matter. If they are not made the theme of obscene lampoons they may count themselves fortunate. There will certainly be verbal lampoons in private."

"Orthodoxy! Orthodoxy!"

---

1   Dr. Lorenz, whom Atherton identifies in her autobiography as a famous Viennese surgeon, took the Steinach Treatment; in 1922, he openly discussed its success in the newspapers. He was described as looking as though he was forty, when he was in actuality in his late sixties. Reading about Dr. Lorenz's rejuvenation, Atherton claimed, convinced her to attempt the treatment.

"Possibly. But orthodoxy is a fixed habit of mind. The average man and woman hug their orthodoxies and spit their venom on those that outrage them. How it may be some years hence, when this cure for senescence has become a commonplace, I do not pretend to say. But so it is today. Personally, no doubt, you would be indifferent, for you have a contemptuously independent mind. But your career and your usefulness would be at an end."

"And suppose I am quite indifferent to that?"

"Ah, but you are not. I will not say that I have killed Mary Ogden during this painful hour, for it is impossible to kill the dead, but I have exorcised her ghost. She will not come again. If you marry this young man it will be out of defiance, or possibly out of a mistaken consideration for him—although he will be an object for sympathy later on. And you will marry him as Marie Zattiany, without an illusion left in that clear brain of yours—from which the mists have been blown by the cold wind of truth. And in a year—if you can stand self-contempt and ineffable ennui so long—you will leave him, resume your present name—the name by which Europe knows you—and return to us. But it may be too late. Vienna would still be laughing. The Viennese are a light-hearted race, and a lax, but when they laugh they cease to take seriously the subject of that good-natured amusement.... It is not aesthetic, you know, it is not aesthetic. Are you really quite indifferent, Marie?"

She shrugged and rose. "It must be time for luncheon," she said. "It will no doubt be horrible, but at least we can have it in here. The public dining-room would be impossible. I will find Mr. Dinwiddie and ask him to order it."

LVI

When the men returned from their fishing trip at six o'clock they saw several of the women on the lake, but there was no one in the living-room. Clavering tapped at Mr. Dinwiddie's door, but as there was no answer, concluded that he and Mary had not yet returned from Huntersville. He was too desirous of a bath and clean clothes, however, to feel more than a fleeting disappointment, and it was not until his return to his room that he saw a letter lying on the table.

It was addressed in Mary's handwriting, and he stared at it in astonishment for a second, then tore it open. It was dated "Huntersville, Monday afternoon," and it read:

"Dear Lee:

"Mr. Dinwiddie will tell you that unforeseen circumstances have arisen which compel me to go to New York for a few days. It is excessively annoying, but unavoidable, and I do not ask you to follow me as I should hardly be able to see anything of you. If there is a prospect of being detained it will not be worth while to return and I'll let you know at once—on Thursday night by telephone; and then I hope you will not wait for the others, but join me here. Indeed, dear Lee, I wish this need not have happened, but at least we had three days.

M."

Clavering read this letter twice, hardly comprehending its purport. She made no mention of Judge Trent. The whole thing was ambiguous, curt. A full explanation was his right; moreover, it was the reverse of a love letter. Even its phrases of regret were formal. Something was wrong.

He put on his clothes hurriedly in order to go in search of Dinwiddie, but before he had finished he heard a sound in the next room and opened the connecting door unceremoniously.

Mr. Dinwiddie braced himself as he saw Clavering's set face.

"Too bad," he muttered, but Clavering cut him short.

"I want the truth. What took Mary to New York?"

"Surely she explained in her letter."

"She explained nothing. There's some mystery here and I want it cleared up at once."

"By God! I'll tell you!" Mr. Dinwiddie burst out. "Mary exacted no promise—I suppose she took for granted I'd not tell you, for she told me what she had written. But if she had I'd tell you anyhow. I'd rather break a promise to a woman than lie to a friend. Believe men should stand by one another. She went down there this morning to meet Hohenhauer."

"Hohenhauer!" Clavering's face turned almost black.

"Yes. Trent telegraphed me yesterday that Hohenhauer was arriving at Huntersville last night and would come up here in the morning to see Mary. He said the matter was most important. I went to Mary's room after you came in from the lake and showed her the message. She was extremely annoyed and said at first that she wouldn't see him. But I pointed out that she couldn't possibly avoid it. Then she said he shouldn't come up here, and she was very emphatic about it. The only thing to do was to take her down. Of course you will be reasonable and see there was nothing else to be done."

"What did that infernal blackguard want of her? And why did she go off with him?"

"She didn't go off with him. She hired a car directly after lunch intending to drive as far as Saratoga and take a train from there. She left Hohenhauer to cool his heels until it was time to take the local for the Adirondack Express. She could easily have taken him along, but I think she was meting out punishment."

"Punishment?"

"Yes. They had a private conference for nearly two hours, and, whatever happened, it put her in an infernally bad humor. She scarcely opened her mouth during luncheon, and as Mary is a woman of the world, used to concealing her feelings, I thought it highly significant. She looked as if she were in a secret frozen rage. Hohenhauer, however, was quite himself, and the meal—corned beef and cabbage!—went off very well."

"What did he want of her?"

"Of that I haven't the vaguest idea. Something momentous, beyond a doubt. If I may hazard a guess, it has something to do with this special mission of his, and it is quite possible that he has asked her to go to Washington—insisted upon it—appealing to her love of Austria. I confess I don't see what she can accomplish there, for she never did have any Washington connections—of course she could get letters from Trent and trust to her personal power and prestige. But let me tell you that she didn't do it to please him. She looked as if she hated him."

"Is he still in love with her? Are you sure he didn't come here to ask her to marry him?"

"If he did he had his journey for his pains—although I can see that it would be a highly desirable combination from his point of view. But he's not in love with her. I'll stake all I know of men on that."

"You are sure?"

"As sure as that I'm alive."

Well, I take the morning train for New York."

"Lee," said Mr. Dinwiddie impressively, "take the advice of an old man, who has seen a good deal of men and women in his day, and stay where you are until you hear from Mary. Some sort of crisis has arisen, no use blinking the fact, but if you burst in on her now, while she is Madame Zattiany, encased in a new set of triple-plated armor, you may ruin all your chances of happiness. Whatever it is let her work it out—and off—by herself. I made her promise she would not leave the country without seeing you again—for I didn't know what might be in the wind—and when she had given her word she added that she had not the least intention of not seeing you again, and that it was quite possible she would return to the camp. If you go down you'll spoil everything."

"I suppose I can trust you, Din, but I've seen plainly that you don't want me to marry her."

"That is true enough. I want nothing less—for your sake; and Hohenhauer would be a far more suitable match for her. But I don't believe you even question my faith——"

"No. I don't. You're a brick, Din. But I'm unspeakably worried—almost terrified. I have never felt that I really knew her. She may have only imagined—but that is impossible! How in God's name am I to sit round here for three days and twiddle my thumbs?"

"Don't. Take one of the men and go off on a three days' tramp. Climb Mount Moose. That will give you no chance to think. All your thinking will be in your muscles."

"And suppose she should return—or telegraph me to go to her?"

"If she returns and finds you gone it'll serve her right. And she won't telegraph before Thursday—if she's going to Washington. Now take my advice and don't be a fool."

Clavering shrugged his shoulders, but he set his lips. "Very well. I won't follow her. Nor will I forgive her in a hurry, either."

"That's healthy. Give her a piece of your mind, have a good row, and then make it up. But let me tell you, my dear boy, that she was horrified at the thought of that man coming up here, and she only refrained from telling you of the summons, so to speak, because she wanted to spare you any anxiety. There's no doubt in my mind that she's as much in love with you as you are with her.... You have none, I suppose?"

"None. Particularly lately. I hadn't told you, but I had intended, in a day or two, to ask you if you would let me have the camp for a few weeks. We intended to marry in Huntersville the day the rest of you went out."

Mr. Dinwiddie whistled. "No wonder she was furious at having her preliminary honeymoon disturbed. But if that is the case of course she'll return. You're more than welcome to the camp, and I'll send whatever you need from time to time. You've only to command me.... It makes it all the more comprehensible. Whatever it was that man said to her, she wanted to get over it by herself before coming back to the place where she had forgotten that Hohenhauers and politics existed. I could see how it was with her here. She looked exactly as she used to in the old days, and I don't doubt felt like it, too. No wonder she resented being forced back into the rôle of Madame Zattiany, or Gräfin—countess—as he calls her. You must let her thresh it out by herself."

"You believe she will come back."

"If that was your plan, I assuredly do. There isn't a spark of human affection between those two, and Mary never placed herself in any man's power. I am more and more inclined to believe that he appealed to her for help in his mission here, whatever it is—and it's not so difficult to guess—and that against her inclination and out of her love for Austria, she consented."

"Well, it's no use to speculate. There's the supper bell. I'll decide in the morning whether I go off for a tramp or not."

LVII

Clavering slept when he first went to bed, for he was healthily tired, but he awoke suddenly at midnight with body refreshed and mind abnormally clear. He knew that he would sleep no more that night, and he put on his trousers and coat over his pyjamas, thrust his feet into bedroom slippers and went out into the living-room. There he put a log on the fire and paced up and down, not unlike a tiger round its cage.

He felt as if black bats were flying about his brain, each charged with a different portent of disaster. Once more the unreality of the whole affair overwhelmed him. How could he have been so fatuous as to believe that he had really won such a woman? He remembered his first impression: that she was on a plane above, apart. They hadn't an interest in common, not even a memory that antedated their meeting a few short weeks ago. She had lived a life of which he knew nothing outside of European novels and memoirs. She had known nothing of any other world until he had introduced her to his friends, and he made no doubt that her interest in them was about as permanent as a highly original comedy on the stage would inspire. There was nothing, literally, between them but a mutual irresistible attraction, and that bond recognized so unerringly by both.

That bond.

Would it hold?

Had this man offered her something that would make love seem insignificant and trivial? She, who had had a surfeit of love long since? Whose eyes had looked a thousand years old until he had given her mind back its youth as the great Vienna biologist had rejuvenated her body.

He was entirely indifferent to her old love affair with Hohen-hauer. It was those years of political association and mutual inter-dependence in Vienna that he feared. He had, when he first met her, appraised her as a woman to whom power was the breath of life. Ambition—in the grand manner—incarnate. She had all the appearance and the air of a woman to whom the wielding of pow-er, however subtly, was an old story. He recalled that that terrify-ing suggestion of concealed ruthless forces behind those charming manners, those feminine wiles, had almost made him resolve to "avoid her like the plague." And then he had fallen madly in love with her and forgotten everything but the woman.

He had divined even before these last miraculous days that she had looked upon love with abhorrence for almost half as many years as he had lived, an abhorrence rooted in a profound revul-sion of body and mind and spirit. For nearly twenty years that re-vulsion had endured and eaten into the very depths of her being.... He had a sudden blaze of enlightenment. She had frequently al-luded to that Lodge of hers in the Dolomites and their sojourn there together, but always in the terms of romance.... She had nev-er given him a glance of understanding.... And she had put off the wedding until the last possible moment.... If she had really been as eager as himself she would have left her power of attorney with Trent and started for Austria six weeks ago. Or the papers could have been sent to her to sign, if her signature were imperative.... And in spite of the fact that everybody had taken the engagement for granted, she had, with wholly insufficient reasons,—as he saw, now that he was removed from the influence of her plausible and dominating self,—refused to announce it. Could it be that in the depths of her mind—unadmitted by her consciousness—she had never intended to marry him? Was that old revulsion paramount? ... Sixteen years! ... A long time, and nothing in life is more cor-roding than habit.

Perhaps—as long as they were down there in New York. But not up here. That he would be willing to swear. There had been another revolution, involuntary perhaps, but the stronger for that; and every shackle that memory and habit can forge had dropped from her. She had been youth incarnate. The proof was in her joy-ful consent to marry him immediately and remain in the moun-tains ... and then her complete surrender of the future into his hands.... She had during those three brief days loved him wholly, and without a shadow in her soul.

But now? Whatever had happened, she was not Mary Ogden tonight, hastening to New York, nor would she be when in her own house on the morrow. She might hate Hohenhauer, but his mere presence would have made the past live again. She must have known when she went down that mountain that even with her strong will and powers of self-delusion, things could not be quite the same again. Not even if she had returned with Dinwiddie. Why in heaven's name had she been so mad as to go? She could have sent Hohenhauer a peremptory refusal to see him and then gone off on a camping trip that could have lasted until he gave up the game. She must have been mad—mad.

And he did not believe for a moment that she had gone to Washington.

She had gone home to think—think.

And if he followed Dinwiddie's advice and remained here she might think too long. And if he followed and insisted upon seeing her, the result might be more fatal still. He knew nothing of those personalities she may have concealed from him. For all he knew she might have depths in her nature as black as the bottomless pit.

And God only knew what the man had said to her.... Should he let her fight it out by herself? What in heaven's name should he do? Whatever happened, this divine interval, like some exquisitely adjusted musical instrument, had been hopelessly jarred out of tune. He almost hoped she would not return. Let it remain a perfect memory.... They could marry in New York and return here, when she was his wife.... If he had not already lost her.... What in God's name was the thing for him to do? He'd go mad if he stayed here, and if he went he might regret it for the rest of his days. Why could not light be vouchsafed him?

Gora.

Fortunately he knew her room for he had carried up her luggage. He ran lightly up the stairs and tapped on her door. A startled sleepy voice answered. He opened the door and put in his head.

"Come downstairs at once, Gora," he said peremptorily. "I must talk to you."

She came down in a moment, clad in a scarlet kimono, her hair hanging in thick braids. With her large round forehead exposed she looked not unlike a gnome, but curiously young.

"What on earth is the matter, Clavey?" she asked as she pushed her chair as close to the fire as possible. "It has something to do with this sudden trip of Mary's, I suppose. Mr. Dinwiddie said she had been called to New York on important business, and the others accepted the explanation as a matter of course; but I'll confess I wondered."

Clavering, still too nervous to sit down, jerked out the whole story, omitting only the old love affair with the man who had exercised so strong an influence on Mary Zattiany's later life.

"You see," he concluded, "there are two things: Austria had taken the place in her affections that women of her age generally concentrate on human beings—it became almost a sacrament. And then—for nearly twenty years she had hated everything in men but their minds. Sex was not only dead but a detestable memory. After that rejuvenescence she had never cast a thought to loving any man again. That mental habit, at least, was fixed. When I met her she was a walking intellect…. I thought I had changed all that … up here I had not a doubt left … but now … I don't know…. Put that cold-blooded mind of yours on it and tell me what to do."

"Let me think a minute, Clavey."

As he resumed his restless march, Gora sent her mind travelling out of the mountains and far to the south, and tried to penetrate the brain of Mary Zattiany. She could not visualize her in the bed of a casual hotel or sitting in the chair of a parlor car, so she skipped the interval and saw her next day in that intimate room of hers upstairs; the room, assuredly, where she would think out her problem.

Gora had studied Madame Zattiany with all the avidity of the artist for a rare human theme, and she believed that she knew her as well as Clavering did, if not better. She had also not failed to observe Prince Hohenhauer's picture, and had read the accompanying text with considerable interest, an interest augmented, not unnaturally, by his exceeding good looks. That same day she had met a Viennese at dinner who had talked of him with enthusiasm and stated definitely that he was the one hope of Austria.

Gora Dwight was a very ambitious woman and revelled in the authority that fame and success had brought her. She was also as disillusioned in regard to men as any unmarried woman could be; although quite aware that if she had lacked a gift to entice her emotions to her brain, she no doubt would even now be looking about for some man to fall in love with. But her pride was spared a succession of humiliating anti-climaxes, and she had learned, younger than most women, or even men, that power, after sex has ceased from troubling, is the dominant passion in human nature.

And Madame Zattiany was twenty years older than herself, and had drained the jewelled chalice to the dregs. And for many years more she had enjoyed power, revelled in it, looked forward, Gora made no doubt, to a greater and greater exercise of it. Power had become the master passion of her life.

Like men in the same case, she had indulged herself, during a period of enforced inaction, with an exciting love adventure. That she had fallen in love, romantically in love, with this young man, whom so many women loved, and who, no doubt, had given her the full benefit of all his pent-up ardors—Gora could imagine those love scenes—she had not questioned, in spite of Madame Zattiany's carefully composed tones when speaking of him, and her avoidance of so much as the exchange of a meaning glance with him in public. Up here "Mary" had ceased to be a woman of the world, she had looked like a girl of twenty: and that she was in love and recklessly happy in the fact, was for all to see. That had been one of her most interesting divagations to the novelist, Gora Dwight—but a phase. Gora was not deluded.

And this man Hohenhauer had brought her to her senses; no doubt of that either to a mind both warmly imaginative and coldly analytical. And what had he come up here for except to ask her to marry him—to share his power? She dismissed the Washington inference with the contempt it deserved. Mr. Dinwiddie was a very experienced and astute old gentleman, but he always settled on the obvious like a hen on a porcelain egg.... What a manifest destiny! What an ideal match.... She sighed, almost envying her. But it would be almost as interesting to write about as to experience. After all, a novelist had things all her own way, and that was more than even the Zattianys could hope for.

Then she remembered poor Clavering and looked up at him with eyes that were wholly sympathetic.

"I don't think there's a doubt," she said, "that Prince Hohenhauer came up here to ask her to marry him. You can see for yourself what such a match would mean for him, for aside from that indisputable genius of hers—trained in later years by himself—she has great wealth and few scruples; and where he failed to win men to his purpose, she, with her superlative charm, and every feminine intuition sharpened by an uncommon experience of men and public life, would succeed. She may hate him, as Mr. Dinwiddie says—for the moment. But even if she continued to hate him that would not prevent her from marrying him if she believed he could help her to power. If it had not been for you I don't believe she would have hesitated a moment."

"Do you mean to say you believe she'll throw me over?" demanded Clavering fiercely.

"I think you're in danger, and if I were you I'd throw Mr. Dinwiddie's advice to the winds and take the morning train for New York."

"Don't you believe that she loves me?"

"Oh, yes. As love goes."

"What d'you mean by that?"

"I mean that Madame Zattiany has long since reached the age when power means more than love—in a woman of that calibre. But you, in turn, have tremendous power over her. Sweep her off her feet again and make her marry you."

"You don't believe she's gone to Washington?"

"I do not. If that was all he wanted of her, why didn't he telephone? I am sure he could be ambiguous enough to defeat the curiosity of any listeners-in. But a man of that sort does not ask a woman to marry him over the telephone——"

"But Din thinks——"

"How long do you think you can stand inaction?"

"Not another hour, by God! I'm nearly mad as it is."

"I thought so. You are about the last man on earth equipped to play the waiting game."

"You don't think she means to return here?"

"Never. She's too much of an artist for one thing. She might be willing to begin a new chapter, but she knows that asterisks in the wrong place are fatal. This interruption has done for your idyl!"

"I had thought the same thing." He sighed heavily.

"Oh, yes, Clavey dear, you are an artist yourself. No matter what happens never forget that it is your destiny to be a great one."

"Artist be damned. If—if—God! if I lose her—I'll never write another line."

"I don't doubt you think so. But you're only just beginning to know yourself. You got a few glimpses, I should think, while you were writing that play."

"Don't mention that play to me. I hate it. If I hadn't let myself go with the damned thing I'd have had my wits about me and would have married her off-hand."

"I wonder. Was she so very anxious to marry?"

He turned cold. Fear flared up again. "What do you mean by that?"

"Well, I don't know that I mean anything. Except that like all women she probably wanted to enjoy the thrilling hopes and fears and uncertainties of that never to be repeated prelude, to the limit. Now, better wake up Larsing and order the car if you mean to catch that morning train. If you don't want to go back to bed I'll sit up with you. You can sleep on the train."

LVIII

He left the next morning in a dense fog. As Larsing rowed him across the lake he could not see its surface nor the wall of trees on the opposite bank, and in a moment the camp was obliterated.

Only Gora and Larsing knew of his departure. Even Dinwiddie was still asleep. Larsing had made him a cup of coffee, and Gora had packed his bag, moving like a mouse in his room. She kissed him good-bye and patted him on the back.

"I'll go out myself in a day or two," she said. "You may need me down there."

The fog thinned gradually and the Ford made its usual comfortless speed down the mountain. When they reached Huntersville the valley was bathed in early morning sunlight, and Huntersville, asleep, shared the evanescent charm of the dawn. It was a beautiful and a peaceful scene and Clavering, whose spirits had descended into utter gloom while enwrapped in that sinister fog, accepted it as a happier portent; and when he was so fortunate as to find an empty drawing-room on the Express, he went to bed and slept until the porter awoke him at Tarrytown.

It was his first impulse to rush direct to Murray Hill, but he knew the folly of doing anything of the sort. He needed a bath and a shave and a fortifying dinner.

He concluded that it would be unwise to telephone, and at nine o'clock he approached her house, reasonably calm and quite determined to have his own way. But the house was dark from cellar to roof. Every window was closed although it was a warm night. He sprang up the steps and rang the bell. He rang again, and then kept his finger on the button for nearly five minutes.

He descended into the area, but the iron bars were new, and immovable. Moreover, a policeman was sauntering opposite. He approached the man in a moment and asked him if he knew whether the house had been open earlier in the evening. Yes, the officer told him, he had seen one of the servants go in about half an hour ago.

Clavering walked away slowly. If Mary had gone to Washington, why had the servants not answered his ring? It was too early for them to be in bed. Then his spirits, which had descended to zero, rose jubilantly. Hohenhauer! It was against him she was barricading herself. No doubt she would feel herself in a state of siege as long as the man remained in the country.

He went to the nearest hotel and telephoned. He was prepared to be told, after an interminable wait, that there was "no answer";

but in a moment he heard the voice of the butler. Obeying a sudden impulse he disguised his own.

"I should like to speak to Madame Zattiany."

"Madame has retired."

He hung up. He had ascertained that she was at home and his spiritual barometer ascended another notch. He'd see her tomorrow if he spent the day on her doorstep. He bought an evening paper, picked out a new play, and spent a very agreeable evening at the theatre.

LIX

His nervous excitement returned next morning, but he forced himself to eat a good breakfast and read his newspapers. He was determined to show her that he was completely master of himself. She should be able to draw no unfavorable comparisons with Hohenhauer, whose composure had probably not been ruffled in forty years. His comparative youth might be against him, but after all a man of thirty-four was no infant, and in some respects he was as old as he would ever be. He knew the value of dignity and self-control, and whatever might come he would sacrifice neither. But he sighed heavily. "Whatever might come." But he refused to dwell on alternatives.

It was ten o'clock when he presented himself at Madame Zattiany's door. As he had hoped, his ring was answered. Hohenhauer was not the man to call on a woman at ten in the morning.

The footman permitted himself to stare, and said deprecatingly: "I am very sorry, Mr. Clavering, but Madame told me to admit no visitors——"

"Did she?" He entered and tossed his hat on a high Italian chair. "Kindly tell her that I am in the library and shall remain there until she is ready to come down."

The man hesitated, but after all Clavering had had the run of the house, and it was possible that Madame believed him still to be in the mountains. At all events he knew determination when he saw it, and marched reluctantly up the stairs.

Clavering went into the library. He was filled with an almost unbearable excitement, but at least the man's assertion that she was at home to no one cemented his belief that she meant to see nothing further of Hohenhauer.

He glanced round the beautiful mellow room so full of memories. After all he had been happier here than he had ever been in his life—until they had gone up to the woods! The room's benignant atmosphere seemed to enfold him, calmed his fears, subdued that inner quiver. Surely she would surrender to its influence and to his—whatever had happened. He knew she had always liked him the better because he did not make love to her the moment they met, but today he would take her by surprise, give her no time to think.

But, as Mrs. Oglethorpe had once told him, a clever man is no match for a still cleverer woman.

At the end of fifteen minutes the footman opened the door and announced:

"Madame is in the car, sir, and begs you will join her."

Clavering repressed a violent start and an imprecation. But there was nothing to do but follow the man; fortunately he did not have what was known as an "open countenance." Let her have her own way for the moment. He could—and would—return with her. For the moment he felt primitive enough to beat her.

She was wearing a black dress with a long jade necklace and a large black hat, and, as he ran down the steps, he had time further to observe that she was even whiter than usual and had dark rings under her eyes.

"It is too beautiful a morning to remain indoors," she said, as she gave him her hand and he took the seat beside her. "We will drive in the Park and then up the river for a bit."

She was completely at her ease, and she was the Madame Zattiany of the night he had met her. But she did not elaborate the rôle, and asked him how he had left his friends at the camp and if he had enjoyed his fishing trip.

"Enough of this," he interrupted, when he had mastered his excitement at being close to her once more. After all, he had expected something of the sort. She was just the woman to fall back on her infernal technique. "I know that you went down to Huntersville to meet Hohenhauer, and that the result of that interview was an abrupt flight from me—possibly from him. I want the truth."

Her face had flushed, but as the color ebbed she looked almost waxen. "I relied on Din——"

"Well, I guessed it and he admitted the fact. And if he hadn't I'd have come after you, anyhow. Your note was enough to tell any man something was wrong. I shall not be put off and I will have an answer to my questions. Do you love me no longer?"

"Oh, yes," she said softly. "I love you." But when he tried to take her hand she drew it away.

"Do you still intend to marry me?"

"Won't you give me a few days more to think it over?"

"No, I will not. And—do you need them? Haven't you already made up your mind?"

She sighed and looked out of the window. They were driving up Fifth Avenue and the bright street was full of color and life. The busses and motors were filled with women on their way to the shops, whose gay windows were the most enticing in the world. New York, in this, her River of Delight, looked as if she had not a care in the world.

Madame Zattiany did not speak again until they were in the Park.

"I have promised to marry you, remember; and I do not lightly go back on my word.... But ... I had intended to ask if you would be willing to let me go alone to Vienna for six months—and then join me——"

"After I had lost you completely! I shall marry you here, today, or not at all. I love you but I'll not let you play with me. I'll go to Austria with you, and you may do as you choose when you get there. You'll belong to me and I'll make the best of it."

"If I married you now it would not be worth my while to return to Austria.... You see, I'd be an American. I'd no longer be Gräfin Zattiany.... I could accomplish nothing.... It is the strangest thing in the world, but I never had thought of changing my name——"

"Until Hohenhauer reminded you, I suppose. Well, I could have told you that myself. I had counted on it, if you want to know the truth."

"Ah! Then you counted on that to—to——"

"To have you altogether. Yes." And then he added hastily: "But up there—you must believe this—I never gave it a thought—after—after you promised to marry me at once."

He doubted if she had listened to this protest that there had been an hour when in the complete baring of his soul he had been above plotting and subterfuge. She was still looking out of the window. He saw her long upward-curving nostril grow rigid.

But she said quietly: "And what do you think you would have done with me, Lee, after we were on the plane of common mortals once more? Transports do not last for ever, you know, and we are not heedless young things with no thought of the future. You have acknowledged there is no place for me here, and there would be no place for me in Europe if I married you. Do you wonder that I came away to think, after Prince Hohenhauer—who, remember, knows me far better than you do—pointed out the inexorable truth? What would you do with me, Lee?"

He stared out of the window in his turn—at the tender greens of the Park. He could hear the birds singing. Spring! The chill of winter was in the car, and it emanated from the woman beside him.

"I don't know," he said miserably. "I only know that I love you and would take any chances."

"But, you see, although it is my misfortune to love you, I recognize that there is a long generation between us. I thought I had spanned it, but—do you realize that we have literally nothing to give each other but love? That we are as unlike——"

"Oh, yes, I realized all that the night you left. But I don't care. Cannot you trust me?"

"There is that long generation, Lee. And it is I who have lived it, not you. Lived it and outlived the woman who began it. The gods in a sportive mood made us for each other—and then sent me into the world too soon.... I must go on. It is not in me to go back nor to remain becalmed. Hohenhauer told me many cruel truths. Those women at my dinner might have enlightened me if I had not deliberately bandaged the eyes of my mind. I chose to forget them at once. But Hohenhauer——" She shuddered. "Well, although I was infuriated with him at the time—what he said was true. Every word. I must go forward. I cannot—cannot go back."

"He appealed to your ambition, your love of power, I suppose——"

"He showed me to myself for exactly what I am," she said emphatically. "No appeal would have made the slightest impression on me if I had really and finally returned to my Mary Ogdenhood up there in the woods of my real youth. My God! What incredible folly! What powers of self-delusion! But we both have that memory. Let us be grateful. I at least shall hold it apart from all memories as long as I live."

"Are you going to marry that man?"

"That is so purely incidental that it is not worth talking about. I came away to think out my own problem. I love you and I believe that I shall always love you—but I don't see any way out. I have killed once and for all that fatal talent for self-delusion that I had thought was as dead—well, as dead as my love for Moritz Hohenhauer; and nothing could be more dead than that. My brain feels like a crystal house illuminated by searchlights, strong enough to penetrate every corner but not strong enough to blind. I could never, if I would, deceive myself again, nor make another mistake, so far as human prescience will serve me."

He looked at her hands. Her gloves were black suede and they made those hands look smaller, but he had an idea that if he lifted one it would fall of its own rigid weight.

He made no comment and she said in a moment: "Perhaps you may have an inspiration. If there is any solution for us, believe me when I say that it would make me as happy as it could make you."

But her hands did not relax.

"What is the solution, Lee?"

He had buried his face in his hands. "There is none, I suppose. Unless you have the courage to drive down to the City Hall and marry me ... and"—he lifted his head with a faint gleam of hope—"remember that you are young again. You have many years to live. You are a woman. Can you go through life without love?"

"Far better than with it. Love is a very old story to me," she said deliberately. "It could never be to me again the significant thing it is even to the woman of middle age, much less to the young. And now—with a world falling to ruins—in the most critical period of its history—to imagine that love has any but a passing significance——Oh, no, my friend. Oh, no! Let those women who have it in their power to repeople the earth which has lost so many millions of its sons, cherish that delusion of the supreme importance of love; but not I! I have had my dream, but it is over. If we had met in Vienna it would never have claimed me at all. In New York one may be serious in the romantic manner when one is temporarily free from care, but seriousness is of another and a portentous quality over there."

"Why did you ask me to wait six months and then join you in Vienna?"

She turned her eyes on him with what he had once called her look of ancient wisdom. There was not an expiring flicker of youth in them, nor in the faint smile on her lips. He had thrown himself back in his corner and folded his arms; he had no desire to attract the attention of the passers-by. But his face was as white as a dark man's can be and his eyes were both stricken and bitter.

"To give you time to get over it," she said. "To write another play. To settle down into your old life—and look back upon this episode as upon a dream, a wonderful dream, but difficult to recall as anything more substantial."

"So I inferred. And you have not the courage to marry me—here—today?"

"No, that is the one thing for which I have no courage whatever. In three months I should hate you and myself. I should not have even one memory in my life that I had no wish to banish—the sustaining memory of love undestroyed I may take back with me now. Courage! I could contemplate going back to certain death at the hands of an assassin, or in another revolution; to stand on the edge of the abyss, the last human being alive in Europe, and look down upon her expiring throes before I went over the brink myself. But I have not the courage to marry you."

Clavering picked up the tube and told the driver to stop.

He closed the door and lifted his hat.

"Good-bye, Madame Zattiany," he said. And as the driver was listening, he added: "A pleasant journey."

THE END

Appendix A: Age and the Body

[This appendix focuses on rejuvenation therapy's claims about bodily change, and it includes excerpts from medical documents surrounding the therapy, including those by Eugen Steinach (pioneer of rejuvenation techniques and collaborator with Atherton's physician, Dr. Harry Benjamin). An excerpt from George F. Corners' book on rejuvenation, which makes somewhat broader social claims regarding the technique, also appears here as evidence of the scope of conversations surrounding rejuvenation treatments. An article by Atherton, "Second Youth" (1939), points to her continued presence in the public conversations surrounding the treatments, while letters to Atherton from her readers suggest the ways in which ordinary readers responded to the novel's representations of rejuvenation therapy.]

1. From George F. Corners, *Rejuvenation: How Steinach Makes People Young* (New York: Thomas Seltzer, 1923), 1-3, 53-55

Has Steinach succeeded where Ponce de Leon failed?[1] Is the secret of youth hidden in a ductless gland? Is it possible to fling away the burden of old age? Can we halt the grim shadow that lies athwart our path? Can man play with Death and win? Can he at least defer the check-mate of the eternal antagonist?

No weightier question has ever exercised mankind. What are wars and kings, tariffs and geographical divisions, compared to the most momentous issue of human life? Oedipus faced the Sphinx.[2] All Sons of Adam face Death. Does Professor Eugen Steinach bring us the knowledge the serpent promised Eve, that shall make us like gods?

It is not possible to answer questions such as these with "yes" or "no." I place before the reader the result of Steinach's experiments and

---

1　Ponce de Leon (1474-1521) is widely credited with discovering Florida while searching for treasure under the Spanish crown's directive. The concept of the "fountain of youth" has been associated with this adventure, though its origins are unclear.

2　When, as a young man, Oedipus arrived at the gates of Thebes, the Sphinx (half lion, half human) asked him a riddle—to name the creature that walks on four legs in the morning, two at noon, and three in the evening— for she planned to kill and eat the youth if he did not answer correctly. Oedipus correctly answered this riddle, responding that the creature is man, who crawls early in life, walks upright as an adult, and who requires a cane in old age. The Sphinx killed herself in frustration that the riddle had been solved. Oedipus would then cross generational lines by killing his father and marrying his mother.

researches, as explained by himself and his fellow workers. In doing so it will be necessary to touch upon intimate phases of life. Technical language cannot be altogether avoided. I shall make my statements as simple as possible.

Steinach claims that he can "arrest within modest limits the process of senility." His hopes go further. His experiments with animals seem to prove that it is possible to prolong life itself. Whether or not experience will confirm all his conclusions, his message is the most cheerful that science has sounded in centuries.

The quest for youth is as old as the world. In every age men have sought to wrest from nature the elixir of life. Even to-day so profound a thinker as George Bernard Shaw toys with the idea of extending man's span to three hundred years by exhorting the mysterious forces of Selective Evolution.[1]

The investigations of the alchemists of the Middle Ages are continued by Twentieth Century science. Jacques Loeb, in the Rockefeller Institute, breeds one hundred generations of flies to test the normal duration of life under specific conditions where neither external accident nor insidious microscopic foes can obscure the issue.[2] By subjecting the insects to low degrees of temperature, he multiplies their span of life.

We know that tissue may live indefinitely, that the heart itself may pulsate outside of the body. But bio-chemistry, the chemistry of Life, has not been able to discover an antidote against Death. We can not even retard measurably the process of deterioration within our own body which is responsible for the phenomenon of old age. We grow old by the poisons we ourselves distil.

Even if we succeed in eluding fatal disaster from without and fatal disease from within, we are killed eventually by the toxins in ourselves. The by-products of Life are the agents of Death.

Hence the world was electrified by the news that Professor Eugen Steinach, physiologist of the Biological Experimental Institute of the Academy of Science in Vienna, had discovered the secret, not of life, but of Rejuvenation.

---

1 Shaw's play cycle, *Back to Methuselah* (1921), deals with characters of an extended life span and with creative evolution (or non-random inheritances determined by environmental factors) rather than Darwin's theory of natural selection.

2 Loeb (1859-1924) worked as a physiologist and experimental biologist; his most famous experiments involved invertebrate marine animals. Loeb was a well-known figure, having been nominated for Nobel prizes. Mark Twain and Sinclair Lewis also wrote about Loeb or based fictional figures on his work.

Steinach does not promise to perpetuate life indefinitely, but he provides an antitoxin that checks the progress of old age. What is more, he re-energizes the body.

"We cannot," Professor Steinach remarked to me, "perform the comic opera bouffe of transmuting an old hag into a giddy young damsel.[1] We have discovered no hocus-pocus that will turn a senile ancient tottering to the tomb into a fairy prince. But, under certain conditions, we can stretch the span of man's usefulness, and enable the patient to recapture the raptures, if not the roses of youth.

"Whether the Steinach operation actually prolongs life, we are not, at present, prepared to state, in spite of certain indications pointing in this direction. Scientific workers in many climes must continue to labor before we can venture to draw more definite conclusions. I am a student, not a dreamer. I place my faith solely in the laboratory. I am interested only in those things which I can compel nature to prove to me beyond doubt or cavil."

[...]

The age to be Steinached depends on the condition of the patient. Incipient arteriosclerosis is usually an indication that the endocrine system is no longer equal to the task of maintaining the resiliency of the organism so essential to its well-being. In women the treatment is most effective at the time of the menopause. Men are more fortunate in that surprising results have been attained even at the biblical three score and ten.

The lives we lead are so complicated, the conditions under which the majority is compelled to live so unnatural, that in most cases, arteriosclerosis and other phenomena of old age appear between forty and sixty. This is the period when most persons should be Steinached for the first time.

The process can be repeated several times, after five or ten years, when the effect of the first treatment wears off. In this manner, vitality may be preserved until an advanced old age. Then, if Kammerer is right, death comes, pleasantly almost as in a dream. The patient dozes away without pain or struggle.[2] It remains to be seen, if this hypothesis is borne out by facts. It has been demonstrated beyond doubt only in animals. The science of rejuvenation applied to human beings is still too young to afford sufficient material for final conclusions.

---

1   Opera bouffe: an opera with a comedic plot, spoken dialogue, and a happy ending.
2   Probably Paul Kammerer (1880-1926), Austrian biologist known for his investment in Lamarckian theory, experiments with midwife toads, and for his pioneering work in seriality theory.

The Steinach operation not merely retards old age, it favorably affects diseases associated with the climacteric period in men and women, especially disorders involving derangements of the endocrine system including diabetes, gout, cancer, metabolistic disturbances of every description, impotence and nervous diseases. It has been known to cure certain forms of insanity.

"The first cases reported by Steinach," Schmidt explained to me, "are now over six years old. So far experience confirms his thesis. However, we can go back far beyond this period. Operations of a similar nature were performed in the United States long before Steinach. Phenomenal cases of rejuvenation were reported by American doctors who had no idea of the effect of vasoligature and vasectomy on the aging Puberty Gland.[1]

"Recent investigations have shown that several patients upon whom vasoligature and vasectomy was performed at an advanced age in connection with other surgical operations still enjoyed an astonishing measure of youthfulness ten years later.

"The phenomena described by Steinach have been observed so universally that there is no reason for concealing these facts, so important both therapeutically and economically, from the public at large.

"We must not expect blonde locks growing in plentiful profusion on bald pates, nor expect to dwell on earth in eternal youth. We can merely assert that medical science has succeeded in a large number of cases in arresting premature senescence and restoring a measure of youthful vigor.

[...]

2. From Eugen Steinach, *Sex and Life: Forty Years of Biological and Medical Experiments* (New York: Viking Press, 1940), 197–208

The clinical application of female sex hormones belongs to the field of gynæcology; in fact, if one sets aside operative gynæcology, one might even say that hormone therapy practically rules this field today. A survey of hormone therapeutics could really fill a book which in scope would not be smaller than the present one. It is impossible here to enter into all those disorders of women in which hormone therapy might be indicated and successfully administered. The purpose of this chapter is to give the reader an idea of gynæcological hormone treatment and one must be content to summarize and compress the vast quantity of material available.

---

1 Steinach argued that vasectomy or vasoligation "rejuvenated" aging men by restoring sexual potency.

Because of its specialized effect and indications, it will be unnecessary to go into detail concerning the corpus luteum hormone, since it plays its principal part during pregnancy.[1] All the more attention can thus be given to the follicular hormone, which is of such great importance for the female functions.

As we know, the follicular hormone reacts not only upon the genital organs, but directly and indirectly upon all organs, in fact upon the whole body of the woman. This multiplicity of hormonic effects corresponds to the variety of manifestations which occur during functional disturbances, and we have therefore to differentiate among a great variety of therapeutic results.

The subdivision of these results into groups will facilitate our survey, and when we so group them they practically automatically fall into two main divisions such as we have already become acquainted with during the experiments concerned with stimulation of the incretory functions of the ovaries. Although gynæcologists never emphasize this point, it must be understood that, as in the laboratory, so also in the clinic, one must recognize two principal categories: *activation* of undeveloped or underdeveloped, that is, insufficient functions, on the one hand; and, on the other, *reactivation* of physiological but no longer adequate functions which have retrogressed through the ageing process.

[...]

No matter how small the deficiency of hormone may be, it can nevertheless cause a variety of symptoms, which may prove to be very harassing. Quite apart from painful menstruation and sterility, such a hormone insufficiency may also cause atrophy of the genital mucous membrane, thus lowering its resistance to external influence. This lowered resistance predisposes to inflammatory processes. Hormone administration in such cases arrests the process of disintegration and promotes regeneration of the mucous membrane. The occasional striking successes in cases of very annoying "nervous" itch (technically termed pruritus) are based on this.

Such pruritic disorders are relieved by hormone therapy, not only when they involve the mucous membrane, but also when they attack the skin. Similarly, other skin disorders, such as eczema, may be influenced; even symptoms which affect dermal appendages such as the nails and the hair—brittleness and ugly blotches on the finger nails, splitting and falling out of hair—may be relieved by hormone treatment. The disease characterized by loss of hair in circular patches, which frequently defies other treatment, may be cured in a surprisingly short time by the introduction of follicular hormone.

---

1   The corpus luteum is what is left of an egg follicle after ovulation; it produces progesterone and helps establish a pregnancy.

If in these cases the improved circulation brought about by the hormones plays an important part, then the same factor may be responsible for the favourable influence exerted in conditions of vascular spasm. For instance, there are cases of migraine in youthful individuals which are the outcome of disturbances of ovarian function. This is shown by the fact that in many cases the beginning of the trouble is observed at puberty, the attacks recurring periodically with menstruation and ceasing during pregnancy.

Dr. Charles W. Dunn, of Philadelphia (*Clinical Medicine and Surgery*, 1934, No. 6), successfully employed sex hormones in patients suffering from headaches, nervous over-excitability, vomiting, visual derangements, and a variety of spasmodic conditions, in all of which the disturbances were distinctly related to the menses, occurring either before, during, or after the period. The intensity of the symptoms seemed to depend upon the degree of hormone deficiency. A great number of the patients who had been previously unsuccessfully treated by other means for varying periods were entirely or partly relieved by hormone therapy. One woman had suffered from a serious migraine for thirteen years. The use of pain-killing remedies could be dispensed with almost entirely, and the author further states that Drouet, Mathieu, and Colleson recorded the same experiences in twelve out of fourteen cases of migraine for which hormone treatment was prescribed.

[...]

The sense of well-being, however, plays an important role in the life of every human being. It is true that the climacteric is a natural condition, and all women must accept the fact that an involution of the ovarian function sets in between the ages of forty-five and fifty-five. But is it really essential that during this time they should endure hot flushes, heat waves, dizziness, palpitation, ringing in the ears, depression, hysterical crying, anxiety, sleeplessness, itching, pains in the joints, irritability, and other tormenting complaints? Further, that they should be prevented by physical inadequacy from following their professions as teachers, singers, actresses, business women? And that those women who have no profession to follow other than that of society should not be able to pursue their accustomed manner of life because during this "dangerous age" they are handicapped by sudden impulses to weep without cause, by the fear of blushing without motive, and by loss of energy, on the one hand, and increased sensitivity and over-excitability on the other? Although the climacteric is in itself to be regarded as a physiological process, it must be admitted that its physical and psychic manifestations, thrusting deeply into life as they do, are barely to be differentiated from symptoms of a genuine disease.

With some women these symptoms occur a short while before the final cessation of menstruation and are termed "preclimacteric complaints." Under this heading must be grouped those cases in which the first faint signs of the endocrine revolution which is noticeably approaching disturb the hormonic equilibrium. As a rule these disturbances first affect the psychic behaviour. A woman thus affected is generally not so much tormented by the realization that she is no longer young, as by the thought that she does not feel old and yet must fear that she has nothing more to expect of life. With this fear that much may have passed them by, that the gates of youth will soon close behind them, some women succumb to a pronounced panic, a condition of increased nervousness. In her world-famous novel, *The Dangerous Age*, which describes the psychic condition of preclimacteric women, Karin Michaelis writes: "If men knew what goes on in women during these years they would flee us like the plague or fell us like mad dogs."[1] These words may rather exaggerate the case and generalize the condition more than is justifiable, but still it cannot be denied that many a marriage which had been happy through a long period of years has been destroyed during the preclimacteric crisis because wives were driven by nervous over-excitability to rash and illogical actions often of far-reaching consequences.

The realization that this behaviour may rest upon a hormonic foundation is of great importance, since thereby a means is offered by which such catastrophes may be averted. Hormone treatment, often in the simple form of tablets, can have the most excellent effect in those psychic disturbances and will help to tide over the period of transition. [...]

Diathermy has proved itself an excellent adjuvant to hormone therapy since through its action on the body the absorption of the hormone by the organism is favoured.[2] More recently diathermy has been frequently replaced by the short waves (short radio waves) or ultra short waves of varying length and intensity.

The application of such a high-tension alternating current, which passes through the organism, produces more or less intense heating not only of the external but also of the deeper tissues, and since warmth relaxes and expands all organs, this affects the blood vessels also, which in turn brings an increased amount of blood to the organ that is being treated. In a notice which appeared in 1925 in the *Wiener medizinische Wochenschrift*,[3] I described how as an outcome of my experiments with animals (which are described in Chapter XIII) I studied,

---

1 Michaelis (1872-1950) published *The Dangerous Age* (1910) in Denmark; it features discussions of women's sex lives, mid-life anxieties, and fear of aging.

2 Diathermy, also known as "deep heating," consisted of the application of heat to bodily tissues beneath the skin.

3 The *Viennese Medical Weekly*, a medical journal.

and successfully applied clinically, diathermy of the whole body and the ovaries. Since then it has become the custom to combine hormone treatment with diathermy, particularly in the climacteric. After each combined treatment the patient should rest for one or two hours.

3. From Gertrude Atherton, "Second Youth: The Latest in Reactivation from one who knows ... a record of new wonders in man's battle against age." *Liberty* (8 July 1939): 17-18, 20

Phyllis Collings, the heroine of Helen Hull's exciting novel, *Frost Flower*, is regarding her father sadly as he rakes the leaves; old and tired but determined to show that he is still a man.[1] Age was a dreadful waste, she thought. That fine mind of his blurring, that exquisite balance and control frittered by moods of irritability. "The approach of senility is a natural phenomenon," he had said to her, "but I resent it." It was an extraordinary arrangement that when a man had learned how to live, when he was mature and wise and really valuable, he had to face the insidious destruction of age.

"The Major," as they called him, had been one of the most brilliant men in his profession, and now in his early seventies he was tottering on the verge of senescence, his body filled with a perpetual weariness, his mind revealing its old vigor in flashes only. Garrulity was growing upon him; his memory was as uncertain as his temper.

This is the real tragedy of age; not the loss of potency, such visibilities as white hairs and wrinkles. Those who scoff virtuously at the reactivation of the glandular constitution assume that it is "smeared with sex," and has no other connotation. But with men of advancing years who have been successful in business, the professions, etc., sex is practically forgotten in their desire to retain their faculties unimpaired, that they may go on working or creating to the end of their days, ever increasing in usefulness to those dependent upon them; possibly to a world sorely in need of mature and disinterested minds. (N.b.: Why do not the members of the Supreme Court of the United States undergo this treatment and defy threats of possible retirement by setting their individual clocks back ten or twenty years?)

But to keep the mind agile and productive the body must furnish the brain with healthy blood, arteries must be soft, all organs must function with the vigor of early middle age.

Let us see what Dr. Norman Haire of London, one of the most distinguished of the Steinach disciples, had to say on this subject.[2]

---

1 *Frost Flower* (1939) was one of Hull's (1888-1971) many novels.
2 Haire (1892-1952) was an Australian-born sexologist, obstetrician/gyneocologist, and proponent of birth control (beginning in the early 20s); he also

After reminding his audience of the enormous strides taken by the medical profession during the last hundred years, he continues on another note: "Under the growing stress of modern life it is probable that we age more quickly than did earlier generations. All the obvious signs of age—loss of physical and mental vigor, changes of the hair and skin, etc.—are only secondary effects. The primary causes upon which they depend are functional and organic changes in the tissues and organs of the body. The functional and structural integrity of any organ is largely dependent on the quantity and quality of the blood supply it receives.... The blood must contain in sufficient amount all the chemical substances which are needed to nourish and activate the tissues; and among these substances are certain complex chemical compounds known as hormones, produced by a group of small but very important organs, the endocrine glands ... glands which lack a duct. Their secretions are carried away by the blood which passes through them. These are called hormones ... and are conveyed by the blood to every organ and tissue so that they may exert their influence on every function or part of the whole organism.

"It is with these endocrine glands that modern research in the field of reactivation, or, as it is too often spectacularly called, rejuvenation, is concerned.... It is frequently remarked that the effects of treatment are due to suggestion ... but it is quite impossible to explain the beneficial effects of such treatment *in animals* as being due to suggestion. One has only to imagine the veterinary or surgeon exhorting his patient, 'Now Fido, the operation which I am about to perform on you will produce a great improvement in your health. Every day in every way you will get better and better,' to see how ludicrous this explanation is."

These brief remarks are taken from Dr. Haire's introduction to a lecture given before a congress in London by an American physician whom, for ethical reasons, I shall continue to call Dr. X. But before going further it is well to dispose of the word rejuvenation. It is said that Dr. Steinach blows up if any one uses it in his presence. Nevertheless, it was used in the beginning by both himself and his disciples, but merely because they couldn't think of a better word at the time, and they never expected it to be taken literally. That is to say, that a man or woman of sixty after taking the treatment would both look and *be* twenty. As well expect a yellow autumn leaf suddenly to turn a dewy green.

Rejuvenation is a loose term that might be used by some one who, thoroughly run down, returns from a sea voyage feeling "twenty years younger." So be careful when interviewing one of these pundits to use

---

explored eugenics, sex education, and the psychology of sex. During the 1920s and 1930s, he was considered an expert on such subjects and centered his practice in London.

the word which exactly describes the treatment—reactivation. Renovation or re-energizing would do as well. To have every organ, tissue, etc., in your body restored to perfect health and started off again on life's difficult track with a sound second wind is quite enough.

Dr. X in his lecture said that "a return of greater usefulness may be accompanied by a certain appearance of youthfulness; the latter, however may be just as much a matter of psychology (or, in women, of the beauty parlor) as of endocrinology. No proof has been offered that any method has prolonged the span of life, although such seems to be the case in experimental animals. Years, therefore, may not be added to life, but that life may be added to years is an indisputable fact."

Here are some of the advances in reactivation that have taken place since my last article appeared in Liberty. One of the most important is that sex-gland treatment has been replaced by deficiency-gland treatment. Another great change in the methods of reactivation owes its triumphs to the work of biochemists, who have been able to produce more and more potent preparations; in other words, hormone solutions, which enable the physician to apply reliable substitution therapy—in simpler language—fluids and pills.

[...]

Dr. X lists the following reasons that among others, motivate men in considering the operation: The desire to improve memory, working ability, physical and mental energy, even the ambition to play a better game of bridge or golf. And in regard to women I may say here that in the avalanche of letters that followed the publication of Black Oxen, and the two magazine articles later, women seldom expressed a desire to take the treatment from motives of vanity.[1] Hard mental or physical work had worn them out, illness, grief, worry. All asked was renewed energies—most of them were self-supporting—that they might be as efficient as in their prime.

Dr. X adds significantly: "It is impossible to say how many Steinach operations have been or are being performed, or how many corresponding treatments have been given to women. The patient, fearful of being ridiculed, carefully keeps his secret."

A man in New York recently asked me why, if the operation was so successful, one didn't hear more about it. There is the answer. It is a curious anomaly that in these days when sex parades shamelessly on the stage, is frankly discussed in fiction, and among young people as naturally as if they were talking of diet, when it comes to any personal application, man coyly hides his head. If I admit I took that operation,

---

1   Atherton's two later articles include "Defeating Old Age" in *Can Women Be Gentlemen?* (Boston: Houghton Mifflin, 1938, 58-65) and "Science after Fifty" in *Pictorial Review* 34 (March 1933): 15, 58.

thinks he, they'll sneer and say I'm just another old fool who wants to be young and frisky again. I never could convince them that not only my enjoyment in mere living but my daily bread depends upon renewed energies. Women are equally reticent. Human nature is still conservative.

4. Readers' Letters to Atherton[1]

Deer Lodge, Montana
November 17, 1935

Dear Mrs. Atherton:

No doubt you are weary of answering such questions as mine. However, if you will advise me in this matter, I shall pass the kindness on to some one else.

I have read a number of your books, including "Adventures of a Novelist" and "Black Oxen" in which you relate your experience with reactivation. I have become interested in this and should like to state my condition to you, as well as to ask you some questions.

I am thirty-nine years of age and have not started my menapause [sic]. My face has aged in appearance, having premature lines due to acne and X Ray scars. I am small and my figure is slender and girlish. I have always been very active and athletic, and still am. I have formed a decided complex about these lines on my face. I imagine I look years older than I am or that my figure indicates. In spite of this feeling about my appearance, I feel young. My friends are young, in the twenties, and I enjoy the things they enjoy.

The following are questions uppermost in my mind. Some of them may seem to overlap.

Do the latest methods cause sterility? I should not want to this happen unless absolutely necessary.

If this treatment is not a success, would it make one older appearing than before and cause sterility?

Does it effect [sic] a woman before her change differently than one who has passed this period? Does it prolong her period of fertility if it does not cause sterility?

Is there a more decided reaction or change in appearance if taken before the change, or more benefit derived?

When the effects of this treatment wear off, does it leave one suddenly old or is it a gradual ageing as in the normal condition?

After the effects of the treatment have worn off, is one older appearing than if the treatment had never been given?

---

1 Letters reprinted with the permission of the Bancroft Library, University of California, Berkeley.

Is the price prohibitive? Can you given me an estimate of the doctor and laboratory fees?

Are there clinics other than at New York where these treatments are given under the direction of competent doctors?

Will you please give me the name and address of Dr. Benjamin to whom you referred in your book?

No doubt these questions sound childish to you; but having taken this step yourself, you must know the hesitancy and fear accompanying such an act. Thank you for your patience in trying to unravel my meaning.

Sincerely yours,
Lynette Blair

New York, April 9th, 1923

Dear Mrs. Atherton

Would you be kind enough to let me know if there are really Doctors in New York who rejuvenate according to the methods you wrote of in Black Oxen[.]

I am deeply interested always in your Books but this subject being new to me (and I do not care to ask my Doctor or any one I know) and am presuming on your kindness to help me find out where one can go and have the right X Ray rejuvenation as I imagine many will claim to use it as Black Oxen has caused such a sensation.

Please accept my sincere congratulations and best wishes.

From an admirer.
Jennie Hall Brickhont

November 21, 1946

Dear Mrs. Atherton:

I'm wondering if you realize how many women admire you, and would like to turn to you for help.

May I take a little of your valuable time to please let me know to whom I may turn for the Steinach Method of rejuvation [sic]. At forty I am so fatigued mentally and physically, I really need some help. Three years ago I went through surgery for hyper-thyroidism and since then I have just become old—I guess that is the only word for it.

I don't want to bore you with details, but I do wish you would let me know if there is a local doctor to whom I may go for the information and help I must have.

In all sincerity,
Virginia Brenner

Appendix B: Theories of Cultural Change in the 1920s

[This appendix charts perceptions surrounding cultural changes in the jazz age, including the moral consternation that accompanied widespread shifts in behavior, clothing, and physical interactions across the sexes. Ben B. Lindsey and Wainright Evans' study of the companionate marriage (which became a focal point for prohibitions about birth control information), outlines the perceived moral offense posed by non-procreative marriages, or the kind of marriage in which Mary Zattiany and Lee Clavering will participate. There will be no maternity in Mary Zattiany's future, so the union that she and Clavering consider is what would have been known as a "companionate marriage," as it had been since the late decades of the nineteenth century. This form of commitment was rooted in the pleasures of intellectual and cultural exploration. By the 1920s, such marriages also meant childlessness—by choice—during an era when public discussions of birth control were illegal because of the Comstock laws. In their book on the subject, Lindsey and Evans define companionate marriage as a union "entered into for love, companionship, and cooperation" by persons who "are not prepared at the time of their marriage to undertake the care of a family." The text continues, supposing that "people who entered [this form of marriage] would openly profess their intention not to have children without special license from the state; and the state would instruct them in scientific birth control, to that end."[1] The text thus imagines a scenario that would allow individuals to be armed with the knowledge of birth control, though this arrangement was critiqued as promoting promiscuous cohabitation and as a likely prelude to divorce. In the context of Atherton's other critiques of American conservatism, the novel hints at the ways in which companionate marriage is a mature and considered choice, but one that is anathema to American culture, precisely because of its logic.

Frederick Lewis Allen's popular history of the 1920s, *Only Yesterday* (1931), also outlines a variety of challenges to social and moral order visible during the era, particularly those specific to the young generation. Allen's assessment of the "Revolution of Manners and Morals" renders few judgments on the social changes it charts, but it does suggest the scale of social change contemplated by Americans of the early twentieth century. Greenwich Village author Floyd Dell's

---

1   Judge Ben B. Lindsey and Wainwright Evans, *The Companionate Marriage* (1936), 175.

generation-specific study of love within family life offers a broad-scale psychological analysis of how the generations think differently about love, sex, marriage, and personal choice in regard to early twentieth-century relationships.]

1. From Ben B. Lindsey and Wainwright Evans, *The Companionate Marriage* (New York: Boni & Liveright, 1927), 176-81

Soon after this incident I had a talk with a young woman whom I had known since her school days. She holds a responsible executive position in a Denver department store. She has been married for a few years, has continued her work, and has no children....

"By the way, Edna," I said, "how many children have you?"

She looked up in surprise. "What makes you ask that? Of course, you know I haven't any."

"Such was my impression," I answered, "but I wasn't quite sure. How long have you been married?"

"Four years."

"No babies—in four years?"

"We couldn't afford them," she said defensively. "Larry was making just about enough to live on in comfort by himself. So was I. If we married, and I gave up my position, it meant that his income would have to support the two of us; and it couldn't be done in comfort. So we decided that we would both go on working till he was making more money. Another consideration was that my health was not quite up to par. It is all right now, however; and so is Larry's income."

"Oh—then you haven't given up the babies?"

"No, indeed. There will be some before long, I hope."

"Let me get this clear—for I am much interested. Did you and Larry talk this all over before you got married, or did you wait till after you were married?"

"Before—of course."

"In other words, you chose the kind of marriage you were to enter, didn't you? And then by previous agreement, the two of you continued to live after marriage much as you had before marriage—except that you moved into his apartment, and that you made a home together, and lived henceforth together in sexual and social companionship. Am I right?"

She laughed. "I see, what you are driving at, Judge. But that was real marriage. We loved each other, and we proposed to stick, and see it through."

"Precisely," I said. "You proposed to stick. Most young people who fall in love with each other propose to stick. They have a similar vision of permanence in their relationship. Some guess wrong, and some guess right. But for those who guess wrong, marriage as we have it is a terribly irrevocable step. For such persons, it would be fortunate if there were a way of backing out. It would prevent many a tragedy. [...]

"But tell me this, Edna—why did you and Larry get married? Why didn't you just go on living in single blessedness? I suppose you know that according to orthodox beliefs, marriage is a religious state, a sacramental thing, ordained by God for the procreation of children. Since you and Larry were leaving out the children, why did you marry?"

"You know the answer to that as well as I do," she said.

"Of course I do. The answer—correct me if I am wrong—is that you wanted to be together; that you could not find the happiness you wanted in being merely engaged; that you endured just as long as you could the strain of resisting the force that was drawing you together—and then, since a *liaison* didn't fit with your notion of what was right and moral, and socially safe, you married. And you benefited very greatly by so doing, both in happiness and health. Isn't that it?"

"With us," she said gravely, "it had become a choice between marriage and a *liaison*. Many choose the *liaison*. Many of our friends had done so and made no secret of it in their own set. But we couldn't make up our minds to it—at least I couldn't. It was against my training, it was dangerous, we might have been found out. And besides, the anxiety and fear and sense of social guilt would all have combined to mar our happiness. I don't mean that I had any religious scruples. I honestly don't think society had any right to keep us apart. We really loved each other, you see. But that is why I mark it off from your Companionate Marriage.[1] We turned to real marriage, and we intended to stay put. It wasn't just an affair."

"Very interesting," I said. "Most young people who fall in love intend to stay put. But you are living in deliberately childless marriage—like many other conventional people who join you in denouncing my views on Companionate Marriage. Don't you realize that this is Companionate Marriage; that you are living in Companionate Marriage right now, and have been for four years?—My dear Edna, I hope this news doesn't

---

1 "Companionate Marriage" is a term for a marriage rooted in a desire for companionship, and while it was not understood as a marriage wherein household duties would be shared equally by men, it did suggest that late nineteenth- and early twentieth-century men would participate more fully in the running of a household and the rearing of children than did the men in previous generations, a change that allowed women more time for extradomestic pursuits. See Margaret Marsh, "Suburban Men and Masculine Domesticity, 1790-1915," in *Meanings for Manhood: Constructions of Masculinity in Victorian America*, ed. Mark C. Carnes and Clyde Griffen (Chicago: U of Chicago P, 1990), 111-27.

shock you; and I hope you don't feel too immoral and promiscuous. But perhaps you will now tell me when you propose to discard your present husband and try another—since that, according to you, would be one necessary consequence of Companionate Marriage. In short, when are you and Larry going to make good on all these dire predictions of free love, trial marriage, and anarchy?"

"But," she gasped, "it isn't. It's marriage—not a companionate thing at all."

"It is marriage," I retorted; "and it conforms in its physical and psychological essentials to what sociologists call Companionate Marriage. There isn't a jot of difference between legal Companionate Marriage and the deliberately childless union of sexual and social companionship which you have preferred to a secret liaison or a long engagement, except that your Companionate is illegal in the sense that it involves the illegal use of Birth Control, and would involve divorce by illegal collusion if you wanted a divorce by mutual consent.[1] I'm proposing to legalize what you now have illegally.

[...]

"Now let me point out to you one thing about these childless marriages that you may not have thought of. Deliberately childless marriages involve, in ninety-nine cases out of a hundred, the use of contraceptives. But this involves a violation of the law that forbids the manufacture and sale of contraceptives and the imparting of contraceptive information. Since this use of contraceptives is against the law, deliberate childlessness is also against the law whenever it involves the use of these illegal contraceptives. This is a form of law-violation which people practice as a matter of course, without scruple. It is winked at by the authorities; and it amounts to a nullification of one of the craziest pieces of freak legislation ever put over in this country. This is a fact. Childless marriage usually involves bootleg Birth Control. And *yet* these marriages, childless by means of utterly illegal agencies, and by a technically felonious breaking of the law, are recognized by church, state, and society as perfectly respectable; and no stigma attaches to persons who so marry and so conduct themselves in marriage.

[...]

---

1   During the 1910s, Margaret Sanger (1879-1966) campaigned for the availability of birth control and in 1921, Sanger, who lived in the then-radical Greenwich Village section of New York City, established the American Birth Control League, later renamed Planned Parenthood. In her early writings and activism, Sanger defied the 1873 Comstock Law, which outlawed both the "obscene" sale and dissemination of information about contraception. The speaker in this piece goes on to describe the law's consequences as creating "bootleg birth control."

"Let me finish with bootleg Birth Control first. I want you to realize what a hideous thing it is that the law of this land should virtually require of you that you either abstain from sex relations in marriage, or that you let nature take its course, and bear children year after year whether you want them or not.

"Get this clear in your mind. It is important. The law of the land forbids anybody to impart contraceptive information to you or to sell you contraceptives. It thereby seeks, forcibly and by statute, to impose ignorance on you, and to prevent you from acquiring information you have a right to as much as anybody in the world, including the fools that made that law.

"The law has no more right to forbid science to instruct you in these matters of scientific knowledge and practice than it has to, forbid you to read your Bible, or Darwin's 'Origin of Species,' or 'Einstein on Relativity.'[1] It goes to these outrageous and unconstitutional lengths for a purpose; and that purpose is, by keeping you ignorant, to trick you *into making a contribution to the population whether you want to make it or not*. Ignorance imposed by law! What do you think of that? You must not be left to judge as to when you will have children or how often. The late Anthony Comstock, and his unclean legions, will take care of that for you in the name of holy chastity. They have rightly named it the Obscenity Law.[2] They put into it all the obscenity they had—but they had as much left as ever when they were through; and they spewed it out into every home in this land. As apostles of prurience and lies the world has seldom seen their like."

2. From Frederick Lewis Allen, *Only Yesterday: An Informal History of the Nineteen-Twenties* (New York: Harper & Brothers, 1931), 88-94

A first-class revolt against the accepted American order was certainly taking place during those early years of the Post-war Decade, but it

---

1 Charles Darwin (1809-82), the British naturalist, is best known for *On the Origin of Species by Means of Natural Selection* (1859), which outlines his influential theory of evolution. In 1905 Albert Einstein (1879-1955) began publishing widely; his initial subjects included the photoelectric effect, for which he would receive the Nobel Prize in 1921, and electrodynamics. In 1923, he published "Fundamental Ideas and Problems of the Theory of Relativity."

2 Anthony Comstock (1844-1915) was an American postal inspector who attempted to enforce moral codes through the circulation of print material. In 1873 Comstock organized a group called the New York Society for the Suppression of Vice. Later that year, he advocated the "Comstock Laws," which made it illegal to deliver "obscene" materials through the mail. The laws were best known for their suppression of materials about birth control.

was one with which Nikolai Lenin had nothing whatever to do.[1] The shock troops of the rebellion were not alien agitators, but the sons and daughters of well-to-do American families, who knew little about Bolshevism and cared distinctly less, and their defiance was expressed not in obscure radical publications or in soap-box speeches, but right across the family breakfast table into the horrified ears of conservative fathers and mothers.[2] Men and women were still shivering at the Red Menace when they awoke to the no less alarming Problem of the Younger Generation, and realized that if the Constitution were not in danger, the moral code of the country certainly was.[3]

This code, as it currently concerned young people, might have been roughly summarized as follows: Women were the guardians of morality; they were made of finer stuff than men and were expected to act accordingly. Young girls must look forward in innocence (tempered perhaps with a modicum of physiological instruction) to a romantic love match which would lead them to the altar and to living-happily-ever-after; and until the "right man" came along they must allow no male to kiss them. It was expected that some men would succumb to the temptations of sex, but only with a special class of outlawed women; girls of respectable families were supposed to have no such temptations. Boys and girls were permitted large freedom to work and play together, with decreasing and well-nigh nominal chaperonage, but only because the code worked so well on the whole that a sort of honor system was supplanting supervision by their elders; it was taken for granted that if they had been well brought up they would never take advantage of this freedom. And although the attitude toward smoking and drinking by girls differed widely in different strata of society and different parts of the country, majority opinion held that it was morally wrong for them to smoke and could hardly imagine them showing the effects of alcohol.

The war had not long been over when cries of alarm from parents, teachers, and moral preceptors began to rend the air. For the boys and girls just growing out of adolescence were making mincemeat of this code.

---

1 Lenin (1870-1924, born Vladimir Ulyanov) was Russian leader of the Bolshevik party who led the October 1917 revolution, then leader of the Soviet state from 1917-24; although Nikolai was never Lenin's name, he was known as Nikolai, supposedly because he signed his letters with the initial "N."

2 "Bolshevism" was a term for the ideological beliefs of communist Russians (Bolsheviks) who came to power during the 1917 Russian Revolution; the name "Bolshevik" derives from the word "majority" in Russian.

3 The "red menace" was a term used primarily during the Cold War era to describe the ideological differences associated with Soviet communists and their presumed threat to democratic states.

The dresses that the girls—and for that matter most of the older women—were wearing seemed alarming enough. In July, 1920, a fashion-writer reported in the *New York Times* that "the American woman ... has lifted her skirts far beyond any modest limitation," which was another way of saying that the hem was now all of nine inches above the ground. It was freely predicted that skirts would come down again in the winter of 1920-21, but instead they climbed a few scandalous inches farther. The flappers wore thin dresses, short-sleeved and occasionally (in the evening) sleeveless; some of the wilder young things rolled their stockings below their knees, revealing to the shocked eyes of virtue a fleeting glance of shin-bones and knee-cap; and many of them were visibly using cosmetics. "The intoxication of rouge," earnestly explained Dorothy Speare in *Dancers in the Dark*, "is an insidious vintage known to more girls than mere man can ever believe."[1] Useless for frantic parents to insist that no lady did such things; the answer was that the daughters of ladies were doing it, and even retouching their masterpieces in public. Some of them, furthermore, were abandoning their corsets. "The men won't dance with you if you wear a corset," they were quoted as saying.

The current mode in dancing created still more consternation. Not the romantic violin but the barbaric saxophone now dominated the orchestra, and to its passionate crooning and wailing the fox-trotters moved in what the editor of the Hobart College *Herald* disgustedly, called a "syncopated embrace." No longer did even an inch of space separate them; they danced as if glued together, body to body, cheek to cheek. Cried the *Catholic Telegraph* of Cincinnati in righteous indignation, "The music is sensuous, the embracing of partners—the female only half dressed—is absolutely indecent; and the motions—they are such as may not be described, with any respect for propriety, in a family newspaper. Suffice it to say that there are certain houses appropriate for such dances; but those houses have been closed by law."

Supposedly "nice" girls were smoking cigarettes—openly and defiantly, if often rather awkwardly and self-consciously. They were drinking—somewhat less openly but often all too efficaciously. There were stories of daughters of the most exemplary parents getting drunk—"blotto," as their companions cheerfully put it—on the contents of the hip-flasks of the new prohibition régime, and going out joyriding with men at four in the morning. And worst of all, even at well-regulated dances they were said to retire where the eye of the most sharp-sighted chaperon could not follow, and in darkened rooms or in parked cars to engage in the unspeakable practice of petting and necking.

---

1 Dorothy Speare's 1922 novel portrays the American girl as an "excitement eater" and as living "from man to man."

It was not until F. Scott Fitzgerald, who had hardly graduated from Princeton and ought to know what his generation were doing, brought out *This Side of Paradise* in April, 1920, that fathers and mothers realized fully what was afoot and how long it had been going on.[1] Apparently the "petting party" had been current as early as 1916, and was now widely established as an indoor sport. "None of the Victorian mothers—and most of the mothers were Victorian—had any idea how casually their daughters were accustomed to be kissed," wrote Mr. Fitzgerald. "... Amory saw girls doing things that even in his memory would have been impossible: eating three-o'clock, after-dance suppers in impossible cafés, talking of every side of life with an air half of earnestness, half of mockery, yet with a furtive excitement that Amory considered stood for a real moral let-down. But he never realized how widespread it was until he saw the cities between New York and Chicago as one vast juvenile intrigue." The book caused a shudder to run down the national spine; did not Mr. Fitzgerald represent one of his well-nurtured heroines as brazenly confessing, "I've kissed dozens of men. I suppose I'll kiss dozens more"; and another heroine as saying to a young man (*to a young man!*), "Oh, just one person in fifty has any glimmer of what sex is. I'm hipped on Freud and all that, but it's rotten that every bit of real love in the world is ninety-nine per cent passion and one little *soupçon* of jealousy"?

It was incredible. It was abominable. What did it all mean? Was every decent standard being thrown over? Mothers read the scarlet words and wondered if they themselves "had any idea how often their daughters were accustomed to be kissed." ... But no, this must be an exaggerated account of the misconduct of some especially depraved group. Nice girls couldn't behave like that and talk openly about passion. But in due course other books appeared to substantiate the findings of Mr. Fitzgerald: *Dancers in the Dark, The Plastic Age, Flaming Youth.*[2] Magazine articles and newspapers reiterated the scandal. To be sure, there were plenty of communities where nice girls did not, in actual fact, "behave like that"; and even in the more sophisticated urban centers there were plenty of girls who did not. Nevertheless, there was enough fire beneath the smoke of these sensational revelations to make the Problem of the Younger Generation a topic of anxious discussion from coast to coast.

---

1 *This Side of Paradise* (1920), the first novel by F. Scott Fitzgerald, was set at Princeton University.
2 *The Plastic Age* (1924), by Percy Marks, featured co-eds at "Sanford" college and reported their entertainments, pranks, and "petting" practices. It was made into a 1925 film featuring Clara Bow. *Flaming Youth* (1923), by Samuel Hopkins Adams, published under the name Warner Fabian, was made into a 1923 film and features a young woman's social as well as sexual coming of age, along with her developing love for her mother's ex-lover.

The forces of morality rallied to the attack. Dr. Francis E. Clark, the founder and president of the Christian Endeavor Society, declared that the modern "indecent dance" was "an offense against womanly purity, the very fountainhead of our family and civil life."[1] The new style of dancing was denounced in religious journals as "impure, polluting, corrupting, debasing, destroying spirituality, increasing carnality," and the mothers and sisters and church members of the land were called upon to admonish and instruct and raise the spiritual tone of these dreadful young people. President Murphy of the University of Florida cried out with true Southern warmth, "The low-cut gowns, the rolled hose and short skirts are born of the Devil and his angels, and are carrying the present and future generations to chaos and destruction." A group of Episcopal church-women in New York, speaking with the authority of wealth and social position (for they included Mrs. J. Pierpont Morgan, Mrs. Borden Harriman, Mrs. Henry Phipps, Mrs. James Roosevelt, and Mrs. E.H. Harriman), proposed an organization to discourage fashions involving an "excess of nudity" and "improper ways of dancing." The Y.W.C.A. conducted a national campaign against immodest dress among high-school girls, supplying newspapers with printed matter carrying headlines such as "Working Girls Responsive to Modesty Appeal" and "High Heels Losing Ground Even in France."[2] In Philadelphia a Dress Reform Committee of prominent citizens sent a questionnaire to over a thousand clergymen to ask them what would be their idea of a proper dress, and although the gentlemen of the cloth showed a distressing variety of opinion, the committee proceeded to design a "moral gown" which was endorsed by ministers of fifteen denominations. The distinguishing characteristics of this moral gown were that it was very loose-fitting, that the sleeves reached just below the elbows, and that the hem came within seven and a half inches of the floor.

[...]

Meanwhile innumerable families were torn with dissension over cigarettes and gin and all-night automobile rides. Fathers and mothers lay awake asking themselves whether their children were not utterly lost; sons and daughters evaded questions, lied miserably and unhappily, or flared up to reply rudely that at least they were not dirty-minded hypocrites, that they saw no harm in what they were doing and proposed to go right on doing it. From those liberal clergymen and teachers who prided themselves on keeping step with all that was new, came

---

1 The Christian Endeavor Society gave rise to the "youth ministry" movement in Christian churches; it was an evangelical, non-denominational movement formed in the late nineteenth century.

2 The Young Women's Christian Association spread to the US from England in the early twentieth century and sought to provide young women with moral safe havens in urban environments.

a chorus of reassurance: these young people were at least franker and more honest than their elders had been; having experimented for themselves, would they not soon find out which standards were outworn and which represented the accumulated moral wisdom of the race? Hearing such hopeful words, many good people took heart again. Perhaps this flare-up of youthful passion was a flash in the pan, after all. Perhaps in another year or two the boys and girls would come to their senses and everything would be all right again.

They were wrong, however. For the revolt of the younger generation was only the beginning of a revolution in manners and morals that was already beginning to affect men and women of every age in every part of the country.

A number of forces were working together and interacting upon one another to make this revolution inevitable.

First of all was the state of mind brought about by the war and its conclusion. A whole generation had been infected by the eat-drink-and-be-merry-for-tomorrow-we-die spirit which accompanied the departure of the soldiers to the training camps and the fighting front. There had been an epidemic not only of abrupt war marriages, but of less conventional liaisons. In France, two million men had found themselves very close to filth and annihilation and very far from the American moral code and its defenders; prostitution had followed the flag and willing mademoiselles from Armentieres had been plentiful;[1] American girls sent over as nurses and war workers had come under the influence of continental manners and standards without being subject to the rigid protections thrown about their continental sisters of the respectable classes; and there had been a very widespread and very natural breakdown of traditional restraints and reticences and taboos. It was impossible for this generation to return unchanged when the ordeal was over. Some of them had acquired under the pressure of war-time conditions a new code which seemed to them quite defensible; millions of them had been provided with an emotional stimulant from which it was not easy to taper off. Their torn nerves craved the anodynes of speed, excitement, and passion. They found themselves expected to settle down into the humdrum routine of American life as if nothing had happened, to accept the moral dicta of elders who seemed to them still to be living in a Pollyanna land of rosy ideals which the war had killed for them. They couldn't do it, and they very disrespectfully said so.[2]

---

1 Armentières lies in northern France on the border with Belgium and was attacked on multiple occasions during World War I. "Mademoiselles from Armentieres" was a popular World War I British song (set to existing French music) featuring risqué lyrics about an older French woman wooed by British soldiers.

2 Eleanor H. Porter's *Pollyanna* (1913) features an extremely optimistic orphan child who comforts herself by playing "the glad game," or finding the positives at every downturn.

3. From Floyd Dell, *Love in the Machine Age: A Psychological Study of the Transition from Patriarchal Society* (New York: Octagon Books, 1973 [1930]), 13-16

The psychic development of the individual from infancy to maturity can be described roughly as proceeding through four stages. The first stage, that of helpless infancy, shows the individual's interests centering exclusively in himself, in his own bodily needs, functions and pleasures. The last stage shows him capable of enjoying responsible relations to society in general (work, and getting along with other people), and in particular to a mate and children (marriage and parenthood). This emotional capacity is psychological adulthood as biologically determined. To be real, it must have been reached in psychic development and not in mere physical fact. On the other hand, it can of course be reached in psychic development under circumstances which prevent its actual or direct accomplishment in physical fact. Thus it is not the fact of marriage or of parenthood that constitutes psychological adulthood, but the capacity for enjoyment of these responsible relationships.

Now between the early infantile state of complete dependence with its wholly self-centered interests, and the adult capacity for the enjoyment of responsible work and love, there is a great gulf to be bridged by the processes of emotional growth. We are enabled to see how great a gulf it is, through observation of those individuals in whom such emotional growth is prevented to an extreme degree. In them the infantile self-centered interests in their own bodily needs, functions and pleasures are manifested now on an adult plane of activity, but not in an adult way. Thus we may find them still cherishing the infantile excitements derived from the anus as a pleasure-zone, making them the center of their sexual lives through pederasty; we may also find childish cruelty become sadism, when conditioned by sex-experiences. We might thus—but here we shall not—run through the catalogue of the sexual perversions, which are simply infantile traits which have failed to be subordinated to the normal adult pattern of sexuality by the processes of psychic growth. Unmarriageability, or unsuitableness for normal marriage, is in general characteristic of the person who, growing up to physical adulthood, remains at a low infantile level of psychic development. Persons who are not grown up emotionally, who are still self-centered children themselves, cannot successfully bear parental responsibilities; and unless they are so fortunate as to be able to achieve a socially useful sublimation of their otherwise unsuitable tendencies through some kind of work, usually artistic, they are likely to have great difficulty in submitting to the adult discipline involved in co-operation with others. This applies more particularly to our modern world, for, as will be seen, the patriarchal regime sanctioned or sheltered a great deal of childishness in adults.[1]

The normal psychic processes, which bridge this gulf between self-centered childish interests and the adult state, comprise two stages, of which the first extends from early infancy to puberty. There is in this period of childhood a play-life which leads on to adult work-interests, and a love-life within the family which prepares for later love-interests outside. The child learns to love others beside himself; and the original 'polymorphous' eroticism of childhood gives way, as puberty approaches, to a primacy of the genital zone, a gradual centering of interest in the opposite sex, and the adoption of a masculine role of aggression or a feminine role of quasi-passive encouragement.[2] This development is dependent upon growth in physical and nervous (including brain) structure, and upon glandular changes. It is incomplete, however, at this stage. For a long time in this childhood period the love interests are still (normally) centered, to a considerable though decreasing extent in the self. And insofar as they flow out to others—parents and nurses, brothers and sisters, playmates, teachers—these love interests only lately and slowly come to involve any emotional preference for persons of the opposite sex. It is, indeed, in childhood that there is formed the emotional habit-basis for all those adult human relations in which erotic attractions are subordinated to the social purposes of work and play.

The immense glandular changes of puberty normally complete this process of psychic development. They enhance the attractions of the other sex by creating specific sexual tensions requiring the sexual act for their relief. These changes thus, in collaboration with other psychic influences, lead normally (that is, in the absence of cultural regulations to the contrary) through parade, flirtation, male rivalry and female encouragement (which latter may characteristically take the form of retreat)—through courtship, in short, to love-choice, sexual mating, parenthood, and family life. This appears to be the normal biological pattern, insofar as it can be distinguished from the results of social education, from the effects of which it is never in practice free. Psychologically it involves a centering of the deepest love-interests in persons

1 Throughout *Love in the Machine Age*, Dell treats the patriarchal regime as the traditional family/social structure and positions modernity as a period during which the patriarchy's cultural significance will wane, though after first setting in motion a period of cultural neurosis.

2 Dell alludes to Freud's sense of "polymorphous" sexuality, which involves the body's multiple erotic possibilities, located in any part of the human form and directed toward any object that could be understood as providing pleasure. Freud located the polymorphous as a developmental stage, predating the adult, erogenous period of human sexuality.

of the other sex. This *hetero*sexuality, as it is called (from the Greek 'heteros', other, or different, or opposite,—but having the sense also of being a 'mate' in that difference, as the one sex is to the other), is one of the two essential qualities of biological adulthood. The other quality, the interest in and capacity for sustained efforts to gain food and shelter, comes with an increase in size and muscular strength and skill, and represents a narrowing and practical intensification of early scattered play-interests (the rest of the early play-interests being taken care of in adult social activities).

Now we have here a simple pattern of emotional development occurring as a result of biological growth from infancy to maturity. If it actually occurred as simply as that, life would be obvious and easy. It would contain no religion, art, crime or insanity. These are due to the strain upon human nature of social deviations from the biological pattern—they are the ways in which the discrepancies between biological impulses and social codes are patched up. These kinds of psychological patchwork can make human life hideous or beautiful; indeed they make it both. We are now, or so we believe, in an economic position which enables us to dispense with much of this patchwork, and we have learned enough to manage the remainder so as to produce more happiness and less misery.

It may, however, be asked at this point why we cannot go back to the simple biological pattern. We presumably cannot do so; but certainly we do not wish to do so. Our civilization is founded upon some of the discrepancies between simple biological impulses and social codes. When we consider what they are—they include fundamentally the incest-taboo and the deflection of a natural interest in anal matters which we apparently share with our remote canine relatives—it is fairly clear that we would not give up these civilized deviations from Nature, even if we could. It is not a question of becoming like savages or primitive folk; they already have created these taboos and built their culture upon them. If we went back to the life of the cave man of the Aurignacian period, a quarter of a million or more years ago, we should still apparently not have gone back far enough to avoid the discrepancies between nature and culture, of which the art of the cave-man presents us unmistakable evidences.[1] We should have to go back millions of years beyond that. We cannot turn and live with the animals, because our germ-plasm has forgotten that way of life, has lost its neat and sufficient little set of inherited adaptations to environment. We must go ahead in our own human way.

---

1 A period during which early humans made and used stone tools and produced art, from approximately 40,000 to 26,000 years ago, during the Paleolithic era; the Aurignacian humans are widely considered the first modern humans.

Appendix C: The Flapper and Other Generations

[This appendix presents images and satires of the emerging flapper culture of the early 1920s, contextualizing the kind of youthful figures represented in *Black Oxen* by Janet Oglethorpe. These pieces, from popular newspapers in New York and Los Angeles, oppose the older generation to the flapper youth of the twenties, with some pieces articulating the hope that the flapper's days of influence are waning.]

1. E.L. Aultman, "What Is a 'Flapper'?" *Los Angeles Times*, 1 March 1922

In our armchair, after tea,
Pondering on the things we see,
Some women's place in history,
    We vainly try to map her:
We take our Webster, tried and true,[1]
And turn the printed pages through
To see what wise old Noah could do
    When he beheld a "flapper."
We note his statement does not jibe
With what the sporty boys describe
As members of the "flapper" tribe,
    Who daily preen and flutter
Along the city's great White Way,[2]
With beads and lace in bright array,
And pulchritudinous display
    To make one stare and stutter.
Some say that she is just as good
As any of her sisterhood,
Though she doesn't dress as she should,
    According to the censors:
While others state that they can see
Her influence is sure N.G.[3]—

---

1 Webster's Dictionary is a brand that descended from Noah Webster's *A Compendious Dictionary of the English Language* in 1806.
2 A section of Broadway, New York, encompassing the Theatre District. The nickname came from the bright lighting of the area, which was one of the first in New York to be lit with electricity in 1880.
3 "N.G." presumably stands for "No Good."

Pray tell who has the right to be
Of mortals our dispensors?
So we suggest there seems a need
Of caution and diminished speed.
Some startling point ere we proceed
    To mercilessly rap her;
As press and pulpit can't agree,
And educators are at sea,
Let's have some learned court decree
    What constitutes a "flapper."

2. Helen Bullitt Lowry, "Mrs. Grundy[1] and Miss 1921," *New York Times*, 23 January 1921

Who has turned over that new leaf for 1921—the new generation or the old?

It is too early to tell yet. In a few weeks, perhaps, the returns may be all in, and we can decide whether those radical youngsters have decided to behave more like their elders or whether those hidebound elders have been convinced that they ought to adopt the ideas of their children; whether, in short, the leaf of the Book of Life was turned forward or backward this New Year's.

Fancy the reproachful expression of the thrifty shade of Benjamin Franklin, if all that print paper and all those shocked tea-table conversations of 1920 were expended in vain and neither side has prevailed on the other to reform!

For whenever two or three elders were gathered together in the last year there was somebody to whisper about the outrageous new customs of the outrageous new generation.

Now, for the benefit of those of the "older generation" who have been imperfectly informed, who have been forced until now to exclaim in abstract terms of those "awful children" without knowing exactly what it is that those awful children do: The truth is that the awful children do some awful things, according to the standards of ten years ago.[2] Ten years ago débutantes were pretending to know less than they knew. Now they are pretending to know more, with all of the consequences that such a pretense brings in its train. I quote from a New York matron

---

1   First mentioned in Thomas Morton's play *Speed the Plough* (1798), Mrs. Grundy represented the power of convention and was a force to be feared. By the 1920s she would have connoted priggish conventionality, or "grundyism."

2   Terms such as "older generation" and "young generation" were common during the 1920s. See Marc Dolan, *Modern Lives: A Cultural Re-Reading of "the Lost Generation"* (West Lafayette, IN: Purdue UP, 1996).

who has looked with concern into conditions because she herself has a young daughter scheduled to "come out" next year:

"Ten years ago punch was served at an entertainment for young people, but the guest who brought in whisky or any sort of alcohol would have been *de trop*. The breach of etiquette would have been so extreme that no amount of social position could carry it off. Nowadays the man who carries a flask of raw whisky to the private home is taken for granted. He is even welcomed by the host as an aid in conserving his own private stock.

"When the punch system prevailed it was easy enough for the experienced hostess to control how much the inexperienced young girls or boys drank at her entertainment. If the assemblage became too hilarious, she could squeeze in a few oranges. Today it is the young men and the girls who do the dispensing and the deciding. Last Summer each youth brought his private roadster to the clubhouse, and between dances it was taken for granted that a little spin should be taken for refreshments. Ten years ago there was no such reason for wanting to get away from the rest of the crowd."

With the Winter season matters grow worse in New York social circles, it appears. Now comes the servant problem, which is making it more and more inconvenient to entertain on a large scale in a private home. Hostesses have found it convenient to entertain in the hotels. Again enters prohibition. It is customary for each man or each clique of men to engage a private room for the evening, because there is no public bar. This is a condition that Mrs. Herbert Shipman points out.

Mrs. Shipman is the wife of the Rev. Herbert Shipman, rector of one of the fashionable Fifth Avenue churches and once for nine years Chaplain of West Point. Her observations, therefore, are not only New York's young society, but of the "smart" young society of West Point, "there" and "now."

"Ten years ago a girl's reputation would be utterly gone if it were known that she had been in a man's hotel room," said she the other day. "Now her obvious reason for going there is 'to get a drink.' The chaperones themselves go for the same purpose. So who is to object? The trouble is that the personal hotel bar has been accepted as an established fact in society."

A physician with many patients in the fashionable "sets" discussed the matter frankly with me.

"This younger generation," said he, "is throwing off the old tradition of one rule for the men and another for the girls."

"Are men of the better class distressed and bewildered by this development?" I asked him.

"Perhaps. But have they a right to be? Men made the rule that they could do things not permissible for the womenfolk, and now the women have decided, to apply the role to themselves. Suffrage is only one small item, remember, in the restless struggle of the last century, which has been for equality of the sexes. The younger generation—in New York and I presume everywhere—is modeling itself after women of a type which defies old conventions, a type which was not common in polite society until recently. The débutante is rouging and painting her lips with frank abandon today. Groups of very young girls and men go to the Broadway jazz restaurants without any chaperone to give them the background of experience. The older matrons have used the servant problem as an excuse to save money and to avoid the work of formal home gatherings—with the result that the young people have left home for their pleasures. Not even the chaperonage of the reliable family chauffeur is left. The girl's mother is 'afraid' to ask him to stay till 1 o'clock, much less to 4 o'clock. The public taxi takes his place.

Not only in the restricted limits of New York society or the wealthy circles of other cities is the older generation bemoaning new manners and morals. A few days ago dear old Wellesley fairly shivered from the shock of a lecture delivered by Mrs. Augustus Trowbridge, wife of a Princeton professor.

To Mrs. Trowbridge belongs the credit for giving circulation to a new colloquialism—"petting parties." She did not explain what a "petting party" was. Apparently she didn't need to. But observers of recent New York social changes infer that she referred to the not uncommon scenes of fondling such as are witnessed at many public places and they had acquired their alcohol at the men's bar. Outside of the "fast young married crowd," the private parties had only punch, or maybe one lone cocktail.

Yet our turkey trot, we were told, was considered downright "scandalous" by the generation that had been Gibson Girls.[1] To each half decade its own shocks!

"'I've stopped dancing," explain the young matrons who have grown stout since their husbands (i.e., ex-turkey-trot partners) have prospered and their feet have sat long afternoon hours beneath the bridge table. "Now, you know, I'm not a prude, but I simply am not willing to go the length those children do—" And at that a choice bit of gossip is related. And one of them, from the secure domestic comfort of a husband, a house, and a cook, gives this advice to a young unmarried woman:

---

1 The "Gibson Girl" was an image created by illustrator Charles Dana Gibson (1867-1944), featuring an athletic, adept young woman with upswept hair and a full figure, of great height, with a long slender neck and small waist. She was often pictured in athletic and social contests with men. The Gibson girl was most popular between the 1890s and World War I and was popularized by Gibson's illustrations in periodicals such as *Century, Harper's Monthly,* and *Life.*

"I don't think that you ought to have an apartment. Some one might misunderstand you. I never thought of two unmarried girls renting an apartment when I used to study in New York."

Those who are married would have those who are not remain perennial boarders, because they themselves never were faced with the problems of 1920. For it is the biological law of the world that each should stop understanding where her own experiences of life leave off.

"And that is the fundamental reason why every generation thinks its own ethics are the best," comments a man who has danced with enough crops of "debbies" to look back over the changes of fifteen years, as well as over one year on the front in France. "But, when all's said and done, did mid-Victorianism make good? The world has tried prudishness for nearly a hundred years now—and were homes any happier? Have husbands been more faithful? Have wives been more efficient home-makers?

"If the Grundys, who are doing all this worrying, would only read history, they'd discover that the world has gone through many lax periods and the human race survived them. Political liberty was the fruit of the eighteenth century—and look at its morals! Isn't it possible that a hundred years from now this generation will be known by the name of the 'generation that won the great war'? Why not let each generation work out its own ethics?"

Not for us!

Everybody has been trying this year as never before to make everybody else live by the ethics of his pet generation. The very blue law propagandists are trying to force the Generation Ago itself to live by the code of Two Generations Ago—turn the leaf back fifty years. And, with everybody trying to reform somebody else, and spending yards of print paper and hours of conversation on the subject, surely somebody ought to have succeeded, or we ought to have a scientific explanation of what becomes of the waste [*sic*] energy.

So one generation or the other must have turned over a new leaf on Jan. 1, 1921. The debate might be settled if we only knew which had done the deed.

3. Alma Whitaker, "Exit Flapper; Enter the Mysterious Woman of Thirty," *Los Angeles Times*, 23 July 1922

Ominous changes in the air. "She" is about to enter upon another era, another phase, to affect a new pose, new poise, new manners, new styles and a new personality.

The skittish flapper styles are registering their last kick. Very short skirts are distinctly passe. Extreme youthfulness is rapidly becoming demode. Obvious makeup utterly outre. And the reckless, impudent, flamboyant, dashing, inconsequential, flippant young person, with her independent devil-may-care attitude, her defiance of the conventions, and her scorn of dignity is passing, passing, passing.

What now is going to be her new pose? What manner of front is she going to exhibit to the world? What demeanor will she adopt to confuse and boggle the naive male? What is her next move in the game?

She has rather enjoyed the reckless era with its sumptuous audacity and flouting of all the traditions. She shows a marked inclination to cling to it for a little longer, to defy the Parisian edict of longer skirts, to continue to bob her hair and show her legs and snap her fingers in the face of Mrs. Grundy. She liked the attention it commanded, the anxiety it fostered, the alarmed criticism it provoked. But she also knows that variety is the spice of life, that the eternal feminine demands disconcerting changes, that to remain the paramount interest in a world of crowded competitive interests she must ever be on the alert for something new. She positively must not be "understood," the male must be kept guessing, maintained on a "qui vive?"[1] footing, bewildered and a little embarrassed. And this flapper attitude has worn itself thin. Even the pulpits are beginning to "understand," to exonerate, to excuse, nay, even to approve. Yes, and even to ignore—the unkindest cut of all.[2]

WHEN SHE WAS "CUTEY"

Just before that she had elected to be merely cutey, with her hair dressed in ultra simplicity, with fluffy coy escaped tendrils over the ears. Dainty little collars and cuffs, plain tailored gowns, severe white satin fronts, all of which was combined with the earnest attitude of a damsel intent upon war work, taking life rather seriously, service and serviceability rampant. It was the civilian counterpart of the Red Cross costume.

All of which you will recall was a marked and fetching contrast to the floppy style which immediately preceded it, the bunchy clothes, the debutante slouch, the hunched shoulders and the slightly elevated tummy. She was a weary limp little creature in those days, rather bored, with hair yanked back off her forehead to conform to the slightly contemptuous arched eyebrow. Any enthusiasm she evinced was confined to a wistful little smile, an obvious effort at tactful congeniality. Hence the trim tailored docilely eager war attitude was a highly becoming contrast.

But just before the flop it was the slit skirt, with its subtle draperies, its hint of naughtiness combined with a touch-me-not hauteur.

1 Idiomatically, "On the alert."
2 *Julius Caesar* 3.ii.183.

Sophisticated elegance was her role then, dashing, daring, sparkling, but a bit overwhelming. A long queenly fishtail, half across the room, jeweled laces, rich silks—most imposing, but artfully modified with that stretch of silken petticoatless leg in chorus girl tights that was so utterly confusing. She strutted in those days with a haughty glide, she smiled with serene superiority and dressed her hair high and queenly—oh, the very quintessence of daring, but haughty sophistication. Today's flapper is daring to be sure, but it is impudence, not hauteur, cheeky, reckless, but not the elegant superciliousness of the slit skirt era.

SLIT SKIRTS

The bolster skirt era of ten years ago was still another pose. She hobbled and hopped, walked with a staccato little jerk, showed a fair modicum of leg, and for a time accentuated her buttock line with a rather lame sort of vulgarity. That phase seemed to indicate a deliberate accentuation of her former thralldom, an exaggeration of the outward and visible shackles to which her inward spirit had ever been heir.

It was the last phase before suffrage came in—and incidentally woman's suffrage came in with slit skirts in California—the first untrammeled stride she had taken for years! And it came in for the rest of the country with bare-backs and knee-length skirts.

But just before the hobble, she had pawed through the sporty, doggy, stage of which Miss Eleanor Sears was a shining example. The mannish clothes, hands in pockets, the boyish stride, the athletic swing to the shoulders, all combined with an ultra practical manner, an air of physical capacity—and it was stylish to be very sound and healthy in those days. Fainting Amelias were decidedly out.[1]

That was a sequence to the Gibson girl vogue—that elegant young lady who so successfully combined ultra-feminism with a taste for sports—who managed to look radiantly healthy, capable, ineffably attractive, slightly superior, haughtily dignified, and pleasantly graceful all in one. She wore her hair mounted high upon her head, artfully exposing her intellectual temples. She wore her skirts long and frilly round the feet for dress occasions, but had a nice taste in trim shirtwaists, sailor hats and trotter skirts for walking-and sport wear. It was she who adopted the divided skirt for bicycle riding as distinct from the less artistic "bloomers" which had a brief, but perilous vogue. Oh, that Gibson girl era had a lot to recommend it—it had the bolster skirt

---

1 Henry Fielding's character in the eponymous domestic novel *Amelia* (1751) features a virtuous heroine wronged in several ways by her husband.

phase and the slit skirt phase and even the demure practical war phase all beaten to a frazzle.

Well, we needn't go back any farther than that. But what is she going to do now? After being flamboyantly frank, telling all she knows and not caring a whoop what anybody thinks of her, tripping around in skittish knee-length skirts, metaphorically putting out her impudent tongue at the world, kicking up her heels, painting her face, bobbing her hair, behaving how she jolly well likes, you can wager something diametrically opposed to all that is in the offing. That was but an exuberant outburst following her new found freedom. But now she is settling down, getting used to her emancipation, growing up.

Ah, growing up. That is the next phase. The fall styles are all designed to present an enchanting woman of 30. That subtle, clever, sophisticated, dangerous "woman of 30" who has lurked through fiction all the way from George Moore[1] to Gertrude Atherton.

The Mysterious Woman   The Flapper

"The Mysterious Woman" and "The Flapper," *Los Angeles Times*, 23 July 1922. The figures closely resemble Countess Zattiany and the flapper in *Black Oxen*.

---

1   Irish writer (1852-1933) influenced by French realism whose writing could be described as realist and naturalist.

Appendix D: Reviews of the Novel and the Film

[This appendix draws from contemporary publications and contains reviews of both *Black Oxen* and the filmic adaptation of the novel, released in early 1924.]

1. Carl Van Vechten, "A Lady Who Defies Time," *The Nation*, 14 February 1923

Between writers of natural temperament and genius, however exaggeratedly they may express themselves, and careful artisans who know how to give their work at least the appearance of art, I cast my vote in favor of the former. On the whole, I prefer the work of Gertrude Atherton to that of Edith Wharton.[1] Usually (not always, to be sure) the work of Mrs. Wharton seems to me to be scrupulous, clever, and uninspired, while that of Mrs. Atherton is often careless, sprawling, but inspired. Mrs. Wharton, with some difficulty, it would appear, has learned to write; Mrs. Atherton was born with a facility for telling stories.

The Californian possesses to the highest degree to the qualities of vitality and glamor. These are two of the essentials of any art, and they are very rare. Their presence explains, in a sense, my really deep and lasting affection for Ouida, a novelist whom I vastly prefer to George Eliot, or even Thackeray.[2] Ouida had vitality, glamour, and imagination. She

---

1 Edith Wharton (1862-1937) was an American author and contemporary of Atherton's who authored fiction, travel writing, and other nonfiction from the 1880s through the 1930s. She was the first woman to be awarded a Pulitzer Prize in 1920. Wharton's childhood, like Atherton's, was peripatetic, for her family moved to England, Italy, and France during parts of her early childhood. Both Wharton and Atherton began their careers after following more conventional family paths, with Wharton marrying Edward (Teddy) Wharton in 1885 and Atherton marrying and having two children by 1878. Based on obvious incompatibilities in the Wharton marriage and on Teddy Wharton's worsening mental state, Wharton and her husband eventually divorced, and she spent her later life in France. Given the similarities in their histories it is somewhat curious that Wharton and Atherton did not (reportedly) meet.

2 "Ouida" was the pseudonym of English-born novelist Maria Louise Ramé (1839-1908) who went by the name Maria Louise de la Ramée. Specializing in sensation fiction and historical romance, Ouida authored over forty novels and various short story collections between the 1860s and the century's turn. George Eliot was the pen name of author and translator Mary Ann Evans (1819-80), whose influential novels of the Victorian era were published between

was so prodigal of her talents, and so sure of them, that she never took the trouble to verify references or to correct her copy, to soften her first impressions or to heighten them. Nevertheless, she was a genius. Some of her genius, restrained and curbed at certain acute angles—for Mrs. Atherton is a finer artist and a deeper thinker than Ouida—has descended on the shoulders of the Californian.

This type of genius is not essentially self-critical and on this account is often likely to flicker unevenly. Nevertheless it is indubitably genius, genius of a higher quality than that possessed by the artist who struggles with words and erases phrases for years in order to achieve his ideal of perfection. It is the genius of Charles Dickens as opposed to the vastly inferior talent of Walter Pater.[1] It is the prodigal genius of a man who feels rather than the careful capacity of the man who takes pains.

Contemporary critics invariably prefer the Walter Paters to the Charles Dickenses. Contemporary American critics allot a more important place to Mrs. Wharton than to Mrs. Atherton. Mistakenly, I may reiterate. "Rezánov" and "The Conqueror," even "A Daughter of the Vine" and "Senator North," are likely to outlive any of the works of Mrs. Wharton, aside from "Ethan Frome."[2]

It is characteristic of this type of genius, as I have already asserted, to produce a very uneven quality of work: one day a "David Copperfield" or a "Pickwick Papers," the next day a "Barnaby Rudge" or an "Our Mutual Friend."[3] I have been told that Mrs. Atherton's genius was never at so low an ebb as in "Sleeping Fires." I cannot speak personally of this novel as I have not read it, but it is improbable that she has ever before published a book that came so perilously near to failure. She has followed it with "Black Oxen," which may be considered her most brilliant book up to date. Moreover it is written with a care and attention to detail which hitherto have been absent from all but her best work.

1859 and 1876. Her private life was considered scandalous because of her open relationship with married critic George Henry Lewes. George Makepeace Thackeray (1811-63) was an English novelist and journalist who was most famous for his satirical novel, *Vanity Fair* (1848).

1 Walter Pater (1839-94) was an English critic, essayist, and novelist who taught at Oxford and whose most influential works include *Studies in the History of the Renaissance* (1873), which drew criticism because of its perceived amorality and eventually caused Pater to resign from his teaching position. Between 1885 and 1887 he composed fiction, returning to essays in 1889.

2 *Ethan Frome* is the title of Edith Wharton's 1911 novella set in a rural New England town named "Starkfield," a place of rigid mores and stoic characters. It met with acclaim upon its initial publication and is considered one of Wharton's most tragic pieces of writing and a departure from her portraits of urban high society.

3 Novels by Charles Dickens (1812-70).

The title is taken from the tag of W.B. Yeats's play, "The Countess Cathleen," and the black oxen are the heavy years that God, the herdsman, goads on from behind.[1] It is a poetic title that has a fine significance, for the heroine of the book, Countess Zattiany, tearing a modern leaf from Samuel Butler's "Luck or Cunning?"[2] and Bernard Shaw's "Back to Methuselah," has succeeded in defying time.[3] A heroine of fifty-eight who (for perfectly good reasons) looks twenty-eight (in the morning or at the opera) is, indeed, a novelty.

Mrs. Atherton is explicit that her heroine's mind is that of a woman who has fully lived her fifty-eight years; otherwise she is young, young even in her capacity to indulge in amorous experience, young in her transcendent beauty. She awakens passion in a young man of thirty-four, and this is the problem: what will happen to an immature male of thirty-four who is in love with a lovely female with a mind of fifty-eight? This problem is intensified by the attitude of the Countess Zattiany's contemporaries, less fortunate in appearance than she, and her juniors, intent upon defending their preserves, in New York society. Mrs. Atherton is content to have her Countess move triumphantly through this rabble, instead of erecting a scaffold for a tragedy by arranging a marriage between the mis-aged pair.

The resemblances, both figurative and literal, between the Californian and her own heroine will be apparent to many readers. According to "Who's Who," Mrs. Atherton was born in 1857 and she published her first book in 1892, thirty-one years ago. But in vitality and youthful zest in fulfilling her self-appointed tasks, she has few equals and no superiors among the "younger" novelists. Perhaps, indeed, vitality

---

1   "The Countess Cathleen" is the title of William Butler Yeats's verse drama of 1892, with a final version performed in 1911 and published in 1912. Set against a background of an Irish famine, Cathleen makes a bargain with the devil, selling her soul so that starving tenants will be spared both hunger and damnation (for they have also sold their souls). The play was first performed in 1899 and reappeared in the Abbey Theatre in 1911 after substantive revisions.

2   Samuel Butler (1835-1902) was a novelist and essayist whose *Luck or Cunning?* (1887) is a piece of nonfiction that explores Charles Darwin's theory of natural selection in light of Butler's criticisms of Darwin's formulation.

3   "Back to Methuselah" is a series of five plays written between 1918 and 1920 and published in 1921 (performed 1922) that involves genetic inheritances based on acquired characteristics (thus embracing Lamarckian science rather than a Darwinian approach to evolution). A central idea is Creative Evolution, or the willing and/or necessary adoption of favorable characteristics. The plays also address Shaw's sense of the widespread post-World War I poverty that he traces to poor governmental interventions into complex twentieth-century lives. His solution to the problem of twentieth-century management is a longer life span, in which increased age (of well over a hundred years) allows humans the opportunity to gain wisdom through experience.

is vouchsafed by providence only to those who have passed the gates of fifty. Certainly, few of our young writers could turn out a book like "Black Oxen" of which the perusal at a sitting would seem almost fore-ordained. "Black Oxen" is a long novel, but, once begun, it does not permit itself to be dropped until finished.

I have not, I fear, left myself space to speak of Mrs. Atherton's "Sophisticates," as she calls the columnists and dramatic critics who congregate at the Hotel Algonquin (which figures in the book as the Sign of the Indian Chief).[1] It will entertain the outside world to discover that at the parties of these Sophisticates the chief amusements appear to be charades, guessing games, and pun contests. Nor can I dwell on the diverting picture of the unregenerate flapper, Janet Oglethorpe, who drinks and smokes and invades bachelors' apartments at what would have been considered improper hours a decade or so ago, or on her superb grandmother, Mrs. Oglethorpe, a type of the *grande dame* that is fast dying out of New York society and soon will be as extinct as the unsophisticated *jeune fille*. Nor have I spoken of the exceedingly novel pivot on which the actions turns, which will certainly be the cause of Mrs. Atherton's receiving letters of query from every dowdy frump who has passed fifty (and has the requisite slenderness) in the United States. "Black Oxen" will more firmly seat its author in the unique place she occupies in our literature.

2. "The New Curiosity Shop, *Black Oxen,*" *The Literary Review*, 7 July 1923 [a satirical review published by *The New York Evening Post*]

I   Lee Clavering's weary eyes—steel blue, half closed—roved over the darkened auditorium.

Twelve years ago he had migrated from pre-civil war Louisiana to Manhattan, the Brains of America—from the ante-bellum to the cerebellum. In that time he had attained the highest position in the gift of the nation.

He was L.C., the premier columnist of America, the King Kleagle of the Kolyumist Klan.[2]

His steel-blue eyes were now, as always, searching with the evergreen hope of finding *the* consummate woman, which proves him romantic.

---

1   This is an allusion to the Algonquin Round Table, the social group of self-styled wits who met at the Algonquin Hotel in New York and who formed the model for Atherton's "Sophisticates." See Introduction, pp. 29-30.

2   A "King Kleagle" is an officer of the Ku Klux Klan responsible for recruiting new members and for directing the actions of other Kleagles within a particular region.

That he found her in a New York first-night audience proves him a character in fiction.

II She sat two seats ahead of him. After the first act she rose to her feet, turned towards him, and, with her opera glasses, swept the house.

Lee saw that Venus rising from the sea had nothing on her (emphasis on *her*, please!). She most exquisitely beautiful woman he had ever seen— the only authentic consummate woman, indubitably.

Clavering's nerves rippled, but the man next him—old Dinwiddie, swell, suave, and sixty—had an apoplectic fit. His eyes bulged, his lips gibbered.

"It's a ghost—Mary Ogden—belle of New York forty-five years ago, when I was a kid—married Count Zattiany—Hungarian—never been back since—"

"Her daughter, of course," suggested Clavering.

"Never had any—to speak of—but that's it—must be—one of the unmentionable—she was a gay one—little liaison now and then—relished by the best of men—"

III Three weeks passed—six, more "first-nights"—and "Mary Ogden" was at every one of them, also Lee Clavering. She was "the talk of the town."

The newspapers were full of the mystery. Crowds followed her everywhere. She bought a pair of gloves—and seven floorwalkers were hurried to Bellevue in seven separate deliria.[1] She went into the Public Library—and the infatuated populace carried off all the books as souvenirs. She walked around the reservoir—and they drew off all the water and sold it for a dollar a bottle.

On the second Sunday 40 per cent of all the clergymen preached on "Mary has chosen the better part."[2]

Never had there been such excitement in New York since Peter Stuyvesant broke his wooden leg.[3]

IV After the sixth "first night" Lee Clavering followed her home. He found her alone in the great city, on her own doorstep.

---

1 Floorwalkers assisted customers and supervised salespersons in a department store. Bellevue Hospital in Manhattan is believed to be the oldest public hospital in the United States and is known for its psychiatric facilities.

2 Luke 10:42, "Mary has chosen the better part, and it will not be taken from her." A reference to Jesus' praise of Mary of Bethany, particularly as compared to her sister Martha, whom Jesus chides for appearing "distracted" in an earlier part of the verse. The verse has been interpreted as affirming the value of a woman who forgoes traditional household duties and focuses on spirituality.

3 The last director-general of the Dutch colony in what would become New York City, Stuyvesant (1612-72) was nicknamed "old silver leg."

"May I?—am I?—are you?—were they?—was it?—whosis?—" he stammered, his temperature rising rapidly.

"Oh!" she said with a faint smile, "I'm locked out—"

"Watch me!" he said.

He tore out the area railing and threw it at a passing taxicab, smashed all the area windows, burst in the door. Entering, he ran rapidly through the house, switched on all the lights, turned on the hot and cold water in every bathroom, upset all the furniture and slid down the banisters from the fourth story to the first. Landing in a heap at the bottom, he leaped to his feet and opened the front door.

"Thank you," she said simply. "Have a drink, Mr. Clavering."

"You know whom I am, then?" he cyrilled in amazement.

"Certainly. Don't you?" she answered.

"I—yes—no———" he murmured, his eyes fixed on her as he poured a drink.

"You will pardon my confusion," he babbled on. "To who—I mean, to wit have I the honor of speaking? How old are you? Have you ever been married. If so, mark a cross within the circle, but not within the triangle. Who *are* you, and if not, what *is* your beautiful name?"

"Marie Zattiany," she answered, with a smile.

"Legitimate or ill—" he paused in mid-flight, dipped his forefinger into the catsup and dreamily drew a red cross on his shirt front.

"Pardon me," he continued, "I was about to ask a personal question. To speak quite impersonally—will you marry me?—if you're of marriageable age."

"How old do you think I am? Don't answer. Come back in three weeks and I will tell you my story."

Outside the house he remembered the shattered basement windows. His Southern chivalry would not let him leave her unprotected. He lay down on the doorstep and slept soundly until dawn.

V Three weeks passed.

"To-night's the night," he cried as he rushed from his apartment.

He charged up the steps, assaulted the door with his fists, found her in the library and forced the fighting from the start.

It seemed to her that her entire body was encircled by flexible hot bars of iron and that her face, her mouth were being flagellated.

"Break away!" she managed to gurgle. "No hitting in the clinches!"[1]

A left hook to the jaw and he collapsed under the table.

When he came to his voice was weak.

"A typewriter, please!" he gasped. "It's stuff for the column." His news sense rarely failed him.

---

1   A boxing term for blows made in close proximity to an opponent.

"Tuesday, October 29—I to M. Zattiany's, the toast of the town, and a mighty mystery, whether she be in truth Zattiany or a mischievous impostor and did kiss and clip her mightily, but the baggage handed me a slapp on the mapp, as a trunk had fallen on me. So I to the mat."[1]

"What next?" he added feebly.

"Have a drink?" she said.

He took three.

"Who are you, woman? Is your real name Zettiany or Jeffries?"

"I am Mary Ogden Zattiany," she answered quietly. "I married Zattiany forty-five years ago. I was twenty-five at the time. Do your own arithmetic."

"Five from thirty is twenty and carry two—think of a number, add a dash of bitters—shake well before using"—his voice trailed to silence and his jaw dropped.

"I hated Zattiany, but his position appealed to my love of power and intrigue—especially the latter. I was besieged by men—and surrendered at discretion."

VI Three weeks passed. Then a wireless telegram—"Wife dead. Must see you immediately on arrival Berengaria. Haffanauer."

The Prince arrived—straight, thin, erect, broke—in his eyes the glance of the Austrian double eagle, now selling at 99 44-500 off for cash.[2]

"Frau Gräfin."

"Why are you here, Excellenz?"

"Because Austria heeds you—I need you. We both need you every hour and—every dollar. Will you marry me?"

"But I am engaged to L.C."

"What of that? Let me state my case. I am about to rehabilitate Austria. I shall annex Germany, Italy, Greece, Turkey, Moldavia, Bolivia, Roumania, Pneumonia, the Jugo and Czecho brothers and all the Balking States.

"And you?" he went on. "You shall be—what you will—queen, empress, my m—er—morganatic wife.[3] The Oesterreich shall shed its

---

1 In this context, "to clip" means to punch.

2 A double-headed eagle was on the coat of arms of the Austrian empire as a sign of the Hapsburg dynasty. The eagle also appeared on the Austrian 100 Corona coin, made of gold and featuring Franz Joseph I (emperor from 1848 to 1916) on one side and the crowned double eagle on the other side.

3 A morganatic marriage was between two individuals of socially unequal backgrounds. Among European royalty, it prevented the transfer of the husband's titles or holdings to the wife or any children. During the ceremony, the groom would hold the bride's right hand with his left hand, earning it the title of a "left-handed marriage."

plumes for your adornment—if only you'll buy a little preferred with a large bonus of very common."

"Old stuff!" she exclaimed disdainfully. "I have the same plan. I shall do it myself—with the aid my husband's column—I, Marie, Countess Zattiany!"

"But no," he answered. "If you return to Austria as Mrs. Lee Clavering—"

"What?" she started aghast. "Mrs. Lee—? Shall I have to take my husband's name? Isn't the Lucy Stone League too powerful——"[1]

"Not in Austria," he said blandly. "No league, whether of nations or denominations, is recognized."

"I love him so!" she moaned. "But this changes everything. I shall never give up the gräfinship. Moritz! I am yours!"

"Sign on the dotted line," he said quietly.

VII   She wrote Lee these verses.

When lovely woman takes to cooing
    And finds what bills she has to pay
For this—though sweet—untitled wooing
    The next boat takes her down the bay.[2]

You should then be up and doing.
    Follow me on Saturday,
Still your happiness pursuing.
    Love like ours will find a way.

But he printed it in the column on Saturday and on Monday married the daughter of an eminent bootlegger.

---

1   The Lucy Stone League, founded in 1921, continues to advocate for women's retention of their maiden names as part of its feminist platform.

2   This stanza mimics the famous (and much-parodied) poem in Oliver Goldsmith's novel, *The Vicar of Wakefield: A Tale* (1766): "When lovely woman stoops to folly, / And finds too late that men betray, / What charm can soothe her melancholy, / What art can wash her guilt away? / The only art her guilt to cover, / To hide her shame from every eye, / To give repentance to her lover / And wring his bosom, is—to die." Interpreted in the context of the novel's representation of seduction, the passage suggests that women who lose their virginity outside of marriage are doomed. The line also appears in T.S. Eliot's "The Waste Land" (1922), specifically in "The Fire Sermon," and reads, "When a lovely woman stoops to folly and / Paces about her room again, alone, / She smoothes her hair with automatic hand, / And puts a record on the gramophone." While Eliot's version of the lines suggests the sexual permissiveness of a modern society, this parody situates Madame Zattiany as the partner most invested in pursuing a sexual liaison outside of marriage.

3. "First National's *Black Oxen* Plays to Capacity Business," *Moving Picture World*, 19 January 1924

The long heralded and much publicized First National screen version of Gertrude Atherton's "Black Oxen" reached New York on Sunday January 6 at the Strand Theatre. The business through the first three days of the week was tremendous and indications are that there will be no falling off, but rather a gain, in attendance during the remainder of the run.

As in two hundred other cities throughout the country "Black Oxen" was long expected by the public because of the serialization of the novel in a local newspaper, each installment of which announced the forthcoming screen version.

Among the critical comments were: *New York Times*: "Frank Lloyd's picturized version ... is a brilliant example of faithful adherence to an in intensely interesting narrative ... The way in which Corinne Griffith enacts this role (Madame Zattiany) would make anyone forgive her for being beautiful ... This is a delightful picture with a well told story ..."[1]

New York American: "But there is an interesting picture and one which will keep Joseph Plunkett, managing director of the Strand, busy counting the box office receipts, if the first day's business is any indication of what he may expect all week ... Corinne Griffith goes a long way toward satisfying the artistic eye with her Mary Ogden. She is beautiful, she is well groomed and she carries herself with a pleasing dignity."

Evening Telegram: "'Black Oxen,' faithfully translated to the screen by Frank Lloyd who with this photoplay makes his debut as an independent producer after ten years of directorial work does not argue for or against rejuvenation. It tells a great story with dramatic portentousness which every seeker after genuine entertainment will like. It also has the advantage of fine acing by a cast which includes Corinne Griffith, Conway Tearle, Clara Bow, Kate Lester, Alan Hale, Clair MacDowell, Harry Mestayer, Lincoln Stedman, and Thomas Ricketts.

Evening World: "'Black Oxen' as a novel is chock full of dramatics and hence has, in the capable hands of Frank Lloyd, blossomed forth as a fine stalwart bit of picture making."

Sun Globe: "'Black Oxen' seems to us a fantastic, brilliant story, fully as good as any of Edith Wharton's novels of society. The picture follows the book operation for operation, one might say, and it is one of the photoplays that ought not to be missed."

---

1 Griffith (1894-1979) was a popular screen actress during the 1920s; she worked for Vitagraph as well as First National and starred in *The Garden of Eden* (1928) and *The Divine Lady* (1929). After the advent of sound film, she turned to writing, real estate, and politics, successfully in all cases.

get this!

Oh! What a clean up this one is going to be.
The critics were right when they said it was a knockout.

In San Francisco—"Black Oxen" broke all records on opening day for any theatre in San Francisco and the second day was larger than first day. In St. Louis it crashed through to phenomenal business.

When Exhibitors Herald said it was "A 'Best Seller' made into a best seller," they certainly hit the nail right on the head.

"Black Oxen" will be the biggest hit of the year.

Opens at Mark Strand
N. Y.—January 7th

Hit No. 7

FRANK LLOYD PRODUCTIONS INC. OFFERS

"BLACK OXEN"

by GERTRUDE ATHERTON
featuring
Corinne Griffith
and
Conway Tearle
Directed by
FRANK LLOYD

FIRST NATIONAL PICTURES

A First National Picture

Advertisement from *Moving Picture World*, 12 January 1924, 89.

A First National Picture

Advertisement from *Photoplay* 25.3, February 1924, 9.

4. Frank Elliott, "*Black Oxen*, Frank Lloyd, First National," *Motion Picture News*, 5 January 1924

With hundreds of newspapers in the country publishing this story in serial form, the picture version is undoubtedly one of the greatest "looked for" features of the season. We are confident that the screen adaptation of the widely read and much discussed book will satisfy everyone. It might be called a self-made box office success.

"Black Oxen" deals with rejuvenation, the topic of the hour, and so to begin with the picture can boast of something new under the sun in the say of a story. And it has another big asset in Corinne Griffith, who gives a vivid portrayal of the role of Madame Zatianny, who, given back her youth through glandular treatment, comes to America, falls in love with a young man, but in the end returns to her native Austria after deciding that she is to [sic] old to marry. The gowns and furs, as well as jewels worn by Miss Griffith constitute a veritable fashion parade which moves throughout the picture.

The production itself is an elaborate one. The settings, especially the interiors are the last word in artistic lavishness.

Every member of the cast does admirable work, especially Conway Tearle as Clavering, but we want to direct everyone's attention to the flapper portrayal contributed by Clara Bow.[1] It is one of the peppiest bits we've seen in many moons.

THEME. Presents idea upon the rejuvenation of a noted Austrian woman who comes to America, astounds everyone with her beauty, falls in love with a young playwright and is about to marry him, when she is made to see the folly of such a move and persuaded to return to Austria.

PRODUCTION HIGHLIGHTS. The interpretation of the role of Madame Zatianny by Corinne Griffith. The gorgeous gowns worn by the star. Clara Bow's work as the flapper. The fine supporting cast. The scene in which Madame reveals her identity. The lavish mounting given the picture. The novel climax. The European episodes.

DIRECTION. Has transplanted the Gertrude Atherton book to the screen in admirable manner, preserving all its romance and appeal. Has brought out some fine work on the part of Corinne Griffith and has developed the makings of a star in Clara Bow. Has kept up the interest in spite of the length of the picture.

---

1 Tearle (1878-1938) starred in close to a hundred films from the 1910s to 1936. Bow was known as the "it" girl after *It* (1927), a film about animal magnetism that cemented her rising stardom. Playing Janet Oglethorpe in *Black Oxen* (one of eight films in which Bow appeared in 1924 alone) was one of her career turning points.

EXPLOITATION ANGLES.[1] Tie up with a book store on big display of the novel and get your photos from the picture as well as cuts into it. Tie up with the newspaper in your town running the story as a serial. The gowns suggest a splash in shop windows. If you can get a pair of black oxen and drive them through the street in front of an old fashioned wagon—great!

DRAWING POWER. Will tax the capacity of the largest and best houses in the land.

SUMMARY. You'll go a long ways before you can grab a better box office feature than this one. Everybody seems to be waiting to see the screen version of the book. The picture is a fine adaptation of the novel, splendidly acted.

★ ★ ★

---

1 These are suggested approaches to marketing and publicity.

Select Bibliography

Works by Gertrude Atherton

"The Literary Development of California." *Cosmopolitan* 10 (January 1891): 269-78.

"The Young Person as a Novel-Reader." *Critic* n.s. 19 (11 February 1893): 86-87.

Before the Gringo Came. New York: J. Selwin Tait, Sons, 1894.

"Divorce in the United States." *Contemporary Review* 72 (September 1897): 410-15.

American Wives and English Husbands. London: Service & Paton, 1898.

A Daughter of the Vine. New York: John Lane, The Bodley Head, 1899.

"The Novel: Its Friends and Foes: A Reply." *Bookman* (NY) 14 (October 1901): 137-38.

The Conqueror: Being the True and Romantic Story of Alexander Hamilton. New York: Macmillan, 1902.

The Splendid Idle Forties: Stories of Old California. New York: Macmillan, 1902.

"Some Truths about American Readers." *Bookman* (NY) 18 (February 1904): 658-60.

"Why is American Literature Bourgeois?" *The North American Review* 178 (May 1904): 771-81.

"Earthquake Reflections." *Harper's Weekly* 50 (23 June 1906): 891.

"Why Have We Not More Great Novelists?" *Current Literature* 44 (February 1908): 158-60.

"Present Unrest among Women." *Delineator* 74 (August 1909): 118.

"The American Novel in England." *Bookman* (NY) 30 (February 1910): 633-40.

"Mating Youth with Age." *Good Housekeeping* 57 (October 1913): 476-81.

"The Woman of Tomorrow." *Yale Review* n.s. 2 (April 1913): 412-35.

California: An Intimate History. New York: Harper, 1914.

The Living Present. New York: Frederick A. Stokes, 1917.

Sisters in Law: A Novel of Our Time. New York: Frederick A. Stokes, 1921.

The Crystal Cup. New York: Boni & Liveright, 1925.

The Immortal Marriage. New York: Boni & Liveright, 1927.

"When a Woman Marries a Man Younger Than Herself." *Red Book* 50 (December 1927): 52-53, 98, 100, 102.

Adventures of a Novelist. New York: Liveright, Inc., 1932.

"Science after Fifty" *Pictorial Review* 34 (March 1933): 15, 58.

"Wanted: Imagination." *What is a Book? Thoughts about Writing.* Ed. Dale Warren. Boston: Houghton Mifflin, 1935. 43-60.

"Defeating Old Age." In *Can Women Be Gentlemen?* Boston: Houghton Mifflin, 1938. 58-65.

——. "Second Youth: The Latest in Reactivation from one who knows ... a record of new wonders in man's battle against age." *Liberty* (8 July 1939): 17-87, 20.

The Horn of Life. New York: D. Appleton-Century, 1942.

"Is 35 the End?" *Saturday Home Magazine* (18 January 1947): 10-11, 15 C/B.

"Youth Lies Not in the Glass." *Saturday Home Magazine* (25 January 1947): 11, 17 C/B.

Biographies and Critical Works

Bauer, Dale. "Refusing Middle Age." *ANQ* 15.1 (2002): 46-60.

Bradley, Jennifer. "Woman at the Golden Gate: The Last Works of Gertrude Atherton." *Women's Studies* 12.1 (1986): 17-30.

Budd, Louis J. "Gertrude Atherton on Mark Twain." *Mark Twain Journal* 21.3 (Spring 1983): 18.

Cucinella, Catherine. "Gertrude Atherton (1857-1948)." *American Women Writers, 1900-1945: A Bio-Bibliographical Critical Sourcebook.* Ed. Laurie Champion. Westport, CT: Greenwood, 2000. 6-11.

Dawson, Melanie V. "Modern Maturity: Middle-Aged Anxiety in Modern American Fiction." *Blackwell Literature Compass* 5 (2008): 1-21.

Ellis, David M. "A Liberated Woman Visits the Adirondacks." *NYFQ* 5.3-4 (Winter 1979): 150-54.

Forman, Henry James. "A Brilliant California Novelist: Gertrude Atherton." *California Historical Society Quarterly* 40 (1961): 1-10.

"Gertrude Atherton Writes Her 56th Book." *Life* 11 November 1946, 95-97.

Hapke, Laura. "The Problem of Sensual Womanhood: Three Late Nineteenth-Century Fictional Solutions." *The Nassau Review* 4.2 (1981): 86-95.

Holt, Marilyn J. "Gertrude Atherton." *Supernatural Fiction Writers: Fantasy and Horror 2: A.E. Coppard to Roger Zelazny.* Ed. Everett Franklin Bleiler. New York: Scribner's, 1985. 777-81.

Jackson, Joseph Henry, "Watch the Parade: Write It All Down," *The San Francisco Chronicle*, vol. 6, no. 25, 1 November 1942, 11.

Kinney, Arthur. "The Other Dorothy Parkers." *The Critical Waltz: Essays on the Work of Dorothy Parker.* Ed. Rhonda S. Pettit and Regina Barreca. Madison, NJ: Fairleigh Dickinson UP, 2005. 114-26.

"Latest Works of Fiction," *The New York Times*, 21 January 1923, BR 14.

Leider, Emily Wortis. *California's Daughter*. Stanford: Stanford UP, 1991.

——. "'Your Picture Hangs in My Salon': The Letters of Gertrude Atherton to Ambrose Bierce." *California History* 60.4 (1981-82 Winter): 333-49.

Makowsky, Veronica. "Fear of Feeling and the Turn-of-the-Century Woman of Letters." *American Literary History* 5.2 (Summer 1993): 326-34.

McClure, Charlotte S. *Gertrude Atherton*. Boston: Twayne, 1979.

——. "Gertrude Atherton and Her San Francisco: A Wayward Writer and a Wayward City in a Wayward Paradise." *San Francisco in Fiction: Essays in a Regional Literature*. Ed. David Fine and Paul Skenazy. Albuquerque: U of New Mexico P, 1995. 73-95.

——. "Gertrude Atherton's California Woman: From Love Story to Psychological Drama." *Itinerary: Criticism: Essays on California Writers*. Ed. Charles L. Crow. Bowling Green, OH: UP of Bowling Green, 1978.

McElderry, B.R., Jr. "Gertrude Atherton and Henry James." *Colby Library Quarterly* 16 (Nov. 1954): 269-72.

Parker, Gail T. "William Dean Howells: Realism and Feminism." *Uses of Literature*. Ed. Monroe Engel. Cambridge: Harvard UP, 1973. 133-61.

Parry, Sally E. "The Fountain of Youth: Scandal and Black Oxen." *Sinclair Lewis Society Newsletter* 12.2 (Spring 2004): 7, 11, 13.

Pennell, Melissa McFarland. "Through the Golden Gate: Madness and the Persephone Myth in Gertrude Atherton's 'The Foghorn'." *Images of Persephone: Feminist Readings in Western Literature*. Ed. Elizabeth T. Hayes. Gainesville: UP of Florida, 1994. 84-98.

Piep, Karsten H. *Embattled Home Fronts: Domestic Politics and the American Novel of World War I*. Amsterdam, Netherlands: Rodopi, 2009.

——. "War as Feminist Utopia in Dorothy Canfield Fisher's Home Fires in France and Gertrude Atherton's The White Morning." *Women's Studies: An Interdisciplinary Journal* 34.2 (March 2005): 159-89.

Prebel, Julie. "Engineering Womanhood: The Politics of Rejuvenation in Gertrude Atherton's *Black Oxen*." *American Literature* 76.2 (2004): 307-35.

Rosenberg, Tracey S. "A Challenge to Victorian Motherhood: Mona Caird and Gertrude Atherton." *Women's Writing* 12.3 (2005): 485-504.

"Sophisticates." *Time*, 13 March 1923, 12.

Stevenson, Lionel. "Atherton versus Grundy: The Forty Years' War." *Bookman* 69 (1929): 464-72.

Stobbs, Janet. "Tracing the Female Triptych of Space: Private, Public, and Power Strongholds in Gertrude Atherton's Patience Sparhawk

and Her Times and F. Tennyson Jesse's A Pin to See the Peepshow."
Inside Out: Women Negotiating, Subverting, Appropriating Public and Private Space. Ed. Teresa Gómez Reus, Aránzazu Usandizaga, and Janet Wolff. Amsterdam, Netherlands: Rodopi, 2008. 125-45.

Weinstock, Jeffrey Andrew. *Scare Tactics: Supernatural Fiction by American Women*. New York: Fordham UP, 2008.

Weir, Sybil. "Gertrude Atherton: The Limits of Feminism in the 1890's." *San Jose Studies* 1.1 (1975): 24-31.

Medical Approaches to Aging

Benjamin, Dr. Harry. "The New Fountain of Youth." *McClure's Magazine* 56.3 (1924): 105.

———. "Steinach-Therapy against Old Age (A Review of Ten Years' Experience)." Manuscript, Bancroft Library, University of California, Berkeley.

Corners, George F. *Rejuvenation: How Steinach Makes People Young*. New York: Thomas Seltzer, 1923.

"Doctor Undergoes Steinach Operation." *The New York Times*, 13 August 1923.

"Gland Treatment Spreads in America: Many Seekers of Youth." *The New York Times*, 8 April 1923, XX2.

Hirshbein, Laura Davidow. "The Glandular Solution: Sex, Masculinity, and Aging in the 1920s." *Journal of the History of Sexuality* 9.3 (2000): 277-304.

Levick, M.B., "Pursuit of the Elixir of Life: Dr. Steinach's Predecessors Had Recipes for Changing Old Men into Young in 1600 B.C." *The New York Times*, 9 September 1923, SM 9.

Morris, Charles Evans. *Modern Rejuvenation Methods*. New York: Scientific Medical Publishing Company, 1926.

"'The New Fountain of Youth': How the Famous Steinach Operation Checks the Progress of Old Age—A Record of Its Success to Date." *McClure's Magazine* 56.3 (1924): 105-07.

"Rejuvenation Lure is Fad." *The Los Angeles Times*, 17 March 1924.

Squier, Susan, "Incubabies and Rejuvenates: The Traffic between Technologies of Reproduction and Age-Extension." *Figuring Age: Women, Bodies, Generations*. Ed. Kathleen Woodward. Bloomington: Indiana UP, 1999. 88-111.

Steinach, Eugen. *Sex and Life: Forty Years of Biological and Medical Experiments*. New York: Viking, 1940.

Works by Atherton's Contemporaries

Dell, Floyd. *Essays from the Friday Literary Review, 1909-1913.* Ed. R. Craig Sautter. Highland Park, IL: December Press, 1995.

——. *Love in the Machine Age: A Psychological Study of the Transition from Patriarchal Society.* New York: Octagon Books, 1973 [1930].

Fabian, Walter [Samuel Adams Hopkins]. *Flaming Youth.* New York: Boni & Liveright, 1923.

Freud, Sigmund. *The Basic Writings of Sigmund Freud.* Trans. and ed. Dr. A.A. Brill. New York: Modern Library, 1938.

Loos, Anita. *Gentlemen Prefer Blondes and But Gentlemen Marry Brunettes.* New York: Penguin, 1998 [1925 & 1928].

Parker, Dorothy. *Constant Reader: A Selection of Articles Originally Published in the New Yorker, 1927-1933.* New York: Viking, 1970.

——. *Enough Rope: Poems.* New York: Pocket Books, 1939 [1926].

——. *Laments for the Living.* New York: Viking, 1930.

Robinson, James Harvey. *The Human Comedy: As Devised and Directed by Mankind Itself.* New York: Harper and Brothers, 1937.

——. *The Mind in the Making: The Relation of Intelligence to Social Reform.* New York: Harper and Brothers, 1921.

Van Vechten, Carl. *Nigger Heaven.* New York: Octagon Books, 1973 [1926].

Wharton, Edith. *The Mother's Recompense.* New York: Scribner, 1986 [1925].

Yeats, W.B. *The Countess Cathleen, Manuscript Materials.* Ed. Michael J. Sidnell and Wayne K. Chapman. Ithaca, NY: Cornell UP, 1999.

Cultural Studies of American Modernity

Allen, Frederick Lewis. *Only Yesterday: An Informal History of the Nineteen-Twenties.* New York: Harper & Brothers, 1931.

Dolan, Marc. *Modern Lives: A Cultural Re-Reading of "the Lost Generation."* West Lafayette, IN: Purdue UP, 1996.

Douglas, Ann. *Terrible Honesty: Mongrel Manhattan in the 1920s.* New York: Farrar, Strauss, and Giroux, 1996.

Ellis, L. Ethan. *Republican Foreign Policy, 1921-1933.* New Brunswick, NJ: Rutgers UP, 1968.

Higham, John. *Strangers in the Land: Patterns of American Nativism, 1860-1925.* New Brunswick, NJ: Rutgers UP, 2002.

Lindsey, Ben B. and Wainwright Evans. *The Companionate Marriage.* New York: Boni & Liveright, 1927.

Miller, Nina. *Making Love Modern: The Intimate Public Worlds of New York's Literary Women.* New York: Oxford UP, 1999.

Miller, Tyrus. *Late Modernism: Politics, Fiction, and the Arts between the World Wars*. Berkeley: U of California P, 1999.

Mott, Frank Luther. *Golden Multitudes: The Story of Best Sellers in the United States*. New York: Macmillan, 1947.

———. *A History of American Magazines*. Cambridge, MA: Belknap Press of Harvard University, 1957.

Stansell, Christine. *American Moderns: Bohemian New York and the Creation of a New Century*. New York: Henry Holt and Company, 2000.

The Flapper and American Youth

"Artist Coffin Sees Flapper's Doom: Predicts Era of Graceful Greek Maids." *The New York Times*, 11 August 1922, 10.

"Blame Girls for 'Snugglepupping' and 'Petting Parties' in Chicago." *The Washington Post*, 12 March 1922, 21.

"Councilman Quinn and the Female Flapper." *The Washington Post*, 22 January 1922, 65.

"Criticizes Campus Girls." *The New York Times*, 16 March 1922, 16.

"Exit Flapper: Enter Woman." *The Los Angeles Times*, 6 August 1922, III25.

"Fashions: Longer Skirts are the Style Now—All Garments Made Loose." *The New York Times*, 21 May 1922, 87.

"Flapper's Cosmetics Alarming Physicians." *The New York Times*, 13 April 1922, 10.

"Grecian Maiden Beauty Replaces Flapper Type." *The Washington Post*, 1 August 1922, 11.

Rowland, Helen. "Exit the Flapper." *The Washington Post*, 5 August 1922, 9.

"Sweet and Twenty-Eight." *The New York Times*, 14 June 1922, 15.

"The Passing of Youth." *The New York Times*, 11 June 1922, 38.

"Wrecks from Flapperitis." *The New York Times*, 20 June 1922, 17.

"Youth at the Helm." *The Los Angeles Times*, 6 April 1922, II4.